50

GIRL
UNDER
WATER

BOOKS BY L.T. VARGUS AND TIM MCBAIN

LT VARGUS
TIM MCBAIN

GIRL UNDER WATER

bookouture

Published by Bookouture in 2020

An imprint of Storyfire Ltd.
Carmelite House
50 Victoria Embankment
London EC4Y 0DZ

www.bookouture.com

ISBN: 978-1-83888-835-0
eBook ISBN: 978-1-83888-834-3

This book is a work of fiction. Names, characters, businesses,
organizations, places and events other than those clearly in the
public domain, are either the product of the author's imagination
or are used fictitiously. Any resemblance to actual persons, living or
dead, events or locales is entirely coincidental.

PROLOGUE

The old man felt the dampness on his cheeks. Confused, it took him a few seconds to remember what tears were like, what crying was like. Billionaires like Dutch Carmichael didn't cry, did they?

"I know I have a tendency to be distant," he said, his voice shaking slightly. "Maybe even a little cold. I know that."

They walked through the upstairs hallway of the Carmichael mansion, the two of them striding over a rich Persian rug and past an original Tiffany lamp. The crystal chandelier hanging over the entryway glinted rainbow shards of light all around them.

"Looking back..." Dutch said, "maybe I could have been more open. More demonstrative with my affection. And not just with you. With everyone."

The old man's cane tapped out a beat on the inlaid wood floor. Pictures congregated in clusters along the wall. Photographs mixed in with paintings. Several blown-up magazine covers featured a younger Dutch—the rugged, self-made tycoon smiling the same wolfish smile in every shot.

He couldn't say what he wanted to say. Couldn't conjure the words to articulate what he felt inside. He'd kept a hard edge about himself for all of those years, fought his way to the top of the cutthroat business world, stayed lean and hard and hungry at the expense of nearly all of his personal relationships. He hadn't known any other way, and whenever he tried to voice any of the softer feelings inside, his mind went strangely blank.

The voice that finally answered him was clear and strong.

"Well, I forgive you. I can't speak for any of the others, of course. But I do. You've always done your best. I think we all know that."

They hugged there at the top of the stairs, and Dutch was overcome with emotion. Joy. Sorrow. Nostalgia. Regret. Things he hadn't felt in years. Things he hadn't let himself feel.

Christ, how had he let his life go this way? Selfish. Alone. Separate from his lover. Separate from his family. Separate from everyone. Greed was a blackness, a corruption that invaded the mind and spread through the body like cancer. It chewed you up.

The family's long history of conflict flickered through his head: fights, feuds, divorces, lawsuits. Dutch's increasing wealth only seemed to make the familial squabbles worse. More heated. More vicious.

"It's all long-forgotten now. Back in the past where no one can change it, where no one can touch it."

The hug tightened. The body in his arms felt so light. Childlike.

Maybe he could make things right after all. There was still time. He was seventy-seven, yes. White-haired and stooped, yes. But he was in good health. The heart and lungs of a forty-year-old, the doctors told him.

He had time to fix it, to repair the broken relationships before the end.

He pulled gently away from the embrace.

"You know, the staff are off on Sundays, but Rosa leaves sandwiches," the old man said. "More than enough for both of us. I'd love it if you'd stay and have lunch with me."

"Well... I only came for a short visit, like I said."

Dutch's eyelids fluttered. He almost let it go at that. Almost.

"Ah, come on. Humor me. It'd mean the world."

A sigh.

"OK. Let's eat."

Dutch smiled and turned to walk the last few paces to the stairway.

He picked his foot up. Wobbled down that first step.

There was a soft scraping sound, and then something bashed him on the back of the head.

Motes of white light flashed in his skull. Popping. Exploding.

The object burst on impact, spreading its shards around him.

Dutch planted his cane, wedged it into the oak floor, and for a second it seemed that would hold him.

Then the cane snapped. Cracked in half.

The old man launched off the top of the stairs. Body cartwheeling into empty space.

His vision whirled. Flashed on the ceiling. The chandelier. The wood of the stairs. And back to the ceiling again.

His upper back crunched on impact, body folding up like an accordion, knees tucking into his chin. But he didn't stop, didn't slow. Gravity wasn't through with him yet.

Tiny moments of his life flashed through his head. Blinking off and on.

Huddled in a tent outside of Da Nang. Drinking warm Coca-Cola and Tiger beer with his men. Laughing about something someone had said. Probably Fanelli. He'd always been the joker of the bunch.

His body rolled over itself. Somersaulting. Downward. Reality swung around and around.

Another flash took him to the birth of his eldest child. The press of the surgical mask against his face. The nurses handing over that tiny bundle. The small child, red and raw like an alien creature. A smile so big it made his cheeks sting.

The wood splintered. His bones snapped. One of his shoes came off and bumped alongside him.

Finally he landed on the polished floor at the bottom of the stairs and stopped moving.

Something popped in his spine. Severed. A tremor ran through him, tingling and throbbing and needling as his nerves began to die. All sensation fading out to nothing.

Numb. Paralyzed. A broken thing. Battered and bloody.

As the last glimmer of consciousness drained from him, he looked up. Saw the menacing silhouette standing at the top of the steps, feet planted shoulder-width apart.

And part of him had always known. Always feared. Always suspected that this might happen—someone close turning against him.

But I never thought it would be you.

CHAPTER ONE

Charlotte Winters thought she was the first one to the office that morning, but when she entered through the back door of A1 Investigations a few minutes before 9 a.m., she heard a voice coming from inside.

"Now you've done it." The voice was barely above a whisper. "You've made a mess of this."

Juggling her laptop, purse, a drink carrier, and a paper bag with two toasted bagels inside, Charlie hurried through to the main office. There she found her new assistant huddled on the floor behind the front desk, cheeks splotched red.

"Paige?" Charlie said.

The girl jumped at her name.

"Oh! Miss Winters!" Paige let out a nervous laugh. "I didn't hear you come in."

Charlie moved to the desk and set the coffee and bagels down.

"What are you doing here so early?"

"Well, you were so excited when your new chair came in yesterday, I thought it'd be a nice surprise if I came in early and had it all set up for you, but…" Paige's eyes strayed to the lopsided configuration on the floor beside her, and her voice went up an octave. "But I'm no good at these assemble-it-yourself things. The directions are always a bunch of gobbledygook, and I wind up with extra pieces by the end."

She lifted a plastic baggie filled with bolts and washers and shook it, jangling the parts together. She jabbed her finger at a piece of paper on the floor beside her.

"Everything is arrows and letters. It might as well be written in hieroglyphics." She pointed at the parts strewn about on the carpet, voice wavering, tears threatening to spill over her eyelashes. "I have no idea what's what."

"She's losing it, sis," Allie's voice chimed in Charlie's head. "You better step in unless you want another meltdown like when she found that sparrow last week."

The voice of her dead sister had a habit of cropping up when tensions were running high.

Charlie's twin had gone missing nearly twenty years ago, and the only trace they'd ever found was her severed foot, which had washed ashore on one of the island's beaches. It was at Allie's funeral that her voice had first appeared, beamed into Charlie's head as if by radio signal or satellite. It was disconcerting at first. Was it real? Evidence of the paranormal? Or was Charlie slightly insane, her twin's death breaking her psyche in half to restore the balance of things, fabricating the voice to fill the void left by Allie's absence?

Whatever the explanation, Allie was attracted to drama. But that didn't mean she wasn't also right. Charlie had only known Paige for a few weeks, but it was already clear she was an emotional creature. Last Friday, a bird had flown into the front office window hard enough to knock itself out and leave a smudge of tiny feathers on the glass. Paige had started sobbing, thinking it was dead. But it had only been stunned, flying away unharmed a few minutes later.

Charlie snatched up one of the cups from the drink carrier she'd set on the desk and held it out.

"Why don't we take a break? Once we have some caffeine pumping through our veins, I bet we'll be able to figure this out."

"Yeah. OK." Paige scooted closer to take the offered drink.

When she settled back on the floor, she sat cross-legged, gripping the cup with both hands and blowing into the opening in the lid. Paige was twenty-three, but sometimes Charlie had a hard time remembering she wasn't a kid. There was something so wide-eyed and innocent about her.

It had been Frank's idea to hire someone to help out at the office. The caseload at A1 Investigations had nearly doubled in the last few months, and with Frank's health problems, it made sense to find someone to pick up some of the slack. Paige was great with paperwork and answering phones. She kept Charlie organized and free to focus on the real investigative work. Charlie was willing to overlook the fact that the girl panicked at the notion of assembling office furniture.

"Thanks, Miss Winters."

Charlie was about to remind her that she'd asked to be called by her first name when the front door opened with a swoosh, letting in a gust of crisp May air.

Charlie turned, expecting the FedEx guy, Ralph. He almost always came this time of day. Instead, a woman stood on the mat just inside the door.

She was tall with red-blonde hair styled in a shoulder-length flip that reminded Charlie of Jackie Onassis. The woman studied the office as she carefully removed a pair of soft leather gloves, her lips puckering in a way Charlie interpreted as disapproving.

"Welcome to A1 Investigations. I'm Charlie Winters," she said, walking over and extending a hand.

"Gloria Carmichael," the woman replied.

She slid a pair of Gucci sunglasses from her eyes up onto her head. The crow's feet around her green eyes suggested she was older than Charlie had first suspected. Late fifties, maybe early sixties.

"I smell money," Allie whispered, and Charlie silently agreed.

Even if she hadn't come in with designer sunglasses and supple-as-butter leather gloves, Charlie would have pegged her as being wealthy. It was something in her posture, her head held high atop her long, smooth neck. The confident note of command in her voice. This was a woman used to having things her way.

"What can I do for you, Mrs. Carmichael?"

"It's *Ms.* Carmichael, but you might as well call me Gloria," she said, still eyeballing the surroundings. "This is... I mean... you're the one who found that missing girl, yes?"

The Kara Dawkins case had made all the headlines, the news outlets in the area painting Charlie as a hero. It had been good for business, but Charlie couldn't get comfortable with all the hype.

"That's right."

Still studying the office, Gloria Carmichael frowned.

"I was expecting something... different."

"Tell her you can go change into a pinstripe suit and fedora if that'll make her feel better," Allie suggested.

Charlie ignored her sister's voice and gestured to the leather couch against the wall. Gloria hesitated a moment before taking a seat, and then Charlie realized she had nowhere to sit herself. Paige had moved her old chair out to make room for the new one.

The half-assembled thing jutted up from the floor, looking more like an abstract sculpture than something someone could sit on. She opted to lean against her desk, but a moment later, Paige hopped up with a wink, which Charlie took to mean she was going to fetch a chair from the back room.

"I'm here about my father. Randolph Carmichael."

Charlie stood up straighter at that. Randolph "Dutch" Carmichael was big news on Salem Island. The founder of Carmichael Investments, a wildly successful hedge fund, had been found dead at the bottom of a stairway in his home a few weeks back. Initially presumed an accident, the police had eventually ruled the death a homicide. Ever since, the press had been going wild speculating the who and why of it all.

"I'm sorry for your loss," Charlie said.

Gloria flapped her gloves in the air in a dismissive gesture.

"I'm not here for sympathy. I want answers. The work of the local police... leaves something to be desired, you might say. I'd like another set of eyes on the case. An outsider. And I've discovered some inconsistencies in my father's estate."

Charlie was about to ask what she meant by "inconsistencies" but was interrupted by a high-pitched squeal. The sound of a harpooned sea creature screamed out from the hall—the awful squawk of Charlie's old chair.

Everything stopped as Paige emerged from the hallway pushing the ancient wooden thing. The chair's shriek was painfully shrill. Ice picks to the ear drums. It sent a wave of shivers up Charlie's spine.

Realizing all eyes were now on her, Paige's cheeks glowed red.

"Sorry," Paige mouthed, wincing as she guided the chair over to Charlie with a final screech for good measure.

Charlie had found a comfortable position on the desk and had no interest in moving to the decrepit chair, but she felt obligated to take the seat now that Paige had gone to all the trouble. She lowered herself onto it, wincing as it wobbled slightly but held her weight.

Gloria frowned from her position on the couch. The look on her face might have been pity.

"You were saying there are inconsistencies with your father's estate," Charlie said. "Could you elaborate?"

"My father had his own way of doing things." Gloria reached up and fiddled with her earring, a pearl set into a gold rose. "He was a maverick when it came to the stock market, as everyone knows, but he always advocated diversifying one's assets, and since he retired from running the hedge fund, he'd become fascinated with the 'unbanking' movement."

"Unbanking?"

"Yes. He began transferring large sums into luxury assets and alternate currencies. Unfortunately, it's not all accounted for. What we've been able to itemize at the house adds up to a few million dollars, and that's not nearly enough. I could bore you with the minutiae, but the bottom line is this: there's about four hundred million dollars missing."

CHAPTER TWO

Charlie's eyebrows shot up.

"Four hundred million dollars?"

Gloria nodded.

"The problem is that my family are a paranoid lot, and the rumors are already flying about where the money has gone." Another gesture sent the gloves slapping against Gloria's thigh. "Cryptocurrency and buried treasure and what-have-you. Items have started disappearing from the house. I wouldn't be surprised if a couple of my brothers are there now, ripping up floorboards and digging holes all over the property. They'll be at each other's throats until the money is found. And then of course there's the elephant in the room: the possibility that one of my siblings murdered my father."

Charlie reached for her notepad but paused at that.

"And what do you think?"

Gloria opened her mouth, her head shaking from side to side.

"I honestly don't know. The inheritance would make for a compelling motive, of course. But now? With the questions surrounding the money and the fact that we can't find his will—"

"His will is missing?"

"Yes. I've spoken with his lawyers and spent hours searching for it myself. I checked the safe in his office but only found a few pieces of my mother's jewelry and some random bits of family paperwork. Birth certificates and such. Then I realized he probably kept a digital copy on his laptop. But I can't find that either. The laptop, I mean."

Charlie tapped her pen against her lip. The details surrounding Dutch Carmichael's murder seemed to grow more complicated by the second: the missing laptop, the estate in limbo, the bulk of his fortune unaccounted for. She braced herself as Gloria went on.

"I'm afraid my siblings are already scheming against one another, convinced *someone* knows something about the money. My father always taught us to put family first. He would have been disgusted to see what jackals we've become. I've been chosen as the representative of the estate, and between itemizing the house and keeping my siblings from turning into absolute savages, my hands are full. I need you to work the murder angle, yes, but I also need someone—an expert—to figure out what my father did with the money."

"You have how many brothers and sisters?" Charlie asked.

With her chin raised, Gloria pierced Charlie with her fierce green gaze.

"Three brothers, two sisters, and you can spare me the Brady Bunch jokes. I've heard them all."

"And your mother?"

"She passed," Gloria said. "Many years ago now."

"I'm sorry."

The gloves flapped again as Gloria waved away Charlie's condolences.

Turning her notebook to a fresh page, Charlie passed it to Gloria, along with a pen.

"I'll need the names and numbers for your siblings and anyone else you think I should talk to. Any close friends of your father's, business associates, that kind of thing."

Gloria nodded as she wrote.

The rickety old chair listed slightly as Charlie leaned her weight against the backrest, and she reached out to steady herself against the desk.

"If you had to take a guess, who's your money on?"

Gloria paused in her writing.

"Pardon?"

"Which one of your siblings do you think would be most likely to attempt to collect on an early inheritance?"

Gloria sighed.

"I honestly can't decide."

"Are they really that bad?"

Gloria looked confused for a moment and then shook her head.

"Oh no. It's quite the opposite. I can't imagine any of them stooping to something so common as murder," she said. "Believe me, I'm no rube. I've watched enough true crime documentaries to know that money is as good a motivator as any. And the truth of it is, as much as my father encouraged us to be independent, we grew up sheltered. Or perhaps 'spoiled' is really the best way to say it. We are used to the finer things. Big houses. Nice cars. None of us have struggled."

"Is there anyone else who would stand to gain from your father's death? Anyone outside the family?"

Gloria folded her hands in her lap.

"As a matter of fact, there is someone who would better fill that role, in my opinion."

"And who would that be?"

"Vivien Marley. His mistress."

Her face tightened when she said it, as if that last word tasted bitter in her mouth.

"His…" Charlie blinked. "I'm sorry… you said your mother was dead?"

"Yes."

"Then… I mean, wouldn't she be your father's girlfriend? Or fiancée?"

Gloria scoffed.

"Absolutely not. Their relationship began when my mother was still alive and continued up until his death. She'll always be the other woman in my eyes. I honestly don't know what my father saw in her. She's barely older than me, for God's sake." Gloria rolled her eyes and laced her fingers together. "What you have to understand is that Mother and Father had an… arrangement, as sordid as that sounds."

"An arrangement?"

Gloria studied her fingernails, the distinct pucker of distaste on her lips.

"He was free to have other women as long as he agreed to never set my mother aside."

"So I guess all that 'family first' stuff was a 'do as I say, not as I do' type of deal," Allie said.

Charlie kept her focus on Gloria.

"But then—"

"You wonder why he didn't marry Vivien after my mother died?"

"Well… yes."

Gloria pinched the large diamond set into one of her rings and spun it around her finger absently.

"I suppose he was a bit old-fashioned that way. His word was his bond. He told my mother he'd never marry his mistress, and I think in some way he felt that even after she died, it would have been dishonoring her to remarry. Anyway, I won't deny that I have a certain bias against the woman. I've never liked her. Perhaps that clouds my judgment. Predisposes me to suspecting her."

Charlie definitely wanted to talk to this Vivien character.

She hadn't been sure what to make of Gloria at first. The woman had an air of snobbishness about her. But Charlie appreciated this sudden admission of a blind spot when it came to her father's lover. She'd found that most people weren't self-aware enough to realize they had them.

"And to be quite blunt," Gloria continued, "Vivien is *such* an airhead that I doubt she would have been able to pull something like this off."

Charlie handed Gloria a clipboard with the standard client contract attached. After a cursory glance at the pages, the woman signed her name to the bottom with a flourish of the pen.

"I'd like to take a look at the house, if I can," Charlie said.

Gloria glanced at the thin, rose-gold Cartier watch encircling her wrist.

"I can do it now, if we're quick about it." She stood and started pulling on her gloves. "You'll follow me over?"

Charlie nodded and grabbed her bag.

CHAPTER THREE

Charlie followed Gloria's Bentley through downtown Salem Island, past the storefronts, and out to the end of the island where most of the wealthy residents lived. The "cake-eaters" as her uncle Frank called them.

"Working a case for the Carmichael family," Allie said, letting out a low whistle. "You're a real hotshot now."

Charlie tried to ignore her, but as usual, Allie kept the conversation going all by herself.

"Six kids. Old lady Carmichael was really pumping 'em out," Allie said. "She probably died just to give her vagina a rest. The ol' dirt nap is one way to stop human beings from crawling out of the damn thing."

Charlie returned her coffee to the cup holder beside her.

"Thanks for that visual."

The truth was, sometimes it was comforting to have Allie's voice in her head. A little piece of her sister that never left.

Other times, she just wished Allie would shut the hell up.

Gloria's Bentley slowed in front of Charlie, brake lights flashing red before swooping into a driveway flanked by two brick pillars. Charlie followed, rolling past a wrought-iron gate with a large copper "C" emblazoned in the center.

A row of weeping willows lined both sides of the drive, their silvery-green foliage reaching almost close enough to brush the roof of the car. The house beyond was a mansion in the truest sense of the word: a Georgian revival masterpiece in red brick and slate tiles with formal gardens and hedges populating the grounds. Charlie's mouth popped open at the sight. It looked like a postcard of an English country house where the queen might stay.

"Damn. This is some classy shit," Allie said.

Charlie parked in front of the main entry and got out, catching a whiff of the spring flowers blooming along the path. As Gloria paused to inspect a silver Cadillac parked nearby, Charlie ogled the place, craning her neck to take it all in.

She struggled to process that this vast estate existed on Salem Island. She'd known Dutch Carmichael was wealthy, but this was next level.

Halfway up the marble steps of the entrance, Gloria turned back. "Are you coming?"

With a final glance around at the exterior of the house, Charlie nodded.

CHAPTER FOUR

As Charlie passed through the front door, her mood shifted. The opulent awe of the exterior gave way to something ghostly inside, something hushed and eerie.

Her gaze drifted up the sweeping staircase, lingering briefly on the crystal chandelier, roughly the size of her car, sparkling overhead.

This was where Dutch Carmichael had met his demise. Tumbling down this long, curving staircase. Snapping bones. Crushing vertebrae.

His maid had found him at the bottom in a pool of crusted blood. Cloudy eyes staring up at nothing.

Charlie gawked at the spot where the body must have lain, the inlaid wood floor polished to a mirror-like sheen. Then her eyes swept back up the stairs.

The tabloids had ghoulishly spread the leaked crime scene photos far and wide, and the graphic images flared in Charlie's head now. The old man's scalp had split and torn at the points of impact from the fall, flaps of skin coming free from the curvature of his skull.

Gloria's heels echoed as she strode beyond the entryway, and the clacking brought Charlie back to the present moment.

"We might as well start here in the parlor," Gloria said, sweeping aside a door across from the cursed staircase.

A man stood in the room beyond with his back to them, pointing his phone at a large oil painting of a woman holding a spiked wheel and a book. The flash on his phone's camera went off as Gloria and Charlie entered. He whirled around as he heard them approach.

"Glori!" the man said, tucking his phone into his vest pocket. Charlie noted that he wore a full three-piece suit with no tie. "I didn't know you were coming by."

Gloria crossed her arms over her chest. Charlie would have been able to read the displeasure in her posture a mile away.

"Likewise," she said, her tone flat.

She allowed the man to plant a kiss on her cheek but didn't exactly look pleased to see him.

The man was familiar somehow. He looked around the same age as Gloria, with sandy hair and a smile he could flick on like a light bulb. It transformed his chiseled features into something softer. More approachable.

He did it now, stretching his mouth wide and letting the skin at the corner of his eyes crinkle.

Instead of smiling back, Gloria fixed him with an unwavering stare.

"What are you doing in here, Wes?"

"Me?" The man's forehead wrinkled. "Well, I was talking with Tucker over at the *Free Press*, and they're interested in doing a feature on Dad. A memorial of sorts. They asked me to write a little something about him, and they also want some photos. I was trying to find the one of all of us at Marjory's cabin from a few summers ago, when we did the surprise party for Dad's seventy-fifth. Do you happen to have a copy somewhere?"

"I'll have to look." Gloria flicked her head at the painting. "And the reason you're photographing the art?"

The man blinked.

"Photographing the… art?"

"Don't play stupid, Wes. I saw you take a picture of the Sabbatini."

"Oh, that!" He waved her away. "Tucker mentioned that Dad's collecting might be an angle they would use in the feature. I thought I could take a few snapshots to give them an idea of what's here."

The man squirmed slightly under Gloria's fierce gaze. His eyes flicked over to Charlie, going wide as he made a show of noticing her.

"Is this her? The crack investigator?"

He moved closer, and Charlie noted how his brilliant white teeth were all the same size and shape, like a row of perfect little breath mints. At the thought, she realized he smelled slightly minty, as if he'd just gargled with mouthwash.

He extended a hand.

"Wesley Carmichael, pleased to meet you."

Of course, Charlie thought. That was why he looked familiar.

Wesley Carmichael, formerly Senator Carmichael. Or Senator Bar-michael as the tabloids often taunted, a cruel reference to his long-standing alcohol problem.

The lurid headlines flashed through Charlie's head. The mugshot where he looked like he was half dead, massive purple bags puckering under his bloodshot eyes. It had started with an arrest for drunk driving, then the media dug up more and more from there. Hookers. Gambling. Still, for the most part, the public forgave these indiscretions, offered him a second chance. When he got arrested with a kilo of cocaine some months later, it effectively ended his political career and his marriage.

"Charlie Winters," she said.

His grip was firm yet gentle, and he gave exactly three pumps before releasing her. A practiced gesture.

Gloria pulled her gloves off.

"So that's it?" she asked, redirecting Wesley's attention. "I'm supposed to believe you came all the way out here to take some pictures for Tucker?"

"What's that supposed to mean?" Wesley sounded more hurt than defensive.

"It means I hope I won't find any other items missing from the house. You know we've only begun itemizing the assets. This all has to go by the book, and no distributions can be made until the estate is closed. The probate judge was very clear about that."

"Damn it, Glori. I told you it wasn't me. You know Jude always had a hard-on for the Picasso—why don't you ask him about it?"

"I did, and he denied taking it. The painting certainly didn't get up and walk out on its own, Wesley. Someone took it. As soon as Father died, the lying started. It's like everything he taught us, every virtue he tried to reinforce, went flying out the window the minute he was in the ground." She sighed. "Meanwhile, being the eldest, I get saddled with all the responsibility of trying to hold everything together."

"Come on, that's not true." He reached out and put a hand on his sister's shoulder. "We're in this together. You know that."

Gloria glanced at Charlie, then to her watch. She swiveled back to face Wesley.

"If that's true, perhaps you can do something for me?" She cocked her head sideways at Charlie. "I told Ms. Winters I'd show her around the house, but I'm supposed to be meeting with one of the appraisers in forty minutes. Could you take over from here?"

Wesley's face relaxed, and he seemed relieved that Gloria had gone from grilling him to asking for a favor.

"Of course."

"If that's alright with you?" Gloria asked, directing the question to Charlie. "I do apologize for passing you off like this, it's just that this appraiser is supposed to be the best, and it was his only opening for the next month."

Charlie shrugged. She'd need to talk to all of the Carmichael clan at some point, and she might as well check Wesley off the list while she had him here.

"It's fine."

Gloria nodded once then slipped her fingers back into her gloves and headed for the door.

"If you have questions or need anything, please don't hesitate to call," she said, turning back before shutting the door with an imposing thud.

Wesley made a sweeping gesture with his hand, flashing his minty smile at her.

"Shall we?"

CHAPTER FIVE

Wesley guided her through the parlor, which featured a large marble fireplace and bay windows overlooking the gardens at the front of the house. Next came the formal dining room with another massive chandelier glittering over the table like a nebula of diamonds.

"I got the impression that Gloria filled you in on what I'm doing here?" Charlie said, pausing to admire the set of antique Delft pottery displayed against one wall of the room.

"Yes," Wesley said. "We're the two oldest, so we've always had a bit of a bond over that. Sort of pseudo-parental figures to the rest, especially now."

Charlie followed Wesley across a hallway carpeted with Persian rugs and into a glass-roofed solarium with a view of the back lawn. Potted plants peppered the space—a lemon tree, a banana leaf palm, and a hibiscus that reached almost to the ceiling. The greenery gave the room a more relaxed feel than the rest of the house.

Beyond that lay a kitchen that could have housed Charlie's entire studio apartment inside. Wesley pushed through a swinging door into a butler's pantry and then jogged up a stairwell that led to the second floor.

Upstairs, they did a quick circuit of a series of bedrooms, all roughly the same size and decorated in the same classic style as the rest of the house.

"How many bedrooms in the house?" Charlie asked.

"Ten bedrooms, twelve bathrooms," Wesley answered. "Including the basement, the house is a smidge under ten thousand square feet."

"Damn. Lot of toilets to clean," Allie said.

Charlie was starting to get a sense of why Gloria had hired her. Itemizing this huge of an estate was going to be a massive undertaking, let alone trying to work the murder angle.

Dutch's suite occupied the west wing of the second floor. They passed a four-poster mahogany bed and entered the study. Books lined floor-to-ceiling shelves, complete with a library ladder to reach the volumes at the very top. It smelled like wood and leather, and the rug underfoot felt like walking on a cloud. There was a large antique safe in the corner, its door hanging open.

The tiger maple desk was free of clutter, which made it seem unused. Like a showpiece in a museum.

Charlie pointed at one of the drawers.

"May I?"

Wesley shrugged.

"I figure that's what Gloria hired you for."

She slid the top drawer open and found a collection of fancy-looking pens, a box of paper clips, and a sterling-silver letter opener. Charlie checked the other drawers and discovered nothing of note. She hadn't expected anything to turn up someplace so obvious, but she still found herself disappointed.

"Gloria mentioned that your father's computer seems to have gone missing."

"I heard that, yes."

"If you had to guess, who do you think might have taken it?"

"Oh, I'm not sure anyone did. I think it's equally likely—perhaps even more so—that he has some secret hiding spot for it."

"Any idea where that secret hiding spot might be?"

"No. And I'm not sure it'd do us much good even if we had it."

"Why is that?"

"Well, my dad was a nut about privacy. You'll notice there are no cameras in the house? My sister, Marjory, lives just up the road. They had a break-in a while back. The intruder trashed her husband's office and stole an extremely valuable coin collection.

They installed a state-of-the-art home security system after that and tried to convince Dad to do the same thing, given he was so close and was a much more prominent figure. But he was adamantly opposed to the idea. Said he didn't need eyes watching him in his own damn house. Anyway, I've gotten off track. My point was really that he had the computer on lockdown anytime he was away from it. Password-protected. I sincerely doubt we'd be able to get into it even if we had it."

A phone trilled, and Wesley slid a hand into his suit jacket. He glanced at the screen and then held it in the air.

"Would you mind if I take this?"

"Sure," Charlie said. "Go ahead."

"Thanks." He tapped the screen and brought the phone to his ear. "Wesley Carmichael."

His voice receded as he exited the study, and Charlie turned around to face the empty office again. She went back to the desk, doing a more thorough job this time of searching the drawers. Moving things aside and checking for hidden compartments. When she satisfied her curiosity there, she moved to the bookshelves. The bottom half of the units on the back wall were cabinets which revealed a set of office appliances—printer, scanner, even an ancient fax machine. Charlie closed the doors and focused on the books themselves. Pulling out an atlas here and a legal reference there, riffling through the pages. Tugging at a few random volumes of a large world almanac collection.

"You're yanking on those almanacs like you think one of them might open a secret passageway," Allie said.

"I'm being thorough."

Allie laughed.

"Oh my God. I was joking, but you really are, aren't you? This isn't *Clue*, you know."

After sifting through the office and finding nothing, Charlie slipped into the bedroom, checking for signs of Wesley in the hallway. It was deserted. Might as well have a quick peek at the old man's bedroom while she was here.

She slid open the drawers of the matching nightstands, peered into the wardrobe, squatted down and looked under the bed. She didn't figure anyone would have a problem with her searching in here, but poking through bedrooms always made her feel like she was violating something. Even the most spartan bedroom was an intimate space. Someone's sanctuary.

Finding nothing, she went back out into the hallway, listening for Wesley. The quiet in the corridor made her uncomfortable, the odd charm of the Carmichael house veering back toward that unsettling murder scene she'd walked into downstairs, all the extravagant features turning sinister and strange, the air seeming to thicken around her. Goosebumps plumped on her arms as she walked through it.

She hurried down the staircase to the main floor, trying to will her heart into slowing. The light refracted through the crystals of the chandelier, a cold glow that decorated the floor with shimmering spikes.

At the bottom of the steps, she finally heard Wesley's muffled voice coming from behind the dining room door. She moved closer to it until his words came clear.

"No, of course I didn't tell her. I'm not an idiot." Wesley sighed. "Regardless, I think she knew what I was up to. And I'm not exactly *alone*, if you catch my meaning."

There was a brief pause, and then Wesley's voice went lower. Charlie leaned in and closed her eyes, as if it might help her hear better.

"I can try, but…"

Charlie held her breath, straining to make out the words.

"OK. I'll have to wait for a moment when no one else is around, but I'll call you when it's done."

Footsteps approached. Wesley was heading for the door.

Charlie dashed away, scrambling up the first few steps of the staircase, then turning back so it would appear as if she were just now coming down.

Wesley was still glaring down at the phone in his hand when he strode out from the dining room, brow furrowed. He caught sight of her on the stairway.

"Find what you were looking for?"

"What I was looking for?" Charlie asked. Had he heard her lurking outside the door?

"In my dad's office," he said, going on with a dry smile, "No smoking guns?"

"Oh," Charlie chuckled. "No. Nothing like that."

"Well, I suppose you ought to see the basement. I doubt there's much of importance down there, but I figure I might as well give the full tour. Leave no stone unturned and all that," he said with a wink.

CHAPTER SIX

When Wesley hit the bottom step, automatic lights flicked on, illuminating the basement. There was a full bar with swivel stools at one end and a rec room area at the other, complete with a pool table, air hockey, and two bowling lanes.

"No ping-pong?" Allie said. "This place is a joke."

Charlie followed Wesley down a hall, where he pointed out the indoor sauna and a home cinema with a digital projector and theater seating.

"I'm assuming Gloria already asked if you know where your father kept his will," Charlie said as they walked.

Wesley sighed.

"Yes, well, I have my doubts about that as well, to be honest. He was a practical man in many ways, and in others, not so much."

"Meaning?"

He paused, thinking. She remembered him making the same face during his senatorial career when a reporter asked a hardball question. A philosophical look, something he must have practiced but which came off as natural.

"This is going to sound strange, but… I don't think my father believed he would die."

Charlie shrugged. "Death catches many people unaware, I think."

"That's true, but I mean it quite literally. The concept of a will was brought up a few times over the years, in an offhand way. He always brushed it off. One time, when I was much younger, I even recall him saying something along the lines of, 'What do I need a will for?'"

"Could he have meant that as a joke?"

"I thought so at the time. But now…"

They'd finished their circuit of the basement, returning to the large room near the stairs with the bar and bowling alley. Wesley moved behind the bar, grabbed a crystal decanter by its thin neck and poured himself a generous serving of Scotch.

"Can I fix you a drink?"

"No, thanks."

"It's not even noon," Allie said. "Dude knows how to party."

"What I think now is that Dad thought of himself as, well… immortal. I've encountered it a few times with other very wealthy, very successful men. It's almost as if they believe their money and power protect them. And they do, from a great many things. They grow so accustomed to that protective bubble, though, that they start to believe it applies to all things. Even life and death. The world so rarely said 'no' to my dad—I think he thought it would keep on going that way."

Watching him guzzle down the Scotch in two swallows, Charlie thought again of the tawdry headlines. The unflattering mugshot. Those purple pouches of flesh sagging beneath Wesley's bloodshot eyes.

"You sure you don't want a drink?" he asked, snapping her out of the montage of memories.

"Tell him you're all set since you finished off that pint of Jack on the drive over," Allie said.

Instead, Charlie said, "I'm good."

Wesley nodded, unperturbed, and poured himself another.

"What can you tell me about Vivien Marley?"

Wesley smirked.

"Ah, yes, the mistress. I know Gloria and Marjory tend to see her as an evil-minded gold digger, but she strikes me as fairly benign. The way I see it, she's no more than a run-of-the-mill trophy wife. They're a dime a dozen in our circle. The only difference is that Vivien didn't actually get a ring out of the deal. I think that's where the distrust comes from ultimately. Gloria's too pragmatic and Marjory's too shallow to understand that there's a very real possibility that Vivien was with Dad out of love."

Wesley smiled again. Charlie wanted to dislike him after overhearing his phone call, but she couldn't quite pull it off. Despite that and the messy history of his political career, she couldn't help but find him charming.

Polishing off the last of his drink, he slammed the glass on the bar. Then he dabbed his fingers at his chin as if he was about to say something.

But then a strident voice cut through from the bottom of the basement stairway, startling Charlie. Loud. Obnoxious.

"Day-drinking again, Wes? Shocker of the decade."

Charlie turned.

The approaching man was in his early thirties, and he looked much like every other middle-aged hipster she'd ever met. Square-framed glasses. Black jeans cut so slim they looked painted on. A short-sleeved chambray shirt unbuttoned just far enough to reveal the topmost edge of a large chest tattoo. Even suspenders.

Wesley's jaw tightened.

"What do you want, Jude?"

So this was Jude. The youngest of the Carmichael brood.

He marched over to where Wesley stood behind the bar and stuck his finger in his brother's face.

"I know you told Gloria it was me who took the Picasso. That's a lie, and you know it. If you keep slandering me, you'll be hearing from my lawyer."

Wesley snorted.

"Good God, Jude. Is that really supposed to frighten me?"

Without another word, Jude picked up the empty tumbler and threw it, narrowly missing Wesley's head. The crash of the glass shattering against the wall made Charlie flinch.

"Stop lying about me!" Jude shouted before turning on his heel and storming away.

When he'd gone from the basement, Wesley sighed.

"The irony is, if Jude had even an inkling of the truth…"

"What does that mean?"

"Oh, nothing. A petty family squabble." Wesley's grimace transformed suddenly into his best senatorial smile. "I haven't shown you the pool yet, have I?"

"Lead the way," Charlie said, though she didn't think his comment about Jude had been nothing.

If Jude had even an inkling of the truth.

Wesley was hiding something, and she wouldn't be in any hurry to forget about that.

CHAPTER SEVEN

Wesley led the way through a set of French doors onto a patio, warmth from the morning sun radiating up from the flagstones underfoot and coiling around Charlie's ankles. Off to the left, an infinity pool hovered over a hillside view, and Charlie's eyes snapped to the figure bobbing atop the water.

"Ah, yes," Wesley said, gesturing that way. "Witness my brother Brandon in his natural habitat."

Brandon Carmichael floated in a pool chair, sunglasses on, a Budweiser tallboy in a beer floatie next to him. Naked, tanned flesh stretched over his muscles and a pair of tight swimming trunks clung to a small portion of his lean body.

"Holy beefcake alert. He's like a Greek god," Allie said. "Charlie, after giving this a lot of thought, I think you should throw yourself at him. Hold nothing back."

"We all mourn in different ways," Wesley said, still addressing Charlie. "Brandon grieves his father by getting drunk in the pool like some kind of beach bum."

He turned toward Brandon, lifting his voice.

"Are you allergic to shirts now, Bran? I don't think I've seen you wear one since the funeral."

Brandon said nothing. He just floated there, motionless. After a beat, Wesley went on.

"How does that work? You try to put one on and your body just rejects it? Sheds it or something, like you're molting?"

Brandon still didn't respond, didn't move at all, his chair slowly rotating in the water like a dead leaf.

"Is he honestly asleep?" Wesley muttered, and Charlie thought she could hear genuine anger creep into his voice.

He stooped beside the pool, dipped his hand into the water and flung several handfuls, spritzing Brandon in the face pretty good.

Brandon jerked awake. Instinctively, he lurched to grab his beer and cupped a hand over the top, holding it off to the side like he was protecting an infant instead of a macro brew.

"What's your problem, man? Beverage!"

Wesley stopped splashing and stood, a carnivorous smile spreading over his face.

"You must have dozed off out here," he said. "I imagine gambling away Father's money can be quite draining."

Brandon ripped off his sunglasses and glared at him. When he spoke, it came out through clenched teeth.

"You think you put on a vest and it makes you superior? Last time I checked, you haven't been gainfully employed in over a decade, Wes. Pretending to be successful might work at the country club, but it doesn't count for much in the real world."

Wesley's lips tightened, his cheeks slowly going red. He said nothing.

Then Brandon's eyes flicked over to Charlie, and after a few confused blinks, his face brightened into a smile.

"Oh, hey! You must be Gloria's investigator."

He tried to paddle his chair over with one hand, the other still clutching the tall boy, but he made no progress. The chair simply turned one way and then the other. Something about the visual struck Charlie as cartoonish—the muscular man excitedly trying to paddle his way over to her, huge smile on his face, big hand flicking at the water—and she had to stifle a laugh.

After a few seconds, Brandon gave up paddling and slid off the chair and into the water. He made sure to hold his beer up over his head like the Statue of Liberty, the red-and-white can the last thing thrusting out of the water after the rest of him went under.

It slowly moved her way as he walked over the bottom of the pool, and Charlie laughed again.

"Don't you have a Phish concert you need to get to or something?" Wesley said as Brandon emerged from the water.

Brandon chuckled and shook his head, his focus still entirely on Charlie.

"I went to one Phish concert—over a decade ago—and this guy brings it up about once a month. Trying to, I don't know, rub my nose in it or something."

Wesley grumbled something about how he'd leave her and Brandon to get acquainted and walked off, and Charlie realized that Brandon had gotten under his brother's skin some—more successfully than Jude, anyway.

"Do you have a minute to answer a few questions?" Charlie said, refocusing on Brandon, who had now climbed out of the pool and wrapped a towel around his waist.

He took a long pull from his beer before he answered, wiped the heel of his hand across his stubbled chin. That roguish smile still beamed on his face.

"I thought you'd never ask."

CHAPTER EIGHT

Brandon stretched out on the cushions of a teak lounger and dropped his beer in the cupholder built into the armrest. Charlie took the lounger next to him, perching on the side and flipping to a fresh page in her notebook.

"What do you want to know?" Brandon asked, rubbing his palms together like someone sitting down to a feast. "Hit me with it."

Charlie raised an eyebrow.

"You seem awfully excited about this."

"Well it's not every day that a charismatic, young private detective wants to interrogate me."

"Charismatic?" Allie repeated. "He's talking about you?"

Charlie ignored that.

"It's not really an interrogation. That's more of a police thing."

He waved her away.

"My point is, I used to read a lot of Dick Tracy comic books when I was a kid. This is a bit of a childhood dream come true. Though with a name like Charlie Winters, I have to admit, I was picturing an old guy in a hat and trench coat."

"I think Gloria was, too," Charlie said. "I suspect I was a bit of a disappointment for her."

"That's only because she has no imagination. Doesn't like surprises. Me, on the other hand?" Brandon lowered his sunglasses so he could wink at her. "I love a good surprise."

Charlie studied him, trying to decide where to start. He had a bit of Wesley's charm, but it was less polished. Rougher around the edges. Even his handshake was similar to Wesley's, but without the practiced, measured quality. This was Wesley without the coaching.

Brandon even looked a bit like Wesley, though he was younger. Her age, maybe a few years older. But his hair was darker than Wesley's, and he was more relaxed. A touch of slouch in his posture. Then there was the blooming beard. She tried to picture Wesley with facial hair. Couldn't be done. It was much too "common," as Gloria would probably put it.

"What did Wesley mean before, when he made the comment about gambling your father's money away?"

Brandon ran his fingers through his hair and groaned softly.

"Pure exaggeration. Dad lent me some money when I was in college. I thought I'd try my hand at playing the market, you know. Walk in the old man's footsteps. It didn't pan out though. So I used the rest of the cash as my bankroll. Got into playing poker. Wes still acts like I'm some Vegas tourist, pissing away my paycheck on the weekends. He refuses to accept that this is how I make a living."

"You're a professional poker player?"

Brandon cocked his head to one side.

"I prefer to think of myself as not having a profession. But gambling is what pays the bills, so… yes. Technically it is my job. I do some sports betting as well, but poker is my main source of income. And Wes has no respect for it. He likes to blame his own gambling for all his other troubles. The drugs, the drunk driving, the hookers. He went through a twelve-step program for it and everything. Now he acts like he's all high and mighty because he gave up his so-called vice. Likes to talk about being 'clean.'" Brandon put air-quotes around the word and smirked. "The thing is, he still drinks like a fish. He may not gamble anymore, but he's far from clean. He's a hypocrite."

Charlie watched him closely when she asked the next question.

"So you haven't borrowed money from your father anytime recently?"

"No. It was the one time, like I said. And I paid him back."

His response seemed honest enough, though Charlie was careful to remind herself that she didn't know him well. It could take some time to learn someone's tells.

"Well, speaking of your father's money," Charlie said, "do you have any idea where the bulk of it went?"

Brandon shook his head.

"Dad was always very tight-lipped about that stuff. Secretive even." He crossed one leg over the other. "This is going to sound ridiculous, but I can't stop imagining him sneaking around the property at night, burying big jars of coins and whatnot. Gold. Silver. But then I always did like pirate stories when I was a kid. The idea of buried treasure being hidden out here makes me kind of giddy even now. I mean, how great would it be if he pulled a Forrest Fenn?"

"A what?"

Brandon slid his sunglasses to the top of his head and leaned in.

"Forrest Fenn was this rich antiquities dealer who hid a treasure chest in the Rocky Mountains. Filled it with a million dollars in gold and precious gemstones and then wrote a poem about it with clues to help people find it."

"When was this?" Charlie asked. "The 1850s?"

"No, this wasn't long ago at all," Brandon said, eyes glittering with amusement. "Actually, someone found the treasure recently. Took them ten years, but they figured it out."

"You think your dad would really do something like that?" Charlie asked, thinking that if it took ten years to find Dutch's hidden riches, she'd be screwed.

"Probably not," Brandon admitted. "But like I said, I'm a sucker for stories about buried treasure. And I can almost imagine him doing something kind of crazy like that."

"He certainly seemed like a larger-than-life character, your dad," Charlie said. "I suppose his death was probably quite a shock for all of you."

"It really was. When Marjory called to give me the news, I thought it had to be some kind of joke. I couldn't process it. I was at the MotorCity Casino in Detroit. Wandered the parking garage for almost half an hour, completely unable to remember where I'd parked."

A strange, rhythmic pattering sound in the distance interrupted their conversation, and it was a moment before Charlie could identify what it was. Hooves. Sure enough, a chestnut horse galloped by a few seconds later. The rider's ponytail streamed behind her as she steered the animal toward the stables on the other end of the property.

"Have you spoken to Dara yet?" Brandon asked, gesturing toward the girl on horseback.

"No."

"Well, that's her on the Arabian." Brandon took a swig of beer. "You know the animals here are worth somewhere in the ballpark of half a million dollars collectively? Dad paid over sixty grand for one of the stallions. Can you imagine? Buying a horse that costs as much as a luxury car? I mean, they're spectacular animals, but I don't have to shovel shit after I park my BMW."

"You don't think he had some sort of emotional bond with them?" Charlie asked.

Brandon snorted.

"Sorry. If you knew my dad, you'd know how hilarious that sounds. He was not a particularly sentimental man." He lowered his sunglasses and rested his head on the back of the lounger. "We had a dog growing up. Molly. An Irish retriever. She was sweet and smart and impeccably trained. He referred to her exclusively as 'that damn dog.' Never once called her by her name that I can remember. I don't recall ever seeing him pet her. She was the equivalent of a footstool that left hair and puddles of drool around the house."

An image of Dutch Carmichael was beginning to solidify in Charlie's mind. Something beyond the staged portraits and fluffy news features. He'd been a stern man. A pragmatist. Perhaps one more interested in increasing his fortunes than bonding with his family.

"As to your original question, about where Dad's money might have gone? I don't know if you've done much research on his company, but he built Carmichael Investments into one of the largest hedge funds in the state. It currently manages over eight billion in assets. He had to be pulling fifty million a year, easy, before his retirement. So the one thing I'm sure of is that there's money *somewhere*, and a lot of it."

Charlie tapped her pen against her notepad.

"What about his charity? The Lamark Foundation?"

"You'd have to ask Marjory about that. The foundation is really her domain."

Charlie made a quick note of that.

"One last question, and then I'll leave you to the very important work you're doing here, poolside."

Brandon grinned.

"Shoot."

"I witnessed an interesting exchange between your brothers earlier. It was more of an argument really."

"Oh yeah," Brandon said, smiling and brushing some imaginary bit of something from his well-toned abs. "They fight all the time. Did Jude throw anything?"

"Yes, actually. A glass tumbler."

Brandon laughed.

"Classic Jude. So melodramatic. He's like a toddler sometimes, I swear to God. Quite the temper on that one, and Wes knows exactly how to push his buttons."

"Well, after Jude stormed off, Wesley said something along the lines of 'if Jude had even an inkling of the truth.'" Charlie raised her eyebrows. "Any idea what he meant by that?"

Brandon's jovial expression faded.

"Look. There's something Jude doesn't know. Something he can *never* know. For his own sake."

"What is it?"

"Jude isn't—" Brandon stopped short, and Charlie waited for him to go on.

"Isn't what?" she asked, when he didn't.

Hand over his mouth, Brandon shook his head.

"I can't. It's not my place. But trust me when I say it has absolutely no relation to what happened to my dad. It's… ancient history."

"Must be pretty serious if he won't spill the beans," Allie whispered.

Charlie considered this. Brandon had been fairly open and seemingly honest throughout the interview, in her estimation, so the sudden hesitation did come as a bit of a surprise. She supposed she could respect the instinct to protect the family secrets. On the other hand, she wondered at his ability to judge whether or not it had any bearing on his father's murder. He was far too close to be impartial, and Charlie preferred to make those assessments herself. But it wouldn't do any good to badger him about it. Better to find another way to sniff the secret out.

"Thanks for your time, Brandon. I appreciate it." Charlie closed her notebook and slid it into her bag. "Do you think Dara would be up for talking with me?"

"I don't see why not. I'd walk you over to the stables and do the whole introduction thing, but the path is gravel, and, well…" Brandon lifted his bare feet and wiggled his toes.

"That's alright," Charlie said, getting to her feet. "I'm sure she doesn't bite."

"Not unless you insult the horses. Then she might." He raised the sunglasses again to look at her. "So that's really it? We're done?"

"That's it."

"That was rather painless." Brandon frowned, almost looking disappointed. "In the movies, the private eye always has to slap the witnesses around some to get them to cooperate."

Charlie shrugged.

"Next time, don't be so cooperative."

Chuckling, Brandon put out a hand.

"It was a pleasure. Really," he said.

When they shook this time, he hesitated a moment before releasing his grip.

"And if you need anything else, you can call me. Anytime."

With a nod, Charlie said, "I will."

CHAPTER NINE

Gravel crunched under Charlie's feet as she approached the stables. She got a whiff of barn smell as she closed on the building—the sweet, grassy fragrance of hay, the muskiness of animals, and just a hint of horse shit.

Stepping through the doorway, she'd expected the odor of manure to be almost overpowering inside, but the door at the opposite end of the stable was open, allowing a light breeze to keep the air circulating and fresh. The floors were concrete and immaculate, not so much as a stray piece of hay.

"Jesus, Charlie. This barn is cleaner than your apartment," Allie said.

Charlie spotted Dara at the far end of the space shoveling some kind of grain into a metal pail. She was dressed for riding in a navy blue polo shirt, black leather boots, and beige breeches with reinforced panels at the knees.

"Dara?"

Hoisting the pail, the woman turned and blinked at her.

"My name is Charlie Winters," she said, extending a hand. "I don't know if Gloria's spoken to you about any of this, but she's hired me to look into your father's estate."

Dara stared at Charlie's hand for a few seconds before releasing her grip on the pail's handle. Her handshake was flimsy and awkward, quite the opposite of the firm grip displayed by her siblings. Her eyelids fluttered, and she didn't make eye contact.

Charlie pressed on.

"Could I ask you a few questions?"

Dara's brow twitched in what Charlie interpreted as a gesture in the affirmative, but before she could get her first question out, Dara had whisked past her with the pail of horse feed.

Charlie blinked then hurried after her. She caught up in front of a stall occupied by a palomino mare with a white diamond in the center of its forehead. Dara dumped some of the feed into a plastic bin anchored to the edge of the stall.

"You're the youngest, is that right?"

"No." Dara grabbed a coiled hose from a wall mount and filled the horse's water bucket. "Jude is the youngest."

"I see."

Charlie was starting to think she'd done something to offend Dara, though she wasn't certain. She'd interviewed hostile people before, and they were usually more than willing to talk—they were just nasty about it. This girl, by comparison, simply seemed disinterested.

Dara entered the stall and murmured something Charlie couldn't make out. She was about to ask Dara to repeat herself when she realized she was talking to the horse.

"Pretty girl," she said. "I know you're grumpy because I didn't take you out today, but it was Gerdie's turn. You get to go tomorrow."

She went over the horse's neck and chest with a wide wooden brush. There was a warmth in her tone. A confidence in her movements.

Charlie was still trying to decide how to get anything from Dara when the horse stretched out its neck and snuffled at Charlie's arm.

She remembered visiting a farm once as a kid and being taught to hold her hand out flat, fingers together, when giving a horse a treat. She did that now, extending her flattened hand so the horse could smell her. The quivering nostrils moved closer. The wet, fuzzy mouth nuzzled her flesh, and then the lips curled back and the horse snorted loudly into Charlie's hand.

Charlie laughed.

"Hester, you old greedyguts." Dara turned to Charlie, smiling for the first time. "She's mad because there's no treat."

She reached into her back pocket, pulled out a small brown nugget that looked like a dog biscuit.

"Here," she said, handing it to Charlie. "These are her favorite."

Charlie set the treat in her palm and presented it to the horse. The velvety snout returned in search of the prize. The lips parted and the treat disappeared into the horse's toothy maw.

Charlie thought she knew how to get Dara talking now.

"I remember the first time I got to pet a horse when I was little. It was so strange to be that close to something so huge. And then they're so gentle. It was magical. I didn't think it would be the same now that I'm grown, but it is." Charlie stroked between Hester's eyes with her fingertips. "They're incredible creatures."

"Aren't they?" Dara agreed, running her fingers through Hester's mane. "And they're so loyal, too. Much more than people."

"Do you come here to ride often?"

"Oh, almost every day. Even on the days I can't ride, I usually come to feed them. I think they need that. That human connection. They get upset if I don't. I can sense it. They're always a little more standoffish if I miss a day. Like when a child pouts."

Charlie nodded, trying to find a way to steer the conversation toward Dutch.

"And what about your father? Did you two ever take rides together?"

Dara's head swiveled from side to side.

"No. He hasn't ridden since he broke his hip a few years back." She stooped and began to pick out clods of compacted straw and dirt from Hester's hooves with a special tool. "But even before that, it was different for him. He doesn't see them as unique individuals the way I do. As friends. They've always been more like objects to him. 'An investment' is what he always calls them. And investments are made to be bought and sold. That's what he says anyway."

Charlie noticed Dara's continued use of present tense. *Hasn't ridden. Doesn't see them.* As if Dutch were still alive.

"And had he?" Charlie asked. "Sold any of the horses, I mean."

Dara dropped the hoof she'd been cleaning and moved around to the other side of the animal.

"I won't allow it. But he likes bringing it up. Maybe *because* it upsets me." She unscrewed the lid of a plastic container and began painting the waxy goop inside onto Hester's hooves.

"That was the last thing we talked about. Argued about, really. A few days before he died. It was probably the only time I ever won a debate against him."

"Won?" Charlie said. "How so?"

"Well, he's dead, isn't he? He can't sell the horses now."

Charlie thought most people would be hesitant to bring up an argument they'd had with a murder victim only days before their demise in such a context. But then Dara had a certain innocence about her. A naiveté that made her seem much younger than she really was.

Charlie wondered if there was a way she might leverage that guileless nature.

"What do you think of the whole thing with Jude?" she asked, careful to keep her tone casual.

Dara blinked.

"What thing with Jude?"

"You know," Charlie said, leaning in as if they were conspiring together. "The big secret."

"Jude has a secret?" Dara asked, then lowered her voice. "It's not some kind of weird sex thing, is it?"

Charlie raised an eyebrow.

"What makes you say that?"

Dara's cheeks suddenly went bright pink, and she chewed her bottom lip.

"Well, one time, when we were in high school, I found some really disgusting pornography in his room."

"Like what?"

Dara leaned in, whispering.

"A *Playboy*."

Allie snorted.

"*Playboy*? I was expecting something raunchy. *Playboy* barely even shows cooter!"

Charlie wasn't exactly a connoisseur of dirty magazines, but she had to agree that *Playboy* seemed the tamest of the bunch.

"No, I don't think that's it," Charlie said, trying to keep the disappointment from her voice.

"Well then, what is it?" Dara asked. "What's the big secret?"

Charlie waved her hand in the air.

"You know, I think I probably just misunderstood something Wesley said earlier. Forget it."

Dara seemed only too eager to get back to grooming the horses when Charlie thanked her for her time.

"You're not really going to let this Jude mystery go, are you?" Allie asked as Charlie exited the barn. "Don't leave me hanging like that. You know I love digging up a juicy family secret."

"Of course I'm not letting it go," Charlie said. "Dara obviously doesn't know what it is, and I don't want her getting curious and poking around on her own."

Allie clicked her tongue.

"Smart. Better to blindside 'em."

That gave Charlie an idea, and she nodded.

"And who better to blindside than the man himself?"

"Wait," Allie said. "You're going to ask Jude about it? I thought the whole point was that it was a secret being kept from him."

"Yes, but there's a chance he already knows. In my experience, families aren't as good at keeping secrets as they think they are."

Allie let out a low laugh.

"I love it when you get sneaky," she said.

As Charlie approached the house, she noted there were four cars parked out front in addition to her own. If she wasn't mistaken, that meant Jude was still here, somewhere.

CHAPTER TEN

Charlie found Jude upstairs in Dutch's study. The youngest Carmichael sat behind the vast maple desk, brow furrowed, thumbing at his phone.

Charlie knocked and his head snapped up, but when he saw it was her, his face softened. He stood, rounding the desk to shake her hand.

"You're the one Gloria hired," he said. He was shorter than his brothers, and his hair was so dark it was nearly black.

"That's me. Charlie Winters."

"I have to apologize for that little tiff you witnessed earlier, between me and Wes." He scratched the back of his neck. "Do you have any siblings, Ms. Winters?"

"A sister," Charlie said.

"Ah." He knocked his knuckles on the desk. "Then you know how it is. A lifetime of petty feuds and old resentments. With what happened to Dad, not to mention the fact that Wes is so obviously jealous of my accomplishments… well, we've had words more than once recently."

Jude sidled back to the leather executive chair, and Charlie took the seat opposite him.

"Speaking of your accomplishments…" Charlie smiled, thinking Jude seemed like someone who would respond to a bit of ego-stroking. "Can I start by asking about your company? Gloria mentioned you're in marketing."

"Well, that's a bit of an oversimplification." Jude leaned back in his seat, kicking his feet up onto the desk. "In a general sense, we're a full-service, independent PR firm, specializing in niche markets."

"Ugh," Allie said. "This guy is way too cool for school."

"I see," Charlie said.

"The way I usually explain it to people is that we take good companies and make them into great companies," Jude said, lacing his fingers behind his head.

Allie made a gagging sound.

"You know, this is exactly the kind of corporate hipster douchebag who gives all of us millennials a bad name," she said.

"That's interesting," Charlie said, thinking it was anything but. "And that's what you do for the company your father founded? Carmichael Investments?"

Jude sighed.

"The thing you have to understand about Dad is that he was old-school. And that was good, in some ways. Tradition has value. An air of authenticity. People trust a company that's been around for a while. But he was very much stuck in the eighties when it came to marketing. He had the name, so he thought if he clobbered people over the head with that branding enough times, they'd buy what he was selling. But the new generation needs more than that. They want to give a damn about something. A message. They want the companies they support and the products they buy to inspire them. To stand for something more than just, 'Buy our shit. Give us your money.'"

Charlie nodded and Jude went on.

"Frankly, I think part of the reason he retired was because he didn't want to change. He had a lot of pride, my old man. Thankfully, his successor is more malleable. Not that he didn't take some convincing, mind you, but I'm used to that. After dealing with my dad, I know how stubborn the old guard can be. Five years ago, they thought I was some kind of rebel here to destroy their perfect system. Now they come to me and want to know how. How do they tap into the zeitgeist? And it's simple, really. You just have to know your 'why.'"

He put air quotes around the last word.

"Your 'why'?" Charlie repeated. They sounded like nonsense words to her.

"*Why* you do what you do. That's what people want to know." Jude suddenly swung his legs back down to the floor and sat forward. "You're a perfect example. I read about you, after you saved that girl. Have you ever thought about hiring someone to manage your image?"

Charlie raised an eyebrow.

"My image?"

"Sure. You've got the awareness now with all the press from saving the girl, but that'll fade, you know. It's only a matter of time." Jude aimed a finger at her. "What's the name of your company again?"

"A1 Investigations… but it's not really mine."

"Ah, see. That's a big mistake right there. You should be capitalizing on your name." He spread his hands in the air as if unveiling her name in lights. "Charlie Winters Investigations. Or maybe The Winters Firm. You've already got the brand awareness, now you craft the message. And the great thing is, with your story, you've already got a winner. You solve problems. You *save* people. Right? I mean, a tire company, you have to finesse a compelling 'why' in there. But what you do? What you've done? It's built right in."

"Well, like I was saying, it's not really my company. My uncle is the one who started it."

Jude blinked.

"What's his name?"

"Frank Winters."

"Never heard of him," Jude said, then laughed as if this was the funniest joke ever told. "See what I mean? If your uncle is a smart man, he'll see this for what it is: a once in a lifetime opportunity to define exactly what Winters Investigations is and solidify it in the mind of the consumer. I mean, your story is solid gold."

"Here's my question," Allie said. "Does this guy watch *Mad Men* reruns? Or does this guy *jerk off* while watching *Mad Men* reruns?"

"Since you mentioned gold," Charlie said, not sure how they'd gotten so off track, "any idea where your father's vast fortune went?"

Jude's brow twitched as if the sudden subject change irked him.

"I honestly have no idea," he said. "And I hope Gloria hasn't instructed you to ask me about that damn painting again, because I didn't take it. If you want to know where things have been wandering off to, I'd look to Brandon."

"Brandon?"

Despite the fact that Charlie already had a pretty good idea of who'd been filching things from the house, she couldn't help but press Jude on his assumption that Brandon was the culprit.

"Sure. He's the biggest mooch of them all. Always borrowing money from someone or another." Jude rolled his eyes. "Say what you will about Marjory and that joke of her position at the foundation—at least she pretends to be contributing."

"And Brandon doesn't?"

Jude barked out a laugh.

"Brandon is a grifter. He likes to see himself as some kind of bohemian misfit with his lack of a *real* job. But he's a phony."

"Pot, meet kettle," Allie muttered.

Charlie hesitated for a moment. This was the perfect time to blindside Jude to get a feel for whether or not he was wise to the big family secret surrounding him. But she couldn't help but feel a twinge of apprehension remembering the scene with Wesley. The way Jude's mouth had twisted into a furious knot. The explosion of the glass tumbler colliding with the wall and shattering into a thousand pieces.

"Jude, I hope you'll forgive my candidness, because I know it's a sensitive subject," Charlie said. "But I was hoping we could talk about your… little secret."

He blinked a few times, seeming confused, and then his face hardened.

"Who have you been talking to?"

"No one. This is something—"

"It was Wes, wasn't it?" Jude's eyes narrowed to slits. "That piece of shit. I should have known he'd tell you all about EloquenTec. Unbelievable. That has nothing to do with any of this!"

Charlie shook her head. EloquenTec? She had no idea what he was talking about.

"Wesley didn't say anything about that."

"Stop covering for him. I know my brother's shady tactics when I see them." Jude jabbed a finger at the top of the desk. "I put everything into that company. We were supposed to be the next hot tech startup, and Wes couldn't have been more gleeful when it crashed and burned. My own brother! I declared bankruptcy. Lost my house. Seven years ago, and he still brings it up. You know why? Because he can't stand that I'm a success now. That the once great Senator Wesley Carmichael has become the biggest loser in the family. Hell, even the family party boy, Brandon, won a big poker tournament in Atlantic City last year. Got his picture in the paper next to Phil Hellmuth. Wes is the shame of the Carmichaels now, and he can't stand it. The disgraced former senator who still straps on his vests every day like he might hold a press conference."

Jude slammed his fists down onto the polished surface of the desk, and the sudden *thud* made Charlie jump.

"I'm gonna beat his goddamn ass the next time I see him. Is he still here?"

"I think there's been a misunderstanding. I wasn't—" Charlie said, but Jude seemed oblivious to her existence at this point.

He was already up out of his chair, and he stalked over to the door, still ranting.

"He's crossed the line this time, alright. Enough is enough."

Left alone in the study, Charlie glanced around. Her gaze fell on the old cast-iron bank safe in the corner.

"I think that went well," Allie said. "Don't you?"

Charlie ignored her. She got up and approached the safe, testing the handle. It was locked.

"What are you doing? Gloria already said she checked the safe for the will," Allie said.

"Yeah. But do you remember what she found inside?"

"Um. Some jewelry or something?"

"And birth certificates."

"So?"

The corners of Charlie's mouth turned up into a smile.

"So?" Allie repeated. "What are you smirking about?"

"Oh, nothing. Just that I think I figured out the family secret," Charlie said, unable to keep the gloating tone from her voice. "And it has nothing to do with Jude's failed tech startup."

CHAPTER ELEVEN

Charlie's gut clenched as she glanced down the grand staircase once more, unable to stop the grisly photos of Dutch Carmichael laid out in the autopsy suite from invading her mind. She didn't know how his children could traipse around here as if nothing had happened. She hadn't even known the man, and the knowledge that he'd been murdered in this very spot filled her with foreboding.

She gripped the banister firmly and started down the steps, careful to watch her footing. Halfway down, she once again heard Wesley's voice coming from inside the parlor.

"I have no earthly idea what you're talking about."

Now there was a second voice, and Charlie recognized it as Jude's.

"Don't bother denying it, Wes. I know what you've been saying about me. Blabbing about my tech startup to anyone who'll listen."

Wesley scoffed loud enough for Charlie to hear it even through the closed door.

"I didn't say anything about your stupid little failure of a company."

"There we go!" Jude said, his voice rising several decibels. "You know what this is? This is character assassination!"

Charlie reached the bottom of the stairs and padded to the front door, wanting to make her escape before things escalated between the brothers. She felt a touch guilty for giving Jude the wrong idea, though it certainly hadn't been intentional. On the other hand, Jude himself had admitted they'd been feuding long before she came on the scene.

Back in her car, a chill settled over Charlie as soon as she was alone. She blinked a few times. Stared up at the house for a moment—the murder scene, she reminded herself.

With all the quirkiness of the Carmichael family on display, she'd almost forgotten that these were murder suspects she was meeting and greeting. Could one of them have really done it?

She took a deep breath and closed her eyes. Tried to push the little twinge of fear and revulsion away.

It didn't help.

Her skin crawled just the way it had when she'd first walked into the house and gazed up that long flight of stairs.

She opened her eyes, breath hitching in her throat. The silence inside the car felt heavy and cold.

The faces of the siblings she'd met flared in her head one by one, her mind studying each, asking herself if he or she could be the killer. Wesley. The disgraced former senator. Charming. Handsome. Hiding something.

Brandon. The muscular party boy floating atop the pool. A gambler. A grifter, according to some.

Dara. The horse girl practically living out in the stables. She'd shown almost no emotion when talking about her father's death. *He's dead, isn't he? He can't sell the horses now.*

Jude. The hipster marketing guru. Raging. Yelling. Shattering a tumbler against the wall.

Gloria. The eldest of Dutch's brood and Charlie's client. She would seem the least suspicious, which was a bit suspicious in its own right.

Charlie's shoulders quivered as the chill inside intensified.

But no. No. She shouldn't draw any conclusions until she talked to everyone. There was still one more sister, Marjory.

And the mistress, of course. Vivien Marley.

CHAPTER TWELVE

Charlie's phone rang, interrupting her thoughts. Gloria's name flashed on the display, and her voice broke in even before Charlie could say hello.

"What did you say to Jude?"

"I asked him a few questions, that's all."

"Well he called me in an absolute frenzy. Babbling about Wesley using you to engage in some sort of smear campaign against him."

Charlie closed her eyes and shook her head.

"Wesley made somewhat of a cryptic comment earlier. Something like, 'If Jude had even an inkling of the truth.' I don't think I was even meant to hear it, but I did. So I asked Jude about it, and I guess he jumped to conclusions."

"And I'll wager Wes was drinking when he made that little quip. Damn him." Gloria clicked her tongue. "In any case, that particular family secret has nothing to do with the case. I can assure you of that."

"So everyone keeps telling me," Charlie said.

"I'm not sure I appreciate your tone, Ms. Winters." Gloria's voice was as sharp as a knife. "I may have hired you to investigate my father's death, but that doesn't give you the right to go sticking your nose wherever you please. Going forward, I'd appreciate it if you kept your questions focused on my father's affairs."

Charlie couldn't help but smirk at that last turn of phrase.

"So you're saying the fact that Dutch isn't Jude's biological father isn't pertinent to my investigation?"

The line went quiet for a moment.

"Who told you? Was it Brandon?"

"No. He was just as adamant as you are that I not pursue the matter. It was only really a hunch until just now."

The anger in Gloria's tone receded.

"That's… I have to say I'm impressed you figured it out on your own. They said you were good, and they were right."

"Is there concern that Jude might have been left out of the will?"

"Of course not," Gloria insisted. "My father said many times that Jude was his son as far as he was concerned."

"Because I have to tell you, that would be a very powerful motive, Gloria. Especially considering the fact that the will itself is missing."

"The whole reason he wanted it kept from Jude in the first place was because he didn't want him to feel any less a part of the family. Or any less his son. No. My father never would have omitted Jude from his will."

Gloria sighed before she went on.

"Image is very important to Jude. As you might have noticed, he tries quite hard to appear hip. The tattoos. The trendy little office space in Detroit. The Tesla he drives. And he loves pretending he's some kind of self-made marketing mogul, despite the fact that half of his accounts come directly from my father's connections. What I'm trying to say is that Jude has always had a bit of a chip on his shoulder. I think it's because he's the baby of the family. But underneath the tattoos and the swagger, he's a very sensitive boy. I'm worried that if he found out the truth, it would quite literally destroy him. So I hope you'll be discreet."

"Of course. Your secret is safe with me. And if it makes you feel any better, Jude had no idea what I was asking about. He thought Wesley had told me about his failed startup."

Gloria groaned but almost sounded amused.

"Those two have always been like oil and water."

Charlie went on.

"Can I ask if this was a new revelation? That Jude isn't Dutch's biological son, I mean."

"I've known for a little over a year, but my father has known for years, ever since my mother died. Apparently she confessed to quite a few indiscretions on her death bed."

"And what made Dutch decide to tell you?"

"Oh, if it were up to him, I don't think he would have ever told me. He much preferred us to all go along as we always had. The only reason I know is because of *that* woman."

"What woman?"

"Vivien Marley," Gloria said, and Charlie heard the distaste in her voice again. "If she had her way, everyone would know."

Charlie adjusted her grip on her phone.

"What happened?"

"She tried to bring Jude's *situation* up at a family function. Making vague references. Asking Jude about his hair and eye color being different from the rest of the family's. Jude missed the hints, but Wes and I didn't."

"Can you think of any reason why she'd want that information out in the open?"

"What better way to drive a wedge between her lover and his children? She enjoys nothing more than to stir up drama and sow discontent among us. I'm telling you, there's something wrong with that woman."

When Charlie ended the call, she flipped back through her notes until she found the page where Gloria had written down contact information for all of Dutch's family, friends, and associates.

Charlie found the number she was looking for and dialed.

"Marley residence," a woman's voice answered.

"Could I speak to Vivien, please?"

"I'm afraid Ms. Marley isn't available at the moment," the woman said. "Would you like to leave a message?"

"I would. My name is Charlie Winters. I'm a private investigator, and I just need to ask her a few questions about Dutch Carmichael."

"And your phone number?"

Charlie rattled off the digits, thanked the woman, and hung up. She peered down at Vivien Marley's name in Gloria's looping cursive handwriting and drew a line underneath it.

After her conversation with Gloria, Charlie was more eager than ever to speak with Dutch's so-called mistress, but apparently that would have to wait.

As Charlie put the car in gear and rolled down the driveway, Allie perked up for the first time in a while.

"So, you're really buying what Gloria's selling? That Jude being a bastard has nothing to do with Dutch's murder?"

"Not necessarily."

"I mean, you said yourself that if Dutch wrote him out of the will, it'd be a hell of a motive."

"I know what I said," Charlie grumbled.

"Well aren't you going to press Jude on it? I thought we were going to be blindsiding people left and right. What happened with that plan?"

"The problem is, I don't know how to delve into it without tipping Jude off. Which I kind of promised Gloria I wouldn't do."

"And she's paying the bills," Allie said.

"Exactly. Pissing Gloria off would be counterproductive." When she reached the end of the drive, Charlie merged onto the road but not in the direction that headed back to town. "But I never promised I wouldn't ask other people about it."

"Who are you going to ask? You've already talked to everyone."

"Not everyone. There's Vivien Marley, for one," Charlie said. "But there's also one last Carmichael who hasn't weighed in on it. And as it happens, she lives just up the road."

CHAPTER THIRTEEN

Charlie studied Marjory's house as she wound up the cobblestone driveway. It was done in a similar style to Dutch's, and while it wasn't quite as large, it was still a mansion by any definition.

Parking next to a massive garage, Charlie followed a sweeping brick ramp up to the front door and rang the bell. A young man with white-blond hair whisked the door open a few moments later.

"Can I help you?"

"Yes. I'd like to speak with Marjory."

The kind of overly cheerful smile often deployed by customer service reps appeared on his face.

"Do you have an appointment?" the man asked.

"Uh… no. My name is Charlie Winters. I'm a private investigator hired by Marjory's sister. I was hoping to ask her a few questions, but if she's busy—"

The man cut her off with something between a laugh and a scoff.

"Of course she's busy. Marjory is *always* busy. If it weren't for me, she probably wouldn't remember to sleep."

"And you are… Mr. Steigel?" Charlie guessed, though she'd envisioned someone older. She doubted that this guy was over thirty.

When he laughed this time, the sound was more genuine.

"No," he said, his cheeks coloring. "I'm Killian. Her assistant."

If Charlie wasn't mistaken, he'd been flattered by her assumption. He pulled the door open wider.

"Come inside, and I'll see if Marjory can squeeze you in."

Charlie moved into the foyer of the house, and Killian disappeared to find Marjory. She took the time to study the space. Just like in Dutch's house, there was a crystal chandelier and a curved staircase that wound up to the second floor, but the decor here was more feminine than Dutch's estate, with walls painted in an array of pastel hues—robin's egg blue, Swiss cream, powder pink.

A few seconds later, Killian returned.

"Marjory's agreed to speak to you." He was wearing the customer service smile again. "She'll be out in a moment. Can I get you something to drink? Water? Coffee?"

"Ugh, this guy is way too peppy," Allie said. "And check out that hair. I'm getting a total *Children of the Corn* vibe."

"No, thanks," Charlie said.

"Or is it *Village of the Damned*?" Allie continued. "Which one has all the creepy, blond kids?"

Killian moved into a room off the foyer, returning to the task he must have been working on when Charlie had rung the doorbell. He lifted a table lamp from the floor and began carefully swaddling it in bubble wrap. The entire room was in a state of disarray, with items pulled off the shelves and large cardboard boxes strewn about.

"Looks like it's moving day," Charlie said, wondering where Marjory and her husband might be going. Into Dutch's estate? Gloria surely would've mentioned that.

Killian glanced up at her and then around at the room.

"Oh…"

Was that guilt in his eyes? Surprise? Embarrassment?

He cleared his throat and found his voice again.

"Actually—"

A woman swooped in from the next room and patted Killian's shoulder.

"We're renovating," she said, fingering one of the charms dangling from her gold bracelet. It was in the shape of the Chanel logo and encrusted with diamonds. "I hope you'll excuse the mess. This room has to be cleared out before we can start working on it."

Charlie recognized Marjory instantly, not because she'd ever met her before but because she looked very much like Gloria. She was a bit younger and her hair was longer, but the family resemblance was obvious.

The woman stepped forward and extended a hand.

"Marjory Carmichael-Steigel."

"Gloria doesn't wear nearly as much makeup," Allie pointed out. "And she's classier. More understated. I mean that Balmain T-shirt Marjory's wearing probably cost about four hundred bucks."

Ignoring her sister's running commentary, Charlie shook Marjory's hand.

"I appreciate you taking the time to talk to me when you're in the middle of a project like this."

"Honestly, I thought the whole thing would be put on hold after what happened to Daddy, but… the show must go on, I suppose. Anyway, it's the least I could do." She brushed her fingers against her assistant's elbow. "Killian, don't forget to label that box as fragile. My Tiffany frames are in there. If they get damaged, I'll throw an absolute fit."

"What did I say?" Allie said. "Classic brand whore."

"Would you like some coffee?" Marjory asked.

"I'm fine, thanks," Charlie said, but Marjory was already turning back to her assistant.

"Killian, be a darling and fetch us some coffee. Ms. Winters and I will be in the formal living room."

"Of course," Killian said, leaping to his feet like a trained dog.

Marjory pulled an iPhone from her pocket and strode out of the room, and Charlie had to hurry to keep up as she followed her deeper into the house.

CHAPTER FOURTEEN

A small white Pomeranian joined them on their trek through the house, trotting alongside Marjory as she walked.

"What now?" Marjory said, her tone annoyed.

Charlie figured she was addressing the dog until she spoke again.

"No. I'm sorry, but this isn't going to work."

Charlie glanced around.

"Pardon?"

Marjory swiveled to face her and gestured at the Bluetooth headset in her ear.

"Oh," Charlie said, but Marjory's attention was already back on her phone conversation.

"I told him three times already how I wanted it done. We shouldn't even be having this conversation."

They veered right and entered a formal living room with a marble fireplace. Two bouquets of pink roses flanked the mantel.

"Well, you tell him that if he can't do it, I'll find someone else."

Marjory perched stiffly on the edge of a sofa upholstered in ivory velvet while her dog climbed onto a pet bed fashioned to look like a miniature version of the couch.

"Jesus. Everything in this place is adorable with a capital A," Allie said.

Charlie tried to sit up straight in the uncomfortable wingback chair she'd chosen.

"Well?" Marjory said. "Shall we begin?"

"Sorry. I wasn't sure if you were finished with your phone call."

"Yes, you'll have to excuse me. I'm in the middle of organizing a big marketing blitz for the foundation."

"And that's the Lamark Foundation? The charity your father founded?" Charlie asked, though she already knew the answer.

"That's right."

"Can I assume the two of you were close then?"

"Goodness, that's a loaded question." Marjory shook her head and tucked a strand of hair behind her ear. "What you have to understand about Daddy is that he was a very practical man. He wasn't particularly affectionate when we were children. Even less so once we were grown."

Marjory trembled slightly as she took a breath, and Charlie realized she was far more upset than she was letting on.

"I don't mean to imply that he was a cruel man. Not at all. He had a wonderful sense of humor. He could be very charismatic when he wanted to. It sounds like a cliché, but when he was on, he'd light up the room."

Charlie thought of Wesley and wondered if he'd learned to charm people by watching his father.

Marjory blinked.

"And I say 'when he was on' and mean that quite literally. He could turn it on and off like a switch, and when you were the focus of that spotlight, it felt like you could do no wrong. But when it was over, when the switch was turned off, it was like the sun moving behind a cloud. The world seemed a little colder. A little darker."

Marjory straightened suddenly and patted her pockets. A look of annoyance crossed her face until she pulled out a piece of candy. The cellophane wrapper crinkled as she wrestled it free from the bright red candy and popped it into her mouth.

"Was that…" Allie's voice was tinged with awe. "Was that a Jolly Rancher?"

Charlie had thought the same thing but was certain she must be mistaken. The idea of Marjory Carmichael-Steigel—in her big fancy house, surrounded by pink roses and white velvet, long nails polished, designer jewelry sparkling—popping candy in her mouth just felt wrong. It was like watching the Queen of England go to town on a corndog at the county fair.

Marjory caught Charlie staring at her as she wadded the plastic wrapper into a ball.

"I'm sorry. Would you like one?"

She reached into her pocket and brought out another Jolly Rancher.

"No thanks," Charlie said.

Marjory shrugged and pocketed the candy.

"I'm trying to quit smoking. *Again.* I hadn't had a cigarette in over a year, but then… with what happened to Daddy…" She trailed off. "I told myself I'd have just the one cigarette at the funeral, but then one turned into two, and that turned into buying a pack, and it's absolutely astonishing how quickly you can slide right back down that slope."

She sighed.

"Anyway, the candy distracts me when I get a craving. I think it's the cinnamon flavor. The way it burns and tingles isn't quite the same sensation of smoking, but it's close enough that it scratches the itch, you could say." She clasped her hands together so tightly her knuckles stood out white against her tanned skin. "Anyway, you asked about the charity, and I ended up ranting at you about my dad's distant emotional state as if you were my therapist, which I'm sure isn't at all what you're interested in hearing about."

"Actually, every little bit helps. Getting a sense of who he was as a person is as important as anything else."

"Well, your original question was about our working together at the foundation. The fact is, he was a figurehead more than anything by the time I came on. He was very involved in the beginning, of course. The Lamark Foundation simply wouldn't exist without him. But once he'd laid the groundwork, his interest waned." Marjory closed her eyes and inhaled deeply through her nose. "That wasn't unusual for Daddy. He liked the beginning stages of things. When everything was fresh and new and maybe even there was some possibility of failure that made it feel dangerous. But once things were underway, when things had leveled out, he'd lose interest. It happened with us kids. It happened with my mother. The charity was no different."

"Had your father made any large contributions in the past year or so?" Charlie asked.

She'd been wondering if the missing money could, in part, be the result of Dutch taking a Warren Buffet approach to dispersing his wealth as he got older. Distributing it to nonprofits instead of his heirs.

"Oh no. There was a yearly allotment given to the foundation for operating expenses, but the majority of our funding comes from donations from the public."

"And he couldn't have, I don't know, secretly been funneling money into the foundation?"

"Absolutely not. We're required by law to keep meticulous records for tax purposes. We know where every cent comes from," Marjory said. "Of course, I'm expecting that he left a significant endowment to the foundation in his will."

"You're certain there *is* a will?"

"Well… of course there is."

"Wesley seemed to think otherwise."

Marjory rolled her eyes and took another piece of candy from her pocket.

"Yes, well, I stopped trusting in Wesley's judgment when he was arrested for possession." Her face grew cold and hard but softened after depositing the Jolly Rancher into her mouth. "I refuse to believe that Daddy would have left things so ill-prepared.

No. There's a will. And the money is somewhere. Frankly, I'm a bit annoyed about this whole business with Gloria not being able to locate the will. It seems extremely irresponsible of Daddy to not anticipate this and make certain that at least one of us knew where to look."

"Any idea where the money could be?"

Before Marjory could respond, there was a faint rattle of china from the hallway and Killian appeared, balancing a serving tray.

Marjory's brow furrowed.

"Killian, darling, you know I like to serve guests with my Imperial Porcelain set from Saks."

Killian's mouth popped open, and he froze.

"I'm so sorry. Do you want me to switch it?"

Marjory rolled her eyes.

"It's too late for that."

The assistant stood there, looking unsure of what he should do.

"It's fine, Killian. Serve the coffee, please."

He fussed about, pouring two cups of steaming, molasses-colored liquid and then offering to add cream and sugar. When Marjory finally dismissed him, she took a sip of her coffee and made a face at Charlie.

"Killian is skilled at many things, but I'm afraid making coffee isn't among them." She replaced her cup in the matching saucer. "But you were asking about the money. I'm afraid Daddy and I never discussed money unless it related directly to the foundation. In fact, when he first talked about the whole unbanking thing, I imagined sacks with dollar signs printed on them. I realize how absurd that is now. I know Trevor—that's my husband—was always encouraging him to start collecting coins, as if Daddy needed another obsession to inevitably lose interest in. First it was art, then the garden, then cars, then horses, which now that I think about it was sort of a logical progression. More and more complicated. More and more effort required to make it work. More to walk away from when he finally grew bored with it."

The corners of Marjory's mouth pulled up into something reminiscent of a smile, but not quite.

"It's funny, really. He was quite good at reading other people, but he was absolutely blind to his own foibles."

Charlie went back to something she'd said earlier.

"Your husband encouraged him to invest in coins, even after his own coin collection was stolen?"

"You heard about that?" Marjory's hand went to her chest, an almost comical display of surprise. "What an awful scenario. Thankfully they only took a few things. The coin collection, as you mentioned. A few pieces of sports memorabilia. All insured, of course, so it really wasn't much of a loss."

"I heard the thief also trashed your husband's office?"

Marjory grimaced.

"Oh yes. *That.* Do you know they—" she leaned in to whisper the next word "—*urinated* on the carpet in there? Listen to me. They? *He.* Of course it was a man. No woman would stoop that low. Disgusting."

"That sounds… personal," Charlie said.

"And completely over the top, if you ask me. I mean, if you're going to break in to steal something, then do it, and be done with it. What's the point of destroying a perfectly good office like that? Fouling it with bodily fluids? We had to empty the place out and completely redo it. New carpet and the works."

"I hope that's not why you're redoing the parlor," Charlie joked.

Marjory's expression was flat.

"What?"

Charlie gestured over her shoulder with a thumb.

"The renovation?"

Marjory's eyelids fluttered in recognition.

"Oh! Of course." She tittered nervously, putting a hand to her mouth. "No. Thank God. And they'd be fools to try it again with the security system Trevor insisted on installing afterward. We've got over a dozen cameras, sensors on every door and window. I still think he went a bit overboard, but better safe than sorry, I suppose."

It occurred to Charlie that if Trevor Steigel was chummy enough with Dutch to offer investment advice, she should speak with him, too.

"Is your husband here?"

"No. I'm afraid not. He's on business in Denver."

"And what kind of business is he in?"

"Biotechnology." At the sound of her phone buzzing against the coffee table, Marjory snatched it up and studied the screen. "Sorry. Jude's firm is the one handling the marketing campaign for the foundation, and he's passed me off to some totally incompetent underling. But then that's no surprise. Jude will take any chance he gets to pretend he's above the rest of us."

Charlie had been wondering how to broach the subject of Jude, and now here Marjory was, practically serving it up on a platter.

"Speaking of Jude," Charlie said, "I thought we might discuss… well, you know…"

Marjory regarded her with a tight smile. Her eyelids fluttered innocently.

"Discuss what about Jude?"

"Holy balls." Allie choked out a laugh. "She's a terrible liar."

"Marjory, I know about Jude," Charlie said. "Gloria just filled me in."

The sweetly ignorant expression dropped from Marjory's face. "She *told* you?"

"I figured most of it out on my own, which begs the question: if nearly everyone in the family knows, and I—a stranger—can suss it out… don't you think there's a chance Jude could too?"

"No. We've been very careful about it." Marjory closed her eyes. "It's one of the reasons that Dara doesn't know. She's too... naive. She'd end up spilling the beans without even meaning to."

Marjory's eyes popped open, and she leaned in suddenly.

"You can *not* tell Jude."

"I wasn't planning—"

Killian rushed into the room, and the air of intimacy that had just settled over the conversation was instantly shattered. He stooped over the back of the couch, practically pressing his lips to Marjory's ear to whisper something.

"Oh, that's just perfect," Marjory said, throwing her hands up. "I'm going to have to cut this interview short, Ms. Winters. Apparently I'm the only one capable of getting things done the proper way."

Charlie saw her chance to discuss the matter of Jude's paternity in more detail dwindling before her eyes.

"You can't give me just a few more minutes?"

Marjory stood.

"I'm afraid not. There's an urgent matter I have to attend to. Killian will show you out." She stepped closer to Charlie to offer her hand, lowering her voice as she did so. "And I must urge you again to please... please remember what I've said. Jude can't know."

Killian led Charlie to the front door, holding it open for her.

"I'm sorry that got cut short, but you have to understand. She works so hard," he said, his head shaking back and forth the entire time he spoke.

Charlie didn't know what to say to that, so she smiled and nodded and exited the house. She dug around for her keys as she followed the brick pathway outside back to her car.

"Cougar alert. Rawr!" Allie said, making a cat noise.

"What?"

"Oh, come on. I know you saw the way Marjory and that boy toy assistant kept brushing up against one another. He practically nibbled her earlobe when he came in to tell her about that urgent phone call."

Charlie unlocked her car and climbed inside.

"I guess they did seem a little touchy-feely."

"A little?" Allie scoffed. "He was practically getting a boner talking about how *uh-maze-ing* Marjory is."

"Anyway, I think I have to put the Jude thing on the back burner until I can talk to Vivien Marley." Charlie started the car. "As far as his siblings are concerned, he has no idea."

"They could be wrong."

"Sure," Charlie said, turning out of Marjory's driveway onto the road. "Though they did manage to keep it a secret from Dara. That's something."

Goosebumps plumped on Charlie's arms as soon as the gate in front of Dutch's estate came into view. Passing the scene of the old man's murder felt like driving past a graveyard.

Charlie glanced up the drive as she passed. A flurry of movement out in front of the house caught her eye and roused her curiosity. She slowed the car, steering over to the shoulder.

"Whoa. What are you up to now?" Allie said. "Are we sneaking? It feels like we're sneaking."

Charlie parked and jabbed the button on the front of the glovebox. The door popped open, and she pulled out a pair of binoculars.

"Yes! Now we're talkin'," Allie said. "I love when you bust out the 'nocs."

Exiting the car, Charlie crept through the gate and crouched down behind one of the willow trees. She trained her binoculars on the front of the house and waited. Less than a minute later, Wesley reappeared.

Through the binoculars, Charlie watched him tote a painting out of the house and load it into the back of his Cadillac.

"What's Wesley up to now?" Allie asked.

"Helping himself to some of Dad's art collection, looks like."

It also solved the mystery of what he'd been talking about on the phone. She wondered who he'd been talking to. One of his siblings, or someone else?

"That rascal," Allie said. "Are you gonna bust him?"

"No."

"No?"

"I'm not getting involved in the family drama," Charlie said.

She trudged back to the car, replaced the binoculars in the glovebox, and slammed the door shut.

"But I *love* family drama," Allie whined.

"I'll tell Gloria about it, but the rest is up to her. For now, I need to go press my favorite member of the Salem Island police force for details on the Dutch Carmichael murder investigation."

CHAPTER FIFTEEN

When Charlie arrived at the Salem County sheriff's office, she spotted Zoe Wyatt at the far end of the lot. She rolled into the spot beside her friend and put down her window.

"Just who I was coming to see," Charlie said, noting that Zoe was still dressed in her deputy's uniform but had been in the midst of climbing into her personal vehicle. "Are you off-duty?"

"Yes, ma'am. My shift just ended, and I've got a hankering for a double cheeseburger from the Lakeside Tavern."

"Mind if I join you?"

"Hop in," Zoe said. "But be quick about it. I skipped lunch, and I'm starving."

Charlie parked and got out, hurrying around to the passenger side of Zoe's car. She pulled the door open to find the seat absolutely piled with a random assortment of stuff.

"Shoot. Just gimme a sec," Zoe said, grabbing her crap by the handful and tossing it into the backseat.

Same old Zoe, Charlie couldn't help but think. Her car may be different—no longer a hand-me-down from her parents—but it was still chock full of clutter just like it had been in high school. From outside, Charlie spotted four shoes—none of them matching—a desk lamp, two sweatshirts, and a hockey stick.

When the seat was finally free enough for Charlie to sit, she slid inside and closed the door.

Zoe reversed out of the parking space and exited the lot. Charlie noticed what appeared to be a zip-up CD case on the floor next to her foot.

Charlie plucked the case from the floor and undid the zipper, thinking it couldn't possibly contain CDs. But it did.

She flipped through the first few pages, scanning the titles: *The Essential Billie Holiday*, *Born This Way*, *Led Zeppelin III*. Most of the CDs were burned, the labels handwritten in Zoe's messy scrawl.

Charlie snapped the case shut and held it in the air.

"Why do you have this?"

"What do you mean?" Zoe asked.

Charlie pointed at the dash.

"There's no CD player in this car."

"Yeah, but my old car had one."

Charlie stared at her, trying to make it clear that this was not an acceptable answer.

Zoe nodded.

"OK, so when I bought this car, I had all this stuff in my old car, and I kind of just threw everything in here with the intention of sorting it out later."

"And that was how long ago?"

Zoe's lips parted as if to answer, but then she seemed to think better of it.

"More or less than a year?" Charlie pressed.

"I don't see why your arbitrary timeline is relevant."

Charlie chuckled. Zoe's refusal to answer told her plenty.

"Look, it's not doing anyone any harm is it? I mean, it's just a case of CDs. And it's not like I don't use this stuff." Zoe gestured in the general direction of the heaps of junk in the backseat. "These are practical items."

"Uh-huh."

"I know what you are," Zoe said, sticking an accusatory finger in Charlie's face. "You're one of those psycho minimalists, aren't you? One of those Marie Kondo cultists who want everyone to throw everything away for no good reason. Well, I'll tell you what I think about that. It's wasteful. This is all good stuff. Useful stuff. And it's mine. No one can make me get rid of my stuff."

"Whoa there, Zoe. Calm down. You sound like Gollum talking about his ring," Charlie said, laughing. "No one is trying to take your *Precious*."

It was solidly between the lunch and dinner rush when they got to the Lakeside Tavern, which meant the place was practically empty. They chose a booth overlooking the water and ordered without even needing to look at the menu: a double cheeseburger for Zoe and a turkey Reuben for Charlie.

After the waitress returned with their drinks, Zoe took a sip of her Coke and raised an eyebrow at Charlie.

"Well? What do you want?"

"What makes you think I want something? Can't a girl go out with her old pal just because?" Charlie asked, blinking with eyes full of mock innocence.

"When the girl in question is you? No. You only come around when you want information."

Charlie made a face before fessing up.

"OK, fine. What do you have on the Dutch Carmichael murder?"

"Let me guess… the daughter hired you. What's her name? Gloria."

"Good guess."

Zoe nodded.

"She was pretty pissed off about the press getting their hands on the autopsy photos. Came down to the station and gave Sheriff Brown an earful."

"How'd that happen, anyway?"

"Some lackey over at the medical examiner's office leaked them, so it wasn't really our fault, but what can you do?"

The conversation was put on hold when the waitress came to drop off their food. When she'd gone again, Zoe jumped back in.

"The thing is, whoever did it came very close to getting away with it."

Charlie squirted a blob of ketchup onto her plate.

"How so?"

"Think about it." Zoe shrugged. "An old man, who needs a cane to get around, found at the bottom of the stairs? Any idiot would come upon that scene and think it looked like he fell."

"So what tipped you off?"

Zoe lifted her burger and took a hefty bite.

"One of the crime scene techs found a broken shard of pottery in one of the air ducts."

"How is that significant?" Charlie asked.

"It had blood on it, and it was a match for Dutch." Zoe wiped grease from her fingers onto a napkin. "The running theory is that the murderer used an ornamental vase that used to sit at the top of the staircase to hit him over the head. Probably thought it was heavy enough that it wouldn't break, and that the wounds Dutch sustained from the fall would cover up any injuries from the initial blow to the head."

"Only things didn't go to plan."

"Nope. The vase broke, and when they tried to clean up, they missed a piece." Zoe took another bite and closed her eyes. "This is the only place in town that can make a decent burger."

Charlie polished off the first half of her turkey Reuben and started on the next.

"OK, let's talk alibis."

"Who should I start with?" Zoe asked, still chewing her last mouthful of double cheeseburger.

"Do the girls first." Charlie got out a pen. "Gloria, Marjory, and Dara."

"Dara was in Farmington Hills watching a horse give birth."

"Really?"

Zoe nodded.

"She documented the whole thing on Instagram, and let me tell you, I will never unsee that. You know what a horse placenta looks like? Because I do."

Charlie snorted.

"Gloria was at home, and we were able to corroborate that with cell phone records."

"Hold on. That just means Gloria's *phone* was at home."

"True," Zoe admitted. "But do you really think she'd hire you to look into her father's murder if she killed him?"

"No, but I don't believe in ignoring the facts, even if they're inconvenient. Unless you have something better than cell phone records, I'm putting Gloria down as not having an alibi."

"Fair enough," Zoe said, slurping at the dregs of her Coke. "That leaves Marjory, who was also at home."

"Alone?"

"Well, her assistant, Killian Thatcher, was there, and he says she never left the house."

Charlie raised an eyebrow. "I sense a 'but' on the horizon."

"Marjory was in her room for most of the day, sleeping off a headache. I guess it's a chronic thing for her. She has pills for it, but they knock her out. So the assistant was in the house with her…"

"But it's possible she could have slipped out without him even knowing," Charlie mused. "And she lives right down the road from Dutch."

"Exactly."

Charlie scrawled this in her notebook.

"OK. What about Wesley, Brandon, and Jude? Brandon mentioned playing poker when I talked to him."

"Indeed," Zoe said. "We talked to the pit boss at the MotorCity Casino, who confirmed Brandon was at the poker table the entire morning and afternoon. Let's see… Wesley was schvitzing at the health club. We couldn't find anyone who could say he was there for sure that day, and they don't have cameras, but he did have a credit card slip for the parking lot just outside the club."

"What about Jude?"

"Jude was at work."

"On a Sunday?"

"Claims he's a workaholic."

Charlie rolled her eyes.

"Any witnesses to that effect?"

"No, but he was all too eager to provide timestamped security footage of him entering and exiting the building."

"And we both know how easy that is to manipulate." Charlie dredged a fry in ketchup and popped it in her mouth. "So it sounds like Brandon, Dara, and Wesley have fairly solid alibis. Marjory's on slightly shakier ground, while Jude and Gloria are pretty much twisting in the wind."

"That's about what we made of it."

"What about Vivien Marley?"

"Ah, yes." Zoe folded her hands together. "The elusive girlfriend."

"Elusive?"

"We keep trying to set up a time for an interview, and she keeps blowing us off. The detectives even paid her a few house calls, but her maid answers the door and says she's unavailable."

Ice cubes clinked as Charlie swirled her straw around in her iced tea glass.

"That's interesting."

"Yeah, so if you manage to track her down, everyone down at the station would be very eager to hear what she has to say."

"I'll keep you posted," Charlie said. "Have you guys found anything that might suggest what Dutch did with all his money?"

"Nah. As far as we're concerned, that's the family's problem to sort through. And from our perspective, it doesn't change the most obvious motive, which is the money. Even without the millions that are supposedly missing, there's the house, the art, the horses, a dozen or so priceless sports cars… those kids will all get a hefty sum."

When the check came, Charlie insisted on paying.

"I figure I owe you lunch and then some," Charlie said, frowning. "It's true what you said earlier, isn't it? I only call you when I want help with a case."

"It's OK." Zoe reached over and patted her shoulder. "I know you're socially challenged."

"Damn." Allie laughed. "Zoe's dropping truth bombs today."

Charlie wrinkled her nose.

"I'm kind of a shitty friend, aren't I?"

"Kinda," Zoe said, winking. "But not shitty enough that I have to stop hanging out with you."

Charlie sighed as she signed the credit card slip.

"I can do better. I swear." She set the pen down. "What's new with you?"

Zoe chuckled.

"Oh, we're doing this now?"

"Sure," Charlie said. "Why not?"

"Well, as it happens, I have some interesting news for once."

Zoe's expression was so pleased that Charlie found herself leaning in.

"Go on."

"I just found out I have a sister."

"What?" Charlie said. Zoe had always been an only child as far as she knew.

"Technically she's my half-sister," Zoe explained. "I guess my dad had a one-night stand back in college. Some girl he met at a party and never saw again. This was years before he met my mother, of course. He had no idea this other daughter even existed! And we wouldn't have known at all except that I got my parents one of those genealogy kits for Christmas."

"No shit," Charlie said.

"I know! I mean, I've read stories like that, but I never thought it would happen to me."

Zoe was grinning from ear to ear, but Charlie wondered if the rest of the family was as delighted as she was about it.

"And everyone is happy about it… I mean, what did your mom think?"

"Oh, she's thrilled. Rebecca, that's my half-sister, she's got three kids. My mom keeps talking about how she's finally a grandma," Zoe said, rolling her eyes but still smiling.

"So you've met?"

"No. She lives in Toledo, and my parents drove down to her place last month, but I had to work." Zoe frowned, looking genuinely disappointed. "But Rebecca's coming up on Saturday, so I'll finally get to meet her then."

"That's really exciting," Charlie said, getting up and following Zoe out of the restaurant. "I'm happy for you, Zo."

"Thanks. You know, I always wanted a sibling. And if I got to pick, I totally would have chosen a sister." Zoe paused when they reached her car and stared at Charlie over the roof. "I was always envious of you and Allie."

"Really?"

"Yeah." Zoe shrugged. "I mean, it seemed like you came packaged with your very own best friend, you know?"

Charlie felt a sudden pang of heartache.

"Yeah," she said, forcing herself to smile. "I guess I did."

Zoe unlocked the car, and they climbed in. The whole ride back, Charlie couldn't stop thinking about how their roles had been reversed. Zoe had gained a sister whereas Charlie had lost one, and now Charlie was the one who was envious.

CHAPTER SIXTEEN

After Zoe dropped Charlie back at her car, she sat in the parking lot for some time, digesting her turkey Reuben and fries plus what she'd learned from Zoe. Gazing out the window, Charlie's mind kept wandering back to what Zoe had said about motive.

Charlie considered the most common motives for murder: greed, lust, power, revenge. In this case, greed was the most obvious choice, given the financial prowess of the victim.

Dutch had six children, if she counted Jude, and all of them were set to inherit quite a bit of money upon his death. What if Dutch had threatened to write one of them out of the will? Alternately, what if he'd decided to leave his vast fortune to a charity for three-legged dogs? With a man as wealthy as Dutch, the possibilities on that front were endless. Nearly everyone in close proximity might have a reason to think they'd profit from his death.

The flesh prickled on the back of Charlie's neck. Once more, the faces of Dutch's children flashed in her head one by one, this time adding a new name to the list:

Marjory, the charity worker and prissy brand whore. Was she having an affair with her much younger assistant?

Gloria. Wes. Brandon. Dara. Jude. Marjory. Did any of them make sense as a murder suspect more than the others? She didn't want to believe any of them could do it, but it was her job to find out the truth.

She drummed her fingers against the steering wheel, wishing for some epiphany to strike. Some jolt of intuition that would make one name stand out among all the others.

And then one did come to mind. The missing piece to the puzzle of those closest to Dutch.

Vivien Marley, his mistress.

She found it curious that the police hadn't been able to question the woman yet. Vivien Marley was arguably Dutch Carmichael's closest confidante, and yet she seemed to be avoiding speaking with anyone about him. It was as if she had something to hide.

Charlie got out her phone and dialed Vivien's number for the second time that day. It went straight to voicemail, and though Charlie left a message, she was beginning to suspect that Vivien Marley was evading her too.

"Have you noticed that Dutch didn't have any grandchildren?" Allie asked.

"What does that have to do with Vivien?"

"Nothing specifically," Allie said. "Just makes you think."

"About what?"

"You don't think it's odd that *none* of Dutch's kids have children of their own? They're all grown adults," Allie said. "It's weird."

Charlie shrugged.

"*I* don't have kids."

"You really want to go there?" Allie said with a snort.

"Go where?"

"It's just I have this theory. That the 'I'm never having kids' bunch got that way because their family is wacko."

"Who said I'm never having kids?" Charlie asked.

"I just assumed."

Charlie said nothing, hoping Allie would drop it.

"I mean, you're not getting any younger," Allie went on. "Those eggs of yours are probably halfway to hardboiled by now."

"That's not how it works," Charlie grumbled.

"Regardless… what are you waiting for? Your AARP card?"

Charlie's phone rang, and she couldn't help but hope it was the elusive Vivien Marley returning her call. But when she glanced at the screen, she spotted her mother's number flaring on the display this time. It was an odd time for a call. Her mother usually waited until later in the evening.

"Mom?" she answered.

"No," the woman said, and Charlie recognized the voice of her mother's nurse. "It's Elaine."

The edge in the nurse's voice betrayed how upset she was. Elaine was normally serene. Patient. Unflappable. It was what made her such a great caregiver for her mother.

"Hey, Elaine. What's up?" Charlie asked, gritting her teeth and waiting for the bad news to come.

"I'll tell you what's up. I quit. She's done a lot over these last three years, Charlie, let me tell you. But she went too far this time."

"OK, slow down," Charlie said. "Tell me what happened."

"My brand new phone. She up and threw it into the pot of soup I was making, that's what happened."

Charlie's fingers tightened on the steering wheel.

"Oh, Elaine. I'm so sorry."

The woman went on as if Charlie hadn't spoken.

"That was a twelve-hundred-dollar phone. A gift from my husband so I can take professional-quality pictures of my grand-babies. Ruined."

"I'm sorry," Charlie repeated. "And of course I'll replace the phone."

"That's all good and well, but I'm done, Charlie."

Charlie felt a pang of panic run through her at the idea of losing Elaine now.

"Elaine, please. I'll give you a ten percent raise."

"No. No way. This is it. I have to draw a line somewhere. I hate to do it to you, because you're a sweet kid, but you should have heard the way she was screaming at me, hollering about how my 5G was giving her a brain tumor. I will not stay in this house another minute."

Charlie clamped her mouth shut. She was afraid if she opened it now, she might scream. Her mother had done it again. Driven away yet another nurse. And as frustrating as it was, Charlie couldn't blame Elaine for any of it.

"Don't be sorry," she said, finally. "You've been amazing this whole time, and I don't know what I would have done without you. Please send me the bill for your new phone."

When Charlie hung up, she felt a tremendous weight settle on her shoulders. She was so screwed.

Her mother needed in-home care. Someone who could check in on her on a daily basis and make sure she took her morning and afternoon meds. Help with some of the day-to-day housework— grocery shopping, cooking, cleaning.

The last time Charlie had thought Nancy was well enough to do away with the home nurse, it had only taken two weeks for her to spiral into another paranoid episode. By the time Charlie had realized she was off her meds, her mother had ripped up half the carpet upstairs and sledgehammered several holes in the walls, convinced there was black mold lurking in the subfloor and wall cavities. There was no mold. Only a few grand in drywall and flooring repair and another trip to the inpatient psych facility for Mommy Dearest.

No, her mother needed a dedicated caregiver, and it couldn't be Charlie.

The problem was that private care wasn't easy to come by on Salem Island, and her mother had gone through at least a dozen aides over the years. Elaine was the most recent, and she'd lasted the longest. Almost three whole years. Charlie doubted she'd be able to find someone with half the patience. And whoever was going to deal with Nancy Winters was going to need a boatload of it. Charlie had no illusions about that. The meds made her mother alternately lethargic and agitated, and on her bad days, she was a terror. A petulant, spoiled child in a grown woman's body. Plunking Elaine's phone into a pot of soup was rather mild, as far as her tantrums went, though the damage was on the expensive side.

Charlie watched a seagull pluck at a wadded-up McDonald's bag across the parking lot.

"You know you have to go over there," Allie said. "To see Mom."

"I know."

"So?"

"Just give me a minute, will you?" Charlie snapped.

Charlie shook her head as if that might clear her mind the same way it erased the screen of an Etch A Sketch. Why did her mother have to have one of her meltdowns now, when she was right in the middle of a big case?

"That's not how it works. Shit happens, and you don't get to choose when or where or how," Allie said. "Trust me. I'm kind of an expert."

Allie's refusal to let it go for even a minute annoyed Charlie, but she couldn't deny the truth in her sister's words. No one would have chosen for Allie's life to have been cut so very short, least of all Allie herself.

Charlie sighed and glanced at the clock. It was late afternoon already. Elaine would have been there to watch Nancy take her morning meds, but someone had to be there to make sure she took the afternoon dose. And there was no one to do it but Charlie.

She started the car and pulled out of the parking lot. It was time to go deal with her mother.

CHAPTER SEVENTEEN

The sky off to the west was ominously dark as Charlie drove. It looked like a storm was coming.

Somehow, that seemed fitting as Charlie pulled to the curb outside of her mother's home. She shut off the engine and stared up at the house, noting how little it had changed. The same dusty-blue siding and black shutters. A wind chime she'd made at fifth grade camp dangling near the front door. The fraying rope where there used to be a swing on the big hickory tree in the front yard.

"You're stalling again," Allie said.

"No shit."

Charlie braced herself. She'd visited her mother only a handful of times since she'd moved back. It was better, for a whole host of reasons, that she keep her visits brief and limited in frequency.

She ran through the things she needed to accomplish while she was here so she could be in and out and done as quickly as possible: make sure the afternoon meds were taken, for one, but it would also be wise to take stock of the grocery situation. Nancy didn't drive these days, so Elaine had always taken care of the shopping.

"Don't forget to turn your phone off before you go in," Allie reminded her.

Charlie held the power button on her phone and a message popped up asking her, *Are you sure?*

She couldn't help but internalize the question. Was she sure about turning the phone off? Yes. Was she sure about visiting her mother? Not so much.

Charlie climbed out of the car, crossed the sidewalk, and approached the front door. She took a deep breath and knocked.

She studied the lawn while she waited. She paid a neighbor to keep the grass mowed and was glad to see it had been freshly cut. Nancy complained if it wasn't regularly maintained, and it was one less thing to worry about during today's visit.

Charlie knocked again and counted the seconds as they passed. At thirty, she tried the knob and found it unlocked.

She opened the door a crack and called inside.

"Mom?"

There was no answer, which made no sense. Her mother was always home.

Charlie was starting to get a very bad feeling, and that was when she got the first whiff of it.

Smoke.

She barged into the living room. A haze of sooty air billowed in from the kitchen. Charlie ran that way and found a full pan of bacon crackling away on the stove. Without thinking, she reached for the pan, and her skin sizzled on contact with the blazing cast iron of the handle.

Charlie yelped. Snatched her hand away.

Sucking on the burned spot on her fingers, she used her other hand to turn off the burner. Why hadn't she done that in the first place?

Being here always threw her off her game.

A series of thuds drew Charlie's attention away from the stove, and Nancy Winters appeared in the doorway to the basement. Charlie's mom paused there on the threshold, staring. Charlie always had the distinct feeling that whenever her mother saw her after some time had passed, for a brief moment, she thought maybe Charlie was Allie. Back after all these years. Some kind of miracle.

"Charlie," Nancy said, finally. "What are you doing here?"

Charlie pointed at the pan where smoke was still rising from the charred bacon. "You can't leave things on the stove like that, Mom."

"What are you talking about?" Nancy brushed past her to the stove. "I didn't leave anything on the stove. It's burned because that's how I like it."

Charlie threw her hands up.

"Mom, I literally walked in and smelled smoke, and you were nowhere to be found."

"I was in the basement getting a can of beans from the pantry." She lifted a can of Bush's brown sugar baked beans. "Had a hankering for some beans on toast. Figured I was on my own for dinner since Elaine took off."

Charlie wanted to doubt the story as one of her mother's patented little fibs. But she had the can of beans in hand.

Maybe she'd overreacted, jumping to conclusions based on things that had happened in the past. Seeing what she'd expected to see and constructing a narrative to fit it. *Mom's got a screw loose and can't be trusted to do something as simple as frying up a pan of bacon without burning the house down.*

Charlie felt a sudden rush of guilt.

Emptying the can of beans into a resealable plastic container, Nancy popped it in the microwave.

"Hungry?" she asked.

"No," Charlie said, knowing it was best to keep the visit short-lived. "I just ate."

"Suit yourself."

Her mother shuffled around the kitchen, getting out a plate and silverware and depositing two slices of bread in the toaster.

"Are we going to talk about what happened with Elaine?" Charlie asked.

"What about it?"

"You destroyed her property, Mother."

"I told her a thousand times I don't want those cancer bricks in my house." The toaster dinged, and Nancy snatched up the pieces of toast. "Last time I checked, it's my name on the deed. My house. My rules."

"Why couldn't you just ask Elaine to take the phone outside?"

"Because asking worked so well before? How many times do I have to ask for something so simple before I take action?"

"Well, she's gone now."

Nancy scooped a generous portion of beans onto her plate.

"Good riddance. To her and all the rest, like the thief that came before her."

Charlie grumbled.

"Dominique was not a thief."

"Was so."

"She was not. You said she stole some old VHS tapes—which doesn't even make sense to begin with, because they have no value—and then I found them in a box in the attic a few months after she quit."

Nancy dropped her plate onto the kitchen table.

"She didn't quit. I fired her thieving ass. Other things went missing too, by the way. And those were tapes of your sister's dance recitals, so you just watch your mouth with that 'no value' nonsense."

Charlie rubbed her temples. She wasn't sure why she was even bothering with this line of questioning, but if her mother didn't figure out a way to get along with her nurses, they'd eventually run out.

"I don't know what the big fuss is about anyway. Elaine was useless."

"Easy for you to say," Charlie said. "I'm the one who has to find another nurse."

"What for? I'm perfectly capable of taking care of myself. I've told you time and time again, I don't need a babysitter."

Charlie didn't take the bait and instead let the conversation lapse into silence.

Eventually her mother flipped open her *Big Book of Crosswords* and started a puzzle. That was when Charlie saw the pill organizer on the table and remembered the main reason she'd come. She knew Nancy usually took her afternoon dose with dinner to keep the meds from upsetting her stomach. It was one of the reasons she ate so early. But Charlie hadn't seen her mother take the pills yet.

Charlie watched her finish her meal, and then Nancy puttered over to the sink and rinsed her plate and silverware. After sliding the dishes into the dishwasher, she returned to the kitchen table. Charlie waited for her to take the pills, but her mother only returned to her crossword puzzle.

"Mom?"

Nancy didn't glance up from her puzzle.

"Mom, aren't you going to take your afternoon pills?"

"I already did," Nancy said, still not looking up.

This was classic. If her mother sensed even the slightest gap, she'd wiggle through it. And she apparently thought Charlie was gullible enough to take her word for it.

"Check for yourself. The pill compartment is empty."

From the side of her eye, Charlie scoped the compartment. It *was* empty. Even so, Charlie got out her phone.

"Don't make me throw that thing in the garbage disposal. You know the rules. If you're going to call Elaine, then do it outside."

Nancy's eyes were still glued to her crossword puzzle as she spoke.

Charlie gritted her teeth and went out on the porch, switching her phone on.

Pulling up Elaine's name in her list of contacts, Charlie hammered out a text.

Did you see my mother take her meds today?

Charlie wandered the yard while she waited for a response, noting a few spots where moles had been digging. Charlie would need to address that at some point unless she wanted to hear endless rants about "crippling mole infestations" from her mother for the next several months.

A few moments later, her phone chirped.

Yes. Meant to tell you that. Sorry.

Charlie texted back.

Morning and afternoon?

Elaine's response was faster this time.

Correct. I had her take the afternoon dose before I left. Wanted to make sure she was set for the day.

Charlie went back inside, turning her phone off again.

When she returned to the kitchen, Nancy, still engrossed in the puzzle, said, "Told you."

Charlie gathered her bag from where she'd hung it over the back of the dining chair.

"I'll be back tomorrow to check in and bring some groceries, OK?"

"Where are you off to in such a hurry?"

There it was. The clinginess Charlie had come to expect from these interactions with her mother.

"I have to work," Charlie said, bracing herself for what would come next.

Her mother would come up with some last-minute task that needed to be done. Drag it out for as long as she could. Then she'd try to cajole Charlie into staying to watch *Jeopardy!*. Then to sleep over.

Instead, Nancy only said, "Guess I'll see you tomorrow then."

Charlie closed the front door behind herself, the feeling of anxiety she'd had earlier now replaced by frustration. Had she been unfair to assume her mother couldn't take care of herself? Maybe she really had turned a corner this time. People could change, couldn't they?

"People... change?" Allie asked, her sudden appearance jarring Charlie from her thoughts. "Come on, Charles. You know the answer to that."

CHAPTER EIGHTEEN

The storm came on in earnest as Charlie drove back to the office, the sky growing so dark she had to turn on her headlights. A fork of blue-white lightning split the clouds on the western horizon. The crack of thunder came a few moments later, loud enough that Charlie jumped in her seat while she waited for a traffic light to turn green.

It started to rain then, just a light sprinkle at first. But by the time she pulled into the office lot, the droplets had transitioned into fat blobs of water that splatted onto her windshield, forceful and insistent.

She parked as close to the back door as possible and made a mad dash from her car. She was almost to the door when her right foot found a pothole and plunged into the freezing-cold water within, soaking her shoe all the way to the ankle.

"Son of a bitch," Charlie complained.

The wet shoe squelched as she hurried on to the back door and flung herself inside.

She kicked off her shoes as she proceeded to the front room, where she stumbled on a curious scene. Uncle Frank was bent over next to Paige, offering her a tissue. Charlie wasn't sure, but it almost looked like Paige had been crying again. Before she could ask what was wrong, Frank swung around and saw her standing there in her stocking feet.

"What happened to you?" he asked.

"Mud puddle. Stepped in it."

Frank let out a guffaw.

"You know, you always complain that I still call you a turkey, but not a week goes by that you don't pull an absolute, bona fide turkey move like stepping in a mud puddle."

A stray raindrop ran down her scalp and over her forehead, tickling her skin. Charlie wiped it away.

"I didn't expect to see you in the office today."

Frank stood to his full height and hitched up his pants.

"Oh, I had to pop into town to get some food for Marlowe. He decided just this morning that he no longer cares for the Sea Captain's Choice, which used to be his favorite, by the way. So I picked up a tasty array of alternate flavors. Hopefully one of them will please his discerning palate."

"I would have grabbed some for you," Charlie said, dropping her bag on her desk.

Frank waved her away.

"Nah. Dr. Silva said it was OK for me to start taking short jaunts about town. I need to build my stamina back up now that I'm in remission."

Charlie was flipping through a stack of mail Paige had left on her desk, dividing it into piles of legitimate mail and junk. She froze mid-sort, an offer for a low-interest credit card still clasped in her fingers. Slowly, she turned around to face her uncle.

"Did you say remission?"

Grinning, Frank nodded.

"I did indeed."

This was so unexpected, Charlie almost couldn't believe it. On top of chronic lymphocytic leukemia, Frank had only recently recovered from a bout of meningitis. Charlie hadn't lost hope, but she hadn't allowed herself to be blinded by optimism either.

"This better not be one of your jokes," Charlie said. She didn't think Frank would lie about this, but he had a strange sense of humor. He loved nothing more than to tell her little fibs just to test how gullible she was.

"It's not. Ask her." He aimed a thumb at Paige.

The girl nodded.

"It's true. He told me when he first came in."

Charlie's gaze went from Paige back to her uncle. It was real then. Frank was in remission. Charlie was flooded with a sudden burst of relief. She threw herself at Frank, wrapping him in a hug so fierce she knocked him back a step.

"I knew you'd do it." Her voice hitched. "I knew you'd kick cancer's ass."

He patted her back, chuckling.

"Never underestimate the ass-kicking power of your uncle Frank."

Charlie stepped back, wiping the tears from her eyes.

"We should celebrate," she said. "Something big to commemorate the occasion."

Frank squinted thoughtfully.

"You think they still make those big novelty cakes with a half-nekkid Marilyn Monroe look-alike that jumps out of the top of it?"

Charlie snorted.

"I'll have to look into it."

"In the meantime, it sounds like you've got yourself a doozy of a case."

Nodding, Charlie let herself fall into the lap of the old wooden chair, which groaned. She glanced at her new chair, still in semi-complete state. Would she ever be rid of this ancient, uncomfortable relic?

"Paige told you?"

"She did. The Carmichaels, huh?" Frank whistled. "Pretty big fish. Dutch Carmichael is Salem Island royalty."

"You ever hear any good dirt about him?"

"Nothing too salacious, if that's what you mean. But that doesn't mean that dirt doesn't exist," Frank said. "And I'll tell you something else: if I had a dollar for every time I've seen family dynamics go down the toilet over an inheritance, I'd be richer than Dutch Carmichael himself. This whole thing is bound to uncover a whole lot of ugly family secrets. Every family has them. Some are uglier than others, of course. And in my experience, the richer folk are, the deeper the closets they need."

"Deeper closets?" Paige asked.

Frank waggled his eyebrows.

"Sure. To hide all the skellingtons."

The chair squealed as Charlie leaned back in it. She'd already uncovered one family secret, and Frank's words had her wondering what else the Carmichael family might be hiding.

"Anyhow, Marlowe gets ornery if he's not fed on time, so I should be heading back. But before I go, can I have a word with you?" Frank pointed toward the back office.

"Sure." Charlie got to her feet and followed Frank into the back room.

"Close the door, will you?"

Charlie shut the door behind her, wondering at Frank's sudden need for privacy.

"What is it?"

"Has Paige ever talked about her family situation with you?"

"No," Charlie said. "Why?"

"Well, she was very upset when I came in. I guess she has a rather… turbulent relationship with her father. Hasn't spoken to him in years."

"OK."

"It seems that every few months, he tries to get in contact with her. Stirs up the aunts and uncles and grandparents and has them descend on the girl like a pack of flying monkeys, all wanting to know why she won't talk to her poor old man. Laying on the guilt real thick. Pecking away at her in hopes that she'll cave."

"Ugh," Charlie said, wrinkling her nose.

"Yeah," Frank agreed. "So they just started up with the pecking again in the last week or so, and then dear old Dad himself called her up today. Just a few minutes before I came in."

"Has she blocked his number?"

"Yes, but he called the office phone."

Charlie stared at him.

"This office?"

Frank nodded.

"That takes some big brass balls," Charlie said.

"That's what I thought. Anyway, I figured you should know what's going on, in case he calls up again."

"I almost hope he does so I can set his ass straight."

Frank chuckled and squeezed her shoulder.

"For his sake, then, he better hope he doesn't. Hell hath no fury like a pissed-off turkey." Frank kissed her cheek. "I'll get out of your hair. Sounds like you've got your hands full with this Dutch Carmichael thing. But you should let Paige know where you stand on things. She was pretty shaken when I came in, and I think it'd do her good to know you've got her back."

"I'll do that," Charlie said.

As she watched her uncle slip into his jacket and head out the door, Charlie felt herself tearing up again. Frank's cancer had been a dark cloud hanging over them for months now, and she almost couldn't believe it was over, just like that.

"That's because your life is kind of a shitshow," Allie said. "No offense. But you're used to things not working out for the best."

"I'll take the good wherever I can get it," Charlie said.

Charlie went out into the front room and told Paige what Frank had relayed about her father calling the office.

"Oh, geez. I'm so sorry about that, Miss Winters. I honestly don't know how he got the number."

"Paige, you don't need to apologize."

"But it's just so unprofessional for my family drama to be spilling over into the workplace. Not to mention embarrassing."

"I think that's probably exactly why he called here. It's just another tool to wear you down," Charlie said. "The good news is that now that we know his angle, we can disrupt it. So the next time he calls this number, hand me the phone. I'll make sure he understands that we're not playing his games around here. OK?"

Paige nodded and forced a weak smile onto her face.

"Thank you, Charlie."

"Don't mention it."

CHAPTER NINETEEN

Charlie hopped up on her desk and peeled off her wet sock, draping it over the edge of her wastebasket in hopes it would dry faster that way.

"Did we get any other calls while I was out?"

It felt weird only wearing one sock, so she pulled off the dry one, too.

"Oh, yes. I almost forgot." Paige retrieved a pad of Post-it notes the color of bubblegum. "The first was a lady named Laura Engler. She wants to hire you to prove that her husband is a, quote, 'lyin', cheatin' sack of S.' Except that she said the actual swear, and I just don't feel right saying it, not knowing the man myself."

She passed Charlie the note with Laura Engler's phone number.

"And the second call was from Gloria Carmichael. She said she couldn't reach you on your cell."

"Shit," Charlie said, digging her phone out. She'd forgotten to turn it back on after leaving her mother's house. "Did she leave a message?"

"Just that it was urgent and to call her back as soon as possible."

Charlie dialed Gloria's number. It rang once, and then Gloria answered.

"Ms. Winters, thank God."

Gloria sounded out of breath, and for a moment, Charlie was concerned that something bad had happened.

"What is it?"

"I think I found something," Gloria said, her breathlessness taking on an almost giddy tone. "I've just been going crazy not being able to talk to someone about it."

The enthusiastic note in Gloria's voice eased Charlie's anxiety some. She wasn't in trouble, just excited.

"What did you find?"

Instead of answering, Gloria asked, "Are you at your office?"

"Yes."

"Good," Gloria said. "I'll tell you when I get there. I'm on my way now."

"You can't just tell me what it is?" Charlie asked.

"I'd rather not say it over the phone, to be honest. It's all a bit too sordid for my liking." Gloria made a throaty noise that was sort of a laugh with no trace of humor in it. "Actually, this goes well beyond sordid. If it's true, it's quite disgusting, really."

Charlie fiddled with a pen, clicking the retractable tip in and out.

"Well, I must admit you've piqued my curiosity," she said, glancing out the front window at the artificial twilight brought on by the storm.

"Yes, well, I'll see you in a few minutes."

"Everything OK?" Paige asked after Charlie disconnected the call and tossed her phone onto her desk.

"I think so. She's heading here now," Charlie answered.

Paige sprang up from her seat.

"I think I'll make a fresh pot of coffee so you can offer Ms. Carmichael a cup when she arrives."

"Great idea, Paige," Charlie said, thinking she'd never have thought to do that herself. "You've only been here a few weeks, and I already don't know what I'd do without you."

Paige blinked, looking stricken.

"Are you being sarcastic?"

"No." Charlie frowned and shook her head. "Why would you think that?"

Eyes stretching even wider, Paige's cheeks flushed red.

"Oh geez. I'm so sorry. I have a real hard time detecting sarcasm, and then... well, thank you. For saying those nice things." She scurried off toward the back room. "I'll just get to making that coffee now."

"So… she's weird," Allie said.

"Yeah," Charlie agreed. "Then again, I'm the one having a never-ending conversation with my dead sister, so maybe I'm not the best judge."

Charlie swiveled back and forth in her chair, wondering what "sordid" information Gloria might have discovered.

"Sordid *and* disgusting," Allie whispered with glee. "Don't forget that. It's the best part."

The telltale sounds of coffee preparation filtered out from the back room as Charlie hopped up and began pacing around the office in her bare feet. Hinges squeaking as the cupboard door was opened, and then the soft thud as it closed again. Mugs thunking onto the countertop. The hushed scrape of coffee grounds being scooped from a can. Water sloshing into a carafe. The noises offered a pleasant background track to her contemplation.

For several minutes, the swirling pattern of her thoughts matched the circular path she took around the office. She only broke stride when she got a whiff of coffee from the back room. Paige may be a little strange, but she made great coffee, and Charlie couldn't wait to down a cup of it.

She turned and took one step toward the back of the office but stopped when she spotted Gloria's Bentley pull to the curb across the street. The headlights winked out a moment later. It was still pouring outside, and as Gloria stepped from her vehicle, Charlie saw that she didn't have an umbrella.

She scurried over to the front door and pushed it open. It was a small thing. It would only save Gloria four or five seconds at most, but every moment sheltered from this downpour would be a blessing.

Gloria slammed her car door shut and jogged across the road. When she saw Charlie waiting just inside the door, she lifted a hand in greeting and started to speak, but the words never made it to her lips.

Her head swiveled away, facing something up the street that Charlie couldn't see.

Charlie sensed something was very wrong when Gloria's feet slowed and brought her to a dead stop on the double yellow line. Her eyes went wide.

A millisecond later, Charlie heard it. The fierce roar of a car's engine. Too loud. Too close.

The car lurched into Charlie's field of vision. A sheening blur of red streaking from left to right. Tires sizzling over the wet asphalt.

It veered toward Gloria. Engine screaming out a higher note.

Not slowing. Speeding up.

Gloria's body jerked to life again. She tried to dive out of the way. Too late.

The car tracked her movement. Bashed into her. Through her. The metal slapped and thudded against the softness of her form.

She flew. Limp arms and legs splaying. Shivering with the whims of the wind surrounding her.

The car's brake lights flickered. One flash of red. And then it sped out of view. Engine noise trailing away.

Gloria's body toppled to the road. Scraped over the asphalt. Skidded and tumbled onto the sidewalk beyond.

And then she lay still.

CHAPTER TWENTY

Charlie sprinted out into the rain, the water plastering her hair to her face.

Flecks of loose gravel jabbed into her bare feet as she raced down the sidewalk. Chipped bits of rock. Jagged stone edges gnawing at her like teeth.

Down the curb. Into the street. The surface of the asphalt was wet and cold from the rain, but she could still feel the residual heat baked in by the direct sunlight over the course of the day. It felt strange. Warm and cold and wet and gritty all at once.

None of these sensations quite touched Charlie's conscious mind. They were flitting things, experienced and forgotten all at once.

In this moment, she saw only Gloria.

Charlie felt like she was running in slow motion. Feet pounding over the street. Inching along.

She focused on the sprawled figure in the distance. Sharp and vivid.

Gloria lay face up. Crooked. Draped over the curb on the far side of the street.

There was something awkward in the pose of her limbs. Something wrong with the angle of her neck. Something disturbing about the absolute stillness of her.

Even from afar, some of the wounds were visible. Red creases standing out from the milky flesh. Slashes marring her forehead and cheek. Scrapes exposing patches of flesh on her arms and legs.

She'd landed directly under the marquee of the old Fox Village Theater. The sidewalk below was relatively dry, protected by the wide awning overhead.

Charlie drew closer, and the camera in her mind zoomed in on the blood spreading over the cement. A scarlet pool oozing outward from a gash near Gloria's temple.

It spilled down into a seam in the concrete. Filled the gap. Traced along it. A rivulet the width of a finger stretched out from the rest of the circular pool. It looked black where it moved out from under the glow of the marquee.

Part of her expected Gloria to move. To twitch. To show some sign of life. Anything.

But the figure held utterly still.

Charlie hurdled the curb, more details coming into view as she closed the last few yards.

Gloria's eyes were pinched closed. Wrinkles surrounding them. She looked tired. Older now than before. But also somehow peaceful despite the ragged wounds.

Resting. Perhaps for good. Perhaps in peace.

"Gloria?"

The sound of Charlie's own voice surprised her. Sounded dry in her ears. But strong. Calmer than she felt inside.

Charlie knelt beside the broken figure. The uneven surface of the concrete digging into her knees.

"Gloria, can you hear me?"

Gloria didn't respond. No flutter of the eyelids. No quirk of the mouth. No shudder of the torso.

The words "not responsive" echoed in Charlie's head. Someone else's voice speaking inside her skull now. Clinical. Detached. *Victim was not responsive.*

She reached out her hand. Fingers finding that curved place on the neck where the artery nestled. Checking for a pulse.

Gloria's skin was already frigid. Shockingly so.

Charlie held her breath. Fingertips jabbed into the flesh. Waiting for something. Anything.

"Come on, Gloria," she muttered. "Stay with me, please."

She felt it then. A stuttering pulse. Thrumming. Beating against her fingertips.

But it was weak. Faint.

Charlie patted her pocket, feeling for her phone. But it wasn't there. She'd left it on her desk.

Movement in the periphery of her vision snapped Charlie's head up. It was one of the employees from the movie theater, a teenage boy in a red vest and bow tie. Broom in hand and mouth agape as he took in the horror laid out on the concrete.

Again, Charlie's voice scared her as it came out. Unexpected, even to her.

"Call 911!"

But the kid stayed rooted to the spot, unable to hear her through his own shock. He muttered something she couldn't hear, but there were other voices now. Other people gathering on the sidewalk. Charlie turned her attention to the crowd, recognizing Paige among a cluster of women from the salon next door.

"Oh my God!"

"What happened? Did anyone see what happened?"

"Someone should do something! Has anyone called the police?"

Charlie's eyes found Paige's, and she called out to her.

"Call an ambulance."

For one heartbeat, she thought Paige was stuck in the same trance-like state the movie theater usher was in. But the girl nodded once and sprinted back toward the office.

Charlie leaned in and clasped one of Gloria's hands in her own. "Hold on, Gloria."

CHAPTER TWENTY-ONE

Charlie removed her jacket and draped it over Gloria, knowing it probably did little to warm her, but it was the best she could do.

"What happened to the car?" one of the women in the crowd asked.

For the first time, Charlie glanced around, taking in her surroundings. The car was long gone. The driver hadn't even stopped to see if Gloria was OK.

That thought drew her focus back to the fragile body in front of her. Charlie squinted. Gloria's skin was a ghostly white, her lips looked almost gray.

Charlie slid her fingers down to the spot beneath the chin again and felt for a pulse.

Nothing.

"No, no, no," Charlie croaked. "Gloria, stay with me."

Her mind reeled, scrambling for a solution.

CPR. She needed to do CPR.

It had been a while, and she'd never done it for real. Only on a dummy in a class.

Charlie slid down the jacket she'd covered Gloria with and went through the steps she remembered: probing for the end of the breastbone with her fingertips and then using two fingers as a guide for where to place the heel of her hand. Charlie rested her right hand on top of the left. Straightened her arms. Locked her elbows. And drove the weight of her upper body down.

Gloria's chest held firm through the first few compressions. But on the fourth, Charlie heard and felt a terrible crunch as the cartilage between her ribs gave. Charlie ignored the instinct to stop then, blanked out the voice in her head that worried she might be hurting Gloria. She had to keep going until the ambulance arrived.

She counted out thirty compressions and checked Gloria's airway, pausing to consider the fact that much of her face was a bloody mess of road rash. As gently as she could, Charlie pinched Gloria's nostrils shut and delivered two rescue breaths.

One.

Two.

She waited then, her face next to Gloria's, listening for her breathing to resume.

When it didn't, she began again with the compressions.

Paige returned, phone pressed to her ear. She was saying something, asking questions, but Charlie couldn't answer. Knew she couldn't allow her concentration to be broken, even for a moment.

Charlie's awareness shrank down until she was cognizant of nothing beyond her own movements and Gloria's body.

The next stretch of time progressed in increments of thirty compressions and two breaths. Eventually, she was out of breath, sweating, wondering how long she could keep it up.

It wasn't until one of the paramedics touched her arm and told her he'd take over that she stopped.

All the outside stimulus she'd been blocking out flooded in at once, overwhelming her senses. The red and blue flashing lights of the ambulance. The murmur of the onlookers, a crowd that had tripled in size without Charlie noticing.

The other paramedic was a woman, and she started firing questions at Charlie while she unpacked her kit.

"Can you tell us when you first started delivering CPR, ma'am?" The woman checked her watch. "Since the 911 call?"

"Yes," Charlie said, shaking off the disorientation. "It was right around then."

The woman snapped on a pair of gloves.

"Dispatch said it was a hit-and-run. Is that correct?"

"Yes," Charlie said.

She struggled to her feet, noticing that the rain had let up. Even so, the aftereffects of the adrenaline left her shaky and cold. And why was she barefoot?

"How fast was the vehicle going?" the woman asked. "Could you tell?"

Charlie shook her head, teeth chattering.

"I don't know. Fifty. Maybe faster?"

"And was it a direct hit or more of a side-swipe? Did she go under the car at all?"

"No, it hit her pretty much dead center and threw her up into the air."

The two paramedics exchanged some medical jargon that Charlie didn't understand, and then the woman took a pair of scissors from her bag and cut the front of Gloria's blouse open.

"Charging now," the woman said, pressing a button on a boombox-shaped contraption beside her. There was a digital screen with a heart rate monitor in the center of the device. A defibrillator.

"Heard," the man answered, continuing chest compressions.

A robotic voice came from the defibrillator: "Connect electrodes."

The woman followed the instructions, wiping Gloria's exposed skin with gauze and attaching the sticky pads to her chest. The defibrillator whooped.

"Clear."

"Clear."

Both paramedics removed their hands from Gloria's body, and a moment later, her body pulsed violently.

The male paramedic glanced at the machine and immediately began compressions again.

The woman pulled something from her bag that looked like a clear balloon and placed it over Gloria's mouth, using it to force air into her lungs.

When the defibrillator machine whooped again, the two paramedics prepared for the shock.

"Clear," they said in unison.

Gloria's body convulsed again.

Charlie just stood there, arms wrapped around her own body to ward off the chill she felt. She hoped she never had to perform CPR ever again, but this was somehow worse. Standing by and watching as someone else struggled to keep Gloria alive.

A fire truck arrived, followed by two police cruisers. The growing crowd of first responders urged the onlookers back and quickly blocked Charlie's view of the scene.

Someone took her by the arm and guided her under the awning of a nearby building. Charlie's eyes were still glued to the huddle around Gloria, and the person talking to her had to snap their fingers in her face to finally gain her attention.

Charlie blinked. Realized it was Zoe that had been talking to her.

"Jesus, Charlie. Are you OK?"

"Yeah."

"You're totally spaced out, and you're barefoot, for God's sake. Let's go inside."

"No, I want to stay," Charlie said, resisting Zoe's nudge to get her moving. Reality slammed into her then, and she remembered Gloria's brothers and sisters. "Her family. Someone needs to tell them."

"Don't worry about that. We'll handle it," Zoe said, taking off her uniform jacket and draping it over Charlie's shoulders. "Did you see it happen?"

"I saw... everything. I was standing right in the doorway and..." Charlie trailed off as the horrible scene replayed in her mind.

"OK." Zoe's eyes were filled with concern. "We'll need to get a statement from you in a bit. If you're up for it."

"Of course," Charlie murmured, still watching the cluster of bodies obscuring Gloria from view.

They observed the scene for some time before Charlie detected a shift in the energy. The knot of people around Gloria began to break up, first responders wandering away one by one. She caught a glimpse of the paramedics packing up their stuff, and she thought that meant they'd done it. They'd gotten her heart beating again. Gloria would live.

And then she saw the expression on the female paramedic's face. The hard set of her mouth. The furrow of her brow.

A moment later, a deputy unfurled a white sheet and draped it over the lifeless figure on the sidewalk.

Gloria Carmichael was dead.

CHAPTER TWENTY-TWO

The next hour blurred past. It felt like the rest of the world was distant from her, quiet and hazy, like she was underwater.

A detective came over to take an official statement. Charlie had a hard time focusing on his questions, struggling to concentrate for longer than a few seconds at a time.

The detective's mustached face blinked at her. Lips moving.

"Can you tell me what kind of vehicle it was?"

Charlie closed her eyes and willed the scene to mind. This was important. She had to remember.

But it had all been so fast. Two seconds, at most. Gloria turning at the sound of the engine's growl. The way it struck her below the knees, sent her flying.

"It was a car," Charlie said, starting with the easiest detail first. "A sports car."

Detective Mustache nodded. Waited for her to go on.

She took a deep breath and let it come to her. A smear of crimson slicing through the murk of the rain and colliding with Gloria's body.

"Red." Charlie shivered. "Bright red."

"And did it swerve? Slam on the brakes before it hit?"

"No. It sped up, I think."

She pictured it again. Watched the violent movie play in her head. The approach. The impact. Those red brake lights glinting over the wet asphalt, but only for a second.

"The car's lights were off."

That got his attention. Made his mustache twitch.

"You're certain of that?"

"No headlights. No taillights trailing away. The brake lights flared for a split second, shortly after impact, but that was it."

Detective Mustache's pen flicked over his notepad. Probably writing down some variation of what Charlie was thinking now.

Gloria had been hit on purpose. Dutch's killer had just claimed another victim.

When the police finally wrapped up their work and cleared the scene, Charlie realized how late it had gotten.

"You're going to be OK?" Zoe asked as she walked Charlie back over to her office. "I don't get off work for another hour, but I could come check in on you."

Charlie shook her head.

"I'm alright."

"You sure?" Zoe said, looking unconvinced.

Charlie forced a reassuring smile.

"I'm fine. Really."

It was a lie, but Charlie didn't see what good it would do for Zoe to go on worrying about her.

Zoe waited until Charlie had passed through the front doors before giving a wave and taking off. Paige jumped to her feet at the jangle of the bells over the front door.

"What are you still doing here?" Charlie asked.

"I thought I should wait for you."

"That was good of you," Charlie said. "But you didn't need to stay."

"I didn't know what else to do." Tears formed at the corners of the girl's eyes. "It was just so awful, I couldn't imagine going home and… pretending like nothing happened."

Charlie remembered that same thought turning over and over in her mind when Allie had died. How utterly wrong it felt that her entire world had been ripped apart while the rest of humanity continued on in their routines.

"No. You don't have to pretend like nothing happened." Charlie slung an arm around her. "I want you to go home and take a hot shower. Then make yourself a cup of tea and put on a movie or a TV show you've watched a hundred times that always makes you feel good."

Paige nodded, seeming slightly more at ease.

"Then what?"

Charlie rested her hands on Paige's shoulders and looked her dead in the eye.

"Then you get some sleep so that tomorrow you're ready to help me find the son of a bitch who did this. Can you do that?"

That got a tiny laugh out of Paige. She sniffled.

"Yeah."

"Good," Charlie said. "Now gather up your things, and get out of here. I'll close up."

Paige did as Charlie said, tossing a water bottle and her phone into her purse and slipping into her jacket. As she headed for the door, Charlie called out to her.

"Don't forget to eat something. You won't feel like it, but even if it's just some crackers or toast or something, get some food in your stomach."

Paige gave a dutiful nod before disappearing outside.

The sudden quiet of the empty office seemed to close in on Charlie like a cloud. The exhaustion hit her all at once, and she let herself slump down onto the leather couch.

Her eyes blinked shut. She needed to lock up, haul her ass up to her apartment and get out of her damp, blood-soaked clothes. But just now, she was so tired all she wanted to do was curl up here on the battered old sofa.

Anyway, there was no harm in resting her eyes for a minute.

CHAPTER TWENTY-THREE

The rain pattered down in the dream, rivulets streaking Charlie's face as she stumbled toward where Gloria lay in the street. But the air was thick and wrong, slowing her movements. She tried to run, to get there faster, but the more she struggled against it, the more it seemed to hold her back.

No matter what she did, she couldn't get to Gloria. Couldn't help her. Could only stare at the broken figure sprawled on the concrete.

Powerless.

Charlie woke with a silent scream on her lips. Not because of the dream.

Someone was in the room.

A man's figure hovered over her. Broad shoulders. Hands on her arms, shaking her awake.

Charlie tried to blink away the sleep and confusion. Tried to remember where she was.

Drop ceiling. Harsh fluorescent lighting. Carpet that smelled of the Parliaments Uncle Frank used to smoke.

She was in the office. She'd fallen asleep on the couch in the front room.

That made sense. What didn't make sense was Brandon Carmichael's presence. He knelt before her, eyes wide with concern.

"What are you doing here?" she asked.

"The lights were on, and when I came to the door, I saw you through the window," he said. "I had to see if you were alright."

"I'm fine. I fell asleep, that's all."

There was a note of panic in his voice that seemed overblown given the fact that she'd only been having a nightmare.

"But what happened? Are you injured?"

Charlie realized finally that he was staring at the blood on her shirt—Gloria's blood—and assumed it was hers. She gazed down at the irregular blotches and smears staining the fabric.

"It's… not mine."

He reeled back after a beat, no doubt realizing whose blood it was.

"Oh," he said. "Jesus."

Charlie sat up straighter, the gravity of the situation sobering her up in an instant.

"I am so sorry for your loss," she said.

"Thank you," he said, avoiding her gaze.

It struck Charlie that she didn't know whether the police had told the family that the hit-and-run hadn't been an accident.

"Have you talked to the police?"

"Yes," he said, then shook his head. "Well, Wesley did. He's the one who got the call."

Charlie nodded, thinking that if the only call Wesley had received was the one directly after the incident, then they didn't know yet.

"That's why I came down here, actually," Brandon said. "We're all meeting at the house, and we thought… well, I guess we have questions, seeing as you were there when… when it happened. Not to mention all the stuff with the estate. We're all in shock, but Wesley's kind of freaking out now that he's realized all of Gloria's responsibilities are going to end up falling on him."

He scrutinized the blood on her shirt. The streaks of mascara she hadn't quite been able to wipe away completely.

"But it can wait," he said. "We don't have to do this now."

"No, it's OK." Charlie pushed to her feet. "I'll come."

"Are you sure?" Brandon asked, eying her up and down. "Because—and I mean this in the nicest way possible—you look like hell."

Charlie laughed for the first time in what felt like forever.

"Point taken. I'll take a quick shower and change."

Brandon nodded.

"Should I wait for you?"

"You can go ahead," Charlie said. "I'll be right behind you."

Brandon left through the front door, and Charlie made sure to lock up behind him. As she turned out the lights and headed through the office to the back exit, Allie piped up.

"I think he likes you."

"Oh sure." Charlie laid on the sarcasm. "What gave it away for you? When he told me I looked like hell?"

Upstairs, Charlie made a beeline for the bathroom. She couldn't wait to get out of her clothes, which still felt vaguely damp. Not to mention the blood. She studied the stained shirt in the mirror. The pale blue and white plaid fabric was now a deep red from her sternum to her shoulder.

"It looks kinda cool, actually," Allie said.

Charlie hurried to unbutton the shirt and get it off.

"Don't be morbid."

Rolling it into a wad, she tossed it into the trash bin next to the sink.

"Fine," Allie said. "But I have a question."

"What is it?" Charlie asked, struggling out of her ever-so-slightly moist jeans.

"Why did you agree to go talk to Gloria's family tonight when Brandon said it could wait?"

The shower came to life with a hiss as Charlie turned the faucet handle, running her fingers under the spray to check the temperature.

"Because I want to be the one who tells them Gloria was murdered." Charlie caught her reflection in the mirror and stared into it. Her jaw tensed as she gritted her teeth. "I need to see their faces when they find out."

CHAPTER TWENTY-FOUR

There were two cars parked out front of Dutch Carmichael's house when Charlie arrived: Wesley's Cadillac and Brandon's BMW. It was only when Charlie climbed out that she realized Brandon was still in his car.

She approached the driver's side and peered in through the window. Phone pressed to his ear, Brandon held up a finger to indicate he was almost finished.

Charlie thrust her hands in her pockets and moseyed around the large fountain in the center of the driveway. It towered over her, a shapeless mass of stone lit up in the night.

"Who do you think he's talking to?" Allie asked. "I'll bet it's his girlfriend."

"How do you know he has a girlfriend?"

"I don't." Allie cackled. "But now I know that you're interested."

"I am not."

"Deny it all you want, Charles. I'm sure someone will believe you."

Behind her, Charlie heard Brandon's car door open and shut.

"That was Marjory," he said, tucking the phone into his leather jacket.

Charlie couldn't help but feel a tiny surge of vindication at Allie's wrongness.

"She'll be another half hour or so. She and a friend spent the afternoon driving up to her cabin, only to have to turn around and head back almost as soon as they'd arrived."

"How far away is it?" Charlie asked, following Brandon up the front steps.

He paused and held the door open for her.

"About two and a half hours. Right at the tip of the thumb," he said, referring to the tendency of Michiganders to describe locations in the state as a place on a large, imaginary mitten. "Bad Axe is the nearest town, but the cabin itself is really out in the boonies. No neighbors for miles. No Wi-Fi, if you can believe it."

"Sounds remote."

"Completely. When the weather's nice, it can be a very pleasant drive, especially in a convertible. I like to put Sadie's top down and take the M-25 along the coast all the way up."

"Sadie?" Charlie repeated. "You named your car?"

"Doesn't everyone?"

"I don't."

"That's because you drive a Focus," Brandon said. "If you drove a car with character, you'd have no choice but to give it a name."

"Ah, but I'm a private investigator. Driving a car with no character is the whole point, especially if I'm tailing someone."

Brandon stuck his head into the dining room and then the parlor, searching for Wesley. He paused to squint at her.

"Now that you mention it, I always thought there was something off about Tom Selleck driving that red Ferrari in *Magnum, P.I.*"

They finally found Wesley in the solarium. He was slumped over on a bamboo daybed, a tumbler clutched in one hand. A crystal decanter of booze from the basement bar kept him company nearby.

As they entered, Wesley finished off what was left of his drink and poured another.

"How can she be gone?" he asked, as if continuing some prior conversation.

Tears choked his voice, and Charlie thought that he was more than a little drunk.

"Our Glori. She used to set up these tea parties when we were kids. Of course, I was never interested in that kind of thing, but she had a way of always getting what she wanted. She'd bribe me with candy and sweets. And I'd sit there with her and the dog and her dolls, and we'd make believe we were royalty." His words devolved into a heavy sob. "I can't believe she's gone."

"Hey, Wes. It's alright, buddy. What do you say we go make some coffee before everyone else gets here?" Brandon suggested.

He went to take the glass from Wesley's hand, but in a move like a child shoving a stolen cookie in his mouth, Wesley snatched his arm away and tossed back the remainder of the alcohol before Brandon could stop him. It might have been comical if not for the gloomy circumstances.

Charlie helped Brandon corral Wesley into the kitchen. His weepy monologue continued as they dug through the cabinets to find the coffee-making implements.

"She always knew what to do when things were falling apart. When Mom died, Gloria was the one who held everything together. Kept the family forging ahead. No man left behind."

When they'd finally unearthed the necessary components and had a pot brewing, Brandon turned to Charlie.

"Wait here with him for a minute, will you?" He kept his voice low enough that Wesley wouldn't hear. "If I don't hide the Scotch while Wes is out of the room, any sobering effect the coffee has on him will be short-lived."

Charlie nodded.

At the other end of the kitchen, Wesley had gone unusually quiet. He braced himself on the countertop with both hands and seemed to be staring into his reflection on the marble top. Brandon had only been gone a few seconds when he whirled around to face her.

"You were there." His tone was almost accusing. "You saw it all."

"Yes." Charlie swallowed. "I was there."

"I know you won't want to tell me, but I need the truth. The raw truth." He gripped her arms, leaning in so close that she could smell the peaty scent of Scotch on his breath. "Did she suffer? Was she in pain when she died?"

Images of Gloria's broken body flashed in Charlie's mind. She'd had a pulse for only a brief time after she'd been hit, and she definitely hadn't been conscious. Still, Charlie couldn't imagine that Gloria had felt none of it.

And she'd seen it coming. The memory played in slow motion: Gloria's head turning toward the car in the last milliseconds before it all came undone. She'd known, even if only for a flash, what was about to happen. If that didn't constitute suffering, what did?

"It was quick," Charlie finally said, not wanting to lie outright.

"Hey." Brandon stepped back into the kitchen. "What'd I miss?"

Charlie thought Wesley would release her then, change the subject. But his fingers only clamped down on her tighter.

"Are you sure?" he hissed. "Because the police told me the paramedics worked on her for almost an hour."

Jesus, was that right? Almost an hour? To Charlie, the whole ordeal was a blur that might as well have taken place in ten minutes.

Brandon edged in and gently removed Wesley's grip on Charlie.

"Give her some space, Wes," Brandon said, guiding his brother to a spot several feet away from her. "She's had a rough night too."

Wesley glanced from one to the other, eyes slightly wild. And then he brought his hands to his face.

"Oh God. You're right. I'm sorry."

The coffee machine belched out the last dregs of brew into the pot, and Brandon set about pouring three mugs. He handed one to Wesley, who'd lapsed into another round of staring into the shine of the marble counter. With a nod of his head, Brandon directed Charlie to the far end of the room, passing her a cup.

"Are you sure you're up to this?"

When Charlie nodded, Brandon's hand disappeared inside his jacket and came back with a flask.

"Then we're going to need this," he said, pouring a liberal dash of mystery booze into each mug. "Trust me."

CHAPTER TWENTY-FIVE

The whiskey in the coffee slowly suffused Charlie with a warmth that chipped away at the chill she'd had from being barefoot out in the rain. Little by little, she felt the tension she'd been holding in her neck and shoulders loosen.

The front door opened and closed, footsteps echoing in the entryway.

"Hello?"

Charlie recognized Dara's meek voice.

"In the kitchen," Brandon called.

A moment later, Dara came in looking remarkably fresh-faced. Her long hair was tied back in a French braid.

"I think she's a robot," Allie commented.

"Dara," Wesley said, setting his cup aside and moving forward to embrace her. "Sweet Dara."

And then he started to sob again.

Dara stiffened in his arms, a look of distinct discomfort on her face.

"It's… OK, Wesley," she said.

"But it's not OK. It will never be OK." His voice broke. "She's gone. Our Glori is gone."

After several moments of standing there like a statue, Dara lifted her arm and began patting Wesley's back.

"There, there," she muttered mechanically.

"See?" Allie said. "Robot."

"Should we… do something?" Charlie whispered to Brandon.

He smirked from his position in the corner.

"We *are* doing something."

He took a meaningful drink of his whiskey-laced coffee.

Charlie rolled her eyes and stepped closer to where Wesley still clung to Dara.

"There's coffee if you'd like some."

"Yes," Dara said, sensing this as an opportunity to disentangle herself from her brother. "I would."

Over her shoulder, she heard Brandon sigh.

"Wesley, why don't you pour Dara a cup of coffee?" he suggested.

"Hm?" Wesley released Dara. "Oh, yes. Of course."

He pulled a mug from one of the cabinets and moved closer to the coffee machine.

"Cream and sugar?"

"Just sugar," Dara answered, looking relieved to be out of his grasp.

While Wesley was distracted with his task of acting the host, Dara sidled up to Brandon.

"What's wrong with him?"

"Well, what do you think, Dara? He's upset."

She frowned.

"I know that. But he wasn't like this when Dad died."

"That's because Gloria had the foresight to hide all the booze that day." Brandon gulped at his cup. "She could be a bit of a dictator, but she had a knack for circumventing family drama."

"He's drunk?" Dara sounded as if this hadn't occurred to her before now.

"Obviously." Brandon scoffed. "I got rid of the Scotch when he wasn't looking, so hopefully between that and the coffee, he'll start to sober up soon."

Wesley came over, bearing a full cup of black liquid. He passed it to Dara, who raised it to her lips and drank.

"Thank you."

Brandon held his mug in the air.

"I propose a toast to Gloria," he said. "Where's your cup, Wes?"

Wesley blinked and patted his vest, as if he might have tucked the coffee into a pocket. Finally, he spotted where he'd left his mug on the counter and snatched it up.

"To Gloria," he said, and they drank.

Wesley polished off his cup, prompting Brandon to suggest he refill it. That must have been the goal of instigating the toast. Anything to get more caffeine pumping into Wesley's veins.

They moved to the solarium, and Wesley lapsed into reminiscing.

"I remember when you were about five, you were always wanting to dress up in Gloria's clothes," he said, facing Dara. "Usually it annoyed her, but one time you came shuffling out with your feet stuck in a pair of her heels, and she just thought it was the funniest thing."

"I don't think that was me," Dara said. "By the time I was that age, Gloria was off at college."

The frown lines around Wesley's mouth deepened.

"No, you're right. It was Marjory in the high heels. And she was wearing this sequined headband Gloria had as a top."

Despite his confusion, Wesley sounded less unhinged than before. Maybe the caffeine was finally starting to take effect. Charlie hoped so.

"I feel like I should apologize," Brandon said, sliding into the chair next to her.

"For what?"

"I should have waited until everyone was gathered before I dragged you over here," he said. "This is just wasting your time."

"I'm glad actually." Charlie stared into the rippling surface of her coffee. "It would have been a bad night to be alone."

He was baffled for a beat, and then realization seemed to dawn on him.

"That bad? I guess it would be."

She opened her mouth, intending on downplaying it the way she had when Wesley had asked about it, but this time she couldn't hold back the wave of remembered sensations.

The thundering of the rain on the roof.

The revving of the engine.

The look of surprise on Gloria's face when she spotted the car. Mouth open in a perfect circle. Eyebrows lifted. Hands raised, as if that might ward off the blow.

The sickening thud as the car struck her.

Gloria's body fluttering. Limp.

And the car unperturbed as it mowed her down. A dead-on hit meant to kill.

She was startled out of the recollection by a weight settling on her shoulder. Brandon's hand.

"Charlie?"

With a shudder, she shook her head in an attempt to reset her thoughts.

"Sorry."

"You're the last one who owes anyone an apology after what you've been through," he said, his fingers tightening on her shoulder ever so gently.

She stared into his eyes. They were a deep amber that reminded her of fall. Maple syrup and apple cider and golden-brown donut holes dusted with cinnamon sugar.

The clip-clop of heels sounded in the hall, and then Marjory burst into the room. She froze just past the threshold, her eyes bloodshot and rimmed with red as if she'd been crying. Her mouth turned down in a hard frown.

Brandon jumped up, drawing his hand away from Charlie's shoulder.

"Marjory," he said, crossing the room in four long strides. "You're here. Good. How was the drive back?"

"Hellish," Marjory said, furiously unwrapping one of her Jolly Ranchers and popping it into her mouth.

"How about some coffee?" Brandon asked, steering her toward the kitchen. "We just made it fresh."

"I'm so glad you were able to keep yourself occupied while you waited for me," she said, and Charlie thought she detected a note of sarcasm there.

Marjory's eyes scanned the room as she passed by.

"Jude was at dinner with a client when I called to let him know. He said he'd 'get away when he could.'" Her voice was sharp, almost accusing. "Typical."

Between Dara not being the talkative sort to begin with and Wesley lapsing into a pensive silence, the room went quiet for several moments. Through the wall, Charlie could hear the low murmur of Brandon and Marjory talking, which only seemed to amplify the lull in the solarium.

Wesley muttered something, and both Charlie and Dara swung their heads around to face him.

"What was that?" Dara asked.

Lifting his head, Wesley repeated himself, louder this time.

"I said our family must be cursed."

Marjory returned from the kitchen just as the pronouncement left Wesley's lips, followed by Brandon.

"Don't be an idiot, Wesley," Marjory said, slamming her cup back into the saucer she held in her hand. "No one is cursed."

Charlie was getting a distinct air of hostility from her. It radiated out from her body like waves of heat distortion emanating from a sun-baked parking lot in August. She supposed everyone handled their grief in one way or another. Marjory got angry. Wesley morphed into a sobbing, drunken mess. Brandon played peacemaker. And Dara... well, Dara seemed to be mostly the same as before.

"Then why else do such terrible things keep happening to us? First Dad, now Gloria..."

He trailed off, shaking his head.

There was a beat where no one said anything, and then Wesley's eyes went wide.

"Good God. You don't think this has anything to do with, you know… what happened to Dad?"

Marjory glanced uneasily at Brandon from the corner of her eye. It was the first crack in the furious veneer Charlie had seen. The notion of the two deaths being linked had thrown Marjory off-kilter.

"Jesus." Brandon sighed and wiped a hand over his forehead. "I hadn't even thought about that."

"But Gloria was in a car accident," Dara said, her brow furrowed. "Why would that be connected to what happened to Dad?"

Wesley stared at Dara for a moment before shooting Brandon a meaningful look.

"Don't look at me. I told Marjory what you told me. That was my job."

"See, this is why I never liked this telephone game. Things always get lost in translation."

"What things?" Dara asked, but now the two men were looking at Marjory.

"Marjie," Brandon said. "What did you tell Jude?"

With an irritated roll of her eyes, Marjory scoffed.

"I told him exactly what you told me."

As if on cue, the front door slammed shut. Jude strode in a moment later, face angled down at his phone. When he finally glanced up, it was to find everyone in the room staring at him.

"What?"

Wesley's jaw clenched.

"You were supposed to call Dara and pass on the news about Gloria."

"I did."

"No, Jude. You told her Gloria had been in a car accident."

"Yeah?" Jude said, as if he didn't spot the problem.

"Do I really need to explain the difference between a car accident and a hit-and-run to you?"

"It's been absolutely insane at the office this week, alright? I didn't have time to lay out every little detail." Jude scratched the back of his neck. "I mean, I got the point across, didn't I? Dead is dead."

"Goddamn it, Jude!" Wesley vaulted to his feet, his hands balled into fists.

Jude sputtered out a laugh.

"What are you gonna do, Wes? Smack me around like you did when we were kids?" Jude tucked his phone into his back pocket and got into a fighting stance. "Try it, fuckface. See what it gets you."

Wesley sneered.

"Obviously someone should have kicked your ass a little harder. Maybe then you would have grown up."

Brandon stepped in between them, extending his hands like a boxing referee.

"Will you two cut it out? You're making this worse."

There was an ear-piercing shriek, and the entire room went silent. Dara trembled slightly where she stood next to the sofa, her neck and face splotched pink from the effort of screaming.

"Finally, a reaction," Allie said.

"None of this matters. Dad's dead. And now Gloria. And you're all fighting about stupid, meaningless things!" Dara looked at Wesley. "You said something earlier. About what happened to Gloria being connected to Dad."

"I was just talking," Wesley said. "Look, I'm sure that what happened to Gloria really was an accident—"

Charlie cut Wesley off, sensing her moment to strike.

"It wasn't an accident," she said, getting to her feet. "And there's a very good chance that whoever killed your father is the same person who murdered Gloria tonight."

Wesley was the first to speak, his voice artificially high and shrill. "But why?"

"I think she had found something," Charlie said. "Some piece of evidence that might have implicated the murderer."

"What was it?" Wesley demanded.

"I don't know." Charlie shrugged. "Whatever it was, she wanted to discuss it in person. That's why she came to my office. But before she had a chance to tell me anything…"

She trailed off. Saying all of it out loud made it somehow more real. The full gravity of the situation hit her all at once. Gloria was dead because she'd discovered something too big. Too damning. And the fact that she'd never be able to pass on that information meant the killer was several steps ahead of Charlie.

CHAPTER TWENTY-SIX

"Who could that be?" Wesley asked at the sound of the front door opening and closing. Seconds later, Marjory's assistant appeared on the threshold of the solarium.

"Killian?" Marjory stepped forward.

"What's Marjory's whipping boy doing here?" Jude muttered.

Killian hurried to Marjory's side.

"I came as soon as I heard," he said, embracing her. "It's just awful. Are you alright?"

Marjory started to answer, but Wesley cleared his throat and interrupted.

"I'm sorry, but this is sort of a *private* family gathering."

"Oh, mind your own business, Wes," Marjory snapped.

"No, he's right," Killian said, running his fingers through his white-blond hair. "I only wanted to pay my respects and check in on you. I won't stay."

He stepped away from Marjory, but she grabbed his wrist and tugged him back.

"Why does Killian have to leave, but she gets to stay?" Marjory said, gesturing with her chin toward Charlie. "She's not family."

"I asked her to come," Brandon said.

Marjory crossed her arms.

"And I'm asking Killian to stay."

"Do whatever you want," Brandon said, his shoulder quirking into a shrug. "It doesn't matter to me."

"Yours is not the only opinion that matters, Brandon," Wesley said. "I think—"

"No, no, no!" Dara clutched her head with both hands. "You're already back to arguing, and we still haven't decided what we're going to do about Gloria."

Wesley nodded solemnly.

"Dara's right. Obviously we have to arrange a funeral."

"I'm not talking about a funeral!" Dara's eyes filled with tears. "Someone killed her. And Daddy. We have to *do* something."

"What could we possibly do?" Marjory blinked. "That's for the authorities to handle."

Charlie stepped forward. Gloria had signed a contract and paid upfront for a week of her services. Charlie intended to see this investigation through, but she needed the family on her side. Without their consent, she'd have trouble digging any deeper than she already had. She'd been waiting for the right moment to make her proposal, and this seemed like her best shot.

"There is something you can all do, actually," she said.

The bickering halted. Six faces turned her way.

"Gloria hired me, and even though she's no longer with us, I plan to continue my investigation. It would be easier for me if I have your approval."

Marjory scoffed.

"I told Gloria from the beginning that this whole thing should be left to the police. But as usual, she insisted on doing things her way. She always had to be in charge, even in this. And now look at what's happened! She's dead. And for what? Have you found anything? A single shred of evidence?"

"Well, no, but—"

"Then give me one good reason why I should agree to let you continue your nosing around in our affairs."

Charlie shrugged and kept her tone placid.

"I assume anyone who isn't the murderer would want to find out the truth."

"Excuse me?" Marjory planted her fists on her hips. "How dare you suggest—"

Brandon interrupted, hooking a hand around Marjory's bicep. "Marjie, please calm down."

"You calm down," she said, shaking him off. "I will not have some... professional busybody accuse me of murder in my family home."

"I'm not accusing you of anything. I'm simply asking for your cooperation going forward."

"Of course we'll comply," Wesley said.

Marjory's mouth pinched into a tight knot of fury.

"You don't speak for all of us, Wesley. I agree to nothing. You can't compel me to do anything I don't want to. You're not the police."

"That's true. But there's no law saying I can't run my own investigation parallel to the police. And I feel I owe it to Gloria to see this through."

"Oh please. Surely you don't expect us to believe you're doing this out of the goodness of your own heart?" Marjory spun to face Wesley. "Isn't it obvious what she's doing? This is a ploy to squeeze more money from us to keep the investigation going."

"Actually," Charlie cut in, "Gloria agreed to pay in advance on a weekly basis, so the rest of this week is already paid for."

"There, I think that settles that," Wesley said.

"It doesn't settle anything!"

Wesley rubbed his forehead.

"Marjory, please."

"No, I agree with Marjory," Jude piped up. "This doesn't seem right, having an outsider here making these suggestions."

Dara waved a hand in the air.

"What is it, Dara?" Brandon asked.

"I think we should take a vote," she said, licking her lips. "That's what Gloria always did when we couldn't agree on things."

Wesley nodded.

"Dara has the right idea. Let's vote on it."

Marjory rolled her eyes but said, "All in favor of ending this charade here and now?"

She and Jude raised their hands. Killian, eyes on Marjory, put his hand up as well.

"Oh, for crying out loud. You don't get a vote, Killian," Wesley said. "All in favor of giving full cooperation to Ms. Winters while she continues her investigation?"

It was Wesley and Dara for.

"Brandon, you didn't vote," Dara said.

"I'm thinking." Brandon glanced at Charlie and then back at the group. "I understand Marjory's concerns. Dad was always a fanatic about privacy, and it does feel a bit wrong to let an outsider poke around in the family interests. Then again, I think it's important that we know the truth, no matter how ugly or uncomfortable. I'm voting that we cooperate with the investigation."

"That's it then. We have a majority," Wesley said, turning to Charlie. "We agree to comply with any request you might have, within reason. And I should like to be clear, this doesn't mean we're hiring you independently of what Gloria already paid for. I imagine the rest of the week should be more than sufficient to wrap things up."

Charlie knew she'd won by a nose—Brandon's nose to be precise—so even though the reality was that investigations like this took as long as they took, there was no point in saying so now. Wesley's tone made it clear that this wasn't a negotiation. If she dug up something useful, maybe it would buy her more time down the road.

"Thank you," she said with a nod. "Since I have you all here right now, can I ask where you were today around 4:45 p.m.?"

Dara answered first, which surprised Charlie since up until now, she'd been the least forthcoming of the group out of sheer shyness.

"I was here, tending the horses. Esther got a really bad cracked hoof last summer. Now that it's starting to warm up again, I've been trying to come every day to apply hoof dressing so it doesn't happen again."

Charlie jotted this down.

"And was anyone else here? Any of the staff?"

"No," Dara said, staring at the floor. "But I passed one of the neighbors on the road as I drove in."

"Do you know which one?"

"One of the Tamblins, I think," Dara said. "Ronald or Lynette. I'm not sure which one of them it was. Everyone was driving around with their headlights on because of the storm, so it made it impossible to see who was inside the car. But it looked like their Mercedes."

Brandon was the next to offer up his alibi.

"I was in Northville. I had plans to watch a race at the Downs."

"Were you with anyone?" Charlie asked.

"I was meeting up with friends at the track."

"So they can vouch for you?"

"They can vouch that we had plans," Brandon said. "But I didn't actually make it inside. Wes called and told me what happened, and I obviously came back here immediately."

Charlie got the names and numbers of the friends he'd been meeting anyway.

"If you can think of a way to corroborate that… a receipt from a gas station on the way, or something, it'd be helpful," Charlie said.

"I'll see what I can come up with," he said.

Wesley sighed loudly.

"I was at home," he said. "And before you ask, I was alone. My trainer was supposed to come at four, but I canceled the appointment. I wasn't in the mood. But after puttering around the house for a few hours, I got restless. Decided I'd be better off getting some exercise after all, so I took the kayak out. It's possible someone saw me. There were other people on the lake. Two guys on a fishing boat and a gal on a jet ski, but no one I know. I received the call about Gloria just as I was pulling the kayak out of the water."

"Do you have a security system or a doorbell camera that might have a record of you leaving the house after getting the call?"

"There are door and window alarms, but it's a fairly rudimentary system. No cameras or anything like that."

Charlie thanked him and moved on to Marjory.

"Well, I was in the car from about 3:30 p.m. until I arrived here. My friend Shay was with me the entire time. I suppose you want her phone number?"

"Yes, please."

After taking the number down, she finished with Jude.

"I was with a client all afternoon."

"The same client you were having dinner with this evening?"

"That's right," he said with a nod. "Terrance Ferguson. He's the station manager for WJAZ in Detroit. We're doing a big campaign for the jazz festival this summer."

It sounded more like a brag than an alibi, but Charlie wrote down the details without comment.

"Do you need my alibi, too?" Killian asked.

"Uh… sure," Charlie said, though she hadn't been planning on asking him. There wasn't much for Marjory's assistant to gain from either Dutch or Gloria being dead, but it didn't hurt to have his information, too.

"Well, Marjory sent me to run a few errands, and then I stopped by the office to stuff envelopes for the fundraising drive. The security guard at the front desk would have seen me coming and going."

"And do you remember what time any of that was?"

Killian's nearly invisible eyebrows scrunched together.

"Let's see. I think I probably got to the office around four, and then I lost track of time and didn't end up leaving until almost six."

"Are we done?" Marjory asked when Charlie returned her notepad to her bag. "Or did you have some more invasive questions to ask us while we're grieving?"

"Marjory, for God's sake—" Wesley started, but Charlie interrupted.

"No, she's right. I appreciate the time you've given me, but you need space to process all of this. Individually, and as a family." She lifted her bag and slung it over her shoulder. "I'll get out of your way."

Charlie walked herself out, her lone footsteps echoing in the cavernous front entryway. She glanced up the stairway at the credenza that held a single vase where once there had been two.

Outside, her eyes scanned all of the vehicles parked in the driveway, trying to see if any of them matched the sleek red sports car that had hit Gloria. None of them did.

As she reached the front of her car, she heard the telltale sound of the house's thick oak door unlatch behind her.

"Ms. Winters… Charlie. Wait."

It was Brandon. He hustled down the steps and came around to where she was standing beside her car.

"The rest of my family might not understand exactly what you went through today. That you had to watch Gloria die. But I do." He squinted, studying her face. "I wanted to make sure you were OK."

Again she recalled the sound of the revving engine, the hiss of the tires on the wet street, the reinforced steel of a car's front end colliding with flesh and bone.

Charlie closed her eyes.

"Honestly? I'm not OK. I don't think anyone could be after seeing something that horrific." She opened her eyes and jangled her keys in her palm. "But I'll survive."

"You're a tough lady. Under different circumstances…" He cocked his head to one side. "You know what? Screw different circumstances. Do you want to go get a drink?"

"Now?"

"Sure," Brandon said. "Why not?"

It was an appealing offer, the notion of attempting to erase the events of the day with alcohol. And Brandon was sure to be an entertaining drinking partner. But Charlie knew it was a bad idea, if only from a professional standpoint.

Glancing back at the house, Charlie noticed that Marjory was watching them from a window overlooking the driveway. Probably to make sure that Charlie left and didn't hang around to spy on them from the bushes or something.

"I think they're expecting you back inside," Charlie said, gesturing with her chin toward the window. "As for me, I'm going to head home and sleep for a solid fourteen hours."

Brandon turned and waved at Marjory, who stepped back from the window, though Charlie doubted she'd given up her watch. He sighed and thrust his hands in his pockets.

"I hope you won't take some of what was said tonight personally. Marjory doesn't handle this kind of thing very well. The story Wesley told earlier, about Marjory dressing up in Gloria's clothes when we were kids? That was just the tip of the iceberg. She idolized Gloria growing up." He shrugged. "As for Jude… well, he's just kind of a prick."

Charlie couldn't stop a chuckle escaping her lips.

"Anyway, if either of them gives you any trouble, you can call me, and I'll set them straight."

"Good to know," Charlie said, climbing into her car.

As she took the turn onto the road at the end of the long drive, Allie spoke up.

"You know what I'm going to say, don't you?"

Charlie tried to ignore her.

"I think you should have gone for that drink."

"And I think you should mind your own business."

"You're no fun," Allie whined.

Charlie said nothing. She was already envisioning the sweet sensation of her head hitting her pillow, and nothing Allie could say was going to change her mind.

CHAPTER TWENTY-SEVEN

It was late in the morning when Charlie finally dragged herself out of bed the next day. After dressing and forcing down a piece of toast, she lumbered down to the office.

Charlie let herself in via the back door and went through the motions of opening the office: turning on the lights, opening the blinds, unlocking the front door. Since Paige was only working part-time, on days like today she only came into the office in the afternoon, which meant Charlie would be on her own for the next few hours.

She collapsed into her new chair, which Paige had finished assembling. She had to admit, it was far more comfortable to the old one.

Still, she hadn't slept well the night before. The grisly scene of Gloria's death had been enough of a nightmare when she was wide awake. In sleep, it only got worse.

Pulling her notes out, Charlie began the task of running down alibis for the Carmichael clan. She made a couple of calls, first confirming Marjory's story with her friend, Shay Odell, then reaffirming that Jude had been with the radio station manager as he'd reported. That ruled out both siblings who had shaky alibis for the time of Dutch's death, which was a little disappointing.

She looked at the rest of the names on her list. Wesley, Brandon, and Dara didn't have airtight alibis for Gloria's death, but they did for Dutch's. And even though Charlie was certain the murders were related, one of the first things Frank had taught her about investigative work was to be thorough.

One of Brandon's friends confirmed that they'd had plans, but Wesley's story would be tougher to nail down. Charlie might be able to canvass his neighbors and find someone who had seen him go out in his kayak. She'd leave that for later.

Dara didn't have the phone number of the neighbor she thought she'd passed on her way to the estate, but their information was easy enough to find online.

A woman's voice answered.

"Lynette Tamblin?" Charlie guessed.

"Yes?"

"I'm an investigator working with your neighbors, the Carmichaels. I was wondering if I could ask you a few questions."

"Of course. Is this about what happened to Dutch? What a horrible thing."

"It's related, but indirectly. Did you happen to see anyone over there at the house yesterday evening?"

"Me? No."

"Not on the street? You didn't drive past one of them and wave? It would have been around five o'clock."

"Oh! You know my husband had to run into town around that time because we were out of dog food. Let me ask him," she said. "Hold on, I'll put you on speakerphone."

There was a click and then the woman's shrill voice.

"Ronald."

When no answer came, she called again, this time louder.

"Ronald!"

"Eh?"

"Did you wave at one of the neighbors yesterday?"

"Did I wave at the who-what?"

"There's a private investigator on the phone, and she'd like to know if you waved at someone on our street yesterday evening."

"A private investigator? Sounds like a scam to me."

"Ronald, I don't know how a woman asking whether or not you waved to one of Dutch Carmichael's kids on the street can possibly be a scam."

"One of the Carmichael kids, you say?" He grumbled something Charlie couldn't hear.

"Sir," Charlie spoke up, "do you remember passing anyone in your car yesterday around five?"

"I guess I remember someone driving by. Sure."

"And did you see who it was? Or what kind of car?"

"Nah. I was fiddling with my seat. Someone's always messing with the settings. Tipping the seat too far upright."

"Someone?" Lynette interrupted. "I'm the only other person who drives that car, and I'm not sure what else I'm supposed to do. I can't reach the pedals if I leave the seat as it is."

"So you scoot it forward and don't mess with the back at all!" Ronald bellowed.

"I can't sit like that!" Lynette shrieked back.

Their shouting was blowing out the mic on the speakerphone. Charlie thought she'd gotten about as much useful information from them as she was going to get, which wasn't much. Charlie supposed Dara had correctly identified the car as belonging to the Tamblins. That counted for something, didn't it?

"Thank you for your time," she muttered into the phone. She hung up with the Tamblins still screaming at each other about seat settings.

That was probably as good as it would get for Dara's alibi.

Charlie noticed for the first time that the three siblings who had voted to keep her on were the ones who didn't have a solid alibi for Gloria's murder, while the two who did—Marjory and Jude—had been quite against her continuing the investigation.

"What do you think it means?" Allie asked.

"Maybe nothing."

"So now what?"

Charlie pondered this for a moment and then said, "Coffee."

"That's your answer to everything."

"It's an important part of the job. That's what Uncle Frank told me when I asked him what the trick was to being a good P.I." Charlie got to her feet and headed for the coffee machine in the back room. "He said, 'It's mostly patience and perseverance, but if you find yourself running low on either of those, make up for it with some coffee.'"

CHAPTER TWENTY-EIGHT

Armed with a fresh cup of coffee, Charlie returned to her desk. She took a sip of the near-scalding liquid and stared down at the names scribbled on her list. All of the Carmichael siblings had a solid alibi for at least one of the murders. But there was still one unchecked name. One person who, as far as Charlie knew, had no alibi for either murder.

Thumbing through her contacts, she found Zoe's name and tapped out a text.

Did you guys interview Vivien Marley yet?

While she waited for a response, Charlie searched for the elusive Ms. Marley's address online and jotted it down in her notes. If she couldn't get Dutch's mistress to return her calls, then maybe it was time for a house visit.

The front door opened, and Paige bustled in.

"What are you doing here?" Charlie asked. "You're not scheduled to come in for another hour."

"I know. It's just I couldn't stand to be in my apartment a second longer." She set a white paper bakery box on Charlie's desk and took off her jacket. "My roommate and her boyfriend started a band."

"That bad?"

Paige scrunched her face up.

"I don't wanna say *bad*, because that sounds mean. And I do like music. But they do this thing called 'musique concrète.' Have you heard of it?"

"No."

"It's some kind of experimental thing. Lots of weird noises. They record just random sounds, like the toilet flushing, and her boyfriend uses his computer to distort it. Like he'll speed the sound up so it sounds like something completely different. And then my roommate, she does all this sort of avant-garde singing over it. Sometimes it's sort of like yodeling and other times it's more like that ASMR whispering stuff."

"They got any bangers?" Charlie asked.

"Well, I don't get it, personally," Paige admitted. "But I'm glad she's got a passion for something. Anyway, I cleaned our place top to bottom this morning and baked a little, trying to distract myself from everything that happened yesterday, I guess. But I kind of ran out of stuff to do, and then they showed up with all their music gear. I knew I'd go crazy if I had to listen to that right now."

Charlie nodded with understanding and then pointed at the white bakery box.

"What's in there?"

"Cupcakes," Paige said. "Help yourself."

Charlie lifted the lid and admired the rows of perfectly formed confections. Each one had a flawless swirl of icing on top with a dusting of chopped nuts.

Charlie removed one of the cupcakes and took a bite. The cake was fluffy, and the frosting had a touch of tang from the cream cheese. The chopped nuts on top rounded out the whole experience by adding just a bit of crunch. Delicious.

"Oh my God," Charlie said, talking with her mouth full.

"You like it?" Paige asked hopefully.

"I want to eat only these for the rest of my life. I require no other sustenance."

Paige clapped her hands, obviously pleased by the response.

"I think the raspberry filling needs work. The recipe I used called for store-bought jam, but I think it's too sweet when it should be tart. I'm going to try making my own next time from scratch."

"Well, you're a baking wizard as far as I'm concerned." Charlie polished off the first cupcake and reached for a second. "I can't even make muffins from a box mix."

"I'm sure that's not true," Paige said.

"It is," Charlie insisted. "One time I tried, and they turned green."

Paige laughed.

"That just means you overmixed the berries. I'm sure they still tasted good."

"Nope. They were weird and rubbery."

"That's also from overmixing," Paige said, going on to explain the properties of flour and gluten and the effect of being too zealous with the whisk.

After her third cupcake, Charlie pushed the box across the desk.

"Please hide these from me or I'll just keep eating until the box is empty."

"I know the feeling," Paige said, tucking the lid of the box closed. "I've had five already."

Paige removed the pastries from the desk and disappeared into the back room. Charlie rolled her head from side to side, trying to loosen the soreness in her neck. Her whole upper back and shoulders felt tight today. She wondered if it could be from performing CPR. Was that a thing?

Pens and paperclips rattled as she slid open one of the drawers on her desk, searching for the bottle of ibuprofen she kept inside. The motion of shaking out two of the brown tablets brought on the realization that she hadn't called her mother this morning.

"Shit," she muttered, dry-swallowing the pills and grabbing for her phone.

"Hey Mom. It's me," Charlie said when Nancy finally picked up.

"Was that you on the roof just now?"

Charlie frowned.

"Was I… what? I'm at work, Mom."

"I heard noises."

Charlie's heart started to race. Not this. Not now. She couldn't deal with one of her mother's paranoid episodes along with everything else. Then she remembered Elaine mentioning birds nesting on the house, and she relaxed.

"It's birds, Mom. Elaine said there are some robins nesting in the eaves."

"Well they're making an awful racket up there. Scrabbling and scratching. I wish someone would do something about it. It's driving me crazy."

By *someone*, she meant Charlie, of course. But she couldn't just ask. She couldn't be direct and say, "Charlie, dear, could you get the nest out of the eaves?"

No, she had to be passive-aggressive about it.

Charlie pinched the bridge of her nose and reminded herself it wasn't worth getting dragged into an argument over a bird's nest.

"I'll take a look next time I'm there," she said, finally. "The reason I called is that I wanted to make sure you took your pills this morning."

"What pills?"

Her heart set off again, faster this time.

"Your medication, Mom." It was a struggle to keep the panic out of her voice. "The Lexapro and risperidone."

There was a long pause, and then Nancy said, "I was kidding. I already took them, of course. I'm a grown woman, you know."

Charlie got no sense of calm this time. She only felt exhausted. She needed to get off the phone before her mother gave her a heart attack.

"OK, Mom. I'll see you later."

"When?"

Charlie sighed.

"I'm not sure. I have some things to take care of at work first."

"Well, I need bread," Nancy said. "And creamer."

"I can pick those up before I come."

"Make sure you get the Coffee-mate and not the generic brand. They try to tell you it's the same, but I know the difference. I like French vanilla best, but hazelnut is OK if that's all they have."

"Alright. I have to go now."

Charlie hung up. Lifted her coffee cup. Empty. She half-remembered finishing it off between her second and third cupcake.

Resisting the urge to call out to Paige for a refill—she was a secretary, not a servant—Charlie pushed her chair back and stood.

She paused to stretch her back and shoulders again. Something popped in her neck. It sounded bad but felt pretty good.

A blip came from her phone, and Charlie snatched it up. Zoe texting back, she hoped.

Negative on the Marley interview. Pretty sure she's dodging us. Just like you said she was.

Charlie gritted her teeth. When it came to Dutch's murder, Gloria had suspected Vivien, the mistress, above everyone else. And now she was dodging everyone looking to dig into Dutch's life? Awfully suspicious. Why duck everyone's calls unless she had something to hide?

That sealed it then. Charlie was going to talk to Vivien Marley whether the old lady liked it or not.

But first, coffee.

And maybe one more cupcake.

CHAPTER TWENTY-NINE

Vivien Marley lived in an affluent neighborhood on the southeast side of Salem Island. Bridgefork Heights, or Richfuck Heights as Allie called it, formed a six-block area along the beach—manicured landscaping and spotless mansions loaded with every luxury one could imagine. Wine cellars. Marble floors. The occasional indoor swimming pool. The people here may not be as wealthy as the Carmichaels, but they were close—all firmly entrenched in the top one percent, Charlie knew.

Charlie drove that way, watching the houses along the side of the road get bigger and nicer as she closed in on Vivien's address. The front yards, too, grew larger. While a few were so bold as to showcase a fountain or statue, most were flecked with decorative trees, tufts of exotic grass, various beds of flowers, ferns, and ivies. A few kept it simpler, with massive expanses of green grass that stretched out, put some distance between the homes and the street. In a couple of cases a whole football field's worth of sod stood between the asphalt and the front columns of the house.

"I know I'm harping at this point, but just imagine squandering your riches on something like that," Allie said. "Paying someone to mow the vacant field of grass in front of your house. It's pathological."

As Charlie pulled up to a stop sign, she saw the wrought-iron gates rising up to fill the roadway before her. She double-checked the address on her phone. Glanced over to verify the street name. Yep. This was Vivien's street alright.

She craned her neck to take in the full view. The arched barrier blocking the way in was set between brick columns. At the highest point, it stood around twelve feet tall, Charlie figured. A small booth huddled between the lanes in and out, the shape of a man in a khaki-colored uniform faintly visible within.

Charlie clucked her tongue against the roof of her mouth. Apparently part of Bridgefork Heights was gated, and Vivien lived behind the gate. That was not ideal.

She realized she'd been idling at the stop sign for a good forty-five seconds and took a right. She went down a full block before she circled back to park within viewing distance of the gate. Better to avoid the notice of the rent-a-cop in the security booth if she could. Most weren't too meticulous, she knew, but it was always best to take precautions when one could.

Charlie fished a hand into her glovebox. Pulled out the small pair of binoculars. Peered through the broad glass front of the building.

The security guard's head didn't swivel her way. It didn't move much at all. Instead, it stayed locked on the phone in his hands. Every few seconds, the fingers of his right hand detached from the phone, formed a fist, and punched the air in celebration.

"Must be watching sports," Charlie said.

She was talking to herself more than anything, but Allie never missed an opportunity to offer her own insight.

"Or porn."

"Why would he celebrate while watching porn?"

"Boobs," Allie said, as if it were obvious.

Charlie shook her head.

"Regardless, the fact that he's distracted could be a help."

Charlie started the car and eased it alongside the booth. She rolled ahead slowly, as though any sudden movement might spook the attendant.

As she got close, the glare tinting the glass waned and parted, revealing the security guard beyond the windowpane. He was younger than she'd imagined. Toothy. Kind of cute in a gangly way.

His eyes flitted over to her. He smiled.

"Good afternoon, ma'am," he said. "How can I help you?"

"I'm here to see my aunt. Vivien Marley, 108 Strickland Avenue."

"Okey-doke," he said.

Charlie held back a giddy chuckle at how simple that had been. What was the point of having a guarded entryway if they let people in that easily?

Then she saw the guard eyeballing a clipboard.

"I don't see any guests for number 108 on the list today," he said, his gaze swinging up to meet hers.

"Oh, that's because she doesn't know I'm coming," Charlie said, thinking fast. "It's kind of a surprise visit."

He smiled again.

"That's sweet of you. Your aunt is a lucky lady." He leaned across the booth, and Charlie thought for sure he was about to buzz her through the gate. Instead, he lifted a phone into view. "Give me a minute, and I'll call up to the house real quick."

"Wait!" Charlie said, and the guard froze with a finger outstretched over the dial pad.

Her mind went blank. She had no idea what she was going to say. She just didn't want him calling Vivien Marley and blowing her cover.

"Time to bust out that feminine charm," Allie whispered.

"What?"

"Flirt with him, dingus."

Charlie plastered a World's Sweetest Niece smile on her face.

"I'm Charlotte, by the way," she said, batting her eyelashes. "I didn't catch your name."

"Oh, its, uh, Brad."

"Here's the thing, Brad," Charlie said. "I haven't seen my aunt in ages, and I'd really love to knock her socks off by showing up on her doorstep completely unannounced."

"Knock her socks off?" Allie repeated with a snort. "Who are you?"

Ignoring her, Charlie continued.

"I know that's probably against the rules, but I was hoping you might make an exception just this once," she said, trying to find a tone that registered as "cute begging." "And as a thank you, maybe I could buy you a drink later?"

She tipped her head to the side and fluttered her eyelashes.

Brad blinked hard, his big eyes looking somewhat wet. His hand rose up to swipe at the back of his neck.

"Uh… sorry. It's protocol, you know?"

Charlie noticed that he hadn't denied her request outright. Maybe there was still some wiggle room here.

"And you never bend protocol? Not even for a girl trying to surprise her favorite auntie?"

This time when he tried to smile, it was more like a grimace.

"The only time we're allowed to let people in without prior permission or calling up to the house is for deliveries. I wish I could, really. But I could get fired, and well…"

He leaned out of the booth and glanced both ways.

"Anyway, I get off work at four, so why don't you give me your number, and we can meet up somewhere?"

"No, I'll call you," Charlie said, leaving him looking confused as she turned out of the drive and headed back the way she came.

CHAPTER THIRTY

Charlie headed back to the office, watching the buildings on the side of the road shrink back from mansions to tract homes to the clusters of trailer parks that dotted this side of Salem Island, trying to come up with a plan to get to Vivien Marley.

A chill ran down Charlie's spine when she drove past the spot where Gloria had bled out on the sidewalk. There was still a length of police tape wrapped around one of the columns in front of the movie theater, and the ends fluttered in the breeze.

Charlie averted her gaze. She needed to stay focused. Rehashing that grisly scene for the hundredth time wasn't going to get her closer to finding Gloria's murderer, but talking to Vivien Marley might.

A large man walked out the front door of her office as she rolled past. He was tall and bulky, with ramrod-straight posture and shoulders like an offensive lineman. They must have gotten another walk-in client.

Charlie turned into the alley that led to the back lot. It was a good thing Frank would be able to return to work soon, because even with Paige holding things down at the office, Charlie wasn't sure she'd be able to keep up with all the field work on her own for much longer.

She parked and let herself in through the back door.

"Was that another walk-in I just saw?" Charlie asked, but when she reached the front room, Paige wasn't behind the desk.

"Paige?"

There was no response.

She backtracked to the back room and poked her head inside. Eyed the dining table next to the coffee machine. Empty.

"What the hell?" Charlie murmured.

Then she heard it. A muffled sound coming through the bathroom door.

"Paige?" Charlie stepped to the door and knocked. "Are you in there?"

"Is he gone?"

"Who?" Charlie asked.

The girl sniffled.

"My dad."

And suddenly Charlie realized who she'd seen coming out of the office when she'd driven past. The dude with the upright posture. Paige's father.

"He's gone," Charlie said. "It's safe to come out now."

A few seconds passed, and then the lock on the door clicked. Paige hiccuped as she came through the door, eyes puffy from crying.

"Tell me what happened."

"He just came in. I was sitting here, sorting through some of the old files, like you asked, and he walked right through the front door. Said we had to talk."

Paige's face was bright pink and smeared with tears. Charlie handed her a box of tissues.

"I told him I had nothing to say and that he needed to leave because my boss would be back any minute." Paige dabbed at her cheeks with the wadded-up tissue. "And you know what he did? He laughed. Said he wondered who taught me to be such an ungrateful bitch, because it sure wasn't him."

Paige paused to swallow, and Charlie went to get her a bottle of water from the fridge.

"Thank you," Paige said, taking a sip. "Anyway, I realized then he couldn't be reasoned with, so I picked up the phone and told him I was going to call the police if he didn't leave right then. He got the meanest look on his face, the look he always gets when he's real mad. And he ripped the phone from my hands and told me he wasn't going anywhere. That's when I panicked, because how can you make someone leave when they don't want to? So I ran in here and locked myself in the bathroom."

"Did he hurt you?" Charlie asked.

"Not this time. But I got hit with just about everything imaginable when I was a kid. Switches, belts, spoons, extension cords. And he was a believer in 'company punishment.'"

"What's that?" Charlie asked.

"I have three siblings. A sister and two brothers. And anytime one of us messed up, we all took the beating."

"Jesus."

"Yeah. Between all the mischief the four of us could get up to, there weren't many nights we went to bed without a sore behind. But it got worse the older we got. He started adding humiliation to the mix. When I was twelve, I was babysitting my little sister, and she got some gum stuck in her hair. I was so scared of how much trouble I'd be in if he came home to that mess that I did the only thing I could think of and cut it out with some scissors. Of course that wasn't any less noticeable than the gum, so I ended up in trouble for that instead. After he whipped me that time, he shaved my head."

Charlie's mouth dropped open.

"What?"

Paige nodded.

"Spent the whole rest of the school year getting teased for being bald. Making friends was hard enough as it was, since we moved around all the time," she said, pausing to blow her nose. "Dad was in the army."

Charlie put a hand on Paige's shoulder.

"I'm so sorry, Paige," she said. "That's really awful. I can understand why you want nothing to do with him."

"And that's all I want." Fresh tears sprang to Paige's eyes. "For him to leave me alone! Why won't he do that?"

Charlie knew the reason. She'd known many men like Paige's father. Bullies and brutes, the whole lot of them. And the one thing they had in common was that they were only ever interested in power and control. Leaving Paige alone would be losing power over her. Giving up control. And he wouldn't do that readily.

"Listen, if he comes back, there's a stun gun in my bottom desk drawer. I always keep one in my bag and one in the desk," Charlie said. "And in the meantime, I want you to give me his name and address. I'm going to make sure this stops. Right now."

Paige flung her head from side to side.

"Oh no, Miss Winters. I don't want to drag you into this."

"You didn't drag me into this. He did. No one comes into my office and threatens one of my people."

Paige scrunched the tissue in her hand.

"But what are you going to do? He's got a terrible temper. And he's got friends in high places. Everyone outside the family thinks he's some great family man."

"Don't you worry about that. I'll figure something out."

CHAPTER THIRTY-ONE

When Paige finally handed over her father's information, the first thing Charlie did was call Frank to fill him in on the latest development.

"He actually came into the office?"

"Yep," Charlie said. "Apparently we're dealing with someone with very little respect for the boundaries of others."

"I'll say," Frank agreed. "Let me do some digging on this Henry Naughton. See what shakes loose."

"I was hoping you'd say that," Charlie said, feeling a sudden sense of relief.

Between the Carmichael case, witnessing Gloria's gruesome death, and losing her mother's nurse, Charlie was starting to feel the pressure. It was good to have Frank in her corner.

"How's the case going?"

"Still having trouble tracking down the mistress. She lives in a gated section of Bridgefork Heights."

"Ahh, yes. The high-security hideaway of the uber cake-eaters," Frank said. "Well, you'll need to get creative. I've got a whole collection of magnet decals in the office closet with fake business logos on them. Slap one of those on the side of your car, and you might just get past the gates."

"That's not a bad idea," Charlie said. The gate attendant had even mentioned deliveries. "Thanks, Uncle Frank."

"No need to thank me," he said, sighing dramatically. "Just sharing my vast wealth of knowledge."

Charlie snorted and hung up, already hurrying across the office to the back room. She clicked on a light in the shadowy supply closet. The bare light bulb flickered and buzzed overhead as Charlie crouched down and began digging through the stacks of junk.

The ragged edge of the cardboard box dragged along her searching hand. She plucked it from the pile of supplies, plopped it on the countertop of the little kitchenette, and started flipping her way through.

The jumbo-sized magnets stared back at her. Sheening and vivid. Colorful logos of all shapes and sizes.

A magnet for a maid service caught Charlie's eye. She pulled it out. Turned it over in her hands. It felt a little risky. If Vivien had a maid service come through on a regular basis, which seemed fairly likely, it could be a red flag for the guard in the booth.

Charlie chucked the magnet back in the pile and kept digging. A few seconds later, she stopped on a green magnet with a large pink rose and the name "Amanda's Flowers & Gifts" in curly black lettering. A florist. That could work.

Back in the closet, she dug out the hat that matched the logo on the magnet and blew a fine layer of dust off the brim.

With the ball cap pulled down low over her brow, she didn't look like herself. She looked younger. Blander. Totally believable as a college-aged girl with a part-time delivery job—the standard retail slave.

Staring into her own face in the mirror next to the closet, she couldn't help but remember a book she'd read about Ted Bundy, how he'd learned to drastically alter his appearance with facial hair, styling, hats, doing things to seemingly change the proportions of his features. The subtlest change rendered him nearly unrecognizable, allowed him to elude the police for years. The media had called him a chameleon.

She turned her head back and forth in the mirror one more time. Yeah, this would work.

Upstairs in her apartment, Charlie changed into khaki pants and a white button down shirt. The rest of the outfit, combined with the hat, took her from bland to blandest. It was perfect.

She went back down to her car and affixed the magnet to the driver's side door. It took a couple tries to get it straight, the oblong shape of the thing throwing her off at first. Just as she finally got the positioning right, her phone rang.

Before Charlie could say a word, her mother was jabbering away almost too fast to be understood.

"There's someone here, and I don't know what to do!"

Charlie felt her spine go rigid at the panic in Nancy's voice.

"Someone there? What are you talking about?"

"I went down to get the mail, and this woman popped out of the bushes! Like she was waiting there for me! And she started asking me all these questions!" Nancy paused to take a breath after practically vomiting the words out. "I ran back inside, but she's still out there. I think she's one of those reporters. You remember how they were."

Charlie did remember. When Allie had first gone missing, it'd been a big news story. Allie was photogenic, after all. The pretty type they loved to show photographs of and give dire reports about.

Police are asking for anyone who may have seen Allison Winters the day she disappeared to contact them. Foul play is suspected.

It had been bad enough then, but things ramped up after the foot was found on the beach. Charlie could still hear snippets of the reports in her head. That practiced tone journalists used when dispatching grisly details.

Police are not releasing any information at this time, but many are wondering if the dismembered foot belongs to Allison Winters, a Salem Island teen who has now been missing for several weeks.

News vans had camped out across the street from their house, and more than once a reporter or cameraman had dashed over to try to get a statement from one of her parents.

"Mrs. Winters! Have you heard they found a girl's foot on the beach? Do you think it could belong to your daughter? Are you still holding out hope that she's alive?"

Vultures. Charlie wondered why they might be hanging around again, all this time later. But they did little pieces like that all the time, didn't they? Unsolved cases were perennial material. Evergreen. They probably loved that Allie had never been found. They could go on milking it for years. She could see the headline now: *The Tragic Story of Allison Winters.*

Charlie felt her panic turn to anger. She'd love to tell off one of those reporters right about now. Love to get all self-righteous on their asses.

"I'll be right over, Mom," Charlie said. "If anyone comes to the door before I get there, don't answer it."

In the car, Charlie imagined what she'd say if she did find a journalist lurking outside of her mother's house: *Planning on using our personal family tragedy to boost ratings during sweeps? You can fuck right off.*

"I've got it," Allie said. "You should say, 'I eat morons like you for breakfast.'"

"What? No. That's dumb."

"I heard Judge Judy say it on her show once. And it totally worked, too. The guy was devastated."

When Charlie reached her mother's street, she noticed activity near the front of the house. There was a woman sitting in one of the deck chairs on the porch. The idea that this scavenger had ensconced herself right outside the front door renewed Charlie's fury. She marched across the lawn, fully intending to read this bitch the riot act.

"Excuse me," Charlie said. Her voice was loud and sharp.

The woman stood, blinking in a manner Charlie read as friendly. She really was going to eat this moron for breakfast.

"Can I ask what you think you're doing?" she asked, climbing the porch steps.

The front door opened then, and Nancy came out.

"Charlie," she said, almost seeming surprised to see her.

"Mom, go back inside. I'm handling this."

"Handling what?" Nancy came out and passed the woman a rectangle of paper that looked suspiciously like a check.

Why would her mother be giving money to a reporter?

"Here you go," Nancy said to the woman. "I'm sorry I can't give more, but I'm on a fixed income."

The woman beamed and waved the apology away.

"Oh no! Every little bit helps, and we appreciate it so very much. Here's a receipt for you, since this qualifies as a tax-deductible donation."

Charlie stood there, frozen, her anger evaporating on the spot. The woman thanked Nancy again, smiled at Charlie, and proceeded back down the walk to the street. Charlie watched her go, waiting until she was out of earshot before rounding on her mother.

"So I guess that's who was lurking in the bushes, then? A woman collecting donations for God-knows-what?"

Turning to go back inside, Nancy said, "It was for the local Humane Society, if you must know."

Charlie followed her mother into the house, averting her gaze as she passed the bedroom she and Allie had shared. She didn't need to look to know that everything was pretty much exactly the same as it had been the day Allie went missing. Posters still tacked in place with pushpins. Glow-in-the-dark star stickers scattered over the ceiling. Bottles of perfume and trays of makeup still spread across the top of the dresser.

"Mom, I came rushing over here because I thought you were being harassed by a reporter."

"Oh, is that why you look so sour?" Nancy made a clucking sound with her mouth. "It was just a silly misunderstanding. My imagination ran away from me for a minute."

"And you couldn't call to let me know that everything was fine? I was in the middle of something."

"Oh yeah. I guess the P.I. business must not be going so well," Nancy said, pouring herself a glass of iced tea from the fridge.

Charlie had no idea what she was talking about. Of course, her mother had never approved of Charlie's career choice. Charlie was supposed to "put those book smarts to good use" and "do something the family could be proud of." But why her mother would jump to this specific conclusion, especially when business was actually quite good, was baffling.

"What are you talking about?"

With a flick of the wrist, Nancy pointed at the hat. Charlie had forgotten she was wearing the fake florist get-up.

"Doesn't take a genius to figure out why you'd need a second job."

"No, this is…" Charlie shook her head, realizing it would take too long to explain, and they'd gotten way off-topic. "Never mind. My point is that your phone call worried me. I ran over here thinking you needed help."

Nancy sipped at her tea, shrugging.

"How was I supposed to know you'd overreact like this? No one asked you to drop everything and run over here, did they? I know *I* didn't."

She couldn't believe her mother had the balls to act like *Charlie* was the one who'd overreacted. She threw up her hands and stomped out of the kitchen.

"I don't have time for this," Charlie said. "I have to go. Next time your imagination runs away, call someone else."

"What about the groceries?"

Fingers grasping the door handle, Charlie stopped and glanced back at Nancy.

"The what?"

"You said you'd bring groceries. Bread and creamer. I told you this morning."

Charlie felt her blood pressure surge. Before she could say something she'd regret, she pushed through the door and let it slam shut behind her.

CHAPTER THIRTY-TWO

"She always does this. Anytime she's upset about something, she gets everyone else within reach stirred up, too. Because God help you, if Mother is unhappy, everyone better rush around trying to fix it. And then just like that—" Charlie snapped her fingers "—she decides she's fine. Crisis over. Then she turns it around on the rest of us and acts like we're the ones making a big fuss."

"I still think you should have used the Judge Judy line," Allie said.

Charlie rolled her eyes. Allie wasn't helping, but then that was typical.

After a few minutes, though, it occurred to Charlie that things could have been worse. She should have been glad there weren't reporters hanging around trying to pick at old wounds. That really would upset her mother, and that would be bad news for everyone. All things considered, it was a good thing it had been a simple misunderstanding.

And another good thing: Charlie had finally figured out a way to get to Vivien Marley. By the time she made it back to the gate outside of Bridgefork Heights, it was only a few minutes to four. The shift change would happen any minute now. She waited across the street again, watching from a discreet distance.

Right on cue, the new security guard sauntered up to the gate, a little older and heftier than the youngster he was taking over for. At first, Charlie worried the older man may be more savvy, more discerning, harder to fool. Something about his doughy face told her otherwise, however. The soft chin spoke to the rent-a-cop dream: this guy was here to sit for eight hours, collect a paycheck, and generally do as little as possible.

That made a kind of sense, Charlie thought. This was a gated community that didn't really need a lot of guarding, after all, tucked away in a small town like Salem Island. Anyone driven and ambitious wouldn't be suited to work such a cushy job. They'd grow bored. Restless. So bring out your couch potatoes, your slugs, your narcoleptics, your dudes who want to get paid to sit in a booth playing Candy Crush.

When Brad climbed into his F-150 and sped off, Charlie made her move. She counted to ten and wheeled toward the gate. Some faint twinge of nerves squelched in her gut, but the little burst of adrenaline washed that away. It was time to perform. Nerves were not an option. Total confidence was the only way.

The guy in the booth smeared a finger across his phone a couple times before he looked up. He didn't say anything, just raised his eyebrows, waiting for her to state her business.

Charlie beamed a smile at him nevertheless. Held up the bouquet she'd bought on the way over. A steal at $4.99 for the bundle.

"I've got a delivery for—" she pretended to consult the phony paper receipt she'd had Paige print up "—108 Strickland."

His gaze went to the magnet affixed to the driver's side door, the bouquet of pink tulips in Charlie's hand.

The guard bobbed his head once, and his hand moved to something Charlie couldn't see, some lever or button off to his right.

"A real chatterbox, this guy," Allie muttered, and Charlie realized he hadn't uttered a single word thus far.

A faint buzz emitted, and then the gates swung aside in what felt like slow motion. Charlie drove through the opening and into the sacred inner sanctum of Bridgefork Heights.

CHAPTER THIRTY-THREE

Pride swelled in Charlie's chest as the car thumped over the barrier and moved beyond the gates. Icy tendrils of exhilaration quivered in her torso. Her cheeks hurt from smiling.

"Yeah, nice job and all, but don't go counting your chickens just yet," Allie said.

Charlie couldn't help it. She always felt giddy like this when one of her schemes went to plan.

She felt like she was driving into some secret lair—the fortress where the rich people all hid, secured behind thick metal fencing.

Mansions squatted everywhere in Bridgefork Heights, spaced out on fields of sprawling grass, hulking structures sprouting from the ground. Monstrous brick facades shone out from the sides of the street, arches and spires and turrets. Tangles of ivy clung to some of the walls, bringing a touch of the English countryside to these New World palaces. Other homes sported Greek columns, looking a bit like mini-versions of the White House. They were all gleaming and spotless. Giant toys that had never been removed from the packaging.

She drove slowly, reading the numbers on the houses and mailboxes, trying to take in the whole of the scene. It was tranquil here, so quiet she could hear the hum of her tires rolling over the asphalt, could hear the breath swishing in and out of her nostrils. The faintest trickle of sweat slithered over the back of her neck.

Vivien's house took shape ahead. Another of those strangely curving brick palaces that stood three stories high, squatting at a crooked angle on the back of its grass lot. Gargantuan. None of her internet searches suggested that Vivien Marley had children, and it seemed obscene that one woman lived here by herself.

She kept slowing as she got closer, some instinct increasing her caution little by little until she pulled over to the curb across the street, concealed somewhat by a clump of rhododendron. Hands on the steering wheel, she felt the moisture clinging to her palms.

Something moved up near the house. She flinched.

A side door opened. A dark rectangle of wood swinging outward, tiny among all that brick, and Charlie gasped. The paranoid part of her sensed danger, feared discovery. Someone was onto her already.

A woman appeared in the doorway.

"Looks like a maid," Allie said. "That frumpy shirtdress? Dead giveaway."

Charlie nodded, but she didn't speak.

The woman waddled on stocky legs. It looked like she was straining with something. Shining black plastic: a garbage bag. Heavy from the looks of it.

She dragged it over to the royal blue bin next to the garage, swung the lid wide, and tossed the bag in. It thudded on top of the heap, the weight of it rocking the bin. She then closed the lid and rolled the bin down to the curb. The fat plastic wheels grated over the asphalt of the driveway, each warbling out their own tone, two gritty voices that couldn't quite harmonize.

Charlie looked down at her phone, watching out of the corner of her eye as the maid got close. But the maid deposited the bin and turned back for the house without even glancing Charlie's way.

Charlie closed her eyes. Exhaled. Relief flooded her, tingled in her fingers, flushed her face.

OK. It was time to do this. For real.

She shifted into drive and crawled down the serpentine driveway.

Before getting out of the car, she checked herself in the rearview mirror, made eye contact with the girl in the florist uniform, and gave her a wink for good measure.

The giddy feeling swelled again as she exited the car and lugged the bouquet up to the front door, legs tingly and light beneath her.

She stepped up onto the stoop, which was sheltered by a copper awning. The immense structure looming overhead made her feel small.

Her finger jabbed at the doorbell. Half a beat later, she heard its muffled ring chime through the house, and then the maid appeared.

The woman's eyes moved from Charlie's face to the flowers in her hand and then back again. She smiled.

"Can I help you?"

Charlie put on her best customer service face and pitched her voice an octave higher than normal.

"I hope so. I have these flowers and a singing telegram for Vivien Marley."

The maid's smile died.

"I'll just take the flowers," she said.

Charlie gawked at her for a second.

"Yes, but the client who purchased these… they also ordered—and paid for—a singing telegram. So if you could just get Ms. Marley…"

Charlie thought she could read disdain in the way the maid squinted at her.

"Wait here," the woman said, her voice disappearing with her around the huge oak door.

Charlie leaned forward and tried to peer through the crack. She could only make out a sliver of a table with what she thought was a bowl of magnolias on it. Nothing useful.

She stepped back, once more turned to a speck before the hulking stack of bricks. Tiny. Insignificant.

"What song are you going to sing?" Allie whispered.

"No song."

"What?"

"It's not real. Just, you know… a ruse."

"Well, don't you think you should have a song locked and loaded? Just in case?"

"In case of what?"

"An emergency, Charlie. In case something goes wrong."

"What kind of song is in any way helpful during an emergency?"

"'Sexual Healing' by Marvin Gaye would be my pick. I mean, it really depends on what kind of emergency. We don't know what's going to happen here. Lot of variables. Jesus, use your noodle once in a while."

Charlie went quiet, eyes once again tracing up and down that crack in the door.

"Like, what if we bust into song," Allie continued. "Sexual healing this. Sexual healing that. Right? And then, just as the song peaks, we bumrush this lady, right? Give 'er a forearm shiver. Chop her right in the throat. Muscle our way past her through the door. Boom. We just sang our way in."

"And the song helps *how* in that scenario?"

"What do you mean?"

"I mean, I can elbow a lady in the throat without any musical accompaniment."

"It's a distraction, Charlie. The song lulls them. Reaches them emotionally. Gets 'em thinking about… well, sexual healing, I guess. And then, when they're all buttered up, you know… like, that's when you strike."

The door jerked open then, jarring Charlie out of the conversation. It made her flinch.

The maid appeared in the opening again, smiling like an evil cat.

"Ms. Marley isn't accepting visitors this afternoon. So I'll just take the flowers."

"But—"

The maid reached forward and ripped the bouquet out of Charlie's hands with surprising ferocity.

Charlie's fingers clawed at the empty air. A pointless little gripping motion.

The maid shoved a five-dollar bill into one of the twitching hands. Charlie gaped down at it like she'd never seen American currency before.

"For your time," the maid said and slammed the door shut in Charlie's face.

CHAPTER THIRTY-FOUR

Shock constricted in Charlie's gut. She blinked a few times, still staring at the panes of diamond-shaped glass on the door.

"See?" Allie said. "A gripping song could have changed that outcome, but no one ever listens to me. Hey, why listen to the all-knowing voice in your head when you can go it alone and get shut down over and over? I'm a frickin' specter, Charlie. I know things."

Charlie could hear the smile in Allie's voice. Her sister loved nothing more than rubbing it in.

"You're not a specter."

"Oh yeah? Then what am I?"

"A paranoid delusion, maybe. An auditory hallucination, probably."

Allie gasped.

"How dare you!"

Charlie walked back down the sidewalk toward her car, thankful to have shut Allie up for the moment. That valve in her middle clenched tighter, however, erasing any joy she took from the victory.

She climbed into the car. Sat a moment in the driver's seat, her wrists balanced on the steering wheel. She tried to push the anger down. Thought about the problem still facing her: how to talk to Vivien Marley. She needed a way in. Needed information. But how?

"What's with this lady?" she muttered, half to Allie and half to herself. "It's like she's locked up tighter than Fort Knox."

Allie laughed a touch too hard at that, which made Charlie even angrier. The rage swelled, spread from that clenching in her gut into a heat that crawled up over her shoulders to flush her cheeks.

And now the fury propelled her actions.

She ripped the stupid florist hat from her head. Whipped it into the backseat.

Jammed the key into the ignition. Twisted. Yanked the car into reverse.

It zipped backward. Slalomed up the snaking driveway. Jolted over the little ramp into the street.

As the car jerked to a stop and she shifted into drive, Charlie's eyes snapped to the royal blue bin before her. Her foot hesitated just shy of the accelerator.

The plastic garbage bin still sat at the edge of the driveway. Her eyes crawled over the white logo on the side, over the lid sticking up, the bulging bulk below pressing it open a crack like parted lips.

She smiled. Pictured what might be crammed inside those black plastic bags. Piles of discarded mail. Documents deemed unworthy of keeping.

She no longer saw a garbage bin swirling with flies. She saw eighty-five gallons of information sitting in front of her.

Time to go dumpster-diving.

CHAPTER THIRTY-FIVE

"Wait. What are you thinking?" Allie whispered. "Please tell me it's not what I think it is."

Charlie ignored her. Her hands fidgeted on the steering wheel, knuckles clenching and unclenching. The engine's rumble vibrated into the meat of her palms.

"No," Allie said. "No, I know what you're thinking, and I say no. Let's just talk about this, OK? We're both reasonable adults."

Charlie eased back into the driveway, stopping as the car's trunk pulled even with the trash bin, the brakes squealing loud enough to cut off Allie's words.

Once again, Charlie made eye contact with herself in the rearview mirror. This was her best shot, maybe her only shot. She took a breath. Better to be quick about it.

She lurched out of the driver's seat, a rush of adrenaline pushing her into fast motion. She circled toward the back of the car. Popped the trunk.

Allie was aghast.

"What? In the car?! Charlie, no."

Charlie glanced both ways before flipping the lid of the bin open, yanked out two bags and waddled the three steps to round the rear fender.

"Not in the car, you lunatic! You'll never get the smell out."

Charlie lifted the first bag toward the vacancy in the back of her hatchback, her arm quivering from the strain.

"We're talking permanent ramifications, Charlie. There are things you can't take back!"

Charlie slopped the bag in. It tottered back and forth like a turtle trapped on its back before it settled into a heap. She flung the second bag next to the first, watching it squirm and hunker into place as well.

The two bags just about filled the empty storage space she had available, and the rest of the garbage can looked to be loaded with yard work waste—a matted mess of weeds and dead leaves and grass trimmings.

She slid her hands up onto the trunk hatch, brought it about halfway down before stopping. She blinked at the black plastic mounds protruding from the back of her vehicle. There was a minor problem.

"You're going to pop the damn things like water balloons!" Allie screeched.

Charlie shifted the bags around, flattening them some so she'd be able to close the trunk without any additional squishing from the hatch. It was tight, but she got the trunk latched without popping anything, as far as she could tell.

Then she rushed back around the car, hopping into the driver's seat.

Allie unloaded on her.

"Oh, God. You maniac! What a sickening display. Did you hear how fucking juicy that sounded? Garbage water seeping into the upholstery as we speak. Rotting vegetables. Cat vomit wadded into paper towels. Seafood. Yogurt. Warm beer foam. All of it saturating the fibers back there. You'll never get that stench out, Charlie. Every summer day, it's going to smell like a landfill in here."

Charlie made for the gates, eyes glancing up toward the house in her rearview mirror. She half expected the maid to come running out with a meat cleaver.

"My own sister," Allie said. "A damn garbage picker. I'm telling Mom."

Charlie snorted.

"I'm not joking," Allie said. "I'm telling Mom."

CHAPTER THIRTY-SIX

Back at the office, Charlie wasted no time preparing to pick through her new evidence. She needed floor space to work with, a clear flat area, and she knew the back room was her best hope for that. She briefly entertained working in the parking lot out back—the slab of blacktop was certainly flat and empty enough for the job—but today's stiff breeze made her think better of it.

The clutter in the back room bordered on staggering—apart from the space just in front of the kitchenette, it was essentially a stuffed storage locker. Cardboard boxes. Plastic tubs. A dinette set. Filing cabinets. This would take time, but she could make it work.

Paige helped her tuck the dining room table as far into one corner as they could get it, nestling it up against the stove and counter of the little kitchenette. The chairs were stacked seat down on the tabletop. That was a good start.

Next they shifted some of the many cardboard boxes around. Frank had always been a bit of a pack rat, and the back office fell somewhere between time capsule, legitimate storage space, and something of a purgatory for miscellaneous trinkets and paper garbage simply waiting to be thrown away.

"That probably has some value," he'd say of things like McDonald's Happy Meal toys still wrapped in the plastic and old editions of *Rolling Stone* magazine, though Charlie doubted that even he fully believed it.

Dust billowed everywhere. Little gray clouds that seemed to spread ever wider, trying their best to fill the room. After about ten boxes, Charlie realized her shirt was covered in it—oblong smudges the shade of a pigeon smeared up and down her front. So far, she'd gotten dirtier moving Frank's crap than she had literally picking garbage, which seemed funny after all of Allie's melodrama.

With the boxes stacked up in the corners and a couple stowed under the table for good measure, the center of the floor began to clear at last. Charlie surveyed the area. Bare wooden planks stared up from beneath her feet.

"I never really noticed the floors back here were wood," Paige said, echoing Charlie's thoughts.

"I know. It's usually so cluttered with junk back here, I think I forgot there even was a floor."

Next Charlie flung a blue vinyl tarp over the floorboards. It ballooned and floated down into place in slow motion like a sheet settling over a mattress.

She plucked a pair of latex gloves from the box on the counter and snapped them over her wrists, cool on her fingers, a little tight on the heels of her hands. She tossed a pair to Paige.

Finally, it was time to open these bags, see what secrets lay hidden within.

She untied the first bag, hefted it, moving until the bulging thing hovered over the tarp. Adjusting her grip so her hands slid down to the bottom, she tipped and emptied it.

The garbage slopped out as though vomited from this black plastic stomach. Lumps of it spilled free, tumbling, the pile on the tarp pooling outward from the center.

The second bag was lighter, blotting out most of the blue tarp now. Trash piled upon trash. Garbage all the way down.

Taking a deep breath, Charlie and Paige picked at the trash, spreading and sorting bit by bit until there was some semblance of order.

Then Charlie stood back. Looked at the big picture.

Most of it was useless to her. Packing peanuts. Shards of a broken mirror. Food-tainted paper containers. Evidence that Vivien drank a lot of orange juice and that she had a soft spot for Pringles.

On the other hand, there was a lot of mail. Torn envelopes hung open like mouths, bundles of papers protruding from the tattered places like the tips of tongues. That was good.

Loose sheets of white paper caught her eye. Stacks of them interspersed with the rest of the mess. She didn't know what those could be, and why they hadn't been recycled.

"Maybe I should start picking out the food stuff?" Paige suggested. "If I bag up all the grody bits, it might be less gross to sift through the papers and whatnot."

"Good idea," Charlie said.

Charlie got down on her knees before the pile, rolled her sleeves up, and really got to work. Junk mail was the easiest to check over and dismiss, and there was plenty of it. Colorful envelopes advertising everything from a new almond milk brand to the *hottest* online slot machines. Glossy postcards from used car lots running sales made to look like gigantic scratch-off lotto tickets. All of these she glanced at and dismissed, passing them from her right hand to her left hand to the mail pile without really stopping.

She lifted a bundle of coupons for the local grocery store and a glob of brown goop dripped out.

"Ew, what is that?" Allie asked.

Charlie studied it for a moment.

"Baked beans?" Her eyes scanned the rest of the garbage. "Except I don't see any beans anywhere. Just the juice."

Paige plucked a coffee filter from the pile and squinted at the mystery goo.

"Kinda looks like the sauce that comes on General Tsao's chicken."

"Nah," Allie said. "That's Mesquite barbecue sauce, sure as you're alive. Smell it. You'll see."

Charlie crawled closer to Paige and deposited the soggy flier into the bag of definite trash.

Having separated out most of the junk mail, Charlie moved on to the loose sheets of white paper, which took longer to decipher. The pages sported tightly packed text periodically splotched with a grainy black-and-white photo. They were online articles printed off, she could tell that much. Documents for some kind of research project by the look of it. Lots of stuff about the wildlife in tropical regions, especially Hawaii. A few academic papers about the economies of such regions.

Charlie turned one of the pages in her hand. A wild boar stared back at her from the photo, his eyes somehow cold even through the murky rendering of a dated laser jet printer. The article talked about a rash of feral pig attacks on the big island.

Was Vivien planning on moving? Or had one of her worker's kids been using her computer for some homework project? Charlie wasn't sure, but she set the papers aside, keeping them separate from the junk mail for now.

The non-junk mail took the most time of all. She had to peel the papers out of each envelope, really read them, hoping that just one held some clue about where she might meet up with Vivien, get the jump on her.

A lot of it, while legitimate, was just as useless as the junk. Thank you cards sent by local businesses and charities. Credit card companies sending repeated updates about their terms of service—pages loaded with tiny text that no one ever read.

Charlie found a stack of papers pinned together with a paper clip. No photos this time, just double-spaced text in twelve-point Times New Roman. Charlie let her eyes scan the words. After a moment, she burst out laughing.

Paige's head snapped up.

"Did you find something?"

"Oh, I found something alright."

Charlie cleared her throat and began to read aloud.

"'Broderick's manhood strained against the zipper of his khakis, and he could tell by the sharp outline of Maleah's nipples against her thin silk blouse that she, too, was aroused.'" Charlie snickered. "It goes on from there. In graphic detail."

Paige giggled, her cheeks turning pink.

"Oh, Lordy."

Charlie flipped through the rest of the pages, skimming. She found a mention of the main character, Broderick Sterling, being an ethnobiologist studying the mammals native to the rainforests of Hawaii. That explained the printouts, then. Vivien was writing a romance novel.

"My granny was a big reader," Paige said as they continued their work. "Always had a book in her hand, and her basement was stacked floor to ceiling with paperbacks. She loved nothing more than to spend all evening on the back porch reading in her glider."

Charlie doubted Vivien's attempts at fiction would reveal much—other than a healthy imagination—but she set the papers aside anyway.

"I was there for a visit once and it rained for like three days straight, so I couldn't be outside like I usually was. I got so bored that I decided I'd read one of Granny's books." Paige shook her head. "Oh my word. It was 'throbbing member' this and 'heaving bosom' that. I couldn't look her in the face for the whole rest of the visit. Not that I begrudged her guilty pleasures, of course. Whatever floats your boat, that's what I say. But she was such a strait-laced…"

Paige trailed off for a second, staring at an envelope speckled with coffee grounds, and then she was talking again, her voice going up in pitch.

"Oh, crumbs! I was just starting to think we were picking through all this filth for nothing. And then here it is!"

"What are you talking about?"

"I think 'gala' would mean it's kind of fancy, but that shouldn't be a problem, I don't think—"

"Paige," Charlie interrupted. "What is it?"

"Sorry!" She let out a nervous chuckle. "Here. See for yourself."

The envelope was moist, but the letter inside had been mostly protected from the rest of the refuse. One edge sported a faint coffee-colored stain.

The return address was typed out in fancy script and listed the Bridgefork Heights Country Club as the sender. The logo on the letterhead inside matched it. Charlie's eyes flitted down the letter, devouring it.

You are cordially invited to the 18th Annual Jazz Brunch Gala and Silent Auction to benefit Meals on Wheels. This year's gala features a menu planned by world-renowned chef Bobby Flay and a wine-tasting with some of Napa Valley's top sommeliers. Enclosed, please find your complimentary tickets for you and one guest.

"Holy shit!" Allie said. "Bobby Flay's going to be there?"

Charlie checked the inside of the envelope, squeezing the sides so it fattened and opened like a bullfrog's mouth. Empty. The tickets were gone, of course.

Still, she had something to work with now. If Charlie ambushed Vivien Marley at the gala, there'd be nowhere for her to run. No maid to play gatekeeper this time.

Better yet, she wouldn't even have to wait long. The gala was tomorrow morning.

CHAPTER THIRTY-SEVEN

When Charlie finally got herself into bed that night, she lay awake for some time, restless at the thought of sneaking into the gala.

She was just drifting off at around 2 a.m. when the sound of her phone ringing startled her awake. Squinting through the slit of one eye, she read the name on the screen: Mom.

Charlie picked up, expecting to hear a burst of her mother's paranoid babbling before she could get in even a word. But there was only silence.

"Mom? Are you there?"

"Charlie!" Nancy's voice came out in a hiss. "You have to help me! I think there's an intruder!"

Charlie sat up, feeling an immediate jolt of anxiety. Then she remembered what had happened with the so-called lurking reporter who had turned out to be a woman collecting donations for the local animal shelter.

"Someone is in the house?" she asked.

"No. They're prowling around outside."

"How can they be an intruder if they're *outside* the house?"

"Don't get into semantics with me! I heard scratching, like they're trying to get inside."

"That's probably just the birds on the side of the house."

"Birds?" Nancy repeated. "Do you think I'm an idiot?"

Charlie gritted her teeth. Her mother's chronic tendency to overreact and catastrophize every little thing was exhausting.

Charlie remembered something her mother's psychiatrist had told her before, that there tended to be triggers for Nancy's outbursts. With the little scare Nancy had had earlier with the not-really-a-reporter, it was only natural that she'd have a bad night.

Sighing, Charlie let her head fall back against the wall behind her. She needed to calm her mother down enough so that they could both get some sleep.

"Mom, do you remember earlier when you called me in a panic about there being a reporter outside the house?"

"I wasn't in a panic!"

"Well, it sounded that way to me," Charlie said, patiently. "And then when I got there, everything was fine, wasn't it?"

"I can't believe you're using that against me." Nancy whimpered. "I guess I'm just a burden to you. I'm frightened and alone, and now you won't even help me."

Like a dose of drugs plunged straight into her veins, the guilt went straight to Charlie's head.

She opened her mouth to tell her mother she'd be right there. But she stopped herself. Dr. Kesselman had told Charlie over and over that playing into her mother's guilt trips only perpetuated the cycle. It was something that happened every time Charlie spent too much time with her. Her mother began to grow dependent. Created scenarios that made Charlie feel obligated to intervene.

Apologizing, placating, appeasing.

And it wasn't just tonight, Charlie realized. Her mother had been playing this game all week.

So Charlie did something she'd never done before. Something she should have done this afternoon. She called her mother's bluff.

"If you're that scared, Mom, you need to call the police."

A rush of breath rattled out of the speaker.

"You know as well as I do that the police in this town are worthless." Nancy's voice was hard. The simpering woman from a moment before had vanished. "Well, if you won't help me, I'll just go get your father's old hunting rifle and sort it out myself."

And then the line went dead.

CHAPTER THIRTY-EIGHT

Charlie flopped back against her pillow, fuming.

Had her dad actually owned a rifle? She couldn't remember. He and Uncle Frank had gone fishing all the time, but hunting? She had no distinct memories of that. Then again, here in rural Michigan, hunting and fishing went hand in hand. And plenty of people who never went hunting still had a gun or two around the house.

The more she thought about it, the more Charlie couldn't confidently say her father hadn't owned a gun. It was possible.

"Goddamn it," she whispered into the dark.

She had to hand it to her mother: she was a master at the game. Charlie had called her bluff alright, but then her mother had called hers in return.

The question was, what now? Call the police? That would probably make things worse. Besides, she didn't want to be one of those people who sent the cops to do her dirty work. Especially when all of this was over a pair of robins nesting on the side of the damn house.

Charlie threw the covers aside and climbed out of bed, dressing quickly.

On the drive over, she silently berated herself for letting things go this far. She should have seen it coming from a mile away. It was what always happened. No matter how hard she tried to keep her distance, she always got sucked back in.

This was it then. The final straw. From this point forward, Charlie vowed to keep space between her and her mother. She'd tried saving her, but nothing she'd done had ever worked. It was like the stories about drowning victims who end up taking their rescuers down too because they fight and try to climb on top of them to get out of the water. It wasn't intentional. Sheer panic. Fight or flight. But the rescuers got dragged down anyway, sentenced to the same fate they'd been trying to pull someone else out of.

And just like a drowning victim, her mother didn't know what she was doing. She had no idea she was forever pulling Charlie down into the swirling depths of her misery. For Charlie's own sake, the only option left was to save herself.

At the house, Charlie pulled into the driveway and parked. It was dark, no lights on inside. She wasn't sure if that was good or bad. If she was lucky, her mother had realized it really was the birds making noise and had gone back to bed.

Charlie padded up to the front door and paused there for a moment, looking both ways. No activity outside, as expected. Another of Nancy's false alarms.

Charlie sighed. She twisted the key in the deadbolt, turned the knob, and stepped inside.

She was about to call out to her mother when there was a bright flash and then a bullet exploded through the window over her right shoulder.

CHAPTER THIRTY-NINE

It all seemed to happen at once. The muzzle flash. The bullet whizzing past Charlie's face. The popping sound so loud it felt like it ruptured her eardrums. The glass bursting into a thousand pieces.

She knew, of course, if she could rewatch the scene in slow motion, each little event would occupy its own millisecond. But in the moment, it felt simultaneous. It was only after that everything seemed to slow down.

"Mom!" Charlie's voice sounded dull in her own ears, which were ringing.

There was a long pause. Nancy stared at her from across the room, the rifle still aimed at Charlie's face.

Charlie held her breath, afraid to move. Afraid to blink.

Her mother's eyes were stretched wide, showing too much of the whites. Like a cornered dog. It was the look she always got when things went bad. But things never got that bad when Nancy was on her meds.

And then it hit her, what she should have seen before: her mother had obviously stopped taking her medication. She should have figured it out sooner. How long had she been off her meds, was the question. Had she been skipping doses? Fooling Elaine? Or maybe that didn't matter at all, considering the current situation—the one in which her mother was holding her at gunpoint.

Charlie wasn't sure her mother was even seeing her right now. Her paranoid delusions could be making her see just about anything.

Very softly—not wanting to spook her—Charlie spoke.

"Mom? It's me."

The barrel of the gun hung there in the air between them, trembling slightly. And then it swung away as recognition overtook Nancy's features. Charlie had been standing ramrod-straight, and her shoulders relaxed just a hair now that the rifle wasn't pointing between her eyes. If her mother still knew who she was, then she wasn't quite as far gone as Charlie had worried. That was good.

These were the thoughts swirling in Charlie's mind in the brief moment before her mother whispered the single word that told her that things were indeed much, much worse than she'd anticipated.

"Allie?"

Charlie's blood went ice-cold.

"Allie!" The gun thudded to the floor as Nancy released her grip on it. "Oh, Allie, my baby. I knew you'd come back to me."

Bony arms closed around Charlie, clinging to her as her mother seemed to lose the ability to stay upright. Wilting. Collapsing.

Charlie didn't have the strength to hold both of them up, and she felt her mother's tears mixing with her own as she let herself be pulled down, down, down.

CHAPTER FORTY

Charlie didn't know how long they'd been huddled there on the floor, her mother stroking her hair, holding her tight, face pressed into Charlie's neck, crying and repeating, "Allie, Allie, my baby." Over and over again.

Charlie felt like someone set adrift in the middle of the ocean. Floating aimlessly in the void. Flitting out into nothing.

Her mother had gone through some bad times. Charlie had lost count of the number of breakdowns since Allie had died. But she'd never openly mistaken Charlie for her dead sister. Not once.

Eventually Charlie came back to herself. Realized what she had to do. The awful thing she had to do.

She got out her phone to call the sheriff's department. She was still staring at the dial pad when she saw the lights. Flashes of red and blue twirling among the branches of the trees lining the street.

A few seconds later, a sheriff's cruiser pulled to the curb out front. Two deputies climbed out.

Charlie felt like she was in a dream. Had she called the police already and forgotten? Then her eyes strayed to the broken window beside the door, and she realized a neighbor had probably heard the gunshot, the breaking glass, and called it in.

The deputies were at the door now, angling their guns and flashlights into the house.

"Charlie?"

She recognized the voice.

"Hey Zoe," Charlie said, and the simple act of speaking seemed to break her from her trance.

"Are you guys OK?" Zoe asked, holstering her weapon. "Is anyone hurt?"

"No one's hurt," Charlie answered, thinking that neither she nor her mother was OK.

"We got a call. Neighbors heard gunshots." Zoe's gaze slid over to the broken window. "Did someone try to break in?"

Charlie shook her head.

She tried to decide how to explain everything without upsetting her mother. Nancy had never been violent before, but then she'd always been at least somewhat lucid. Charlie wasn't sure what to expect when she was in such a delusional state.

She wiped tears from her cheeks and leaned back in such a way that she could catch her mother's eye.

"OK, Mom." Her voice sounded hoarse. "It's time for your appointment."

"Appointment?"

"Yeah. Don't you remember? You have an appointment with Dr. Kesselman today."

"Dr. Kesselman," Nancy repeated. "I forgot."

Charlie waited for her to notice that it was dark outside. Long after midnight. Much too late an hour for a doctor's appointment, but her mother was apparently too far gone to notice.

"That's OK," Charlie said, forcing false cheer into her words. "There's still time to get there, but you have to leave now or you'll be late."

"But you're coming with me, aren't you, Allie?" Nancy's grip tightened on her. "I won't leave you."

Charlie caught the flicker of surprise that crossed Zoe's face at hearing Allie's name.

"I'm going to meet up with you there," Charlie said, forcing a calmness in her voice that she didn't feel. "You remember Zoe, Mom? My friend from school?"

Nancy begrudgingly let her eyes wander over to Zoe.

"She's going to give you a ride in the back of her police car. Won't that be fun?"

"Why can't you drive me?"

"I have to stay here and clean up."

Her mother seemed to register for the first time that the window was broken.

"Oh my goodness. I almost shot you!" She clutched Charlie's hands. "I'm so sorry. I didn't mean to, Allie. I thought it was someone breaking into the house. I didn't know it was you. If I'd known—"

"It's OK," Charlie interrupted. "I'm OK. You're OK. I'll get this all fixed up while you go to your appointment. And then we'll see each other later. How about that?"

"I guess so," she said but made no move to release the firm grasp she had on Charlie.

"Come on. I'll walk you out."

Charlie hoisted her mother up with her as she rose to her feet, and they walked outside still bunched together. Charlie was worried that as soon as they reached the cruiser, her mother would dig in her heels and refuse to get inside. But she only gave Charlie one final squeeze before climbing in through the door that Zoe held open for her.

With her mother deposited in the back of the cruiser, Charlie went over what had happened with Zoe.

"Holy hell. You're lucky she's got such bad aim."

"It wasn't bad enough," Charlie said. "I actually felt the heat of the bullet zipping past my face. It was close."

"Jesus." Zoe sighed. "And she's really convinced you're Allie?"

"I guess so. She must have quit taking her meds." Charlie wiped a hand down her face. "It's my fault. I should have seen it coming. Anytime her routine gets disrupted, even a little, she goes noncompliant. And this whole week has been one giant disruption."

Zoe frowned.

"Don't be so hard on yourself. I can't even get my dad to take a daily multivitamin." She sighed. "It's hard, taking care of our parents. They still see us as kids, I think. They don't trust us to know what's best, because they've spent most of their lives with the roles reversed."

Charlie's eyes roamed over to where her mother was hunkered in the backseat of Zoe's cruiser. She was only a dark silhouette behind the glass.

"So what's the drill, exactly? You can do a psychiatric hold for forty-eight hours, right?"

"That's right. We'll take her to the hospital. She'll be screened to determine her mental state, and probably they'll institute a treatment plan right away. Usually they go with some kind of injection. Everything after that depends on how she responds to the treatment. Sometimes the two days back on meds seem to clear things up, and they consent to further treatment."

"And if she doesn't consent?"

"Then you'll need to do a Kevin's Law petition, also known as a Petition for Assisted Outpatient Treatment. It's a court-ordered mandate that the individual seek and comply with ongoing treatment."

There was a chill in the night air, and Charlie wrapped her arms around herself.

"But hey, don't worry about that just yet." Zoe reached out and put an arm on Charlie's shoulder. "Let's take this one day—or night—at a time. OK?"

Charlie nodded.

A door opened across the street, and one of the neighbors crept out to see what the ruckus was all about. Glancing around, Charlie noticed lights on in other houses that hadn't been on when she'd arrived. A curtain flapped next door.

She gestured back at the broken window.

"I guess I'd better start cleaning up."

"Call me if you need anything," Zoe said. "Even if it's just to talk. I mean it."

"I will," Charlie said, but she knew she wouldn't. It wasn't the Winters' way to burden others with their problems.

Zoe climbed into the cruiser beside her partner, who Charlie realized hadn't uttered a word the entire time. She thought maybe she was glad for that. It had made the whole thing seem less official. Like Zoe was only doing her a favor as a friend, versus the truth, which was that she'd had to have her mother hauled away by the police.

The low rumble of the cruiser idling changed pitch as Zoe put the car in gear. The spinning lights on the roof winked out.

A small white hand pressed itself to the window in the backseat. Her mother. Charlie raised a hand and waved, forcing a weak smile to her face.

The car pulled away from the curb, gravel crunching underneath the tires. At the end of the block, the vehicle turned onto a side street and within seconds had disappeared from view.

As soon as it was out of sight, the full weight of the night slammed into Charlie. She turned and looked at the broken glass littering the porch. The gaping hole in the front window.

Charlie sighed and went inside to find a broom and some duct tape.

CHAPTER FORTY-ONE

Charlie double-checked the piece of cardboard she'd taped over the broken window. It didn't offer much in the way of security, but at least it would keep the cold and the bugs out. That would have to be good enough for now.

She swept the last few bits of broken glass into a dustpan and walked around to the side of the house to dump it in the garbage bin. As she closed the lid, her eyes scanned the street. The lights in neighboring houses that had been on when the police had been here were all out now. The show was over, she supposed. Everyone back to bed.

Back inside, she picked up the rifle. Charlie unloaded it and tucked the rounds into her pocket. She'd have to take the gun with her. There was no way she could trust her mother with it ever again. And while she was at it, she decided to ask Uncle Frank if he knew of any other guns in the house.

It struck her that Allie had been oddly silent given everything that had happened. Then she remembered that Allie never spoke to her here. For some reason, she was always completely silent in their childhood home.

Charlie knew she should leave. She was exhausted. But she was also wired and jittery from the adrenaline that came with almost being shot.

She left the rifle unloaded on the living room sofa and wandered down the hall to her old room. She avoided this place, usually. Hated the way it felt like a tomb. She hadn't slept in here since Allie had gone missing. When it had first happened, she spent most nights waiting up on the couch, the whole family holding out hope that any moment, Allie would find her way home and come bursting in through the door.

After, when any hope of her return had gone for good, Charlie took to sleeping on the futon in the basement. The bedroom they'd shared since the day they were brought home from the hospital in matching pink hats and striped swaddling blankets was too painful to be in. A reminder of everything she'd lost.

Aside from the odd vacuuming or dusting, nothing had ever been touched in here. Her mother hadn't allowed that.

Charlie went to the old Sony boom box between their beds. To her surprise, it actually powered on. She wondered if there was a CD inside. Something of Allie's, since she'd always been fanatical about controlling the music.

Charlie's thumb found the play button. Was this a mistake? Did she really want to wake this dragon?

She pushed play.

The song started with strange plucking sounds. More ambient than melodic. The bass, guitar, and drums came in together a few seconds later, heavy and grungy. Charlie knew what it was immediately: "You Know You're Right" by Nirvana. It had been a big hit the year Allie disappeared. Played non-stop on the radio. And when that wasn't enough, Allie downloaded it and played it a few thousand times more.

Charlie had closed her eyes when the song started, but at the first chorus, her eyelids snapped open. The song had dredged something up. A memory long-buried.

Charlie moved to the closet, ducked inside, and found the removable panel that offered access to the bathtub plumbing on the other side of the wall.

"Jackpot," she said, pushing the panel aside and revealing Allie's secret stash.

She removed the goodies one by one. A pack of Marlboro Reds with three cigarettes remaining. A condom. An unopened bottle of Bacardi rum.

The last item made her burst out laughing. It was a copy of *Playgirl* magazine from 1981 featuring Burt Reynolds on the cover. Allie had thought it was the funniest thing ever when they were sixteen.

Charlie unscrewed the top of the Bacardi and sniffed it. She didn't think booze went bad, but then she wasn't really an expert.

She sipped at it, and the sharpness made her cough. When she'd recovered, she took a longer drink. The warmth of the alcohol spread down her throat and into her belly. Fiery and pleasant.

She sat down on the end of her old bed, wishing she had someone to call. Someone who would wrap their arms around her and tell her everything would be OK. Even if it was a lie.

CHAPTER FORTY-TWO

Charlie woke to rays of morning sun streaming in through the curtains of her childhood bedroom. Squinting, she peered out at the now half-empty bottle of Bacardi a few feet away. She'd only intended to have a few sips of rum while she wallowed in her sorrows.

She lurched to her feet. The gala. She'd almost forgotten about it.

Her head throbbed so violently that she had to steady herself on the edge of the bed. Her mouth tasted the way a wet dog smelled, and the room felt like it was lurching like a ship on rough seas.

She forced herself upright, tottered out into the hall, fleeing her mother's house. She couldn't miss the gala. She needed to talk to Dutch's mistress, hungover or not.

The sun tried its best to pierce her brain as she sped back to her apartment, stabbing ice picks of bright light through her eyeballs. Her phone rang, and when she saw Zoe's name on the screen, her mind flashed back to the previous night.

"How are you holding up?" Zoe asked once Charlie had picked up.

"I guess that depends on how things went at the hospital," Charlie said.

"Yeah, sorry I didn't call before. Anytime I work a night shift like that, I end up crashing pretty hard when I get home. I just woke up."

"Don't apologize," Charlie said. "I should be thanking you."

"All part of the job, ma'am," Zoe said in an overly folksy accent that made Charlie think of a cop show from the 1960s. "Anyway, things got a little heated at the hospital. She wanted her regular doctor, who wasn't on call. Eventually they got your mom calmed down enough to give her some meds, and that helped. So she's compliant for now, and that's a good sign."

"Yeah," Charlie said, hoping Zoe was right.

"Nancy's at the Henry Ford Urgent Care center for the duration of the hold," Zoe explained. "They usually prefer to keep visitations to a minimum during the forty-eight hours, but I might be able to pull some strings if you think seeing her would help."

"Honestly, I think visiting right now would make it worse, if anything," Charlie said.

She wondered if that was the truth or a convenient thing to tell herself. She thanked Zoe again before hanging up.

At home, she took ibuprofen with her coffee and then chugged two glasses of water. By the time she'd finished showering, she was feeling mostly better.

She got out her laptop and did some background research on Meals on Wheels while she forced down a piece of toast with peanut butter and blackberry jam.

"It's Meals on Wheels," Allie said. "They take food to old people. It's not rocket science."

"I know, but I might have to blend in while I wait for the right moment to approach Vivien Marley. I'd like to at least seem like I know what I'm there for."

"You'd be better off brushing up on your golf lingo and the latest ways to shelter money in the Caymans. That's what these rich bastards are going to be talking about. They probably go to so many of these things they can't keep them straight. They get liquored up at the free bar, write a check, and swap stories about the different positions they employ whilst banging their secretaries," Allie said. "What you should really be worrying about is getting ready. If you screw around and miss meeting Bobby Flay, I will never forgive you."

Obnoxious though she may be, Allie was right.

Charlie rushed to her closet. Ripped out the bridesmaid's dress from her cousin's wedding and started putting it on. It was a tea-length affair in blush-pink lace with an asymmetrical hem. Based on the photos she'd looked at from last year's gala, it wouldn't look out of place.

After dressing and administering a quick lacquer of makeup, she studied her reflection in the full-length mirror on the back of the bathroom door.

"What do you think?" she asked. "Brunchy enough?"

"Super brunchy," Allie said. "Brunchtastic, even."

Charlie took one last look at herself in the mirror and nodded.

Time to talk to Dutch's mistress, once and for all.

CHAPTER FORTY-THREE

The Bridgefork Heights Country Club was all dolled up when Charlie arrived. A red carpet stretched from the sidewalk up to the entrance, and a short line of people waited for their turn to pass through the front doors.

Charlie joined the line, forcing herself to breathe slowly and deeply. To stand still and upright. To believe she belonged here.

The line moved quickly. There was a teenage boy at the door taking tickets. Someone's son or grandson who had gotten roped into ticket duty.

The older couple directly in front of Charlie handed their tickets to the kid, and as they passed through the open doors, Charlie stuck with them.

"Oh, uh… excuse me? Ma'am?" the kid called after her.

Charlie kept going, pretending not to hear, which actually worked a surprising percentage of the time.

The kid was more persistent than she'd anticipated, though. He caught up to her and tapped her on the shoulder.

She whirled around and raised her eyebrows in what she hoped was a haughty manner.

"Sorry, miss. It's just that, uh, I need to get your ticket?" His Adam's apple bobbed up and down when he swallowed.

"Of course," she said. "I already gave it to you."

He blinked.

"Um… are you sure? It's just that, well, I don't think I got it?"

"Just now, you mean?"

He nodded, looking somewhat relieved.

"Oh, I see your confusion." Charlie smiled and placed a hand to her chest. "I came in earlier, with my husband. We gave you our tickets then. But I forgot something in my car, you see. I just nipped out for a moment and was coming back just now."

"Oh… I see," the kid said, sounding like he only half-believed her.

Charlie went to Plan B. She whipped her head around.

"There he is now," she said, pretending to see her fantasy husband in the crowd. "Darling!"

She dashed into the throng, still shouting for her darling and waving her hand in the air like an idiot.

From behind her, the kid tried to call her back to the door.

"Wait a minute, miss," he said. "Ma'am, come back, please!"

She put as much distance between her and the kid as possible, dodging back and forth between the other guests. A server stood nearby wearing a black vest and white gloves and holding a tray of hors d'oeuvres. Charlie ducked behind him and used the cover to glance back at the door.

The kid was back at his post, collecting tickets. Good. He'd given up on chasing her.

Charlie took a deep breath. The air was thick with a miasma of expensive perfumes and colognes. A toxic cloud of Chanel N°5, Shalimar, and Miss Dior. The collective stench seemed acrid, Charlie thought, like something that would effectively keep insects away.

She was past the first obstacle for the day, at least. Now she needed to find Vivien Marley and wait for just the right moment to corner her.

Her eyes searched the room, and after a few moments, she realized that was going to prove more difficult than she'd hoped.

Charlie had seen photos of Vivien and thought she had a good grasp of what she looked like: a fit, older blonde. The kind of woman you expected to see married to a senator or anchoring the evening news. But now that Charlie was here, she realized that Vivien

Marley was a type, and roughly half the women in the room were the *exact same* type. It was only made worse by the fact that they were all done up in a similar manner with their sensible hairstyles and modest formal attire.

Charlie pulled out her phone and tapped Vivien's name into the search bar. She scrolled through the photo results, trying to find a good, clear shot of her face.

After comparing photos to faces for a few minutes, Charlie spotted her in the far corner, near a table with flutes of mimosas and champagne set out on it. Vivien bent over to whisper something to the woman filling the glasses.

"She's got a great rack for an older gal," Allie said.

Charlie couldn't argue with the sentiment, despite the crass way Allie had put it. For someone old enough to be her mother, Vivien Marley was in fantastic shape.

"You think they're natural?" Allie asked. "Or is that eight hundred ccs of liquid saline doing all the work?"

Charlie edged closer to the table where Vivien was, scooping up a mimosa when she got there. Vivien was now chatting with a squat gentleman with glasses and a comb-over. Charlie tried unsuccessfully to eavesdrop on their conversation, but a string quartet had started playing across the room, and all Charlie was able to catch was something about the man's granddaughter "heading to Dartmouth this autumn."

"God, rich people are hilarious," Allie said, putting on an affected aristocratic accent and attempting to mimic him. "Dartmouth, you don't say! Ahem, ahem. Autumn. Foie gras."

Charlie bit her lip to keep from chuckling. Sometimes the worse Allie's impression was, the funnier it seemed.

Vivien finished up her talk with Mr. Dartmouth, Esq. and moved on.

"She's getting away," Allie hissed.

"I've got my eye on her, don't worry," Charlie assured her.

"Why don't you just walk up and hit her with questions? You know, use the element of surprise like a weapon and bludgeon her with it."

"Because, if she makes a scene, I'll get thrown out of here in a heartbeat," Charlie said. "You think this kind of function would look kindly on some lowly peon harassing one of their esteemed guests? If I get her alone, I might have enough time to talk my way past her defenses."

"OK. That's smart, I guess," Allie admitted.

Charlie shadowed Vivien Marley for a solid ten minutes, always careful to keep a discreet distance. Eventually, Vivien broke off from the group she'd joined, striding over to the tables where the silent auction was set up. She gave the items there a cursory glance before exiting the banquet hall and moving in the direction of the restrooms.

CHAPTER FORTY-FOUR

Charlie was waiting by the sink when Vivien came out of the stall.

She was taller than Charlie had realized now that they were up close. Towering over her, Vivien flapped a hand.

"Oh, nothing for me, dear." She had a rich, deep voice that reminded Charlie of Kathleen Turner.

"Um… what?" was the most eloquent thing Charlie could think to say in response to this.

"Aren't you here to offer mints, etcetera?"

Charlie frowned.

"No…"

"Oh my God, this is hilarious," Allie said. "You're more dressed up than you've ever been in your entire life, and she still sniffed you out as the servant class."

Charlie had expected this to go much differently. She'd planned to sidle up beside Vivien and pretend to recognize her from somewhere. Get her talking. But Vivien mistaking her for a bathroom attendant had thrown her off.

"Lipstick on a pig, right?" Allie said.

Screw it, Charlie thought. *I'll just hit her with it, then.*

"My name is Charlotte Winters. I'm a private detective."

Vivien's big blue eyes got bigger. Her ample chest rose as she inhaled deeply. And Charlie knew with certainty that she was about to scream for security.

Instead, Vivien threw back her head and cackled.

"Oh, this is just marvelous! Did you sneak in here just to talk to me?"

Momentarily stunned, it was a few seconds before Charlie could summon a response.

"Well… yeah."

Vivien laughed again, this time reaching out and touching Charlie's arm. It was a strangely intimate gesture, like they were old friends.

"Ask her when Bobby Flay is getting here," Allie whispered.

Charlie ignored her sister.

"My God!" Vivien said. "I'd heard the Carmichael rugrats had hired someone to sniff around after Dutch's money. Now I wish I would have had a moment to return your call sooner. I've been missing out on all the fun."

"So… you weren't intentionally avoiding me?"

"Of course not. That would be rude," Vivien said, brushing this notion aside with a wave of her hand. "I've just been so busy with the last-minute details."

"Last-minute details for what?" Charlie asked.

"For today. I head the committee that organizes the gala. It's practically *my* event."

"Oh."

"Wait." Vivien's eyes narrowed to slits. "If you didn't know this was my event, how did you know I'd be here?"

Charlie wondered how to proceed. Vivien had gotten a hoot out of the whole scenario up until now, but rifling through her personal refuse might cross a line. Charlie weighed it for a moment before deciding to take a gamble.

"I stole your garbage," she admitted. "Found the invitation letter."

"You stole my *garbage*?"

Reading the shock and horror on Vivien's face, Charlie thought she'd made a mistake telling her the truth. But then Vivien let out another scream of laughter.

"That's absolutely priceless! My garbage! Oh, you're too much." Vivien latched onto Charlie's wrist with a hand bedazzled with sparkling rings and bracelets. "Come with me."

Vivien dragged Charlie back to the banquet hall, introducing her to various people they passed as a "real-life private investigator."

"Do you know how she found me today?" Vivien asked a woman in a chiffon gown embroidered with a flower and dragonfly motif. "She went through my trash bins! Can you imagine?"

Vivien howled again at the thought, but the woman in the dragonfly gown didn't seem to find the notion quite so entertaining. She arched a perfectly shaped eyebrow and glanced at Charlie as if she might have some sort of communicable disease.

"Charming," Dragonfly said, her voice high and rasping.

When Vivien tried dragging her before another unsuspecting group, Charlie wriggled free.

"I think that's enough show-and-tell for today, don't you?" Charlie said.

"Oh right. I suppose I got a touch carried away." Vivien reached out and snatched two canapés from a server passing by with a tray. "Here, try one of these."

It looked like a miniature ice cream cone studded with black sesame seeds and filled with salmon and caviar. It was small enough that Charlie could pop the entire thing into her mouth, and she did.

"Isn't it divine?" Vivien asked. "They always suggest salmon puffs for this kind of event, but I think the cornets are so much more elegant."

It was salty and crunchy, and there was some kind of creamy filling Charlie hadn't seen upon her initial inspection. She had to admit it was pretty tasty.

"Do you realize that salmon cornet might have come from Bobby Flay's blessed hands?" Allie said. "From his fingertips to your lips, Charlie. Ask her if we can meet him."

Charlie didn't care one way or the other about Bobby Flay, but if she didn't ask Vivien about him, Allie would probably whine the rest of the night.

"So, uh... speaking of the food... is Bobby Flay actually here? I saw his name mentioned in the invitation letter."

Vivien's face soured for the first time since Charlie had approached her.

"He is not. He was *supposed* to be, but he backed out at the last minute, the weasel." Vivien's hands clenched into fists. "I could wring his little ginger neck. He owes me, and he knows it. But I don't suppose you went to all the trouble getting in here just to ask me about that?"

"No, I didn't," Charlie said. "I wanted to talk to you about Dutch. About his murder."

Vivien's eyes filled with tears.

"The idea that one of those wretched brats took him from me is just too much to bear. It sickens me."

Charlie grabbed a cloth napkin from one of the tables and handed it to Vivien.

"You think one of the Carmichaels is to blame?"

"Of course," Vivien said, sniffling and fanning her moist face. "Who else?"

"I hate to be so brash about this, but can you tell me where you were the day Dutch died?"

"You think *I* killed him?" Vivien asked. "What possible reason could I have?"

"Well, there's the money."

Vivien sputtered out a humorless laugh.

"Darling, Dutch's moronic progeny didn't tell you this because I suppose they don't know, but if one of us was to be considered the gold digger in the relationship, it wasn't me."

"What does that mean?" Charlie asked.

"I know everyone refers to Dutch as a billionaire—even he did himself—but he was what we in the Ten-Figure Club refer to as an 'in name only billionaire' or a 'billionaire with a little b.' His 'b' came from his net worth—an estimated figuring of all of his assets, including his business interests, which is practically an imaginary figure."

"OK," Charlie said. "So he didn't have a billion in liquid assets… but who does?"

Vivien smiled.

"You?"

"My dear, I was born wealthier than even most of the one percent can imagine. I had no use for Dutch's money." Vivien wadded up the napkin and tossed it aside. "Anyway, if you still insist I provide an alibi, you can ask any number of individuals here tonight. I was right here in this room, chairing the gala committee meeting the morning Dutch died."

Vivien put a hand to her chest as she spoke.

"We were supposed to have dinner that evening. No one told me what happened then, either. No one called. When I got to the house to meet him, the coroner was wheeling him into a refrigerated van." She had a faraway look in her eye and sounded as if she were talking to herself more than to Charlie. "Gloria was there, and when I asked her what had happened, I saw such loathing in her eyes. I thought maybe for once she would see that we had at least one thing in common. We both loved her father dearly. I should have known better."

The glazed-over look in her eyes faded, and she snapped her head around to face Charlie.

"Do you know that they kept me from the funeral? I couldn't even say a final goodbye to him." Vivien crossed to one of the tables and helped herself to a glass of champagne, tossing it back in two quick gulps. "This autumn would have been our twentieth anniversary."

Charlie realized she had better get on with her questions before Vivien was too lit on grief and sparkling wine to be of any use.

"Speaking of Gloria, and I'm sorry I have to go down this road again, but can you tell me where you were the day she died, Thursday afternoon around four forty-five?"

Vivien's eyelashes fluttered, and she gazed up at the ceiling.

"Thursday afternoon… I was at home."

"Was anyone with you?"

"Yes. A few people from the committee." Vivien pointed them out to Charlie. "Mitzi Graves and Kassandra Meroni. We were taking care of a few last-minute details. Who was picking up the flowers, had the ice sculptures been ordered yet, that kind of thing."

She waved the one called Mitzi over.

"Mitzi, darling, can you tell this young woman where you were on Thursday from four o'clock to five thirty?"

The woman's thick eyebrows knitted together.

"Is this a trick question?" Mitzi asked. "I was with you. Finalizing everything for the gala."

Vivien turned to Charlie.

"Is that sufficient?"

"Yes, thank you," Charlie said.

Mitzi was dismissed with a flick of Vivien's wrist.

"So is that it?" Vivien scooped up another glass of champagne and crossed her arms. She seemed much less amused with Charlie than she had been a few minutes before. "Any other meddlesome questions you'd like to ask me?"

"I'm really sorry," Charlie said. "I know this isn't easy. And for what it's worth, I can tell you genuinely cared about Dutch."

Vivien's chin quivered slightly.

"Thank you. It's nice to hear someone acknowledge that," she said, blinking away fresh tears. "I don't think I realized until now just how much it's always bothered me that his kids see me as some kind of money-grubbing bedmate."

The term "bedmate" suddenly reminded Charlie of whatever secret Gloria had uncovered.

"I actually do have one more question," Charlie said, biting her lip. "And I have to warn you that it's potentially offensive and probably sensitive. I'm hoping that disclaimer will be enough that you won't have me forcibly removed from the premises immediately."

A small spark of Vivien's intrigue from earlier seemed to return then.

"Oh this sounds good. If you didn't have my full attention before, you have it now." Vivien sipped her champagne. "Let's hear it."

"Were either of you ever unfaithful to the other?" Charlie said, feeling her cheeks grow hot with embarrassment at this line of questioning. "Or was Dutch maybe into anything… I don't know… weird? In the bedroom, I mean?"

Laughter sputtered from Vivien's lips.

"About the kinkiest thing Dutch Carmichael was into was oral sex, and I don't think that counts for much these days." After another chuckle, Vivien lowered her voice. "And as for infidelity, that wasn't really possible since we had an open relationship. I met Dutch when he was still with his wife, and I'm not a big enough fool to think I'd be the one to convert him to monogamy."

Charlie blew out a breath. She'd gone to all the trouble to get here, and it seemed Vivien Marley was going to turn into yet another dead end.

"Now I have to ask *you* something," Vivien said, seeming to have recovered her original sense of curiosity.

"OK," Charlie said. "Shoot."

"What on earth led to that last line of questioning? I can't imagine the ludicrous things people must be saying about Dutch if you felt compelled to ask such a thing."

"It's nothing like that," Charlie said. "Just before Gloria died, she told me she'd found something. All she would say about it over the phone was that it was 'sordid.' Does that bring anything to mind? Anything at all?"

"My God, no." Vivien took a drink and tittered. "Sordid? How absolutely bizarre."

"Do you know if Dutch had a will?" Charlie asked.

She was grasping at straws at this point, but she figured she might as well milk Vivien for any information she might have while she had her attention.

"I assume so," Vivien said. "He liked to do things his own way, but he wasn't an idiot. Why?"

"Well, if there is a will, no one can seem to find it."

"Have you looked on his computer? He kept his entire life on there." Vivien emptied her glass and reached for a third.

"Also missing," Charlie said.

"Really? And you've checked the safe?"

"The big bank safe in his study?" Charlie asked.

"Goodness, no. That's a collector's item. Dutch might have kept a few things in there from time to time, but nothing he truly wanted secure," Vivien explained. "There's a hidden wall safe."

"You can show me where it is?" Charlie asked, feeling a sudden thrill. Maybe this wouldn't be a bust after all.

"Of course," Vivien said. "Shall we go now?"

"Don't you have to… I mean, won't you be missed?"

Vivien waved this notion aside.

"I doubt they'll even notice I'm gone. We've been doing this long enough that once we actually get to the day of the event, the whole thing runs like clockwork," Vivien said. "That's the secret to good event planning. It's all in the preparation."

"OK, great." Charlie slid her phone from her clutch. "Now the question is, which one of Dutch's kids do we call?"

"For what?"

Charlie stared at her.

"To let us in the house."

Vivien clicked her tongue.

"We don't need them for that, darling," she said, pulling a key ring from her own purse. "I have a key."

CHAPTER FORTY-FIVE

They took Charlie's car over to the estate, as Vivien informed her on their way out of the country club that she didn't drive. On the way, Charlie puzzled over Vivien Marley's relationship with Dutch Carmichael. She wasn't at all what Charlie had imagined after the descriptions she'd heard from the Carmichael children. She was so vivacious. So free-spirited and self-possessed. Why would she settle for being Dutch's mistress and never his wife?

"I have a question," Charlie said after several minutes of hemming and hawing about whether or not she should ask it and risk offending Vivien.

"Yes?"

"Well, I'm curious about something, though I should state upfront that it has absolutely nothing to do with my investigation. This is pure, unadulterated nosiness," Charlie said. "You're free to not answer."

Vivien raised an eyebrow.

"Haven't you figured out by now that I'm not shy about much?"

"It's just that you said this fall would have been your twentieth anniversary, and I can't help but wonder why…"

"Why Dutch and I never got married?"

Charlie nodded, feeling a little sheepish for prying.

"Gloria mentioned some sort of arrangement her parents had. That he was free to see other women as long as he never divorced her," Charlie said. "She said it was his way of honoring her, to never marry again after she died."

Vivien let out one of her cackles that made her sound borderline insane. It was a full thirty seconds before she could bring herself to speak.

"Oh my. That's rich." She wiped a tear from the corner of her eye. "Dutch's way of honoring her. My, but Gloria was naive under all her stoicism, wasn't she? At least when it came to her father."

Vivien inhaled deeply, staring out the window at the trees flickering by on the roadside.

"Dutch proposed to me six months after Helena was buried. And many times since," Vivien said. "He wasn't the one opposed to marriage. I was."

"Why?"

"My father was what some might call 'old-fashioned,' by which I mean that he was a misogynistic twat."

Charlie couldn't help but snicker at the word coming from Vivien.

"Well, he was," Vivien insisted. "The trust fund I inherited when I turned eighteen came with a laundry list of stipulations. I could go to college, but my choice of major was limited to a select few my father deemed 'appropriate for women.' He didn't want me having an actual career, you see. But the big one was the marriage incentive. If I were to marry, the funds available to me through the trust would have doubled."

"And that's a bad thing?" Charlie asked.

"Yes, because the other half of the clause stated that my husband would automatically become the trustee of the trust fund. He'd gain absolute control of the money. In *my* trust fund. It's the exact opposite of what most people do. The last thing any rational person would want is for the spouse of their child to gain control of the trust. But my father did precisely that, and he did it by design. In his mind, the woman was always to be subservient to the man. *Husband knows best.* I was expected to be a perfect little brood mare, just like my mother."

Vivien turned to face her.

"And before you think the reason I didn't marry Dutch is because I didn't want him to have access to my money, that wasn't it, either. My father died years ago, and that means I now have complete autonomy over the entire estate. But his attitude toward marriage and a woman's place in it soured me on the prospect," Vivien said, then let out a heavy sigh. "If I'm being perfectly honest, the real reason I never married was purely to spite my father. I hope his corpse is rolling around in his grave knowing I won. Just spinning down there like a rotisserie chicken."

Her white teeth glinted in the sunlight as her mouth spread into a wicked smile.

Charlie supposed she could appreciate Vivien's justification, as petulant as it was. But there was something else she didn't understand.

"Dutch's kid's must know you're… well, independently wealthy," Charlie said. "Why do they act like you're some…"

"Gold-digging whore?"

Vivien's grin turned even more impish as she said the words.

"Well, yeah," Charlie said.

One of Vivien's shoulder's quirked into a shrug.

"I suppose it's what they want to believe. And I should say, the boys have always been civil, if not exactly warm. The younger girl, too. Dara. She's a bit of an odd duck," Vivien mused. "I have a nephew with Asperger's, and while I'm not one to make armchair diagnoses, I have always wondered. Now Marjory, on the other hand… that one is a greedy little pig, and I assume she thinks I'm the same. That's how people are, you know. They think everyone thinks the way they do. You've met her husband?"

Charlie shook her head.

"Trevor is a darling man. Smart as a whip and sweet as a newborn kitten, but you should see the way Marjory looks at him. Like he's something filthy stuck to her shoe. And the way she speaks to him." Vivien shook her head. "But he's loaded, and I think that's all she's ever seen in him. Trevor has cerebral palsy as a result of something that happened during his birth. His parents won a malpractice suit against the hospital, and Trevor inherited fifty million dollars on his eighteenth birthday. He invested it in a biotech startup, made a fortune. Anyway, it's always been painfully obvious to anyone who cares to look that Marjory's only interest in Trevor is his money."

Vivien's assessment of Marjory struck Charlie as especially harsh. And despite her own feelings about Marjory, perhaps a bit unfair.

"Why would she marry him for money when she's rich herself?" Charlie asked.

"Marjory? Rich?" Vivien said. "You must know that Dutch was quite strict with his children when it came to money. He paid for their education, of course. But there were no trust funds for the Carmichael children. They had to earn their own way."

"Yes, but surely Marjory receives a decent salary heading the foundation."

Gripping the door for support, Vivien doubled over with laughter.

"Oh God, no. I'm sure her salary is no pittance, but it's probably barely enough to cover the property taxes on that house of hers."

Charlie wasn't sure if she should trust Vivien's take on wealth. When someone was born a billionaire, did any number with fewer than nine zeros at the end suddenly become a trifling amount?

"And what about Gloria?" Charlie asked. "She certainly wasn't your biggest fan."

"Ah. Well, with Gloria there were two strikes against me. The first is that I'm fairly certain she saw me and Dutch together once, back when her mother was still alive. She had a curious habit of lurking in doorways. Almost like she wanted to catch people doing naughty things. She always struck me as a suspicious sort. Convinced everyone around her was up to no good when she wasn't looking. Anyway, I can imagine how she would have felt about catching her father fooling around with another woman."

Charlie nodded, thinking that was exactly the kind of thing Gloria wouldn't be able to forgive.

"So what was the second strike?"

"I don't suppose you know the story of Gloria's marriage?"

Charlie shook her head.

"Her husband left her for his much-younger secretary. A tale as old as time. She'd tolerated me before, but things changed after she and Roger got divorced. I became a representation of the *other woman*. The floozy." Vivien pursed her lips and looked a bit sad. "It's too bad. I got the sense we could have been great friends if things had been different. I was sorry to hear about her passing."

The words echoed in Charlie's mind as she turned onto the road leading to the Carmichael estate. *Her passing.* The words were too clean and mundane to describe what had happened to Gloria. Charlie pushed that thought aside, though. She needed to keep her mind sharp.

"Do you have any idea what Dutch might have done with the bulk of his money?" she asked Vivien. "Gloria said there were hundreds of millions of dollars unaccounted for."

"I haven't the faintest," Vivien said. "I've always found money-talk dreadfully boring, to be quite honest. It's fun to spend but nothing sucks the energy out of a room faster than financial chatter. Except maybe religion."

The gate was closed when they reached Dutch's driveway. Charlie stopped the car just short of the metal bars.

"I don't suppose you have the gate code?"

"Of course, I do," Vivien said with a knowing smile. "One-nine-six-seven. The year he made his first million."

Charlie climbed out and punched the sequence into the number pad beside the gate. There was a clanking sound and then the gate parted with an electric hum.

As Charlie guided the car up the drive, she glanced over at Vivien. "One more nosy question, if you don't mind?"

"Go ahead."

"How did your father make his money?"

Vivien snorted.

"By marrying my mother. She was the sole heir of David Fernsby, the founder of Fernsby Pharmaceuticals. I assume you've heard of it?"

"Of course," Charlie said. Everyone had heard of Fernsby Pharmaceuticals.

"Yes, my father gained his fortune through pure nepotism. Not a dime of it was earned on his own." Vivien smiled. "I've always thought that was ironic."

Charlie parked beside the now familiar Apollo fountain and shut down the engine. They undid their seatbelts and climbed out. At the door, Vivien produced the key from her purse, slid it into the lock, then paused.

"You know, I was perfectly calm all the way over here, but now my heart is racing!" She giggled quietly. "Is your job always this exhilarating?"

"Rarely. Ninety percent of it is sitting around waiting for something to happen."

"Or digging through a stranger's garbage?" Vivien asked with a wink.

"Exactly," Charlie said.

Vivien tutted and twisted the key.

"I suppose that's for the best, or I'd be tempted to become a P.I. myself just for the high."

She opened the door and let it swing wide, revealing the darkened entryway before them. With a mischievous glint in her eye, she turned to Charlie.

"Shall we?"

CHAPTER FORTY-SIX

Charlie followed Vivien upstairs to Dutch's bedroom. They passed by the bed and the wardrobe and entered his private study. Vivien paused just inside, seeming to study a painting of a ship.

"Get the lights, will you?" Vivien asked.

Despite the empty driveway, darkened interior, and obvious hush that said the house was empty, Charlie hesitated. It was silly, of course. She had the family's permission to investigate, and anything she found was for their benefit. But she couldn't help but feel she was trespassing. Treading where she shouldn't. More than that, she felt like she was being watched. Maybe it was because she'd brought Vivien with her, knowing that Dutch's children probably wouldn't approve of her being here.

Charlie shook off the irrational unease and flipped the light switch. The recessed lights in the study flared overhead.

Vivien lifted the painting from the wall, revealing a safe behind it.

"I wasn't supposed to know about this," Vivien said. "Dutch was very secretive. But I saw him open it once, when he thought I was asleep in the other room."

Charlie stepped forward, studying the combination dial.

"Any idea what the combination might be?"

"Try 40-21-35."

Charlie's eyebrows rose at Vivien's instant response.

"They're my measurements," Vivien said. "Same as Jayne Mansfield."

As Charlie spun the dial, she couldn't help but think Vivien had sounded quite proud of this.

"I mean, wouldn't you be?" Allie asked. "Although—and I have to preface this by saying that Vivien has a rockin' bod, no doubt about it—there is no way she has a twenty-one-inch waist."

Charlie stopped on the first number.

"I don't think that's even physically possible," Allie continued. "Not unless you have some ribs removed or something. All doubts aside, I should have known Vivien's big bajungas would play a role in all of this."

"And Dutch... he knew your measurements?" Charlie asked, carefully reversing back to the second number.

"Yes. He asked me once, and then wrote it down in a little book. At the time, I thought it might be something he did... collect the measurements of his conquests." Vivien chuckled at the thought. "Goodness, I miss him."

Charlie finished entering the combination. The handle turned easily, and the front of the safe popped open with a *thunk*.

Behind her, Vivien squealed with delight.

Charlie tugged at the handle, and the metal door swung aside, revealing...

Nothing.

CHAPTER FORTY-SEVEN

Hands on hips, Vivien clicked her tongue at the empty safe.

"Well, this is an anticlimax."

The light in Dutch's bedroom suddenly clicked on. Charlie and Vivien whirled around in tandem to face the open doorway.

"Looking for this?"

Brandon Carmichael leaned against the wall of his father's bedroom, a black rectangular device in his hands. Dutch's laptop.

"Yes, actually," Charlie said. "We were."

She managed to keep her voice calm and level even as her mind reeled, searching for an explanation for Brandon's presence. Had he been here the whole time? Or had he followed them? And what about the laptop? How long had he been in possession of it?

"Guess I beat you to it, though not by much," he said, smiling in a way that Charlie took as gloating.

She expected him to take off then, scampering away with his prize while laughing maniacally the whole time like a cartoon villain. Instead, he crossed Dutch's bedroom and held out the computer to her like an offering.

"Here you go."

"I don't understand," Charlie said. "Where did you find it?"

"Right there where you were looking. In the safe."

"When?"

"About an hour ago."

"How did you get in? The gate was closed, and there aren't any cars in the drive," Charlie said.

"I parked on a side street and cut across the property. I suppose I don't need to ask how *you* got in." His eyes slid over to Vivien. "Hello, Vivien."

Vivien bobbed her head.

"Brandon."

His gaze swung back over to Charlie, lingering on her dress.

"I have to ask, do you always dress this formally when breaking and entering?"

"Obviously," Charlie said dryly. She drummed her fingers against the laptop. "Did you know the computer was in the safe all along?"

"No. But I figured it had to be in the house somewhere," Brandon said. "Unless someone had taken it. But that's what I came to find out. I figured I'd search the place top to bottom, and if I didn't find the computer, it probably meant one of my siblings had already gotten to it."

"Sounds like you don't trust them very much."

"You've met them, and Gloria must have told you what they're like. What *we're* like." He crossed his arms. "They're not bad people. But they all have their own ideas of how this should be handled. I'm sure you've figured out by now that Wesley's been helping himself to the art collection. It's only a matter of time before the whole lot of them are in here picking the place clean. Without Gloria here to keep us in line, it'll be every man for himself."

"Unless you find a will."

"Exactly. And if there *is* a will, it's on that laptop." He gestured at the machine in Charlie's hands. "I knew I had to get it before anyone else."

"And then what?"

"Well, turn it over to you, of course."

"You planned on giving it to me all along?"

"Of course. That's why Gloria hired you, isn't it?" Brandon pointed a finger at her. "Besides, you're the only one I can trust to be impartial. The only one with no dog in this fight. I figured it'd be better to let you handle it from here."

"Why not just take your pick of everything?" Charlie asked. "You got in here tonight. You could have loaded up your car with priceless antiques."

"Because first of all, the house and what's in it is peanuts. If we can figure out what my old man did with the real money, there won't be a need to squabble over scraps. Everyone will get his or her fair share," Brandon said. "And that's all I'm really interested in. I don't need the whole pie. I only want my piece of it. This way, we see what's on the laptop, and will or no will, we all move on. I just want the truth, you know? Unvarnished."

Charlie could respect this particular blend of self-interest mixed with honor. In some ways, it wasn't all that different from what Gloria had said when she'd come into the office that first day. Had that only been two days ago? It was hard to believe.

She had to stop herself from replaying the hit-and-run in her mind again. Instead, Charlie stepped to the tiger maple desk and set the computer down. Then she opened the laptop and powered it on.

"Have you looked at what's on it?" she asked, internally wondering if he could have already tampered with any of the files they might find.

Brandon shook his head.

"I'm not a big computer guy," he said. "As soon as I found it, I knew I'd be better off letting you take the lead."

They fell quiet as the computer booted up.

"Do either of you mind if I smoke?"

Charlie shook her head.

"If you'll give me a puff or two," Vivien said as Brandon placed a cigarette between his lips.

He shook a second cigarette from the pack, but Vivien waved her hand at him.

"Oh I haven't really smoked for years. I only want a drag."

Brandon lit up, and a tendril of tobacco smoke twined around his head. He looked like the Marlboro Man or something. He inhaled and then passed the cigarette to Vivien.

The computer finished loading, and Charlie slid into the chair behind the desk, brushing the touchpad with her thumb. Brandon and Vivien leaned in on either side of her.

A box appeared, asking for a password.

"Any guesses?" Charlie asked.

"Try the combination for the safe," Vivien suggested.

Charlie had her doubts that Dutch would use the same code over again, on top of the fact that six digits wasn't a very secure password. But she didn't have a better idea.

"Speaking of which," Charlie said, entering the sequence of numbers, "how did you know the combination, Brandon?"

"Dad had this little book he jotted things down in. Ideas, appointments. I saw that written in there once."

"You saw the combination once and remembered it?"

"It's a worthwhile skill to have when you play cards for a living."

The computer beeped and red text appeared: *Incorrect login information.*

Charlie realized that both Brandon and Vivien had mentioned Dutch carrying around a small book. If he'd written the safe combination in it, maybe he'd also kept the computer password there.

"Any idea where the book is now?"

"I haven't seen it since before he died," Brandon said. "I guess I assumed Gloria had it. She didn't mention it?"

Charlie shook her head.

A moment later, Brandon snapped his fingers.

"What about Red Sabazios?"

Charlie had no idea what he was talking about, but Vivien nodded enthusiastically.

"Oh, that's a good one."

"It was the name of his favorite horse," Brandon explained and then spelled it out for her.

Charlie typed in the letters and hit enter.

Incorrect login information.

"Damn," Vivien said. "OK, what was that phrase in Latin he liked so much? The one about wolves and dogs."

"*Lupus non timet canem latrantem.* No wolf fears a barking dog."

Charlie used her phone to look up the spelling of the Latin to make sure she entered it correctly.

Her finger hovered over the enter key this time, hesitating.

Incorrect login information. This device has been locked.

She glanced from Vivien to Brandon and then back at the computer.

"Well, shit."

"Now what?" Brandon asked. "There has to be a way to get in even without the password. I mean, this must happen all the time these days."

Charlie smiled.

"I know a guy."

CHAPTER FORTY-EIGHT

After returning Vivien to her gala with a promise to keep her updated if anything exciting developed, Charlie swung by her apartment to change into normal clothes and remove some of the many layers of makeup caked on her face. Satisfied, she went back down to her car and drove over to meet Mason.

Her mind wandered along the way. If she'd gone into the gala thinking of Vivien as a viable suspect in the recent Carmichael deaths, she thought it no longer. Numerous holes had been poked in any motivation the mistress might have had to kill Dutch, and when it came down to it, Charlie's gut just didn't buy it. She liked Vivien.

Unfortunately, that left Dutch's own children as the primary suspects going forward, a thought she was glad she didn't have to dwell on just now. She'd arrived at her destination.

Mason Resnik ran Dank of America, a marijuana dispensary that bordered on futuristic. No novelty bongs. No hemp necklaces. Mason's establishment was a high-tech marvel. Retina scanners and hydroponic gadgetry set among plate-glass sliding doors that looked like something from an Alex Garland movie—sleek and, above all, professional. Mason also happened to be Frank's main computer guy, and now, Charlie's as well.

Charlie showed her ID to the security guard at the entrance of the building. The laptop felt warm tucked under her arm. Her palm and fingers wrapped around the underside of the metal case like strange barnacle growths.

Her eyes lingered on the mystery box while she waited—the matte black rectangle with a chrome Gigagbyte logo standing out from the center. She'd looked up the brand, as she hadn't recognized it. Gigabyte was a Taiwanese computer hardware company primarily known for producing motherboards. They also manufactured high-end gaming laptops, some of the more expensive and powerful models on the market. That seemed curious. This piece of gear packed far more computing power than Dutch Carmichael would ever need, unless he wanted to play *Fortnite* at the highest possible frame rate, which Charlie doubted.

Handing her license back, the guard buzzed her through the doors. A woman with short spiky hair was waiting for her.

"Charlie Winters?"

Charlie nodded.

"Mason said I should bring you up to his office," the woman said, using her fingerprint to unlock a door that swept aside with a pneumatic whooshing sound. "I'm Lisa, by the way."

She beckoned Charlie through before leading the way down a glass-walled passage that bisected the showroom slash grow room.

Green was the first thing Charlie saw. Healthy-looking marijuana plants thrust their leaves in all directions, bushy-looking things that had been organized in neat rows from one end of the huge space to the other. The ultimate cash crop now that the laws had changed. Something about the neatness of the plants made her think of one of those hedge animals—the green cropped, manicured, and coiffed into the shape of an elephant or giraffe.

Lisa guided her through the corridor and Charlie's shoes clattered on the smooth cement floor. The sound echoed around the giant chamber of this factory turned dispensary, whispers and flutters bouncing everywhere like scattered applause.

Rustic brick walls spoke to the building's past when it had been a dry goods warehouse at the turn of the previous century. But these days, the plants and gadgetry made these industrial details seem modern. Hip. Everything was clean and functional and somehow hooked up to the Wi-Fi with a little blinking light to prove it. It looked like a trendy brewery or coffee shop in Brooklyn or something, Charlie thought.

Stepping through the high-tech gates and into this industrial yet luxe setting, Charlie couldn't help but feel like she was walking into a spy movie. This would be the villain's lair, she supposed.

"No, Mr. Bond. I expect you to hit the vape," Allie said in one of her terrible accents.

The door to Mason's office was closed when Charlie reached it. She rapped her knuckles lightly against the wood.

"Enter," a voice said from inside. It sounded like Mason's voice, but the delivery seemed odd. Formal.

She eased the door open and stepped into the room.

At first it looked like there was no one there, the space beyond the large desk vacant. The oversized office chair faced away from her, with only the back visible. A large fish tank gurgled on the wall beyond that, bright orange and yellow fish darting around everywhere inside, but otherwise the room lay silent. Motionless.

"Hello?" Charlie said after a second.

Mason swiveled the chair around to face her and then leaned back. An odd smile quirked the corners of his mouth. Charlie realized he was messing with her.

"Well, well, well. Charlie Winters, I presume." He drummed his fingers like one of the James Bond villains she'd been thinking about only moments before. "And what brings you to my humble multi-million-dollar marijuana dispensary?"

"Hey, Mason."

When she didn't play along, he dropped the act. His posture went back to normal, and he scooted his chair up to the desk. His eyes fell to the little black box in her hand.

"So this is the laptop you texted me about?"

"Dutch Carmichael's laptop, at your service."

He sniffed a little laugh.

"*The Billionaire's Secret Laptop* could be a pretty good romance title, I bet. You'd need to load it with *Fifty Shades of Grey*-style fornication, or whatever the ladies are into these days, but... Anyway, let's have a look."

She set the laptop on Mason's desk, and he spun it around to face him.

"Gigabyte, huh? Pretty sweet rig for an old man."

"That's what I thought," Charlie said.

"Guess he could afford it. It'd be kind of disappointing if he had an Acer or something."

He opened the laptop. Powered it on. Little blue lights blinked to life along the front of it.

"So, not to rush you or anything, but how long does this kind of thing usually take?" she asked.

Mason leaned back in his chair.

"It depends. If all he's got is the standard out-of-the-box security that comes with Windows, it could take literally a minute." Mason pulled a flash drive from a drawer in his desk and connected it to the laptop. "Let's see what we've got."

Charlie slumped down in the chair opposite him. It felt good to get off her feet after marching around in heels for half of the day.

"Interesting," Mason said from across the desk.

"What is it?"

"I managed to bypass the main login, but someone was a stickler for encrypting their files," Mason said, still tapping away at the keyboard as he spoke.

"That sounds good for security. Bad for us."

"Yes and no. Trying to hack the encryption itself would take far too long. But if we figure out the key, then we don't need to hack the encryption."

"And you can do that?"

Mason's own computer was also on the desk, and he slid it closer and typed something into it.

"Depends on how long the password is. Could be two hours. Or ten. Or never, if it's long enough." Mason paused to grin over at her. "The good news is that his Windows password was only eight characters, and people are creatures of habit."

Moving to a bookcase built into one wall, Mason removed a third laptop from one of the shelves. He brought the computer to his desk and arranged the three machines in a semicircle around himself.

"Anyway, all we can do is try. If I can't crack it in the next twelve hours or so, it's probably a lost cause, but I'm feeling pretty confident."

"Are you sure you're up for this now?" Charlie asked.

"I'm looking forward to it, actually. Makes me feel like I'm in college again, pulling an all-nighter before finals." He gestured at a wet bar in the corner. "You want anything to drink? There's a fridge behind you. Coconut water and Monster, mostly."

"Like it could have been anything but coconut water and Monster," Allie said.

"And there are snacks and stuff in the cabinets next to that."

Mason didn't break eye contact with the computers even as he spoke to her. That little smile quirked his lips again, and excitement gleamed from behind his glasses. He rolled up his sleeves. Cracked his knuckles.

"Let's do this."

CHAPTER FORTY-NINE

Mason's fingers clattered at the keyboard, pounding out strange, stuttering rhythms. The little clicks reminded Charlie of drumbeats in some foreign musical genre. Exotic. A little alien.

His eyes never stopped moving, even if his hands did. He squinted in concentration, eyebrows expressing every little frustration and glimmer of hope. His dilated pupils flicked back and forth from screen to screen. He looked like a predator closing on his prey.

Charlie sipped at a coconut water as the hacker worked his trade. She'd sat across from him for about forty minutes now, watching him drawn deeper and deeper into a trance as he worked. They'd conversed a little at first, but his side of the dialogue shrank from normal sentences to choppy fragments to monosyllabic murmurs and finally to nothing as his mind sank into the task at hand. He hadn't said a word in at least twenty minutes. Charlie didn't think he was actually aware of her presence in the room anymore, let alone able to hear anything she said.

Charlie stood. Stretched. Her stomach grumbled a little, so she wandered over to the cabinets next to the mini-fridge.

A full kitchen's worth of cabinetry occupied this side of the office, cupboards rounding a corner and running floor to ceiling. That seemed excessive. Charlie opened a couple of the doors, curiosity twitching in her skull now.

A rainbow of brightly colored bags stared back from the cabinet shelves, and she and Allie both laughed a little at what they'd found. She quickly checked the other cupboards, confirming her suspicion. Every cupboard, top and bottom, held pretty much the same thing:

Doritos. Seemingly every Dorito flavor imaginable tucked inside in full-sized bags, stacked at least ten deep in rows as neat as the plants out on the main floor.

"This might be the most extreme flavor I've ever seen in one place," Allie said.

Nacho Cheese, Cool Ranch, Flamin' Hot Limón, Blaze, Spicy Sweet Chili, Poppin' Jalapeño, Salsa Verde, and the oddly intriguing Flamas, which featured a giant chili pepper and a couple of angry red Doritos engulfed in flames on the bag.

"I guess this is on brand for both the stoner and hacker sides of your personality, eh?" Charlie said.

Mason didn't respond. His eyebrows jumped and then crunched down into a wrinkled knot that slowly released, and his fingers continued to tap out those endless, lurching rhythms.

Charlie's phone buzzed, and she pulled it from her pocket to find a text from Brandon.

Find anything yet?

Charlie typed out a four-letter response.

Nope.

As she moved to return the phone to her pocket, it buzzed again.

Well, can you let me know?

Charlie tucked the phone back in her pocket without responding. She didn't want to make any promises right now, to Brandon or anyone. Not until she knew what was on the computer.

Selecting a bag of Flamas Doritos and another bottle of coconut water, Charlie settled into the sofa positioned near the snack bar. It didn't look like much. A big blocky thing in dark gray velvet.

But as Charlie sank into it, she quickly decided it was the most comfortable piece of furniture ever.

The Doritos had a surprising kick to them, which was followed by a subtle citrusy aftertaste that vaguely reminded Charlie of Froot Loops, for some reason.

She watched Mason for a while, shoveling chips into her mouth and timing the seconds between his blinks. Thirty-four seconds. Forty-eight seconds. A minute and six seconds.

Eventually her phone rang. She expected it to be Brandon, bugging her about the computer again, but instead, it was Frank.

"Are you busy?"

Charlie glanced down at the bag of chips in her lap.

"Not particularly."

"Well, I think I've got a solution to our problem with Paige's father, but I could use some backup."

"Now?" Charlie asked.

"If you can," Frank said. "It shouldn't take more than an hour."

Charlie's gaze slid over to where Mason was still fixated on the computer. He probably wouldn't even notice she was gone, and it wasn't like she was playing an important role in his work.

"That shouldn't be a problem. I'm having Mason check something out for me. Can you pick me up at the dispensary?"

"I'll be there in ten minutes," Frank said.

Frank hunched over the steering wheel, spine looking crooked, body looking withered. He still hadn't regained the bulk he'd had before chemo. Charlie wondered if he ever would.

But if his frame showed signs of age, the bright gleam in his eyes portrayed the opposite. Intensity. Zeal. Life.

"Did I ever tell you about Big Jim Driskell?" Frank asked, eyes flicking from the road for just a second.

Charlie chuckled before she answered.

"No, and I kind of think I'd remember the name."

"Well, the nickname isn't ironic. He's a walking, talking side of beef. Probably six foot five, two-fifty or two-sixty. Anyway, he was a war hero way back when. Saved a bunch of lives in the first Gulf War, I believe it was. Lost an eye in the process. A side of beef with an eyepatch."

A faint smile played at Frank's lips as he talked.

"He's a nice enough guy. Stoic, though. No real sense of humor to speak of. But he's always been good to me. Anyway, I've seen what happens when people cross him. Just once. A group of mouthy frat boys at the tavern. An argument over a game of pool, yeah?"

Charlie nodded.

"Big Jim just leveled this mob of college boys. Five of 'em. Looked like something from a comic book. Right hook knocked the first one out cold. Left uppercut lifted the next one straight up and then dropped him in a heap. The third and fourth converged on him and he cracked their heads together like coconuts."

Charlie couldn't help but picture it like a superhero movie. A hulking Goliath wearing an eyepatch knocking frat guys about.

Frank went on.

"And then the fifth guy? He tried to run. Jim wasn't having that. He went at him with a broken beer bottle. Thankfully a group of guys pulled Jim off before he could spear the guy in the neck, which looked for all the world like what he was aiming to do."

Frank shook his head.

"This was ten years ago, but he hasn't lost that fire."

"And why is this coming up now?" Charlie asked.

Frank tossed a manila envelope in Charlie's lap. She opened it and found a handful of eight-by-ten photographs of a man and woman in a variety of romantic poses. Holding hands, kissing. In one, the man even had his hand on the girl's ass.

Charlie recognized the man in the pictures as Paige's father, Henry Naughton. But the girl was a stranger to her.

"Who's the girl?"

"A nineteen-year-old college student by the name of Cindy Driskell," Frank said, raising an eyebrow.

"Big Jim's daughter?"

"That's right. And I can tell you right now that Jim wouldn't be amused to find her running around with a married man twenty-five years her senior."

They pulled up into the driveway outside Henry's place. The house was blue with white shutters and a row of hydrangeas planted in front of the porch. The garage door was open, and Charlie could see someone standing over the open hood of an old Ford truck. Paige's father sported a white undershirt smudged with grease.

Frank climbed out of the car, and Charlie followed his lead. She checked that her trusty stun gun was within easy reach in her bag, just in case.

Paige's father watched them approach. Unblinking. He smeared a greasy hand over his shirt and sipped his Miller High Life.

"Henry Naughton?" Frank said, and Charlie thought she could hear the adrenaline in his voice.

"Who wants to know?"

"I'm Frank Winters. I work with your daughter."

Some of the tension seemed to sag from Henry's rigid figure, but his glare didn't break. He still hadn't blinked since they'd pulled up.

"That's right. The professional snoop." He sipped his beer before he went on. "If you're out looking for a lost kitty, I haven't seen it."

"No," Frank said. He stopped a few paces shy of the garage door. "No lost cats today. We're here to tell you to leave Paige alone. No calls. No visits. She doesn't want to hear from you. Doesn't want to know you. Doesn't want anything to do with you at all."

Charlie could see the muscles in Henry's jaw flex and unflex a few times. When he spoke, it came out through clenched teeth.

"You shouldn't have come here, old man. To my home. And you sure as shit shouldn't have spoken to me that way."

"Careful who you threaten, tough guy," Frank said, his voice getting loud. "I'm not a little girl you can kick around."

Henry lurched, a rigid flash of brawn leaping at them.

Charlie went for her stun gun, but Frank was faster.

He spritzed pepper spray in Henry's face, the little hiss bringing Charlie's attention to the can in her uncle's hand.

Paige's father wheezed and buckled before them, folding up and dropping to the ground as though the chemicals had chopped his legs out from under him. His figure twitched and writhed on the cement driveway. He cupped his hands over his face, but Charlie could still make out the tears flowing down his cheeks.

When Henry was down, Frank gave him a kick in the ribs, the toe of his boot cracking into the torso. And then Paige's father coiled into a fetal position, pulling his limbs into a ball like a crushed spider.

Frank plucked the manila folder from inside his jacket. He peeled a few of the photos out and dropped them, floating down onto the crumpled figure.

"If you get to thinking about some kind of retaliation, just imagine how much worse you'll get it if Big Jim Driskell ever chances upon these photographs, yeah? A married, middle-aged guy lying with his nineteen-year-old daughter? It's technically legal, of course, but somehow I don't think ol' Jim will see it that way. Can't imagine your wife will look kindly on it either."

Henry peeled his fingers away from his face to pick up one of the photos. His eyelids fluttered over and over, tears streaming down from puffy, red eyes. He couldn't stop blinking.

"Anyway, it was nice talking to you," Frank said. "Leave Paige the fuck alone, and we won't have the pleasure of doing it again."

Charlie clapped her hands when they were back in Frank's car.

"Damn, Frank! That was awesome!"

Frank tried to stifle a smile and failed.

"I only wish Paige could have seen it," Charlie said. "I bet she wouldn't be scared of him anymore after seeing him curled up on the ground, crying like a baby." She shook her head. "Were you planning on hitting him with the pepper spray the whole time?"

"I was only going to show him the pictures. Lean on him a little. But after hearing Paige describe him, I figured I'd better go in with a Plan B in case our friend Henry got feisty." Frank inhaled. "I didn't realize how much I'd missed all this, and I'm not talking about kicking a fella in the ribs... though that felt good. But the investigative work? Tailing him around town. Finding his weakness. Waiting for the money shot. I think I'm ready to come back. I'm going to talk to Dr. Silva, see what she thinks about me returning to work on a part-time basis."

"Really?" Charlie asked.

Frank nodded.

"What do you think about tag-teaming cases with your uncle?"

Charlie rubbed her palms together.

"I can't wait."

CHAPTER FIFTY

When Charlie returned to Mason's office, he was in exactly the same position as when she'd left: eyes on the computer, fingers tapping away at the keyboard.

"Have you moved at all since I've been gone?" When Mason didn't respond, she snapped her fingers. "Is there a point at which I need to douse you with ice water or something to snap you out of this?"

"I'm good," he murmured.

Charlie frowned and stepped closer to the large wall of glass overlooking the St. Clair River.

"Whoa," she said, feigning shock. "Mason, check this out. There's a whole barge full of naked people floating down the river. It must be the Annual Nudist River Cruise."

"Neat," he said.

The ruse worked better on Allie, who said, "What? Where? I don't see any naked people."

Realizing that she was effectively invisible as far as Mason was concerned, Charlie gave up and returned to the velvet sofa. She was probably better off letting Mason stay focused anyway. The less distracted he was, the faster he'd hack the laptop. At least she hoped so.

Charlie sighed. It felt good to just relax for a few minutes. The last several days had been draining, and the lack of sleep was starting to take a toll.

She settled deeper into the cushions of the couch and closed her eyes, wondering what they might find on Dutch's laptop if they got in. Photographs of the sordid and disgusting variety? The elusive last will and testament?

"Maybe a damning letter from Dutch himself, naming his murderer," Allie suggested. "You know, the kind that starts out with, 'If you are reading this, it can only mean that I am dead. In that event, you must know the only person who could have killed me was…'"

Charlie snorted softly, her eyes still closed.

If only.

Charlie jerked awake. With sleep still muddying her thoughts, it was a moment before she recognized her surroundings. Brick walls. Floor-to-ceiling plate-glass windows. Velveteen couch as soft as a cloud.

Ah, yes. Mason's office.

Her gaze slid over to Mason's desk, where he still hunched in front of the computers.

"How long was I out?" Her voice was thick with sleep.

To her surprise, Mason actually looked up from the screens this time. He checked his watch.

"Ninety minutes. Maybe two hours."

"Why didn't you wake me up?"

He shrugged.

"You looked so peaceful over there, drooling on my ten-thousand-dollar sofa."

Charlie's mouth dropped open, about to ask if he'd really paid that much for a couch. But there were more pressing matters at hand.

"And? Did you crack it?"

"Not yet. But I think it'll be soon. I've got a feeling." He lifted a steaming mug to his lips. "I just made a pot of coffee if you want some."

Charlie went to the coffee machine and poured herself some liquid caffeine. While she drank it, she checked her phone and found several missed calls and texts that had accumulated during her nap: Marjory. Brandon. Wesley. Jude. The only Carmichael who hadn't tried to reach her was Dara, and Charlie supposed that wasn't really a surprise.

Charlie listened to the first voicemail, cringing instantly at the sound of Marjory's shrill voice.

"I was willing to go along with this little charade because it was what the family wanted. But now that I know you're currently in possession of my father's property—property you obtained under dubious circumstances, I might add—I'm done. That computer belongs to the estate, and we have a right to know what's on it. If you don't turn it over to me immediately, I'll have no choice but to contact the authorities."

Charlie rolled her eyes. Convenient that the computer belonged to "the estate," and yet Marjory had demanded it be given to her personally. And what was she talking about, dubious circumstances? Brandon had willingly handed over the laptop. It wasn't like she'd stolen it.

On the other hand, there was one truth to what Marjory had said, and that was that they had a right to know what was on it. Emphasis on *they*.

It was why she hadn't responded to Brandon's text. She was working for the Carmichael family as a unit now, not any one of them individually. The fact still remained that one of them had most likely killed Dutch and Gloria, but she still had no idea which one it might have been. It wasn't right to play favorites. Gloria had wanted things played straight. And so did Brandon.

Charlie nodded as she realized what she needed to do. The only fair way to handle this was to make sure everyone got the same information at the same time.

She checked the messages from the rest of the family. Jude and Wesley weren't quite as accusatory as Marjory had been, but it was clear they weren't happy the computer had been taken from the house. Brandon's text warned her that Marjory knew about the computer, was angry about it, and was probably about to send the rest of them after Charlie.

Too little, too late, she thought.

Charlie called Brandon.

"Word got out about the computer, huh?" she asked.

"I'm really sorry about that," Brandon said. "I mentioned it to Marjory, totally misjudging how she'd react. Now she's whipped the whole lot of them into a frenzy. Even Dara, which is surprising. She usually stays out of the drama."

"It's OK," Charlie said. "I think I've figured out a way to please everyone. Round them up and meet at the house. In a few hours we'll either have the computer cracked, or we'll have to give up on it as a lost cause. If we do get access to your dad's files, we can all look at them together. Either way, I'll return the computer, and order will be restored."

"Alright," Brandon said. "I'm on it."

Charlie hung up and approached Mason's desk.

"I don't mean to rush you, but the Carmichaels are getting antsy. I promised them I'd meet them at the estate. With the computer. That means we've got a few more hours, at best."

Mason eyed her over the edge of his coffee cup. "Is that a challenge?"

"I'd be happy to give you however long you need with the computer, but Marjory Carmichael is pissed I even have it at all." Charlie rubbed her eyes. "If I don't return it soon, she'll make a stink."

"That Marjory can be a pitbull, eh?"

"You know her?" Charlie asked.

"Sure. We contribute to the 5K fundraiser the Lamark Foundation does every year." Mason shrugged. "I actually know her husband better. We've been discussing the possibility of teaming up to do a study together. Right now everyone's focused on CBD and THC, but there are over a hundred other cannabinoids in pot. Most of them haven't been researched thoroughly, but Trevor Steigel thinks they could have applications in treating multiple sclerosis, various cancers, and who knows what else."

Mason tipped back his mug and finished off the last dregs of his coffee.

"Anyway, why don't we just head over there now? I can pack up my gear and bring it with us."

"Really? You don't mind?"

"Mind? I'm not too proud to admit I'm a little curious to find out the stunning conclusion of—" Mason spread his hands wide "—*The Billionaire's Secret Laptop*!"

Charlie smirked.

"I don't know how this is possible, but you've gotten even dorkier since high school."

"I take that as a compliment," he said, aiming a finger gun at her. "Anyway, let me get all this stuff packed up, and I'll follow you over to the house."

CHAPTER FIFTY-ONE

When they arrived at Dutch's estate, Charlie recognized the vehicles belonging to the three elder siblings out front. She was secretly relieved she wouldn't have to face Marjory alone.

As it was, Marjory pounced as soon as Charlie stepped through the door.

"You! I don't know where you get off taking it upon yourself to hack into our father's personal property. Exactly what kind of crook did you hire to—" Marjory's words halted abruptly when she spotted Mason enter behind Charlie. "Mr. Resnik? What are you doing here?"

"Hello, Mrs. Steigel," he said. "Fun fact: before I got into the medical marijuana business, I went to school for computer forensics, which is really a fancy way of saying I've got a degree in ethical hacking."

To Charlie's surprise, Mason's presence seemed to shut Marjory up. She followed them into the solarium and threw herself onto the chaise longue, pulling one of the cinnamon hard candies from her pocket and unwrapping it.

Charlie helped Mason set up at a large mahogany desk at one end of the room, and he got back to work cracking Dutch's encryption key. Dara showed up some time later and then Jude. Marjory and Wesley busied themselves making coffee and then tasked Dara with handing out cups of the steaming brew to everyone.

At one point, Marjory sniffed the air.

"Does anyone else smell that? It's like… piña colada or something."

Charlie inhaled. Marjory was right. There was a definite scent of pineapple and coconut coming from somewhere.

"Jude!" Marjory whirled around and stomped over to where he stood near the window. "Put that away this instant. You know there's no smoking in the house!"

"I'm not smoking. I'm vaping." He let out a tremendous cloud of smoke. "There's a difference."

"If you're going to be an asshole, at least have the decency to do it outside," Wesley said.

"Oh right, *I'm* the asshole," Jude said, pushing through the doors and muttering something about the rest of them always teaming up against him.

After her third cup of coffee since her nap, Charlie asked Dara to show her to the nearest restroom. She locked herself inside, realizing this was the first bathroom in the mansion she'd given any close attention to. It was no less luxe than the rest of the house, with a marble-topped vanity that looked like it must have been reconstructed from an antique and had legs carved to look like lion's feet.

Charlie washed her hands and dried them on a towel so plush she wanted to curl up in it and take another nap. She switched off the powder room light and stepped back into the hallway, where she found Jude waiting for her.

"Ms. Winters… can we talk?" His eyes darted around as if someone might be listening. "Privately?"

Charlie shrugged.

"Sure."

Jude led her upstairs, glancing back over his shoulder the entire way. Charlie was getting an awfully paranoid vibe from him, and she didn't like it.

They passed through Dutch's bedroom and into his study, and Jude closed the door behind them. It occurred to Charlie that she'd left her purse downstairs, which meant she didn't have her stun gun on her person.

"You think he's actually going to attack you or something with everyone else in the house? He'd have to be an idiot," Allie said. "Although, he has acted like kind of an idiot in the past, huh? OK. You're right. Better safe than sorry."

"I apologize for being so secretive, but I honestly don't trust the rest of them to not eavesdrop on our conversation," Jude said.

"That horse head bookend on the shelf looks like cast iron," Allie whispered. "That'll do some damage to a skull. Any sudden moves, and you grab the horse and clock him with it. Right in the vape hole."

"What's up?" Charlie asked.

She felt a bit more relaxed now, as Jude's demeanor had shifted somewhat once they'd reached the study. He seemed less tense.

"What's it cost to get the first peek at the computer?"

Charlie blinked.

"The cost?" She shrugged. "Mason's fee is pretty nominal, but that's figured into what Gloria paid me already."

Jude rolled his eyes in pure disgust.

"No. You don't understand. I want exclusive access. Before anyone else."

Crossing her arms over her chest, Charlie narrowed her eyes at him.

"Why? What's on there that you don't want anyone else to see?"

"I have no idea what's on there. But I don't trust these people. Gloria, I had faith in. She always tried to be fair. But Wesley? I don't care if he's my brother, the guy is a raging prick. He's always been an asshole, especially to me. He'll try to screw me over just because he can."

"I'm still not sure what you're asking me to do. Everyone is here. The second Mason gets into the computer, they're all going to know."

"Make up a story, then. I don't care how you do it. Just give me a day with it—by myself—and then we can bring the rest of them in on it." Jude pulled out his wallet. "So… I'm thinking, what? A thousand? I have five hundred on me, and I can hit up an ATM."

Charlie waved her hands.

"I don't think so."

"OK," he said, shrugging. "I thought a thousand was fair, but I guess you're holding all the cards. Fifteen hundred? I might have to wait until tomorrow to get another five hundred out from the ATM, unless I can find a branch for my bank nearby. I know there isn't one on the island."

"Sorry, I'm not doing this," Charlie said, brushing past him and moving for the door.

"Two thousand dollars."

"No thanks. This conversation is over."

Charlie turned the handle and opened the door a crack, but Jude pushed it shut.

"What's wrong with you? I just offered you two grand."

"I don't care how much it is," Charlie said. "I'm not for sale."

Jude laughed. It was a cruel sound. Humorless.

"Oh please. Cut the innocent act. You're a P.I., not Mother Teresa."

Charlie tried to heave the door open, but Jude was using all of his weight to keep it closed.

"Let me out, please."

"What is it? Is Wes already paying you under the table? Is that it?" He snickered and shook his head. "I should have known."

"You need to let go of the door and let me pass."

Jude's face was inches from hers now. She could smell the cloyingly sweet fragrance of the piña colada vape on his breath.

"Who the fuck do you think you are to give me orders in my own father's house? You think being some snooping bitch Gloria hired gives you some special powers here or something?"

Charlie's gaze strayed to the cast-iron horse head on the shelf over his shoulder. If this little shit didn't let her out of this room in about ten seconds, she was going to be sorely tempted to brain him with it.

A knock came from the other side of the door.

"Everything OK in there?"

Charlie recognized Brandon's voice and felt relief wash over her. It would have been difficult to explain exactly how necessary it had been to clock Jude with a metal statue, after all. Better for everyone if she didn't have to.

Jude's resolve wavered at the sound of Brandon's voice, and he released his hold on the door. Charlie whisked it open, but Jude barreled through ahead of her, no doubt rushing to get away from the scene.

An image of the car speeding away after hitting Gloria flashed in Charlie's mind, freezing her on the spot.

Brandon reached out and touched her arm.

"Charlie? You OK?"

She blinked the memories away.

"Yeah."

"You sure? What happened? Did he corner you in here?"

"He tried to bribe me to give him access to the laptop ahead of everyone else. When I said no, he got angry."

"Jesus, I'm sorry." Brandon scowled. "Jude's always had a bit of a temper. He stabbed me with a pencil once. He was twelve."

"Yikes. And ouch."

"He didn't hurt you, did he?"

Charlie shook her head. "I'm fine."

"I'll have a talk with him," Brandon said.

"Please don't."

"Well someone needs to set him straight," Brandon insisted. "It's not right for him to act that way."

Charlie sighed and closed her eyes.

"I know, but I think it's better if we just try to keep the peace until Mason cracks the encryption."

"If you insist," Brandon said, playing up his disappointment. "But when this is all over, I owe him a punch in the nose."

They didn't have to wait long. Less than twenty minutes after Charlie and Brandon rejoined the group in the solarium, Mason held his hands in the air.

"I'm in."

CHAPTER FIFTY-TWO

Charlie scooted a chair over so she and Mason could go through the contents of the laptop together. The Carmichaels gathered behind the desk, intrigued at first. But after about ten minutes of skimming extremely mundane documents—certificates of pedigree for Dutch's many horses, a spreadsheet with Dutch's to-read list, copies of all of Dutch's email correspondence—the family lost interest and left Charlie and Mason to do the dirty work.

Jude got out his vape pen, but after a pointed look from Wesley, he scoffed and went outside. Brandon and Dara started a game of checkers. Marjory sucked down Jolly Rancher after Jolly Rancher until her phone rang and she moved into the kitchen to take the call. The room was strangely quiet for some time. The calm before the storm.

Charlie and Mason spent the first hour searching for the will with every combination of search terms and phrases they could think of. When that proved fruitless, they moved onto Dutch's photos, which took even longer. There were several hundred gigabytes of pictures on the laptop—snapshots of family functions, headshots and promotional images for Dutch's business, professional photographs of Dutch's many horses. But the one thing they all had in common was they were totally benign. Nothing remotely sordid in any of them.

It was past five when Dara suggested she might go get some food for everyone, which Wesley declared an "outstanding idea."

She came back forty minutes later with a tray of sandwiches, which Marjory promptly complained about.

"Ham, salami, capicola. Everything has pork in it. I don't eat hog," she said, scowling as she set about picking everything off her sandwich but the lettuce and the cheese.

Charlie and Mason each grabbed a sandwich and returned to their task. Having combed through the most obvious files and documents first, Charlie suggested they go back and peruse the few hundred email exchanges Dutch had saved. And so began another hour of tedium.

Dutch arguing with an interior designer about what shade of red an accent wall in one of the conference rooms should be. He wanted "Elk Tongue" while she favored "Sangria."

Dutch inquiring about something called a "Demonzapper," which Charlie eventually figured out was the name of a horse.

Dutch demanding a contractor reimburse him for an antique sconce that had been damaged when workers were repairing some of the brickwork on the garage.

Dutch scheduled lunches, brunches, tee times, and racquetball sessions with friends and colleagues. He did a surprising amount of administrative stuff like this himself, working through his private email, not seeming to delegate these kinds of tasks to assistants or secretaries. Perhaps that made him a bit of a maverick or lone wolf, but it also made his correspondence that much more of a chore to wade through.

Charlie lost track of time until Marjory burst into the room from the kitchen sometime later. She stormed over to Charlie's side of the desk and put her hands on her hips.

"How much longer is this going to take?"

"I'm not really sure." Charlie glanced over at Mason. "There are thousands of files here. Without any idea of what we're looking for, we have to go through them one by one."

"You're supposed to be looking for the will. Can't you just search 'last will and testament' or something like that?"

"We tried that," Mason explained. "We tried every combination of search terms and file types we could think of, but we didn't find anything."

This time, Mason's charm wasn't enough to quell Marjory's fit. One of her Jolly Rancher wrappers was in her hand, and when she squeezed her fist, the plastic crinkled.

"Well, I'm tired of waiting. And I still don't like the idea of two outsiders going through Daddy's things. I think you should leave, the both of you."

Wesley got to his feet.

"Marjie, the family agreed—"

"I don't care what the family agreed!" Suddenly, she burst into tears. "I just want this to be over already."

Wesley put an arm around her and pulled her close.

"Oh, Marjie. I know you do. I think we all feel that way. These last few weeks have been hell." He guided Marjory back toward the kitchen. "Why don't we make everyone some tea? Some of that vanilla chamomile you like so much?"

As Marjory and Wesley disappeared into the kitchen, Charlie turned to Mason, expecting to exchange some kind of knowing glance about the uppity rich folk. But Mason wasn't looking at her. He was staring at the computer screen, his brow furrowed.

"What is it?"

"Read this email and tell me what you think."

The first thing Charlie's eyes locked on was the sender's address: gkentwood@carmichaelinvestments.com

"This is from the vice president of Dutch's old firm."

"Read it."

The subject read: *PROBLEM.*

Her gaze slid down to the body of the email.

Dutch,

The Silvestri and Walsh accounts have requested substantial redemptions this morning. We're talking seven figures. The main account is pretty much tapped out. Thoughts?

Greg

Charlie shook her head.
"I don't get it."
"Read the response," Mason whispered.
Charlie scrolled down and read Dutch's email back to Greg.

Greg,

There should be enough in my JPM account to cover the redemptions. Let me check, and if not, I have a few big fish on the line. I can try to reel them in this week.

Dutch

That did get Charlie's attention. There was something off about it, but Charlie wanted to be certain it was what she thought it was.

"My retirement account consists of some novelty two-dollar bills my uncle got me for my birthday when I was ten and an old Pepsi Gotta Have It card, so I'm far from being an expert on this stuff," Charlie said. "But a redemption is like a withdrawal, right?"

Mason nodded.

"Right. This Greg guy is saying that two of their account holders want to withdraw money. A lot of it. That's not so unusual. But what first caught my eye was when he said the main account is tapped out. Because first of all, 'tapped out' doesn't sound great. But then

Dutch says there should be enough money in *his* account to cover the redemptions. By law, clients' money should be kept separate from personal or business funds." Shaking his head, Mason went on. "To top it all off, Dutch says the thing about having a few big fish on the line… It sounds to me like he's saying if they get some new investors to give them money… I mean, it sounds like some Bernie Madoff scheme."

"It's not exactly hard evidence," Charlie said. "But it looks bad."

They scrolled through more correspondence, focusing just on emails between Dutch and Gregory Kentwood. There were several similar messages from Kentwood, who seemed increasingly panicked about the state of their accounts.

In one, he wrote:

The Legrands were in today, grumbling about closing their account out entirely, but I just managed to convince them to stay. We're on thin ice, Dutch.

For the first time, Charlie had an idea of where Dutch's massive fortune had gone. Or rather that it hadn't gone anywhere. It had simply never existed.

Could the great Dutch Carmichael have been a fraud all this time? She shouldn't let herself think that. Not yet. It seemed the most likely explanation, but this kind of thing was hardly her area of expertise.

"What are you going to do?" Mason asked, his voice low.

"I mean, I have to tell them, right? It's what they hired me for."

Charlie's eyes flitted about the room from one Carmichael to the next, wondering how each of them would react to the notion that their inheritance had probably just gone up in a puff of smoke.

"So… I don't mean to be a dick, but I think I'm gonna duck out now," Mason said, already packing up his gear.

Charlie smiled.

"No, I get it." She patted his arm. "Thanks for your help."

"Any time."

Marjory and Wesley came back in the room just as Mason was leaving. Marjory frowned as she watched him slip into the hallway.

"Where's he going?" Her head whipped around to face Charlie. "Are you done then?"

Charlie chewed her lip, bracing herself for what would come next.

"I think we all need to have a little talk."

CHAPTER FIFTY-THREE

"That's outrageous!" Marjory shouted when Charlie explained what she and Mason had found. "There's just no way that it's true."

"It's not definitive evidence, but I think the authorities will want to take a closer look," Charlie said, shrugging.

"Are you sure the emails are legitimate?" Wesley asked. "Isn't that something that can easily be faked?"

"Why would your father encrypt fake emails that seem to implicate him in fraud on his own computer?" Charlie asked.

"Well when you phrase it like that…" Wesley said.

But Marjory wasn't finished with her outburst.

"This is some kind of smear campaign. Someone obviously hired you to come in and destroy our family, and I will be damned if I allow that to happen!"

She lurched for the computer, sending it skittering across the massive desk. Charlie darted around and barely managed to keep it from falling off the far end of the desk.

When her attempt to destroy the computer failed, Marjory picked up a lamp and hurled it at Charlie. She side-stepped it rather easily, which only seemed to enrage Marjory further.

She screamed and tried to rush Charlie, hands out in front of her like claws—to attack Charlie or destroy the computer, Charlie didn't know. It took Brandon, Jude, and Dara to drag Marjory out of the room and into the kitchen. When they'd gone and some semblance of order had returned to the room, Wesley heaved a sigh.

"I assume you plan to deliver that to the police?" He gestured at the laptop now clutched tightly to Charlie's chest.

"I have to, legally. It might be evidence of fraud," she said.

Wesley ran a hand through his hair.

"Could you do me one small favor?"

"What?"

"Hold onto it for just a little while. Give us a day to get things figured out, as a family?"

After a moment of hesitation, Charlie nodded. Wesley walked her out to the entryway, holding the door open for her.

"And I apologize for Marjory. She's not herself lately. I think Gloria's death in particular has hit her harder than any of us realized."

Outside, Charlie climbed into her car and nestled the laptop safely in the passenger seat beside her.

"Dude, really?" Allie said. "You're gonna sit on this bombshell just because Wesley asked nicely?"

Starting the car, Charlie scoffed.

"No. I told him that so he'd let me leave without a fuss." She put the car in drive and headed toward the road. "I'm going straight to the police with this."

CHAPTER FIFTY-FOUR

As the Carmichael mansion disappeared from view behind her, Charlie glanced at the clock on the dash. It was getting toward evening, and she wanted nothing more than to go home and sleep the rest of the day. The sooner she got the computer to the police, the better.

She didn't know what exactly Wesley had meant when he'd asked her to give the family time to "figure things out." Maybe he'd only meant that they'd prepare themselves for the shitstorm that would inevitably rain down when the public discovered the truth about Dutch's firm. But she couldn't help but wonder if what he really wanted was an opportunity to grab anything he could from the house and bank accounts before the Feds descended upon them like buzzards.

She entered a rural stretch of road with woods crowding the shoulder, too thick to see through. Everything was shady over here, what was left of the fading light blotted out by tree branches, creeping vines, and moss.

Charlie couldn't stop glancing over at the laptop on the seat beside her, like if she let it out of her sight for longer than a minute, it might vanish. It might not have led her to the will, but what she had found was important, even if she didn't know the exact extent of its meaning yet.

A Ponzi scheme. Was it really possible the Carmichael fortune had been a sham all along? Dutch Carmichael's face had been plastered on so many magazine covers for decades. He'd become synonymous with the term "billionaire," the human avatar of success, and all the while he'd sat atop a rotting empire merely pretending at greatness?

A fake. A phony.

She shuddered at the thought. Surprised that it would affect her this deeply. Perhaps it was the size of the lie that got her.

Could it be a misunderstanding? She didn't think so. The emails were straightforward evidence of extreme neglect and carelessness at the very least. It had to be deliberate, she thought. Dutch seemed the meticulous type, even scheduling his own meetings and lunches. Everything was intentional with him.

The car snaked around turns now, the road going curvy here along the water's edge. The dark woods densely packed the area to her right, but the expanse of Lake St. Clair glistened on her left, open water that reached out to the horizon.

She looked out over the choppy blue waves at the bottom of a small cliff, the jagged decline making it seem as though the water lay at the bottom of a flight of stairs. Sunlight glittered against the roiling surface, refracting jewels of white that made her squint.

The steep drop-off and deep waters on this side of the island made it a favorite swimming spot for the local kids in the summer. When tourists clogged the beaches, the Salem Island natives would flock here instead, away from the crowds of out-of-towners. She'd spent hours here with Allie, jumping off the sheer edge into the water below, perfecting swan dives, and trying to see who could make the biggest splash with a cannonball.

Charlie brought her eyes back to the road, and again her gaze crept over to the laptop resting on the passenger seat.

Her stomach gurgled. Some part of her was nervous, restless, overcome with anticipation, though she didn't know why. She just needed to get the laptop to the police and be done with this part. The law would take over after this short car ride across town. Simple. Routine. So why was her chest so tight?

The red car flashed in her head again. The sound as it struck Gloria. That lone flare of the brake lights. And then it had sped away as if Gloria had been nothing more than a raccoon or a squirrel. Roadkill.

She remembered running out into the road. Her bare feet touching the warmth of the asphalt. Her eyes locking on the broken figure.

The fluttering of Gloria's chest. The blood trickling from the corner of her mouth.

She had seemed so small in that moment. So fragile. A baby bird knocked out of the nest.

Yes. That was why Charlie was nervous. Because nothing was quite what it seemed with this case. Because the threats were everywhere, circling her like predators, hiding in plain sight.

She gripped the wheel tighter.

Just get the laptop to Zoe, that was all she needed to do. Turn over the evidence. She'd figure out the rest later.

A movement in the rearview mirror caught her eye and interrupted her thoughts.

The car rose up over the hill behind her. The fluctuating shade from the trees made it hard to make out at first—a sports car, she thought, but was it gaining on her? There was something aggressive about the way it moved, flickering through the dappled light, getting closer every second.

She could see it finally. Really see it.

It was a sports car, for sure. Red and sleek.

Just like the one that had hit Gloria.

The car built even more speed as it hurtled down the hill. Faster. Faster. It erased the space between them. Raced up behind her.

Then it fanned out into the next lane. Moving alongside her.

Charlie could hear the panic in Allie's voice as she spoke.

"It's… it's going to—"

The sports car bashed into her fender, its front end jamming her rear end into a fishtail.

The Focus went squirrelly. Skidding. Out of Charlie's control. She strangled the wheel. Jerked it.

Watched the world spinning around her. The car careening toward that empty space where the road ended and the drop to the water began.

And the glitter from the lake flickered over her. Blinding light that twitched and shook, constantly moving, making her squint.

Cold adrenaline surged through her. Numbed her hands.

But she remembered to steer into the skid. To go with the swerve and regain control.

She drifted all the way to one side of the road and then the other, leaving black streaks behind her.

The Focus fought back, the wheel forcing her to overpower it with sheer muscle, but she got it under control once more.

"Jesus, that was close," Allie breathed.

The sports car raced forward again. Closer and closer.

Charlie jammed on the accelerator. Needed to outrun it or at least try.

The red car kept gaining, though. Drawing up on her.

Charlie strained to see the face behind the steering wheel in the rearview mirror, but there was a murk to the glass. A darkness. She could only make out the outline of shoulders hunched over the steering wheel.

The sports car veered for her again. Charlie managed to evade it, swerving and accelerating out of danger.

The next time the fenders collided, she wasn't so lucky. Metal crunched, and the back of the car went weightless.

The world spun again. Faster this time. It felt like the wheels were lifting off. Betraying gravity. Leaving the road.

She plummeted over the edge of the cliff. Falling.

The shimmering top of the lake became a never-ending wall hurtling toward her.

The front end of the car hit the surface with a crack.

The impact snapped her neck forward, smothering her face first in the inflating airbag.

Something popped and went hot at the top of her spine. Pain flashed bright white inside her head.

All of reality seemed to suck away from her then. Muted. Distant.

Unconsciousness lurched up to swallow her. A spiraling darkness in her skull.

But she fought against it. Dragged her eyelids slowly open. Lifted her head.

She watched the world outside the car as though it were a movie projected on a screen. Quiet and far away. Everything a little blurry, shifting into that soft focus.

The displaced water heaved away from the hood, rolling outward, a receding bulge.

The vehicle drifted. Started to sink. Angled so the front end pointed straight down.

Charlie's eyelids drooped again. The darkness closing in, pressing on her. She fought it. Strained to open her eyes again. Even managed to pull her chin back up from her chest for a moment.

But then the wet rushed back to surround the sedan. Enveloping it. Pouring over the hood. Spilling up onto the tilted windshield.

Charlie lost consciousness just as the car broke through to the dark water below.

CHAPTER FIFTY-FIVE

Water babbled in Charlie's consciousness. Dripping. Gushing.

She opened her eyes. Confused. Blinking.

Her head throbbed as soon as the light hit, and she closed her eyes again. Brought a hand up, cold fingers brushing at her temple.

It felt like she'd been bludgeoned. The hurt beat along with her blood. The headache jabbing a box cutter into her skull behind her left eyeball—thrumming tendrils of pain outward from the epicenter.

She peeled open her eyelids a second time.

She was in a car. Did that make sense?

She blinked again. Squinted as though it might help her concentrate, might help her understand her surroundings.

Blood.

That was the first thing she saw. Blood smeared on the pillow before her. But it wasn't a pillow. It was an airbag. Deflating now.

More blood trickled from her nose. Splattering into a pool of red on the wilting airbag.

She smeared her fingers across her nostrils.

The sound of running water seemed to grow louder. Stole her attention away.

The car leaned. Drifted in the water. Slowly submerging into the lake. It felt like it was floating, but it was sinking in slow motion.

The memory flashed in her head. The moment her car had struck that glittering surface. The wet rolling away and coming back.

Water lapped up onto the hood to touch the windshield. Soon it pressed at every window.

It was sinking faster now. The car tipping forward.

A spray of water came in through the cracked passenger-side window. Pattered onto the seat next to her. Puddled on the upholstery, turning it darker in a semicircle.

The pressure made the glass creak against itself. Sharp noises in time with the lapping of the water. Brittle and gritty. Glass scraping glass.

More cracks appeared all at once in a misshapen spiderweb, as though something solid had hit the window. Faint hairlines fanned out from the original crack.

Then the glass burst inward. Water spewed in. A steady flow laced with shards that just kept coming.

The surging wetness flopped onto Charlie's lap. The cold of it so shocking she gasped as it tumbled over her legs to the floor.

Gallons and gallons and gallons. Endless wet ripping into the car.

Charlie fumbled to release her seatbelt. Jabbing two fingers into the button until the belt zipped past her. Retracting.

Her fingers found the door handle. Pushed.

The door didn't budge.

She bashed her shoulder into it, but there was too much water. Too much pressure.

She needed another way out.

She swiveled in her seat, water splashing up from her lap with her movement. Her eyes snapped to the broken passenger window where the water rushed in.

A few shards of glass still jutted there, a jagged row of teeth.

She leaned back. Kicked through the gushing water to try to clear out more of the glass, widen the opening.

She cleared away the pointed bits piece by piece. Felt them snap away, cleaved like peanut brittle at the hammering of her heels.

The cold seeped into her flesh as she worked. The water's icy grip tightened around her.

And her skin contracted little by little until it felt too tight for her body.

She needed to get out now, before the numbness became total, made swimming to shore impossible.

She sat up. Lurched over the center console. Took a deep breath. And threw herself into the opening.

She crawled into the place where the window should be. Gripped the frame and pulled herself toward the empty air between them.

The small nubs of remaining glass dug into her palms, fingers, the heels of her hands, breaking the skin, shredding her.

Water surged against her chest. Sloshed up onto her neck and chin. Tried to push her back.

The cold shuddered through her. Thrummed fresh tremors in her muscles. The numbness bloomed in her limbs first, spreading quickly to her core.

She fought through the current, shaky arms easing her forward. Her head poked out of the sinking car. Into the open. Into the light.

And her legs kicked behind her. Pushed off the seat and center console the best they could. Thrashed at the surface of the water overtaking the car.

Her shoulders, too, exited through the broken window. Almost there. Almost free.

The car tilted away from her as the water tugged it harder. Gulping noises vented from somewhere in the submerged part of the front end. Slurping. Sucking. Bubbles bursting to the surface all around her.

The car was going down fast now, and it wanted to take her with it.

The sinking ceiling slammed into her back. Bumped her hard enough to break her grip.

She fumbled to regain her grasp on the door. Numb fingers scrabbling over upholstery, over metal, over glass, over the rubber trim. She couldn't get a hold of anything.

Her head dipped under the surface as the car plunged into the depths. Water stung her eyes.

The deep wanted her. Its suction drawing her downward, taking her, absorbing her into its cold and dark.

The top of the window frame pressed harder into her back, slicing at her, cold metal catching just under the shoulder blades.

Her arms shook, the sensation draining from her fingers. Sucked out by the cold.

She couldn't hold her breath much longer.

Her feet flailed at the churning water. She kicked harder, sought something solid to push herself off of, but she found only the empty wet.

She fought to get her shoulders upright. Angled her legs downward. One of those beating legs caught something solid. She pushed off.

That propelled her into the breach, jolted her rump past the threshold of the window opening, and then the car was behind her. Under her. A sinking thing growing blurry as the water took it.

She swam for the shore.

CHAPTER FIFTY-SIX

Charlie's clothes dragged as she swam, and the shoes on her feet made her kicking feel pointless. It was a short swim, but her fingers and toes were completely numb by the time she finally felt the sole of her shoe kick against the sandy bottom. With hands like claws, Charlie dragged herself up on the beach and lay on her back.

She sucked in deep lungfuls of air, held them each for a fraction of a second before she let them out. Anything to slow her breathing, make the world around her stop spinning.

Her mind reeled. Shock not quite letting the reality of the situation sink in.

Someone had just tried to kill her.

Why? What for? How could any of this be real?

The questions only made panic well in her again, so she pushed them away. Focused on her breathing.

She stared at the sky, at the clouds scudding off toward the east. The wooziness died back, the world steadying around her.

She listened for cars out on the road above. Heard none. Just the breeze pushing off the water, scraping over the asphalt, whistling a little where it touched the rock face of the cliff between her and the road.

She pictured the red sports car again. Its sleek body was angular in places, rugged and thin in a way that reminded her of a praying mantis or an Apache helicopter. It was a model she didn't recognize, which was uncommon. Even with Salem Island being as small as it was, the tourist trade brought all manner of vehicles around. Every luxury brand was represented on a regular basis, especially on the sporty side. Fleets of Lexuses, BMWs, Mercedes, and their ilk rolled through the strip. She saw Jaguars almost daily in the summer months.

Whatever make and model the car was, it was something exceedingly rare around here. Foreign. Probably expensive. She couldn't be certain, but it was likely the same one that had killed Gloria. The color was right, the size, the speed, the growl of the engine.

She rolled onto her stomach to crawl further onto the shore. She passed the line where the sand gave way to the rockier stuff, which was drier, and then she lay back down. The sharp edges of the stony land jabbed into her lower back, but the prospect of drying off even a little made it seem worth it.

Slowly the feeling crept back into her body, each part of her coming to life one by one.

Again, she felt how taut her skin had become, all of it rumpled into goosebumps, pulled tight over her. And her body struck her as so strange just then. A weird skin sack housing these organs, and somehow that was who she was. What made her real. It seemed impossible.

The clouds kept racing past overhead. Unperturbed. Totally unaware of the crash, of the girl shivering on the edge of the water.

The image of the laptop flared in her head, that black mystery box resting on the passenger seat. The evidence. She'd lost it.

She sat up and looked out over the water, as though she expected the car to have bobbed to the surface at her convenience. But the choppy blue lake waved back empty-handed.

She needed to call Zoe. Maybe law enforcement could still salvage the hard drive. It seemed like a long shot, but she didn't know.

Her fingers wriggled into her pocket. Pulled her phone free.

It was dead, of course. Water-logged. Fat beads of condensation glared out from behind the blank screen.

"Well, that's a kick in the beanbag," Allie said.

Charlie closed her eyes. Gritted her teeth. Listened to her heart knocking against her chest, the angry backbeat to her frustration.

She took a breath. Held it for several heartbeats before she let it out.

Then she picked herself up off the ground. The cool breeze pushed her wet clothes snug against her body, and the renewed chill sent another shudder through her.

She'd have to walk to one of the houses down the road. Ask to use the phone. Maybe get a towel, if she was lucky.

She started her way up the rocky bank, shivering all the while.

CHAPTER FIFTY-SEVEN

Dusk was descending by the time the police diving team arrived. Charlie watched them suit up as the sun set over the lake, staining the surface orange. Police lights twirled around her, adding splashes of red and blue to the puddling sunset.

Charlie glanced over her shoulder at the cop cars parked at angles up on the edge of the cliff above. It looked like they had all parked as dramatically as possible, jackknifing into place, which Charlie found funny. Maybe it made sense.

Even before all of this, the Dutch and Gloria Carmichael cases had to be the most excitement local law enforcement had had in months. Throw in the prospect of a car getting purposefully run off the road? Attempted murder? Precious evidence trapped at the bottom of the lake, possibly destroyed?

"It's a small-town cop cream dream, so hold nothing back," Allie said. "Roll up on the scene with the lights flashing and the siren blaring. Park like a maniac. Treat yourself."

Charlie huddled on the small scrap of beach, a blanket from the ambulance draped over her shoulders. She squeezed the thick fabric together at the front of her neck, clasping it there like a shawl.

She was still wet, and her legs were cold as hell. Wet denim clung to the backs of her knees, pressing its chill into her every time the wind blew.

Many sets of feet crunched over the rocky part of the shore and down into the sand. Some moved all the way to the mesh point where the waves lapped up onto the shore. Probably most of the

Salem Island sheriff's department was swarming the narrow beach right now, anxious to be part of the action.

All eyes locked on the divers as they waded into the shallows and swam out to where the car had gone down. They treaded water there for a moment, and then they disappeared beneath the surface, one and then the other.

Everyone on the beach fell quiet. Waiting. Watching.

Charlie swallowed. Nervous. Her throat suddenly felt dry, slightly sticky.

A few minutes later the divers bobbed up to the surface, and each one gave a thumbs up to the men standing next to the machinery on the shore.

There was a bit of hollering near the tow truck, and then the winch started up with a metallic groan. Spools wound. The cable slowly pulled taut and then started reeling in Charlie's car.

The surface of the lake shifted. Disturbed circles rippled outward from where the cables entered the water. Bubbles roiled in the center of them.

After several seconds, the rear bumper appeared. It sloshed up and out, the trunk and rear tires following its lead into the open.

The back half of the car lifted out of the murky water at an angle. Runnels of water sluiced down everywhere, little streaks following after the bigger rivulets.

The coils kept winding, and the car glided the rest of the way out of the murk, moving toward the shore. A bulge of water surged along with the vehicle, a wave created by the displacing of the large object.

When the car reached the shore, four of the uniformed officers swarmed the vehicle. Charlie focused on one of them as he moved to the passenger-side door, realizing only after that it was the burly officer that she'd been standing next to moments ago. He reached out, his gloved hand squeaking on the wet door handle. Then he ripped it open and jumped back.

Water spilled out of the door. Everything below window level held water, the cabin of the car absolutely full, though that was changing rapidly before her eyes. Dark lake water gushed out and slapped at the sand and pebbles below, somehow smooth and violent at the same time.

As the water drained, Charlie spotted the laptop. It'd gotten knocked around some, the jostling of the crash wedging it between the seat and center console, one side of the black box jutting up from the gap there.

Charlie sucked her teeth at the sight of it. The slightest twinge of nausea wormed in her gut. Some bodily instinct told her, rather forcefully, that Dutch's laptop was beyond salvation, but she knew she shouldn't think that. Between law enforcement and Mason, maybe they could still figure something out. In any case, they had more information to go on now, a place to keep looking. Emails could be subpoenaed, after all. And it couldn't be easy to conceal a billion-dollar lie once people knew what to look for.

Gravel crunched somewhere behind Charlie, footsteps crossing the beach and drawing up on her. She turned to find Zoe striding over, thumbs looped in her belt, a faint smile on her face.

She handed Charlie a pile of dry clothes.

"Are you sure you don't want me to take you home?" Zoe asked for probably the tenth time. "You've gotta be freezing your ass off."

"I told you, I'm OK. Thanks for the clothes, though. Changing into something dry will make it that much better. Anyway, this is more excitement than I usually get on a Saturday night. I don't want to miss out." Mentioning what day it was suddenly jarred something loose in Charlie's memory. "Hey… wasn't today the day you were meeting your sister?"

"That's correct. Your call interrupted dessert."

"Oh crap," Charlie said. "I'm sorry, Zoe."

Zoe waved her away.

"Don't worry about it. If anything, I think Rebecca was kind of impressed. Now she can go back home and tell all her friends what a hero her little sister is." Zoe pulled her phone from her pocket and swiped at the screen. "Check this out, though. We took our first selfie together."

Charlie took the phone Zoe held out to her and studied the photo.

"Oh my God. She looks exactly like you," Charlie said. "Same smile. Same nose. Same freckles."

Zoe beamed.

"Pretty wild, right?"

As Charlie returned the phone, a burst of chatter erupted from Zoe's radio.

Zoe frowned down at her radio and then up at Charlie.

"Did you catch that?"

Charlie shook her head. It had been too garbled. Too frantic.

Next came shouting from up on the road behind them. Zoe snapped her head that way, and they both stared up toward where all the cruisers were parked.

Blue and red lights lit the darkened area, each glowing orb spiraling in endless circles. It almost made it look like some kind of backwoods rave, Charlie thought.

Quiet followed the initial surge of voices, but then the babble started up again. Louder this time.

"Well, they sounded awfully excited about something," Charlie said.

"Excited in a good way or a bad way," Zoe said, not quite making it sound like a question.

They exchanged a quick glance and Charlie shrugged.

A dark figure rushed down the hill alongside the cliff. Charlie couldn't see his face, but she could tell by the crew cut and the way the silhouette highlighted the cut of his uniform that he was another of the many officers buzzing around the scene. His broad shoulders bounced as he traversed the winding path.

He picked up speed as he hit the flat of the beach, rushed up to Zoe.

"Deputy Wyatt? We just got word that there's another accident site. There's a car wrapped around a tree a couple miles up the road. We've got eyes on it now, securing the scene."

Zoe didn't say anything, probably waiting for the same thing Charlie was waiting for.

The officer swallowed before he spit it out.

"It's a bright red sports car."

CHAPTER FIFTY-EIGHT

A fleet of law enforcement vehicles swarmed the area around the car wreck. The sound of tires crushing gravel into the sand was almost constant as cruiser after cruiser settled in, two lines of them huddling along this rural road.

Charlie finished changing into the dry clothes in the back of Zoe's car, and she instantly felt warmer. The long sleeves even covered the bandages on the heels of her hands. After that, the two of them hustled to the crime scene on foot and ducked under the yellow police tape.

The busted vehicle came into view. Despite the dying light, Charlie could make out that it was a red sports car alright, and without a doubt the same one that had run her off the road.

The front end wrapped itself around a thick tree trunk, metal twisting and bending at impossible angles. Shards of steel, or possibly aluminum, jutting outward from the point of impact like the remnants of an exploded cigar.

Swirling flashlight beams surrounded them as they approached the wreck, swinging from the car to the ground, off into the woods, and back again. Zoe got out her flashlight and joined in.

"So we've got the driver, yeah?" someone asked.

A female officer replied.

"Negative. The responding officers cleared the vehicle. Empty. Any occupants fled the scene, probably on foot."

When the first officer responded to this new information, most of the urgency had drained out of his voice.

"A bunch of us thought… I mean, a wreck like that? You don't figure anybody's walking away too quickly."

The female officer shook her head.

"We ran the plates, though. Vehicle's registered to Randolph Carmichael."

Charlie perked up at this, though she realized after a moment she should have guessed that from the beginning. Her shoulders sagged.

On the way over, she'd hoped that identifying the owner of the car would be the key to discovering who'd killed Gloria. But any one of the Carmichael clan could have let themselves into Dutch's garage and taken the car. And every single one of them had been at the house. Had probably presumed she was on her way to the police with the smoking gun.

Another crew came in, hauling equipment from the cargo door of a van. They jogged right up to within a few feet of the crash site and started setting up industrial rigs of lights.

"Almost looks like they're prepping this thing for a magazine cover shoot," Allie said.

Soon the spotlights clicked on, one set after another. Everything at the scene seemed to come to an abrupt halt, as though everyone held their breath to look upon the car wreck anew.

One by one, heads started turning toward Charlie. Finally someone asked the question they were all thinking.

"You sure this is the vehicle that you tangled with back there?"

Charlie nodded.

"That's the car. I'm certain." Probably the one that killed Gloria, too, but she couldn't prove that yet, so she left it unsaid.

The crime scene techs moved in after that. Snapping photos. Processing and documenting the exterior of the car.

Zoe came trudging back through the undergrowth, flashlight aimed at the ground.

"What we've got here is a Hennessey Venom GT. Extremely, extremely rare. Wanna guess who this one is registered to?"

"Dutch Carmichael," Charlie said.

Zoe rolled her eyes.

"You cheated."

With the outside of the car processed, the crime scene techs popped open the doors and moved to working the interior. Zoe and Charlie stopped talking to focus on the action.

From Charlie's angle, the car looked to be spotless inside. She doubted they'd find anything. This car had been crashed on purpose. After the damage it had sustained from driving her off the road, it was the only logical thing to do.

"Got nothing in the glove box," one of the techs said. "I mean literally nothing. Not even a speck of dust."

"Same with the center console," another tech said. "Nothing. Whole thing looks wiped to me."

"Got something!"

One of the techs retracted his arm from beneath the driver's seat. He held up something in tiny tweezers. Charlie couldn't see what it was, but it seemed to glitter in the spotlights, some tiny twinkling star clenched at the end of the tweezers.

The glowing expression on the tech's face seemed to fade as he examined it closer. His smile turned down.

"Just some garbage," he muttered.

He jammed the shiny bit into an evidence bag. Labeled it.

Charlie and Zoe moved closer to see.

"Can I see what you've got there?" Zoe asked.

"This?" The tech waggled the evidence bag then handed it over to Zoe. "All yours."

Zoe turned the baggie over in her hands. Then she extended her arm to hold it up to the light. Charlie gasped when she saw what was inside.

The rest of the scene went quiet apart from the faint buzzing of the light bulbs.

Heads turned. All eyes latched onto Charlie. Waiting.

"What?" Zoe said, her voice small and clear in the silence.

A candy wrapper shone within the plastic sheath of the evidence bag. Clear cellophane with red edges and instantly recognizable printing across the center:

JOLLY rancher.

CHAPTER FIFTY-NINE

Charlie and Zoe ripped across Salem Island to Marjory's house in Zoe's cruiser. The thrum of the tires against the asphalt vibrated up through the floor to prickle in Charlie's feet.

"You're sure about this?" Zoe asked. "It's a popular candy, you know."

"Trust me. She sucks them down like they're her only source of sustenance. I watched her eat about twenty of them earlier today."

Charlie pressed Zoe's phone to her ear, the ring chiming away, reaching out to Marjory's cell phone and, so far, getting no answer. And Charlie could understand that. If *she'd* just run someone off the road, she'd probably screen calls, too.

Her jaw clenched and unclenched as she listened to the phone ring. And ring. And ring. Something urgent pattered in her pulse now, that hot surge of blood twitching in her neck, its pace quickening.

Frustration. Of the blend of emotions coursing through her, frustration was the strongest.

Because finding the candy wrapper in the sports car slash murder weapon sure seemed like a big reveal, right? It pointed an accusatory finger at Marjory, lit it up in flashing neon lights.

Except Marjory couldn't have possibly been driving the car when it had hit Gloria. She had an airtight alibi for that window of time. She'd been on her way to her cabin with a friend. So what did any of this mean? And what did it have to do with the damning emails on Dutch's computer, found and then lost almost as quickly? It was yet another strand in a tangled mess.

The ringing cut out. Marjory's voicemail greeting took its place, and Charlie hung up.

"Still no answer," she said, her voice flat, concealing her annoyance.

She clenched her jaw so hard that the muscles along it shook.

Her eyes closed. Squeezed tight. Pink splotches floated in the darkness invading her head.

"Talk to me," Zoe said. "What are you thinking?"

Charlie looked over, and Zoe's eyes met hers for a moment before shifting back to the road.

"I don't know," Charlie said. "But if I were Marjory, and I'd just done what we think she did—not to mention murdering Dutch and Gloria—I'd run."

Full darkness had descended by the time they zipped closer to the house. Moonlight flitted through the trees as they sped down the road, but otherwise the blackness alongside the car was near total as they drove through this wooded stretch.

The cruiser's headlights pierced the murk. Lit the way forward. Glowed bright where the reflective paint made a dotted yellow line down the center of the asphalt.

"Here we go," Zoe muttered.

Charlie followed her gaze to Marjory's mansion in the distance. No lights shone in the windows.

They pulled into the driveway and followed the serpentine blacktop strip up toward the house. Zoe killed the engine, and then they were out, rushing to the front door.

"Wait," Zoe said, stopping dead in her tracks some six paces shy of the stoop.

Charlie bumped into Zoe's shoulder then stopped as well. Her eyes snapped to Zoe's face, found her brows creased, her lips pressed into a tight line.

"What is it?" Charlie said.

Zoe drew her weapon from her holster. Kept it pointed at the ground. She spoke in a whisper.

"Front door's open, and all the lights are off."

Charlie wheeled her head that way. Scanned for confirmation.

The front door lay open a few inches, something sinister about the shadowed gap.

Charlie blinked. Chills crawled over her back and shoulders as she peered into the crack, but she couldn't look away.

Darkness spilled out of the chasm, a gaping blackness that felt very wrong.

CHAPTER SIXTY

Zoe pushed the door open, and a wedge of moonlight sliced into the foyer. The glow wasn't strong enough for them to see much beyond the faint grid of the tile floor.

The deputy stepped through the doorway first, and Charlie followed. They milled around in the dark for a second, both of them fidgety, unsure of how to proceed.

Charlie fumbled her fingers along the wall, feeling for a light switch and failing to find one.

Zoe cupped a hand to her mouth and bellowed into the darkness. "Sheriff's Department. Anyone here?"

They both went still. Listened.

No response.

Charlie finally found a light switch and flipped it on. Recessed lights clicked on in the high ceiling, far overhead, and the foyer formed around them, as though congealing just now from the darkness.

Everything looked to be in perfect order. Spotless. Exactly the same as when Charlie had been here a couple of days ago.

Charlie licked her lips. With the front door hanging open, part of her had expected to find the place trashed or at least some signs of a struggle. It was somehow creepier to find the place so neat and still, ready and waiting to be the centerfold in next month's *Martha Stewart Living*.

Zoe took a few steps forward, boots echoing off the tile.

She tensed, eyes narrowing. She raised her gun, extended it before her, arms shaking it a little.

There was a small yip and Marjory's dog emerged from the shadows. Charlie knelt, scooping the tiny creature into her arms.

"Christ," Zoe muttered.

She sighed and lowered her weapon again.

They crossed the living room, reaching the point where the house branched off in various directions. Again, Zoe cupped a hand to the side of her mouth.

"Salem's County Sheriff's Department! Answer me if you're there."

Still nothing.

Charlie set the tiny dog down in the kitchen with its food bowl and returned to the hallway.

Zoe gestured toward the dining room, indicating she would take the lead and clear the area, but something caught Charlie's eye upstairs. From this angle, she could just make out a glint of light under one of the doorways of the second floor.

She grabbed Zoe's shirtsleeve and pointed up at the glowing sliver. Zoe gazed up at the faint light and then at Charlie and nodded.

Charlie could feel her heartbeat in her neck as they tiptoed up the stairs. A steady glugging of blood gushing all through her.

No noise at all emitted from the lit room. No flitting shadows or other signs of movement disturbed that narrow bar of light under the door.

At the top of the stairs, they turned left, closing the last six paces to the door. Zoe raised her weapon again and gave a little hand signal for Charlie to whip it open and get out of the way.

Charlie's hand drifted to the knob. Grasped it. Twisted.

Locked.

Zoe held up a hand. Nodded. She pointed a finger to the center of her chest and then pantomimed that she would kick it in. Charlie nodded and stepped aside.

Zoe took a breath, shoulders heaving up and then down. She counted down with her lips. Charlie held her breath.

Three.

Two.

One.

Zoe took two steps forward, building momentum. Then she lifted her right leg and cracked it into the door just beneath the knob.

The jamb splintered around the latch and burst out of the way, flung like a piece of balsa wood. It rebounded off the doorstop, shivering out a brittle tone.

"Salem County Sheriff's Department!" Zoe yelled, her gun once again raised in front of her.

Apart from the trembling door, nothing in the room moved. Charlie took it in one piece at a time.

It was a bathroom. All white tile accented with pastel pink here and there. The bank of lights over the vanity were blinding, made Charlie's eyes sting where they gleamed off all that porcelain.

Charlie and Zoe exchanged another glance before filing into the room, with Zoe leading the way. Three steps in, the rest of the room came into view.

The first thing Charlie saw was the blood. Thick red clouds of it fluttered in the bathwater.

A straight razor rested on the side of the tub, folded into an acute angle but not quite closed. Gummy red droplets clung to the blade.

Marjory lay motionless in the water, chin slumped against her sternum. Her skin looked gray against all the white in here. Ashen. Drained.

Red slits gashed the length of each forearm, presumably where she'd used the razor to open herself up. To watch her life spill into the bathwater, little shudders of it pulsing out until they stopped.

Charlie and Zoe stood motionless for a moment. Silent. Stunned.

A single drop of water gathered at the tip of the faucet and dripped. Plopped into the water in the tub, the wet sound loud in the quiet.

Concentric circles rippled outward from the point of impact. The tendrils of red undulated along with the water's movement, billowing around the utterly still body of Marjory Carmichael.

And then Zoe lurched forward, reaching for the figure in the tub. "She's still breathing."

CHAPTER SIXTY-ONE

When the paramedics finished locking the gurney into place, Charlie climbed into the back of the ambulance and buckled herself into one of the seats. In the few seconds it took one of the EMTs to occupy the driver's seat, the other had started an IV on Marjory and set up a drip on one of the stands in back.

Within moments, the ambulance was tearing down the road. Juddering over potholes. Siren screaming every time they passed through an intersection.

Charlie swayed with each bump along the way, her face angled to watch the figure sprawled on the gurney.

Something about the slackness in Marjory's cheeks looked utterly lifeless, not unlike a body in a casket, though the shaky rise and fall of her chest betrayed this vision. The gray undertone to her skin only looked darker in this lighting. Charlie couldn't get over her complexion, no matter how long she stared at it. She didn't look pallid, sickly, or peaked so much as straight-up gray.

Between the color and the grim expression unconsciousness had etched onto Marjory's face, Charlie found her nearly unrecognizable. She pressed her lips together as guilt crept into her belly.

Should she feel guilty, though? She wasn't sure.

She'd rushed to Marjory's place to accuse her of… what? Eating candy in her father's sports car? Did she have proof of anything beyond that? Not really.

Instead they'd found her nearly dead by her own hand. The whole scenario came with some whiplash effect, she supposed. A little guilt might make sense here and now.

Then again, maybe this suicide attempt was a kind of proof. Nothing definitive, of course, but it spoke to some dark possibilities, didn't it?

Maybe. Maybe not.

The fact remained that Marjory had an alibi for the time when Gloria had been killed. Didn't that make her an unlikely suspect to have run Charlie off the road in the same car?

Charlie watched the still figure on the gurney as her mind raced over these thoughts, the cadaverous face pointed up at the ceiling. Eyes closed.

Why did none of this make sense?

Charlie didn't want to think about it just now. Didn't want to ask herself a bunch of questions that couldn't be answered.

The paramedic in back aimed a no-touch thermometer at Marjory's forehead and frowned at the reading. Opening a small door near the floor, she pulled out two more blankets and draped them over the pale form on the gurney.

The ambulance lurched to the left and angled up a ramp, tires screaming a little.

Charlie turned to watch out the windshield, and the khaki facade of the hospital rapidly grew larger as they approached. Then everything started happening very quickly.

The ambulance parked, and the EMT in back threw the rear doors open. They unloaded the gurney and wheeled Marjory up onto the sidewalk, her limp limbs flopping like noodles with every jostle. Then they jogged off toward the building where glass doors waited, open and ready.

Zoe's cruiser came to a halt behind the ambulance a moment later, and the two of them hurried to catch up with the paramedics.

A team of doctors and nurses were waiting for them, and everyone was talking at once, barking out commands or saying encouraging things, though Charlie couldn't really understand any one of the voices.

She felt wrong exiting the shelter of the back of the vehicle, striding up onto the sidewalk. Exposed. Cold wind whipped at them, an endless gust that seemed to slam into the concrete wall of the hospital. It smashed her hair to the left side of her face, twisted a strand of it under her nose to flap around like a flag.

Zoe stopped, and Charlie pulled up beside her.

"We should hang back," Zoe said. "Call the family and everything."

"Right," Charlie agreed.

They stood and watched the gurney wheel through the gaping place where the glass doors of the hospital had slid aside. The building swallowed Marjory like a mouth, her and the two paramedics vanishing into the structure.

Everything seemed quiet for a beat, apart from the endless hiss of the wind. And then the doors glided shut.

CHAPTER SIXTY-TWO

After Zoe contacted Marjory's family, the wind eventually drove the pair of them inside to one of the small waiting areas.

"None of this makes sense," Charlie said, seating herself on a hard bench.

"What do you mean?"

"Well, there's an obvious motive for Marjory to kill Dutch, which is the inheritance. But why kill Gloria? And how? Marjory has a solid alibi for the time of Gloria's death." Charlie sighed. "But let's say, for the sake of argument, that her alibi falls apart. Let's say Marjory *did* kill Gloria. What was her motive then?"

Adjusting her glasses on the bridge of her nose, Zoe pursed her lips.

"You said Gloria was coming to you with information. Maybe she'd found proof that Marjory killed their father."

"Maybe."

Charlie had considered this herself. She didn't know if it fit.

"But there's another problem," she said, turning to face Zoe. "If Marjory was driving the red car that ran me off the road, I think we can assume she was trying to keep me from taking the computer to the police, right? She wanted to keep a lid on the Ponzi scheme."

"Right."

"OK, well whoever was driving the red car saw me go off the road and into the water. They would have believed their efforts were successful."

Zoe frowned and then began nodding slowly as she put it together.

"So then why would she run home and off herself?" Zoe said. "She shut you up and destroyed the computer in one stroke by running you off the road, or at least she would have thought so. Trying to kill herself after that doesn't really make sense."

"Exactly."

Zoe's eyes went wide.

"You think it means someone's trying to set Marjory up?"

"I don't know what I think right now," Charlie said, massaging her temples. "But something about this doesn't add up."

They lapsed into silence for a moment, and then Zoe spoke again.

"On the other hand, if Marjory is somehow responsible for killing Dutch and Gloria, it would be a pretty powerful reason to try to commit suicide. I mean, if I'd gone to all this trouble—murdering my family members and all that—only to find out the fortune I was after didn't exist, I'd feel pretty low."

"Yeah," Charlie said. "In some ways, Marjory's suicide attempt is the one part of this that has some logic to it."

Her gaze slid over to the door, where she spotted Wesley and Brandon making their way down a hallway toward the waiting room.

"Zoe, do me a favor," Charlie said quickly.

"What's that?"

"Marjory's family is here, and I don't want to mention the crash to them. Nothing about my run-in with the red car at all."

"Why not?"

"I don't know. It's just a feeling."

Zoe shrugged.

"Fine with me. They'll find out sooner or later, but there's no reason we have to tell them about it now."

They rose to their feet as Marjory's brothers entered the waiting area. While Zoe explained the exact state they'd found Marjory in, Charlie tried to assess the two men, analyzing their responses.

Wesley did most of the talking, his eyes stretching a little wider than usual, which gave him a perpetually surprised look. Beside him, Brandon barely uttered a word, but Charlie could see his jaw clenching and unclenching. One shocked and one grave. Normal enough reactions, given the circumstances.

"Oh my God!" Wesley said for the third time, running a hand through his hair. "Was there a note?"

It was a second before Charlie realized he meant a suicide note, but Zoe had apparently taken his meaning right away.

"No, sir," she said.

"I still don't understand why she'd do this," Wesley muttered, staring at the floor.

Zoe and Charlie exchanged a glance, and then Zoe cleared her throat.

"Have you spoken with any of the staff here about your sister's condition?"

Wesley nodded.

"Yes. She's with the doctors now. They had to give her a blood transfusion, and there were some additional complications because she apparently took sleeping pills on top of the…" Wesley trailed off, apparently unable to find the words to describe what Marjory had done to herself.

"But they're expecting her to pull through it," Brandon finished the thought.

"That's good," Zoe said, tucking her thumbs in her belt. "We'll need to talk to the lot of you at some point—"

"About what?" Wesley asked, and his eyes darted over to Charlie.

She'd forgotten about Wesley asking her to hold off on delivering the computer to the police. She pondered that for a moment. Had he asked her that and then come after her in the red car to get rid of the evidence once and for all? If so, he should have been surprised to see her standing here, alive and well, when he'd first come in.

"… a few questions about some matters concerning the family, that's all," Zoe was saying. "Anyway, we don't need to do that now. You all have your plate full at the moment, and we certainly understand that."

A nurse entered with a stack of forms she needed the family's help filling out, and Zoe and Charlie moved into the hallway to give them some privacy.

"So I'm heading out now," Zoe said. "You want a lift home?"

Charlie thrust her hands into her pockets and gave a shake of her head.

"I'm gonna stay. I want to be here to observe when the rest of Marjory's siblings show up."

Gripping Charlie's shoulder, Zoe gave it a friendly squeeze.

"Well, be careful, will you? The whole lot of them seem like a nest of vipers, if you ask me."

It wasn't long after Wesley and Brandon had finished up the paperwork with the nurse that Jude and Dara arrived. Dara ran ahead, her long hair swaying behind her.

"Is she going to be OK?" Dara asked, her face streaked with tears. "Have they let you in to see her yet?"

Embracing her, Wesley shook his head.

"She's still in the ICU, but the doctors are very optimistic."

"Oh, Marjie," Dara sobbed. "Why would she do this?"

"Well, the police didn't find a note," Wesley said, his eyes flicking over to Charlie as he lowered his voice. "But I suppose the obvious conclusion would be that it was all the stuff with Dad."

"Shit. Yeah," Jude said. "That's what happened to Bernie Madoff's kid, right? Same exact thing."

Charlie hoped that Wesley's pointed look wasn't a subtle suggestion that he thought it was her fault that Marjory had attempted suicide. She'd only been the one to uncover Dutch's deception. Then again, the phrase "don't shoot the messenger" existed for a reason. Someone, somewhere, had wanted to shoot the messenger.

"It's just one disaster after another, isn't it? We can't catch a break." Before anyone else could speak, Jude whirled around, searching the room. "Where's Trevor? He's Marjory's husband, for God's sake."

"He's been out of town," Wesley explained. "I called him from the car. He's getting the first plane back."

Jude threw himself into a chair and crossed his arms.

"Well, he should be here."

"Be sure to tell him that when he gets here, won't you?" Wesley said sarcastically. "I'm sure it will help things."

Spittle flung from Jude's mouth as he sat forward to shout at his brother.

"Oh, fuck off, Wes! Just fuck all the way off, OK?"

Wesley only raised his eyebrows and shook his head.

"What about Percival?" a small voice asked after a few minutes had passed with no one speaking.

It was Dara. Charlie had noticed when she'd first entered the room that she had dark bags under her eyes and seemed paler than usual.

"What's that, Dara?" Wesley said.

"She's asking about Percival," Brandon explained. "Marjory's dog."

Jude scoffed and muttered, "You can't be serious."

"Enough." Wesley didn't say any more than that, but his tone made it clear that this was a warning.

Jude responded by holding up his middle finger, though he remained silent.

From her seat in the corner, Charlie cleared her throat.

"Marjory's dog is fine," she said. "I made sure he had food and water before we left the house."

Charlie kept waiting for someone to ask how they'd known to go to Marjory's house in the first place, and then she'd have to explain about Dutch's red car and the candy wrapper they'd found, but so far no one had asked. She supposed they were all still in shock. They'd had a lot to digest in one day. Still, it was only a matter of time before someone started trying to line up the events and began to wonder.

Thankfully, Dara only nodded and said, "That's good."

"He's gonna shit and piss all over the place," Jude said. "Marjory's gonna be furious. I mean, if she even makes it."

"Goddamn it, Jude!" Wesley slammed his fist down on the arm of his chair. "Why do you always have to look at things that way? It's like you want everything to go poorly."

Jude shrugged and crossed one leg over the other.

"I'm just telling it like it is," he said. "Being *honest*, which is a concept I know you have no comprehension of. Is there a class you have to take when you become a politician that removes your ability to be authentic?"

Wesley wiped a hand over his face.

"I swear to God, Jude, one of these days…"

A malignant grin spread across Jude's mouth.

"One of these days… what, Wes?" He leaned forward, the knuckles of his fingers turning white as he squeezed his hands into fists. "You're gonna teach me a lesson? Kick my ass? Finish the sentence, dickface."

"Jude." Brandon kept his voice low, but the tone was sharp enough that Jude's head whipped around to face him.

When he had his brother's attention, Brandon continued.

"Shut. Up."

An angry breath puffed out of Jude's nostrils. After several minutes of tense silence, he spoke again.

"Do you guys have little meetings or something?"

"Now what are you talking about?" Wesley asked.

"It just seems like a team effort, you know? How the lot of you are all equally shitty to me. It's never one-on-one, which would at least be fair." Jude's right leg bounced up and down. "It's like you're always working together."

"Oh, please," Wesley said, and Jude repeated him mockingly. "*Oh, please.*"

"That's not true at all, Jude," Dara protested. "In fact, I think it's really unfair of you to say that."

Jude laughed bitterly.

"Jesus Christ! You're literally doing it *right now*." He shoved himself to a standing position. "Forget it. I'm gonna go find somewhere I can vape in this godforsaken place."

"Why does he always act like this? Like it's a contest or something?" Dara asked.

Charlie was barely listening by then, though. She was still stuck on something Jude had said before he stormed out.

It's like you're always working together.

And suddenly Charlie thought she had an idea of how Marjory having an alibi for one murder but not the other could make sense.

If she'd had an accomplice.

CHAPTER SIXTY-THREE

A tingle spread over Charlie's body. She stood. Mumbled something about how she'd be right back. Walked out into the hall on legs going numb.

She thought moving might stave off some of the pins and needles, but it was no help. The surface of her flesh throbbed with electric jabs and twinges that only seemed to gain intensity with each passing second. All those nerves lurching and spitting inside. Overloaded.

By the time she pushed through the door into the restroom across the hall, she felt like she was floating over the ceramic tiles.

She leaned forward, bracing herself on the end of one of the sinks. Splashed cold water on her face, eyes closed. The thoughts tumbled rapidly in her head.

If Marjory hadn't acted alone, it opened up a number of possibilities. She had an alibi for the time of Gloria's death, but the day Dutch was murdered, she was in her home, just up the road, sleeping off a headache. Or so she'd said. And while her assistant, Killian, had vouched for this story, he hadn't been in the room with Marjory. He couldn't account for her whereabouts other than that he'd seen her that morning, before she'd retired to her room. She could have slipped out to murder her father and snuck back to the house without Killian even noticing she was gone.

An accomplice. Yes. The more she thought about it, the more it made sense.

Charlie opened her eyes. Stared into her wet face in the mirror. Blinked a few times. Cold droplets formed along her jawline and plummeted to the sink below.

But who would the accomplice be? Charlie's mind kicked back into hyperdrive, riffling back through all that happened, searching for some telltale detail, some overlooked clue. Marjory and Jude had been against the idea of Charlie continuing her investigation. But Jude was the other sibling with a solid alibi for the time of Gloria's death, being with a client all day, so he was out.

A husband would make a likely enough accomplice, but Marjory's husband had been out of town. Then again, had anyone checked that? Or had Charlie and the police taken Marjory's word for it?

In any case, Charlie knew what she needed to do next: go back to Marjory's house and look for clues.

She nudged open the bathroom door with her elbow and glanced in the direction of the waiting room, where the remaining members of the Carmichael family still sat. She considered telling them she was leaving but decided it was better to keep them in the dark for now. Could she really trust any of them?

It was only once Charlie was outside on the sidewalk that she remembered her car had just gone for a swim in Lake St. Clair.

"Crap," she murmured, reaching for her phone. But that had also been destroyed.

Back inside, a hospital employee directed her to a row of courtesy phones near the entrance. Charlie called her uncle Frank.

CHAPTER SIXTY-FOUR

Charlie parked Frank's Buick down the street from the house, around a bend that kept it just out of sight from Marjory's driveway. Despite her clandestine parking job, she strode purposefully up the drive and to the front door, as if she were an expected guest.

She'd been the one who'd closed up, when they'd been here with the ambulance, and she was pretty certain she hadn't locked the door behind her. Sure enough, the door knob turned easily when she tried it, and she smiled to herself. Had her subconscious mind somehow known she'd be returning here tonight?

Charlie opened the door and stepped inside. There was a noise, and she froze. A weird mechanical chime. One note.

What the hell was that?

Her eyes swiveled to the right and she spotted it. A sleek white box set into the wall with a number pad and a bunch of buttons on it. And then Charlie remembered her first conversation here with Marjory, when they'd talked about the break-in and the high-tech security system her husband had insisted on installing.

She took a step toward it and saw a message blinking on the small LED screen: *ALARM OFF.*

That was good, but Charlie swore Marjory had said something about cameras everywhere, and she had no idea whether those were also off.

Shit. Video evidence of her breaking and entering? That was definitely *not* good.

OK. Think.

Just then, Marjory's dog trotted out from the back of the house.

Ah. Yes.

Charlie wasn't breaking and entering! She'd come here to check on precious… what was his name again?

Percival. That was it.

Charlie lifted the dog and carried him with her into the kitchen. There was still plenty of kibble left, but Charlie dumped the water bowl and refilled it, mostly to look busy.

There was a leash by the back door, so Charlie hooked it to Percival's collar and took him outside. He spent several minutes distributing his pee on various flowering plants and bushes before Charlie led him back inside.

With the possibility of being on camera, she wouldn't be able to snoop around the place quite like she'd hoped. But there was nothing to stop her from taking a cursory peek here and there. Maybe there'd be something obvious just sitting out for her to see.

She wandered from room to room with Percival hot on her heels, but nothing leapt out at her. In fact, the only thing that really struck her was the room just off the foyer. When she'd first come to the house to talk to Marjory, her assistant Killian had been packing boxes in the room. Marjory had explained they had to clear out the room for a remodeling project. And while the boxes were gone, the room wasn't bare. There was still furniture and bookcases half-filled with stuff: thick books, a copper globe, framed photographs.

Charlie spotted spaces on the shelves where things had obviously been removed, marks on the carpet where perhaps a small table had once stood, but on the whole the room looked far from empty. It was more like *half* the things had been taken from the room. And that didn't make sense.

Unless…

Rushing from one end of the house to the other, Charlie checked the rooms along the way, noting empty hooks on the wall where a painting might have hung. A side table without a lamp. She ended up in the formal living room where she and Marjory had talked back on the first day she'd taken Gloria's case. The coffee table was gone.

Just then, Charlie's pocket buzzed, which confused her until she remembered she'd grabbed the spare cell phone from the office before coming here. She didn't recognize the number and hoped it was Marjory's husband returning her call.

"A1 Investigations."

"Ms. Winters, hello. This is Dr. Kesselman."

Charlie squeezed her eyes shut. Her mother's doctor. Great. Just what Charlie needed right now, on top of everything else.

"Hello, Dr. Kesselman," she said, forcing some semblance of a smile into her voice. "How are you?"

"Wonderful now that I've reached you. I know it's late, but I left several voicemails today and finally decided to try the backup number I had on file."

"I'm so sorry. My phone died today, and I haven't even had a chance to check my voicemail," Charlie said, not wanting to get into exactly *how* her phone had died. "What can I do for you?"

"Well, I was mostly calling to make sure you were on board with your mother's treatment plan. After some discussion, we've decided that some time in an inpatient facility is the best option right now."

Charlie blinked.

"We…" Charlie repeated. "My mother agreed to this?"

"It was her idea." Dr. Kesselman sighed. "I think almost harming you was somewhat of a wake-up call for her."

The air around Charlie suddenly felt heavy. Taking care of her mother was Charlie's responsibility, whether she'd asked for it or not. And she'd failed. Maybe it wasn't her fault, but she'd failed and now Nancy needed inpatient treatment.

"I've arranged for her to be transferred to the Cedar Grove Healing Center tomorrow," Dr. Kesselman went on. "I can give you their number and information if you'd like to arrange a visit at some point soon."

"Of course," Charlie said, her mouth working on autopilot now.

After hanging up, Charlie let her head fall back into the cushions of the couch. She felt like crying but fought the urge.

Percival hopped up beside her, and Charlie swiveled her neck to regard him.

"Why do I have the feeling you're not supposed to be on the furniture?" she asked.

The dog flopped onto his belly, resting his head on her lap. Charlie chuckled.

"OK," she said. "You win."

Stroking the dog's head, Charlie stared up at the gloom clinging to the vaulted ceiling and let the tears run down her cheeks.

There'd been a noise. A strange, one-note chime. And it was familiar somehow.

Charlie woke on the couch in Marjory's house, having dozed off. She looked around.

A small desk lamp lit one corner of the expansive living room, but the shadows swelled to fill most of the space. Boxes of moonlight reached through the windows and stretched over the floor, but they could merely cut slices out of the dark and leave the rest untouched.

A thud came from the direction of the front door, and Charlie realized suddenly what the noise had been.

The security system beeping because someone had just entered the house.

Charlie jumped up from the couch, forgetting that Marjory's dog had crawled into her lap. Percival tumbled to the floor in front of her, and Charlie had to scramble her feet to avoid trampling the small creature. The frantic, clumsy movements sent her tripping across the room, where she spilled into the hallway and slammed into the wall.

The figure in the foyer staggered backward, arms lifted defensively. Charlie recognized him quickly from a few of the photographs in the house. Trevor Steigel.

A pair of crutches protruded from his elbows, and Charlie wondered exactly what kind of damage they could do if swung into someone's skull. Not wanting to find out, she put her hands out and spoke.

"I'm so sorry, I didn't mean to startle you like that."

To Trevor's credit, he regained his composure quickly. The feet of the crutches came down with a *clack*, and he took a bold step forward.

"Who are you?" he demanded. "What the hell are you doing in my house?"

Percival yapped excitedly, perhaps sensing the alarm in his master's voice.

"My name is Charlie Winters. I'm an investigator hired by the Carmichaels. I was the one who… found Marjory."

Trevor stopped stalking toward her. The rigid tension in his shoulders relaxed infinitesimally.

"I see." He sighed. "And why is it you're in my house?"

Charlie pointed at the dog, who had stopped barking.

"Percival. The family was concerned about him being here alone, so I volunteered to come check on him, and I… sort of dozed off on your couch," Charlie said, adding a sheepish smile for good measure.

"Of course." He nodded and then paused to squint at her. "You said your name is Charlie Winters?"

"That's right."

"Ah, so you're the one who left approximately twenty messages on my voicemail?"

Charlie grimaced.

"Yes. Sorry. It's just that it's very important that I talk to you."

"Can it wait?" he asked, suddenly sounded exhausted. "I drove straight from the airport to Marjory's bedside, and I only came back here to get a few hours' sleep before I return to the hospital first thing in the morning."

"How is she?" Charlie asked.

"She's stable now. But they have her pumped full of sedatives, so no one has been able to speak to her yet to figure out what on earth she was thinking." He made a move toward the door. "If you come back in the morning—"

"You and Marjory are getting a divorce," Charlie said, spitting out what had been on her mind since she'd first noticed the state of the house. The bare spaces everywhere as if someone had removed only half of the items.

Trevor slowly swiveled to face her.

"I didn't mean to blurt it out like that, it's just... I really need you to answer a few questions. And it really can't wait."

Closing his eyes and then blinking a few times, Trevor finally nodded.

"Very well," he said. "Though would you mind if I have a drink first? I have a feeling I'm going to need it."

CHAPTER SIXTY-FIVE

Everything in the vast kitchen was white. White marble floors. White marble counters. White cabinets. White walls. Even the vase of tulips on the counter was white.

Trevor moved to the fridge and removed a bottle of tonic water and a bottle of gin from the freezer.

"Can I offer you a gin and tonic?" he asked as he reached for a glass in one of the cabinets. "I don't usually drink at this hour, but given the circumstances…"

He finished the thought with a shrug.

"No thanks," Charlie said, settling on one of the stools across the wide island from where Trevor stood to fix his drink.

She waited until he'd mixed the two liquids, added ice, and sipped the concoction before she dove in.

"Can you think of any reason Marjory would have done this? Had she seemed depressed lately?"

He rolled his eyes to the ceiling.

"There was the divorce, of course. We hadn't told anyone yet," he explained. "That was how she wanted it, and I went along, because… I suppose I thought it would make things easier to let her decide that side of things."

"I take it you initiated it then? The divorce, I mean."

"Yes. And to be clear, it was something that was decided well before her father passed. If I could have known everything that would have transpired since I announced I wanted to separate, I would have waited. God knows I'd already waited years as it was. What would another few months have been?" He shook his head.

"The financial ramifications alone would have been difficult for her to adjust to, but to add on top of that the death of her father and her sister… well, perhaps that's enough to break anyone."

He went silent, and Charlie spurred him on.

"And by financial ramifications, do you mean that the majority of your household income comes from your endeavors?"

"That's correct. And based on our prenup, she… well, it's quite specific. Marjory is to receive a single fifty-thousand-dollar payment upon the finalization of the divorce. A modest sum to almost anyone. But based on Marjory's lifestyle? It's not much. And now, with all the uncertainty surrounding her father's estate, I believe she'd be close to broke. At least in the short term."

Charlie considered the pains Marjory had taken to hide this detail. The story about remodeling the house to cover up the real reason she was packing her things. How even her family didn't seem to be aware of her impending divorce.

"I see," she said. "I mean, I can imagine that would be a lot for anyone to deal with."

When Trevor spoke again, his voice shook a little.

"Our marriage may have failed, but I didn't want… I mean, I'd never have dreamed that she'd hurt herself or anything like that. I just… I think…"

He trailed off again, just shy of divulging something, Charlie thought. She thought about asking him outright whether he thought Marjory was capable of murder, but something told her to take the subtle approach. Besides, the fact that Marjory would have been ruined financially after their divorce was an even stronger motive for her to murder Dutch in an attempt to cash in on her inheritance early. Charlie chose her next words carefully.

"Can I ask why the marriage… fell apart?"

Trevor studied her for a few seconds and took a long drink.

"It's all a bit complicated… but to begin with, I should explain that I have epilepsy. It's a rather common coexisting condition for those of us with cerebral palsy. When Marjory and I first met, I was having a bit of difficulty controlling my seizures. They left me quite weak and impacted my mobility, so I was using a wheelchair more frequently at the time. I think that gave her certain misconceptions about my... capabilities."

Trevor's tone was pointed. It was a few seconds before she grasped his meaning.

"You mean... sexually?"

"Yes," Trevor said, his demeanor matter-of-fact. "I had a somewhat sheltered upbringing. My parents are devout Christians, and I was raised believing all those virtuous things about waiting to have sex until marriage. On top of that, I was a very shy young man. I think it's part of my nature, but... having a disability that marked me as being different from my peers didn't exactly help me in the social department."

Trevor brought his shoulders up into a shrug.

"My point is that our wedding night was, you could say, something I'd been anticipating for a very long time." The smile he gave her then was tight and not altogether pleasant. "Only it became abundantly clear that Marjory had been under the impression all along that the reason I'd never... *initiated* anything before was because I wasn't able to have sex. And so began our marital woes."

"So you and Marjory have... never...?" Charlie said before realizing what an intrusive question it was. She held up a hand. "I'm sorry. You don't have to answer that."

"Please. I've been over this topic with so many therapists and marriage counselors at this point that I almost can't remember what it feels like to be embarrassed about it anymore." Ice cubes tinkled as Trevor swirled the contents of his glass. "Marjory found it within herself to, on occasion, join me in our marital bed. But only because she wanted children, you see. "

He took a long drink before setting the glass down on the counter.

"For a long time I thought it was me. That she found me... unattractive. But a few years back, we started going to counseling together, and she managed to convince me it was just... who she was. That she wasn't interested in that part of a romantic relationship. And she and the therapist even had a word for it: asexual. And of course it made sense logically, but it was more than that. I *wanted* to believe it, because it meant that none of it had anything to do with me. Had nothing to do with my disability." Trevor paused, shutting his eyes. "I was such a fool."

Charlie had been following him up until this point, but now she was confused.

"Sorry... are you saying Marjory isn't asexual?"

"That's exactly what I'm saying."

"But how can you know?" Charlie asked.

It seemed like the kind of thing you had to take someone's word for. Unless you caught them doing the very thing they said they had no earthly interest in.

"Marjory was having an affair," Charlie said, answering her own question.

"Yes," Trevor said, his mouth settling into a grim line. "Yes, she was."

CHAPTER SIXTY-SIX

The next few seconds passed with neither Charlie nor Trevor uttering a word. The only sounds were the hum of the fridge and the small crunches of Percival eating kibble.

"You caught her?"

"In the act? No." Trevor wiped a hand over his brow. "Nothing quite as sleazy as that. But Marjory keeps a journal, you see. And in it, she writes quite openly about her… escapades."

"A journal?" Charlie asked, unable to hide her interest.

"Yes, and lest you think me some kind of snoop, I happened upon it quite by accident. Marjory likes to think of the second floor of the house as *her* domain."

He gestured in the direction of the stairway at the front of the house.

"Stairs can sometimes be difficult for me, but I *can* climb them. Marjory just likes to believe I'm less capable than I am. I went up in search of Percival's nail clippers one day, and there it was, just sitting out on her dressing table. It was even open, like she'd left it there right in the middle of recording an entry. And I suppose curiosity just got the better of me. The irony is, I'd spent the first few years of our marriage practically obsessing over the idea of Marjory sneaking off to be with another man. Once I found out about her supposed asexuality, I felt like a jerk. Was I really that jealous? That insecure?" He let out a dry half laugh. "Only it turns out I was right all along."

"Who was Marjory having an affair with?" Charlie asked, thinking that whoever it was would be an ideal candidate for an accomplice.

"I don't know. She describes a great many things in the journal, but one thing she never mentions is a name." Suddenly Trevor's posture seemed to collapse. "I'm sorry. But are we about done? I really would like to sleep at some point tonight."

"Yes, and I appreciate you taking the time to answer my questions," Charlie said, hopping down from her stool. "I just have one last request. Before I go, could I take a look at Marjory's journal?"

"Take it with you, for all I care." Ice cubes clattered into the sink as Trevor dumped out his glass. "It should be on her dressing table upstairs. At the top of the steps, first door on the right."

Charlie padded down the hall and climbed the stairs. Her eyes strayed to the bathroom door where she and Zoe had discovered Marjory earlier this evening, and she quickly redirected her gaze.

Pushing through the door and into Marjory's room, she found the journal right where Trevor had said it would be. It was a small book with gilt-edged paper and bound in pale pink leather, the style with a strip of leather wound around it to keep it closed.

"Ugh, even her journal is so prissy it makes me want to barf," Allie said.

Charlie scooped up the book. Flipped through pages filled with an intricate scrawl. Tiny and neat.

She was itching to dive in now, but it was late, and she'd promised Trevor she'd leave. Tucking the journal into her bag, Charlie strode back to the stairs.

Trevor was waiting near the door to let her out when she reached the bottom of the staircase.

"One more question, and I swear it's the last one," Charlie said.

"Yes?" Trevor said, holding the door open.

"You said Marjory doesn't mention a name, but if I asked you to guess who she was having an affair with?"

Something like a laugh puttered out of his nostrils.

"I have my suspicions. Yes."

He fell quiet for a long moment after that. Charlie didn't press him.

"Her assistant. Killian Thatcher."

CHAPTER SIXTY-SEVEN

A little before noon the next day, Charlie drove over to where Zoe and a few other members of the sheriff's department were surveilling Killian Thatcher's home. Law enforcement had already been there for a few hours, but Charlie had overslept. With everything that had happened the previous day and night, she felt it was justified.

She parked on a side street and approached on foot, spotting Zoe sitting at the end of Killian's block in a silver Toyota Yaris.

Charlie peered in through the passenger window, waved, and then climbed in beside Zoe.

"Brought you a coffee," she said, passing the steaming cup over to her friend as she peered out at the houses on the street. "Which one is it?"

Zoe took the coffee and pointed with her free hand.

"Thirteen Sycamore Lane. The little brick guy over there."

The house was a dinky box of a home, albeit a clean one with attractive details. Tan brick with black shutters and a well-kept yard.

"You said on the phone that Killian Thatcher has priors?"

"Just one," Zoe said, lifting the cup to her lips and taking a sip from it. "An aggravated assault charge back when he was in college. But the charges were dropped."

"Why?"

Zoe shrugged.

"Nothing in the file to indicate why, but my guess would be that if he's ended up working this closely with Marjory Carmichael, he probably knows people."

"It's like he was born with… what do you call it?" Allie said. "That, uh, silver spoon or whatever in his mouth. Remember that show? *Silver Spoons*? With Ricky Schroder? Well, I kind of figure this whole deal is pretty much exactly like that show."

Charlie wanted to ask when Allie had ever watched an episode of *Silver Spoons*, but that was beside the point. And there was at least one part of what Allie had said that struck her. Killian Thatcher kind of looked like Ricky Schroder.

"What do you think about this angle?" Zoe said. "About Thatcher being Marjory's accomplice, I mean? He's her alibi for Dutch's murder, so right away that seems a little suspicious, right?"

"What about his alibi for the day Gloria was killed? He told me he was at Marjory's office most of that evening."

"That's where it gets good. There's a front desk with a security guard, and he confirms Killian coming and going."

"But?"

"But there's a back freight entrance. Marjory's supposed to be the only one who has keys for it, but who's to say she didn't lend them to Killian that day?"

"What about the timeline? Could he have made it across town to run down Gloria and then back to the office in time?"

"One of the detectives timed it earlier. He could do it with time to spare." Zoe paused to guzzle some coffee. "And I'm thinking, if it was him behind the wheel for that murder, maybe he was the one who ran you off the road. Meanwhile, realizing Dutch's fortune was a sham, Marjory tries to take the easy way out."

Charlie nodded.

"It'd make sense. Whole thing seems like an episode of *Dateline Mystery*."

Zoe's eyes went wide.

"Oh man, I love that show. Can you imagine if this ends up being featured in an episode? We might be on TV! On *Dateline*!" Zoe's gaze softened, and she went silent for several seconds, imagining it. Finally, she shook herself from the fantasy. "So what did the husband say?"

"He said the entire affair is pretty much laid out in here," Charlie said, pulling the journal from her bag. "And like I said before, Marjory never names him, but Trevor Steigel had no doubts that Killian Thatcher was the man."

"That's it, then? Marjory's journal?"

Charlie riffled through the pages.

"Yes, ma'am."

"Anything else interesting in there?" Zoe waggled her eyebrows.

"A little whining about politics at the Lamark Foundation and some grumbling about her husband, but the bulk of it is about meeting up with her secret manfriend."

"OK," Zoe said. "So here's what I'm thinking. We've got a little crack in the armor to work with, what with Marjory being laid up in the hospital. We need to pounce. Now. Prove that this assistant here is her lover and accomplice. With Marjory out of commission, maybe we can trip one or the other of 'em up. Keep 'em separated. Sheriff wants us to sit on Thatcher for the time being. We'll probably haul him in and question him eventually. Especially if he makes a move to get out of town. But if we can get some leverage on him in the meantime, that'd be ideal."

"Leverage," Charlie said. "Like proof of the affair?"

A wide grin split the bottom half of Zoe's face.

"Great minds think alike. I'm thinking that while we keep an eye on the guy, you finish reading the journal. See if there's anything that might implicate him or lead us to some hard evidence of their affair. Maybe they met at a hotel or something, and we can get footage from the security cameras or something like that. Whatever it is, there's gotta be something in there we can use once we get down to interrogating him."

Charlie opened her mouth to agree, but before she could, the front door of the brick house opened. Zoe gasped, and then she and Charlie went absolutely quiet. They both stared at the door.

An arm swung into the opening, and then he stepped out onto the stoop, closing the door behind him.

Killian Thatcher looked well dressed as always. Polo shirt. Khakis. Slightly formal for what must be his day off. His blond hair seemed wet, long strands slicked to his scalp in a side part. He seemed to hesitate, looking both ways before he stepped out onto the front walk. Almost like he could feel their presence, even if he didn't look their way.

His body language must have gotten Zoe's hackles up, too. They both ducked down in their seats.

"Is he bolting?" Zoe hissed, her whisper shrill and harsh.

He didn't move toward the car in the driveway to leave. Instead, he trotted down toward the curb. Opened the mailbox. Pulled out a wad of grocery store and fast-food fliers with a couple of envelopes tucked on top of the glossy paper.

"Not bolting," Charlie said. "Not yet, anyway."

On the way back, he dumped the load of junk mail in the green trash can tucked up against the side of the house. Then he disappeared back inside.

"OK," Zoe said. "Little bit of an anticlimax there, but… I don't know. He feels right to me. Do you think?"

Charlie could only nod in response. When she really searched her feelings, she thought it was possible. It could fit, could make sense.

"You'll keep me posted on the stakeout?" Charlie asked, reaching for the door handle.

"Naturally," Zoe said. "Same goes with you and Marjory's sex journal, yeah?"

"Sure thing."

As Charlie slid out of Zoe's car and headed back to where she'd parked, she stared down at the journal clasped in her fingers, thinking that the truth might well lie in the pages inside.

CHAPTER SIXTY-EIGHT

Charlie tipped her head back, the coffee mug clinking against her top teeth, and then the dark sludge poured in. It didn't taste good, but at least it was hot.

She slammed the mug down on the counter, refilled it, and then took it back to her desk. She could feel the zing in her eyes as the fresh caffeine entered her bloodstream, little electric throbs trying their best to wake her.

The last few nights of tossing and turning in awkward places had done their damage, however. It'd take more than coffee to undo this kind of exhaustion.

Marjory Carmichael's journal lay open on the top of her desk. Her neat handwriting filled the pages, front and back. Small text. Long paragraphs. A slog to get through.

Cover to cover, it was a constant stream of secret rendezvouses, liaisons, interludes, and so on. Marjory was so blasé about the affair in her entries, Charlie couldn't believe she hadn't kept it under lock and key. The one thing she hadn't done was use a proper name or any other kind of identifier for her potential accomplice. Instead, her mysterious lover was known simply as "he."

Her writing style, too, left something to be desired. Something about it was so formal, so populated with tedious details, rendering even a torrid love affair dull.

We made love as the sun set. The sky overhead was a glorious pastel arrangement of pink and lavender and peach. It reminded me of a

dessert I had on my last trip to Paris, a little crème tart topped with
fruit and different-colored macarons.

"I'm surprised she doesn't describe her guy's junk the same way," Allie said. "Dear diary, his manhood reminds me of a baguette I had in Lyon. It was fresh from the oven, still warm, and slathered with locally churned butter."

Charlie couldn't help but snort out a laugh.

She paused to yawn and stretch, giving her eyes a short break before returning to her task. She was going back through the journal now, focusing on the various locations Marjory had written about. So far, she'd described being "in the woods" quite a few times, particularly meeting "him" there. Other passages, seemingly referring to the same instances, mentioned being "along the water" or "on the water."

In and of themselves, these water references seemed fairly useless. When you lived on an island, you were never far from the lake. Still, the combination of woods and water seemed to be referring to a usual meeting spot. If she could suss that out, maybe it'd lead her to some hard evidence.

Charlie took a sip of her coffee. The heat tingling as it crossed her tongue. She got back to reading.

I guess we went a bit overboard with the Cabernet last night,
and he had a bit of… "trouble" when it came time to perform.
Thankfully, there was still some of the Viagra left from when we
experimented with it last year. I'd considered throwing it away,
but decided it might come in handy, so I'd tucked it in our little
hiding spot. A lucky move, or his overindulgence might have
spoiled our evening.

Allie snorted. "No one likes a soggy baguette."

Over the course of the next hour and a half, Charlie's eyelids grew heavier and heavier. The tiredness only strengthening no matter how much caffeine she threw at it.

The words squirmed on the page. Tired eyes flicking back and forth, trying to chase them down. Mentions of the woods or the lake woke her up some at first, but the endless drone of banality had worn down the effect.

She was nodding off when the phone rang. That finally jerked her awake. She checked the display: Zoe.

She thumbed the button. Brought the phone to her ear. "Hey Zoe."

"Tell me you've got something definitive in that journal." Some note of distress in Zoe's voice caught Charlie's ear.

"Not yet," Charlie said. "Why?"

"Looks like Killian Thatcher is making a move. For real this time."

"What do you mean? He ran?"

"Tried to. Bought a plane ticket to Switzerland at a travel agency here on the island. We had to arrest him before he left our jurisdiction."

Charlie sat forward in her chair. Suddenly, she was wide awake.

CHAPTER SIXTY-NINE

Charlie's chair squeaked as she rolled it back from the desk. She switched the phone to her right ear, considering what it might mean that Killian Thatcher had been trying to flee the country.

"But this is a good thing, right?" Charlie said. "In that it makes him look pretty guilty, I mean."

Zoe sighed.

"Sure. But it also means we now have a ticking clock. We wanted to slow-play it, watch him while we gathered info. But now that we've got him in custody, we have forty-eight hours to charge him or let him go. So if you can find anything in that damn journal, we need it like ten minutes ago."

Charlie's eyes flitted over the journal still lying open before her, those tightly packed lines of tiny text.

"I'm working on it. It sounds like they had some kind of regular meeting place, and I might be able to figure out the location."

"Anything concrete, you let me know right away. Something dramatic would be great, but any kind of leverage would be a help. Armed with some info, we can lean on him a little bit. Get under his skin. Give him the impression that we already know everything, that resistance is futile, so to speak."

"Well, I'll keep at it," Charlie said, already feeling a renewed sense of purpose. "You got him sitting in the interrogation room now?"

"Oh yeah. We'll let him stew a bit. He hasn't lawyered up yet, so at least there's that. He seems oddly calm so far. Personally, I don't care for the too-cool-for-school act, but I've learned to not read too much into that kind of thing. Anyway, I'll let you get back to it."

Charlie hung up, and her index finger traced along one of the scratches on the heel of her hand. The tiny cuts from the broken glass had all scabbed over, and she'd removed the bandages this morning.

She freshened her coffee and returned to the task at hand. Marjory rambled on about a disagreement at work for a few pages—something about putting together a pamphlet and needing some quotes, someone forgetting to bring in a magazine that seemed to slowly get blown out of any sensible proportion.

Then Charlie found something useful. Her eyes snapped to the word "boat" and raced down the page.

We were on the boat again this afternoon when calamity struck. We went way out in the water, the way he likes to do, out so far you can't see the shore any longer. It was sunny enough when we disembarked, but that changed all too quickly. Storm clouds gathered above us, the sky gone black. The water grew choppy, waves flinging themselves at the boat.

And then the sky opened up, and the heavens wept with incredible gusto. It poured. A forceful deluge unleashed, something biblical about it, a wrathful God out to punish. It didn't seem like drops so much as sheets of wet pounding the boat, watery explosions splashing up everywhere around us. We were both soaked to the bone within thirty seconds.

By the time we got back to the cabin, we were shivering and completely saturated, clothes and hair alike. So wet that even when we stripped down, a sheening layer of water clung to every inch of our skin. Our bodies shook like mad, teeth chattering. We hopped into the hot tub, which stung like crazy at first, and it still took a good five or ten minutes to stop the trembling.

Charlie's eyes drifted back up to the beginning of that last paragraph. She read it out loud.

"By the time we got back to the cabin."

Cabin. The meeting place—along the water, in the woods—was a cabin.

CHAPTER SEVENTY

Charlie's hand shook as she found Trevor Steigel's name in her contact list and punched the button to call him. With her hands half-numb, it felt like the phone was levitating next to her ear, a floating object mashing itself to the side of her face.

He picked up after two rings.

"Ms. Winters. I suppose I should have known I'd be hearing from you again."

Charlie winced at the mild tone of annoyance in his voice.

"Yes, sorry to bother you, but I had a quick question."

"Go ahead."

"In Marjory's journal, she mentions a cabin in the woods. And of being out on the water in a boat. Does that sound like somewhere familiar to you?"

"Of course. She must be talking about our vacation home on Lake Huron."

"Vacation home. Right."

"It's right at the tip of Michigan's thumb, not far from the town of Bad Axe. More trees than humans up that way. That was the idea, I suppose—have a place to get away from it all. No cell service. No internet. The only real link to the outside world is the landline."

Charlie remembered hearing mention of the cabin before. It was where Marjory had been headed when Gloria had been killed.

Her mind whirred, trying to think of a way to ask her next question without being too direct about the affair.

"Do you think it's possible Marjory was using the cabin as a… um… meeting place?"

Trevor made a noise. Not quite a chuckle, but almost.

"It's funny. Marjory always calls it a cabin, but this is more like a full-blown lodge—the mansion version of a cabin. Anyway, she's always really loved it up there. We had a big to-do for Dutch's seventy-fifth, and Marjory chose that as the location. Naturally, he didn't care for being cut off from technology for more than a few minutes and only stayed one night as I recall. Anyway... I wouldn't be surprised at all to find out that she's been using it for her dalliances. Unlike her father, she really, truly loves it out there."

Charlie was practically bouncing in her chair now. She had to stop herself from shouting the next question.

"Would there be any way to confirm when she might have been up there? I was thinking if it's a gated community, there might be a log to track the comings and goings."

"Well, I think maybe I've failed to get across exactly how rural this place is. The biggest town for seventy miles has a population of around two thousand souls. I wasn't exaggerating about the trees. They probably outnumber people a thousand to one up there. Maybe more. So no, there's no gate. There's not even another building within four or five miles, I'd guess. It's just the house, the lake, and a whole lot of nothing."

Charlie grimaced and squeezed her eyes shut.

"I see."

"But to answer your first question, I installed a state-of-the-art security system up there," Trevor continued. "I know Dutch hates that kind of crap, but, well, I ain't Dutch. I'm not going miles away from civilization unprotected."

Charlie's eyes snapped open.

"Cameras?"

"Absolutely. Cameras everywhere. Video and audio. I even paid extra to have them set up a bank of monitors in a utility closet. Looks like something out of a spy movie. Anyway, it's all motion-activated. Being that we sometimes go months at a time without using the place, the cameras and hard drives only kick on when someone enters one of the rooms. Anyway, yeah. There should be plenty of video of, well, whatever she's been up to of late."

Charlie plucked a pen from the mug on her desk and went to work scrawling down the address and some basic directions to the place.

"There's a keypad next to the front door," Trevor said. "I'll text you the code."

Charlie thanked him and was already halfway out the door and unlocking Frank's car before she'd hung up the phone.

CHAPTER SEVENTY-ONE

The tires juddered over the pocked bridge to the mainland. Charlie used voice commands to dial Zoe as she drove.

"I think I've got something," she said when Zoe picked up. "Marjory has a cabin on Lake Huron. It's mentioned a lot in the journal as a point of contact with Marjory and her loverboy. According to the husband, there's a pretty elaborate security system up there. Motion-activated cameras and the whole nine yards. So I'm heading up there. Hopefully I'll find footage of young Killian and his cougar girlfriend in flagrante."

"That sounds like a scoot," Zoe said.

"Yeah, it's up near Bad Axe. Close to the tip of the thumb. The drive will take a couple hours, and apparently cell service is nonexistent. I might have to wait until I'm driving back before I can tell you what I've found."

"Well, I'll keep my fingers crossed that you find the dirt." Zoe huffed, her breath audible over the phone. "We're gonna need it."

"How's the interrogation going?"

"Oh, our Mr. Thatcher is a smug one. We're playing it subtle for now. Making indirect mentions of a possible relationship between him and Marjory. He claims he has no idea what we're talking about."

Charlie merged onto the highway heading north.

"You think he's being truthful?" she asked.

"Hard to say. I figure we'll know more around the three-hour mark or so. That's kind of the magic number in my experience. Lots of guys are real cocky for those first couple hours, but then they start to wear down. The cracks start to show, and they get twitchy."

"Well, give me a call back if anything happens before then," Charlie said. "Might have to leave a message if I'm out of cell range."

"Will do. Good luck, my friend."

Charlie hung up and settled in for the long drive.

Civilization seemed to fade as Charlie trekked north. The buildings thinned out, and trees and overgrown thicket rose up to take their place. Soon it was all plant life. Shades of green dominated the roadside, flecked with the periodic dark earthen tones of tree trunks. All those leaves waved at her, but she couldn't decide if they meant to say hello or goodbye.

Most of the ride was quiet. Focused. Intense. Charlie tumbled the facts of the case in her head again and again, trying to stay objective, trying not to get her hopes up about what she might find at the cabin. But once she got to within ten or fifteen miles of the destination, the nerves spilled over into talk for Allie.

"You could probably start a kickass cult up here," Allie said.

"Oh yeah?"

"I mean, you've got all the privacy you could want. No meddling government. No nosy neighbors. Just gotta set up a badass compound, and let the isolation do most of the heavy lifting. Think about it, once you get this far away from the city, all you have to do is go out in the woods at night, and it feels like anything is possible."

"Not a lot of available recruits nearby," Charlie said. "Unless you want to start a cult of trees."

According to the population density map she'd checked before departing, the humanity in this region sharply declined from the 5,000-plus people per square mile in Detroit to a mere 1 to 10 per square mile in the part of Huron County where the vacation home was located. Hard to believe only 115 miles of road could separate such utterly opposing ways of living, Charlie thought.

"You truck the dupes up from Detroit," Allie said. "Not like it'd be hard to pry them out of that hellhole."

They took a right onto a private dirt road, Hideaway Lane. Charlie slowed to keep the flinging gravel from beating the hell out of Frank's car.

"This is it," Charlie said. "The house is about two miles down this road."

Charlie swiveled her head, really taking in the surroundings now. More pines mixed into the trees here, and vines seemed to tangle up in things, tentacle-looking tendrils draped up and down the foliage.

They wheeled around a curve and the washboard surface of the road sent a series of shocks through her body. Her palms tingled against the steering wheel, and she slowed further until the shaking receded.

And as they reached the end of the bend in the road, there it was.

The house jutted up from the land, a hulking structure that towered over the pine trees surrounding it. Trevor was right. This was no mere cabin.

Four lodge pole columns stood out from the front of the building, wood stained as dark as mocha. The pillars must have been at least fifty feet tall and fat enough to conjure thoughts of sequoias. The rest of the plank facade was slightly lighter in shade, perhaps the color of caramel, Charlie thought.

"Iced mocha," Allie said.

"What?"

"That's the color you're looking for. Iced mocha is slightly lighter than mocha. Let's be real, caramel is a step too far into the dreaded tan region."

"If you say so."

Charlie turned into the driveway, a long strip of spotless, interlocking pavers that gashed a gently curved pathway up to the house. The tires jostled over the seams in the geometric pattern beneath. Concrete made to look like dark-stained brick. The angular pattern made for a stark contrast to the rough and rustic look of the woods all around. Order amongst all the chaos.

The house came into full view as they moved toward it, the encroaching pines and a few rows of decorative bushes unblocking their view in stages.

Behind the house, the land sloped quickly down toward the lake, and for just a moment Charlie could see the pathway leading from the house to the water. A dock protruded into the lake, with a large boat lashed to it, gently bobbing with the waves. The fading daylight shimmered on the surface of the water, the glowing shapes shifting, disappearing, and reappearing as the wetness endlessly fluctuated.

The curve of the driveway slid these things out of view, the large house slowly filling Charlie's vision as she got close. She parked in front of a garage large enough to store at least four or five cars. Then she killed the engine and sat in the quiet for a moment, just looking up at the gigantic lodge. Finally, she undid her seatbelt and climbed out.

She crossed over the driveway and stepped onto a smooth concrete walk that snaked up to the front door, and the foliage reached out for her. Clumps of fern and wispy elephant grass. All of it a little too manicured, a little too presentable in this otherwise pastoral setting. A bit of the bourgeois family background creeping in where it didn't belong.

When Charlie reached the front door, she paused to take one last look out over the grounds. Everything was very still here in the wilderness, and it would be dark soon.

Then she turned, found the keypad, and punched in the code.

CHAPTER SEVENTY-TWO

A vaulted ceiling, crosscut by exposed wooden beams, stretched nearly to the heavens in the front room. A large stairway sloped upward in the center of the room, more of that mocha-colored wood heading up some twenty feet to the second floor.

It smelled like pine in here, that bracing green odor of crushed pine needles.

"Wood details accented with wood," Allie said. "Keep it simple."

Charlie stood just inside the door and took it all in. The house made her feel small, threatened to swallow her whole.

She turned back to swing the huge front door shut, and the sound of it closing echoed loudly in the empty space. Charlie flinched at the way the *thud* reverberated through the house.

Charlie pushed herself deeper into the cabin, moving past the stairway to take a quick glance around the downstairs. She didn't need to search the whole place. She reminded herself of that. Still, she thought maybe taking a quick peek into some of the rooms and getting a feel for the place would strip it of some of its strange power. Demystify it. Reduce it to the bougie vacation lodge it was. Nothing more. Nothing less.

To the right of the front room she found a den with a river rock fireplace—finally something prominent that wasn't brown. And a room off of that looked like a full-blown sports bar. Flat-screen TVs lined the wall behind the glossy wooden bar, fully stocked with booze. It even had stools and a brass bar running along the front of it. A dartboard occupied one corner, and a pool table was sprawled in another.

The kitchen looked industrial, like something that could legitimately serve as a restaurant kitchen at a place seating perhaps forty to sixty people, everything gleaming silver-gray. She peeked into the walk-in freezer and a pantry, both loaded with food. Crazy for a place that a small group of people used sporadically.

"Isn't it weird?" Allie said.

"What?"

"How no matter how much time you spend around rich people, you can't get used to the way they live?"

Charlie walked back to the front room. No more putting it off. She needed to head upstairs and get a look at that security footage.

She took a breath and started up the steps, wood creaking beneath her feet, creepy and loud in the quiet. Jarring. It made her stop and listen for a second.

Saliva welled in her mouth, and she swallowed. She tried to be quieter as she climbed the rest of the way, even if there was no one else here.

At the top of the steps, she checked a couple more doors, looking in on luxurious bedrooms with huge wooden four-poster beds covered in Pendelton throws and mounds of pillows.

Behind door number three, she finally found the utility-closet-turned-security-station, which she recognized by the bank of screens Trevor had told her about. Eight wall-mounted flat-screens completely filled the wall from the middle up. Blank, dark, and still. She couldn't help but be a touch disappointed, even if she knew it wouldn't last long. Still, even in its lifeless state, it was certainly the most elaborate security system she'd seen in a private residence. There was no denying that.

She took a seat in the small chair, a menagerie of controls laid out before her. Buttons. Switches. Faders.

She found the appropriate buttons, flicked on the screens, watched them come to life. The empty rooms of the lodge took shape on one screen after another, the live feeds coming up in stunning clarity until brilliant color filled all eight monitors.

CHAPTER SEVENTY-THREE

Charlie glanced once more at the screens, and all the empty rooms of the lodge gazed back at her. Nothing moved on any of the monitors, save for the fronds of a potted fern whisking gently in the front room, a furnace vent blowing them around. These were the live feeds, though. She needed to figure out how to access the archived footage.

Again, she ran her fingers over the assemblage of buttons and switches before her, scanned the variety of shapes and colors.

"What do you think that big red guy does?" Allie said, her voice suddenly hushed with reverent excitement.

Charlie ignored her, still looking for something that seemed likely to open the system's control menu.

"That one there, I mean," Allie said. "See it? It's like the shape of a stop sign."

Again, Charlie said nothing.

"Ohh…" Allie said, her voice increasing in volume. "Purple triangle! Charlie, for the love of God, push the purple triangle!"

Instead, Charlie fingered a small black button in the bottom left corner of the panel that read, "Main."

"What?! No!" Allie sounded like a toddler throwing a tantrum. "What part of 'purple triangle' did you not understand, idiot?"

The screens flickered to black, and then a blue menu popped up on the screen directly in front of her seat. White text listed the various options. It took Charlie a second to realize that it was a touchscreen. She leaned forward and tapped the "Video Archive" icon.

A new list populated the screen, generic file names and timestamps. She selected one of the most recent videos first.

Her own figure appeared there on the screen, peeking into the kitchen. She took a few steps into the room, poked into the walk-in freezer and pantry. She was slightly embarrassed to hear herself talking to Allie out loud. On video, the one-sided conversation made her look crazy.

"Looking a little slouchy, Chuck," Allie said. "Better get that posture righted before old age sets in, especially if you want to bag a man with some money before it's too late. Trust me, last thing any man of means wants is a hunchback."

Charlie scrolled back a few videos to the first one today. Clicked it. Watched herself walk through the front door. She realized that the video kicked in with the door already halfway open, so the motion-sensor took a second to trigger. That could be significant, depending on what she found later.

Anyway, all the videos from today were of her. That made sense. She needed to dig deeper.

She tried the last one before today, dated three days ago. A cleaning lady vacuumed the upstairs hallway, then another of her dusting. OK. Fair enough. A place like this would have a lot of staff coming and going. It was a huge place to keep up, especially to the exacting specifications of the ultra-wealthy.

She'd jotted a few notes from Marjory's journal in her phone, and she checked them now. She scrolled to the last date confirmed to have involved Marjory being at the cabin with her paramour. That'd be a good starting point. She tapped it.

The monitor fluttered, and then Charlie saw Marjory drying herself in the upstairs hallway. A towel wrapped around her body, held in place with one hand. The other arm worked at swishing a second towel at the back of her hair, which was sopping.

Charlie remembered the story about getting wet in the rain and then warming up in the hot tub. This must be that, she thought. So her adultery square-dance partner would be there, somewhere.

Motion in the corner of the screen caught her eye. A door behind and to the left of Marjory swung open, and the bright light of the bathroom shone out, all the lights above the vanity glowing white-hot. Marjory turned to face the motion.

And Charlie saw an arm appear there in the doorway—a man's arm. The rest of his upper body swung into view. Based on the motion of his arm, she could tell he was brushing his teeth, but he was facing away from the camera.

"Is that Killian the loverboy?" Allie said. "I can't tell."

It could be, Charlie thought. The size was about right. Tall and lean. Some muscle to him, enough to not be considered skinny, but no real bulk to his build.

The hair was wrong, though. Too dark. At first, she thought it could just be the wet making it look darker, but no. This was dark brown hair, nearly black. And Killian was, as Allie had mentioned several times, as towheaded as a kid in *Village of the Damned*.

Marjory walked off the screen, and the video cut out.

Charlie scrolled down, tapped an earlier video. The screen flickered, and an error message popped up. Something about missing data.

She tried another. Got the same error message. She tried several more before she gave up.

All the files before the drying scene had been erased.

CHAPTER SEVENTY-FOUR

Charlie sat very still, staring at the last of the error messages. Some new fury spiraled in her head. Made her grit her teeth.

Nothing. No evidence. No win.

She pushed herself off the corner of the desktop where the security console lay, the office chair thrust backward with a forceful jerk. It butted into the wall behind her.

Then she stood. Stormed out into the hallway. Paced a few steps down and then back.

Now what?

She replayed the short snippet of video in her mind as she paced the hallway. Saw the flash of a man's arm appear there in the doorway. Saw his back, his dark hair.

It'd seemed such a close thing, the truth right there, close enough to touch with the tips of her fingers, but it had all come to nothing. Missing data.

"If it'd make you feel any better, I saw all the fixins for grilled cheese down in the kitchen," Allie said. "A couple of those bad boys would really hit the spot, would they not? Have you eaten anything today?"

Charlie mumbled her answer, but her mind worked at something else, another memory flashing in her head.

"I ate a couple of Nutri-Grain bars on the drive."

"Wait. Aren't those Paige's?"

A memory from earlier in the day flickered in Charlie's mind. Something she'd read in the journal.

"There was a hiding place," Charlie said, freezing in place.

"For the Nutri-Grain bars?"

"No. In Marjory's journal." Charlie started moving again. "She talked about a hiding place at the cabin. Remember? The story about Marjory's dude drinking too much and needing to take Viagra?"

"Like I'm going to forget the story about loverboy not being able to get it up. That was the only decent laugh in the whole journal."

Charlie walked down the hall with purpose now, peeking in doors along the way. So far the bedrooms had been the same size, but she had a feeling that wouldn't be the case for all of them.

"Looking for the master suite, I take it?" Allie said.

Charlie nodded.

"It's no sure thing, but it seems the most likely place for a hiding spot," Allie said. "I mean, it sounded like Marjory loved bringing guests up here. What do you expect to find, though? Naughty photographs?"

"Well, if loverboy had a prescription for the Viagra, and the bottle is still there…"

"It'd have his name on it," Allie finished the thought. "Charles, you magnificent son of a bitch."

Charlie shrugged.

"It's at least a place to start. There's no way we can search this entire house."

At the far end of the hall, the last bedroom held what she sought. The master suite was a good three times the size of the guest bedrooms, and the high ceiling gave it a cavernous feel. Paintings of mountainous landscapes and hunting parties hung on the walls. In the center of the room, a double-sided fireplace divided the bedroom from the en-suite bathroom with columned openings on either side.

"What is with the bathroom being completely open to the bedroom?" Allie asked. "That's just weird and gross."

"Yeah." Charlie's voice echoed in the vast space. "It does seem weird to intentionally not have bathroom doors."

"Of course, if you absolutely *want* to watch your spouse take a shit, this is the only way to go," Allie said.

Charlie chuckled as she rifled through the drawers on the nightstand. But that wouldn't be much of a hiding place, would it?

She checked the obvious places: under the mattress, the HVAC vents, the far recesses of the large walk-in closet. She was nearly ready to give up when something in the closet caught her eye.

On the wall the closet shared with the master bathroom, there was a small, hinged door. Charlie crouched down before it. The panel was just like the one in the closet of the bedroom she'd shared with Allie growing up. The one Allie had always used as her secret stash spot.

"No way Marjory is as clever as I am," Allie said. "She's not on my level."

Charlie opened the hatch and peered inside. The light in the closet wasn't enough to reveal what was in there, and she had to stick her hand into the dark cavity and feel around.

Her fingers brushed over pipes and wires until finally they grazed something that crinkled. Plastic.

She pulled out a sandwich baggie containing a collection of pills in various size. Two shades of pale blue stood out from the otherwise white tablets.

"Oh-ho-ho! What have we here?" Allie said. "I'm thinking Viagra, Valium, Cialis, and Xanax. The perfect party. In order."

Just when Charlie had given up on the stash spot as containing solely pharmaceuticals, a solid black nub emerged from the jumble of pills. She couldn't tell what it was at first, but she opened the bag and plucked it out of the mess.

The little rectangle rested in the palm of her hand. The exterior looked featureless at first—solid black, smooth. Then she saw the seam running around about a third of the way down, and she knew what it was.

Sliding a thumbnail into the creased space, she popped the lid off, exposing the little metal mouth with the blue plastic held within. A USB connector. It was a thumb drive.

"Just doing some mental math here," Allie said. "We've got a thumb drive in suspiciously close proximity to a bunch of boner pills. Which leads, I think, to the question of the day: is there a sex video on the thumb drive, or are there *a bunch* of sex videos on the thumb drive?"

Allie giggled as she reached the end of her joke, but Charlie barely heard her. She was rushing back down the hallway to the security console.

She found a USB port just next to the purple triangle and plugged the thumb drive in. A circle wound around and around itself on the center of the monitor, and then a list of thirteen files popped up—all of them MKV extensions, which meant they were video files. The names themselves were generic, AK40001, AK40002, etc.

"Could be some of the deleted security videos," Charlie muttered as she sat in the office chair and rolled back up to the desk.

"Are you kidding? These are sex tapes, Charlie. I say tread lightly. I know this kind of thing turns your stomach."

"What? Shut up. Turns *your* stomach."

Charlie reached out for the screen, touched the first file on the list with the tip of her index finger. The screen snapped to black.

Then the video came to life. Right away, she could see that it was one of the deleted security videos. She recognized all of the gleaming stainless steel in the kitchen, the angle looking down from above.

And then she saw Marjory draped face up over the counter, a dark-haired man on top of her, his shirtless back to the camera. Kissing. Groping.

Unreal. This could be the accomplice, but she still couldn't see his face.

Most of the lights were off, one fluorescent bulb on the opposite side of the kitchen lighting the scene in long shadows. The system seemed to auto-adjust for the lack of light, though, so the details were plain enough. Too plain for Charlie's taste.

The shirtless man pawed at the buttons of Marjory's shirt. His face slid down her neck, kissing all the while. The muscles in his back rippled as he climbed onto her fully, mashing her down onto that stainless-steel counter top.

Marjory's face contorted in some ecstasy that almost looked like a snarl. Her hands fumbled to undo his pants.

"Gross," Charlie whispered.

"C'mon, the kitchen counter?" Allie said. "Food is prepared here! This isn't... isn't... sanitary."

Charlie moved a finger to the menu button on the console, but then she stopped herself. The outstretched finger trembled just shy of the screen. Her eyes widened.

The man lifted himself, his hands finding the corner of the countertop, triceps flexing. Then he turned, and the side of his face came into view at last.

Charlie gasped. Her eyelids fluttered. She couldn't make sense of what she was seeing at first. Couldn't process the information.

It looked like... But that couldn't be...

Brother and sister?

Another hard blink turned everything black for a second. When she opened her eyes again, the face on-screen was now almost fully in view, and there was no doubt left.

It was Brandon Carmichael.

CHAPTER SEVENTY-FIVE

Charlie's mouth dropped open. She couldn't think. Couldn't breathe.

She stared at the screen, Brandon's figure frozen there, draped over Marjory, a carnivorous look in his eyes.

"Marjory and Brandon," Allie said, her voice blank from shock. "That's… that's *incest.*"

A chill gripped the backs of Charlie's arms, and she shivered. She yanked the thumb drive from the USB port and tucked it in her pocket.

When Charlie replied, she was surprised to hear the strength of her own voice, the clarity of her thoughts.

"Keeping something like that secret would make for the ultimate motive," she said. "This must be what Gloria figured out. Fits the 'sordid and disgusting' bill, don't you think?"

"Holy shit," Allie said. "Uh, yeah. That would explain… a lot."

"It fits," Charlie said, talking to herself as much as Allie now. "If Gloria found out about Marjory and Brandon, they'd stop at nothing to hide their secret. And while Marjory had an alibi for that crime, Brandon didn't."

"And Dutch?"

"Marjory's alibi has always been weak. I think the whole story about sleeping off a headache is a lie. She let her assistant see her that morning and then slipped over to her father's house without anyone knowing she was gone."

"Jesus." Allie's voice was just a little hiss now.

"It's still not hard evidence that they did all of this, but… it paints too perfect of a picture, doesn't it? My gut believes it. Brandon and Marjory. Working together. Now I just have to prove it."

Even as the puzzle pieces snapped into place in her mind, she struggled to think straight somehow. There was something else she needed to do here…

Her hand patted at her pockets. Felt the bulge of her phone there on her left hip. Yes. That was it. She needed to call Zoe. Let her know about all of this. The man they were interrogating was innocent. Marjorie's accomplice was Brandon Carmichael.

She dug the phone out. Scrolled to Zoe's number on the contact list.

She blinked down at it, overwhelmed at the prospect of pressing this button. Lights spun in her head, her vision blurred. These were symptoms of shock, she knew.

She closed her eyes. Sucked in a deep breath. Let it out slowly. Centered herself.

When she opened her eyes, she finally was able to take in the lack of bars in the upper corner of the phone. No cell service out here. Of course, she knew that.

"OK. No cause for panic. I'm pretty sure Trevor mentioned a landline," she said aloud, again talking to herself more than to Allie. "And if I can't find that, I can drive down the road until I get some bars. If I head toward Bad Axe, I should get something sooner than later."

Just as she went to stand, the front door slammed shut downstairs. The thud seemed to shake the whole house.

"Oh, *shit*," Allie said.

CHAPTER SEVENTY-SIX

Charlie's eyes went wide. Her heartbeat thundered in her chest. She didn't dare breathe.

Someone was here. With her. Now. In the cabin. She could hear them downstairs.

The heavy footsteps clattered across the floor, loud in the stillness.

"It's probably a maid or something, right?" Allie said.

Charlie said nothing. She slipped the stun gun out of her bag and let her finger find the trigger. Then she glanced at her phone, saw that little "No Service" staring back from the upper left-hand corner. And she didn't know where the landline was.

Instinct told her to run. Scramble out into the hallway. Duck into one of the bedrooms. Find a place to hide.

The security closet felt like a trap. A cell. If anyone came close, she'd have no way out. And if it was who she thought it was downstairs, this might well be the first place he looked.

She didn't run, though. She froze. Waited. Listened.

She heard the intruder's feet hit the stairs like sledge hammers thumping down on each tread.

THUMP.

THUMP.

THUMP.

The wood moaned and creaked, deafening in the quiet.

Charlie turned back to the bank of monitors. Splayed fingers shaking over the console. Eyes scanning back and forth, flickering too fast to focus on anything.

Panicking.

She forced in a deep breath. Found what she needed.

She clicked a couple buttons to get the live feeds back on the screens. All the rooms showed empty on the monitors—blank and motionless, save for one.

And there he was. Broad-shouldered and dark-haired. His flannel shirt a blur of red on the monitor.

He bobbed as he ascended the stairs. Face mostly expressionless except for some glint of darkness in his eyes.

Then he disappeared off the edge of the first monitor and reappeared on another—the one showing where the staircase met the second-floor hallway. He moved left to right, sloping upward alongside the banister.

He tilted his head, a ripple passing over the muscles in his jaw.

Brandon Carmichael climbed the steps, a handgun dangling from the end of his arm.

CHAPTER SEVENTY-SEVEN

The footsteps grew louder. Closer.

Charlie flipped the switch to turn the monitors off and saw copies of herself reflected in the blank screens. Blinking. Trembling slightly.

The stun gun wouldn't do much good against a nine millimeter. She tucked it into her hip pocket.

Then she spun to her right. The door into the security closet was open a crack, and she reached for the knob. Clasped her hand around it in slow motion.

Her mind raced. Tried to come up with options. Play out plausible scenarios in her head.

Should she hide here? Or chance a trip out into the hall? Which would buy her more time?

Brandon would know she was here. He must. The car out in the driveway wasn't hers, but why else would he have the gun in his hand?

She was the next obstacle to overcome. The next threat to the family secret. The open loop that needed closing.

Yes. He'd know why she was here.

She took one last breath and held it. Edged the door open as quietly as possible. Needed to be quick and quiet as she bent low and shuffled into the hall. Into the open.

She pulled the door most of the way closed behind her, not quite daring to latch it and make a noise.

Then she tiptoed a diagonal path across the hall, suddenly exposed and vulnerable. The five paces felt endless.

She dared a glance to her right. Couldn't quite see the top of his head jutting up from the staircase.

Any second now, he'd be there. Right there.

When she reached the opposite side of the hallway, she ducked into a bedroom and eased the door shut behind her. The wood settled into the jamb without a sound, but the latch clicked when it caught. A faint snick of metal on metal.

She hunched her shoulders. Waited for some change in the rhythm in the footsteps. A pause to indicate that he'd heard the click.

But no. The thumps carried on as before.

She took in the room around her. A queen bed took up most of the floorspace along the far wall. An oversized quilt was draped over it, reaching almost to the floor—rust-red fabric patched with cream and gold, with bears and moose and ducks embroidered onto it.

A cherry-wood dresser huddled opposite of the bed. More of those dark wooden details lined the windows and ran a border around the middle of the room.

At first glance, she didn't see anything of immediate use. No blunt objects or other makeshift weapons at the ready, not that they'd do her much good in a gunfight.

Charlie's head snapped back the way she'd come. Her eyes scanned up and down the crease where the door and its frame meshed, lingering on the brushed brass doorknob.

No deadbolt. No way to lock herself inside. That left her without much choice. She could hide here for the moment, but she'd ultimately need to keep moving. Avoid him. Get to the car.

His footsteps changed as they reached the top of the steps. Muffled by the lush carpet.

She heard him trail down the hall. Move to the security closet. That metallic snick of the latch replaying as he opened the door.

Silence.

He paused there for what must have only been a few seconds even if it felt longer. Then the footsteps started up again, coming her way.

Charlie scrambled underneath the bed. Churning her arms and legs. Wishing for the patch of darkness there to swallow her, those flaps of bedspread to conceal her.

The rough Berber carpet grated at her elbows, and her shoulder blades grazed the wooden planks that formed the supports for the mattress. It smelled like dust and old potpourri.

She flattened onto her belly and wriggled the last stretch like a worm. Inching. Hip bones shuffling her forward until she was fully concealed, reaching back to cover her entryway with the bedspread just as the bedroom door burst open.

His shoes stood there in the doorway, the rest of him cut off by the quilt shielding her view.

CHAPTER SEVENTY-EIGHT

Brandon Carmichael stepped into the room. A single step. Then he stopped.

The soles of his shoes squished the carpet. Bent the pile downward in semicircles around the balls of his feet. It made the floor look warped.

Charlie heard the faintest wind flutter between her lips, and she reminded herself to hold her breath. To make no sound.

Her eyes snapped upward. Looked where the gun would be. Then where his face would be.

But the bedspread and frame blocked her view. She saw pale planks of wood. Saw one of the ducks on the blanket smiling at her.

He took a few steps forward.

Careful movements. Precise. Feet rocking heel to toe.

The carpet tilted under the treads of his shoes. Molded to his every touch.

All Charlie could see were the cuffs of his jeans nestled over a pair of Adidas.

The shoes stopped at the foot of the bed. Feet set wide. Just more than shoulder-width apart.

He stood there. Motionless. Silent.

Charlie's skin prickled and itched at the knowledge of how close he was.

Her breath constricted in her throat, and she blinked. Scraped her bottom lip against her teeth. Felt the pattern of the carpet etching into her palms. Dared not move.

Sweat leaked down from her hairline, snaking down her temple and tickling over her cheekbone. The saltiness clung to the corner of her mouth.

He let out a sigh. But how to read it? Frustrated? Aggressive? Resigned? Disappointed?

He shifted his weight. And Charlie's mind moved a million miles per second, imagining his face appearing next to hers against the carpet. A cocky smile playing at the corners of his lips.

Instead he turned. Squared his feet toward the open doorway. Paced across the room, back the way he'd come.

Charlie scraped her bottom lip against her teeth again. Felt the sharp little bones grate at the soft pink flesh.

Some disbelief welled in her. Made her blink several times. Verify what she was seeing.

Brandon's feet stepped through the doorway and moved out of sight.

She listened. Strained to hear through the sound of her pulse thudding in her ears. Fought back the panicky feelings that fought for her attention.

The footsteps trailed away. Heading down the hall. Probably planning to work his way down. Room by room.

This was her only chance.

No hesitation this time. No thinking. She slithered out from under the bed.

CHAPTER SEVENTY-NINE

Charlie peered through the open doorway.

He was there. All of him now, not just the feet. A walking shadow at the far end of the hall. He turned right and disappeared into a bedroom doorway. Perfect.

She darted into the open. Heart punching in her chest.

Her eyes focused on the top of the stairwell. Trying to zoom in on it like a movie camera.

She hunched down, instinctively making herself smaller. If she beat him to the steps, she could beat him to the door. If she beat him to the door, she could beat him to the car.

Then? Spill out onto the road, into the night, into the open. Into some place with cell service. Far away from here.

As the wall cut off to her left and the banister took shape there, Charlie got an overwhelming urge to leap over it, hop it like a subway turnstile. Of course, she'd plummet some twenty-five feet and snap both of her ankles, but the urge to flee was so strong that—to the panicking part of her brain—this strategy made perfect sense.

Instead she closed on the top of the stairs. Eyes flicking to the bedroom doorway in the distance. Waiting for him to emerge and see her.

He didn't.

She hit the steps. Flying downward. No longer worried about sound.

She could do this. Win this race. Beat him outside. Get to the car. Get gone.

She hit the landing and vaulted herself over the banister to bypass the last ten or so steps.

Flying. Soaring. Weightless.

Then the ground came rushing up. Too fast. Too hard.

She landed on hands and knees, body folding on impact. Compacted into a tight ball ready to spring for the door.

His feet pounded down the steps behind her. Faster than before.

The massive slab of dark wood was within arm's reach.

Hand extending. Fingers clenching.

She jerked open the front door and raced into the night.

CHAPTER EIGHTY

Charlie slammed the door behind her. Wood cracked against wood. She heard its echo shiver off the siding of the house. The great clap rolling upward and outward.

She banked left onto the front walk. Picked up speed as she slalomed through the foliage, traversing that snaking path to the driveway.

Her feet felt light now, skimming over the concrete.

Decorative plant life snagged at the arms of her shirt. Raked at her skin. Cold and prickly.

The branches wagged back and forth upon releasing her. Snapping and shaking. Leaves swishing out sibilance where they fell against each other.

She barreled on. Listened for the door behind her. Sprinting past the largest of the shrubs. And there it was.

Frank's Buick. So close now. A floodlight over the garage shimmered a yellow pool where it touched the glass of the windshield.

She ran for it. And a glow blossomed in her skull. A flare. A blaze. A lightness that drove out all the darkness.

Hope.

She could do this. Would do this. Was already doing it.

She stared straight ahead. Unblinking. And she saw only the car now. Nothing else was quite real.

It seemed to float ever closer like a mirage on the horizon. A gleaming, shimmering thing. Not quite tethered to the ground from her vantage point.

She arrived at the car, her forward momentum crashing her outstretched hands into the driver's side door. Then the rest of her body hit, pinning her arms against the vehicle for a second before she pulled herself off. Got her body back under control.

And a jolt of fear came over her. A delayed reaction that sent cold electricity shooting through all her nerves. Her chest flitted. Sucked in a ragged breath.

Those couple seconds lost to clumsiness, to impatience. Would they matter?

Trembling, she reached for the handle. Panic thrusting pins and needles into her fingertips.

Some part of her was sure that something would stop her here. Just shy of opening the door. Just shy of touching that door handle.

But then it was there. The chrome in her hand, in her grip. Cold metal.

She opened the door. Swung it aside.

The big front door of the lodge ripped open behind her. The door making a sucking sound as it peeled away from the frame.

Brandon's footsteps clattered toward her. Already growing louder.

And the driver's seat lay open right before her. Ready. Waiting.

But something was wrong. She felt it before she understood why.

She glanced down and saw that both tires on this side of the car were flat.

CHAPTER EIGHTY-ONE

She took off again. Wheeling around the rear end of the car.

Her feet scuffed over the blacktop. Threatened to slide out from underneath her as she cut sharply at the bumper.

But then she was moving again. Darting forward. Accelerating.

She crossed the driveway. The hard asphalt underfoot quickly transitioned to the soft of the grass.

Brandon was closing on her. She could hear him.

He yelled something into the night. Three syllables. Voice sharp and raspy. Full of rage.

But she couldn't make out his words. Adrenaline surged through her veins and blocked out everything else.

Run.

Run for the darkness.

She moved out of the perimeter of the exterior lights. Into the relative blackness beyond the side of the garage. Angled herself away from the house.

And she picked her knees up higher. Pushed off harder.

Her toes dug into the soft earth. Exploded upward from the ground with all the force they could muster. Propelled her onward.

She moved into the pines huddling on this side of the property. Darker still. Cover to be had among the boughs. If only temporarily.

Pine needles brushed at her. Scraped at her arms. Tousled her hair. Coarse bristles.

Faint swishing sounds accompanied her. Needles whispering to her with each step. Excited by the chase.

Something sizzled and crashed to her left. Startled her until realization arrived a second later.

Water. The waves of Lake Huron surging up onto the beach and rolling back.

She couldn't see it through the foliage, but it must be close.

She veered away from the water's edge. Wanted to get deeper into the cover of the woods, into the dark. The beach would be too open.

Soon the pines around her gave way to thicker oaks and maples. Fatter trunks. Higher limbs.

The spaces between the trees widened. Parts of the ground laid bare. Silvery moonlight spilling through the gaps to dapple the dirt and dead leaves underfoot.

She felt exposed without all the interlocked pine boughs wagging around her. Ferns. Prickers. Dense green covered the ground in tangles, reaching up waist-high in places.

She worked hard to keep going. Picking out the best path she could in this mess of greenery. Trudging through the snarls of foliage.

And she heard him crashing along behind her. Somewhere not so far back there. Knees and feet beating their way through the bush. Breath heaving through his teeth.

She swiveled her head. Glanced back.

Some disturbance ruffled the green. Stalks and stems thrashing. Leaves all aflutter.

But she couldn't see him. Couldn't pick out his shape among the moving bits. Even if he must be within twenty or so feet by now.

A louder crash erupted. His footsteps stopped.

He'd fallen, she realized. Hard from the sound of it.

Something between a smile and a grimace spread over Charlie's face. She picked up her pace and focused on the path ahead again.

He yelled something into the night. One syllable. Probably a curse.

She veered harder right now. Partially circling back the way she'd come in a wide arc. She'd take a chance here. Try to outsmart him.

The fall would have rattled him. Frustrated him. Confused him. He'd focus on charging ahead. Try to make up lost time. He'd make too much noise to hear her coming back the other way.

She could hear him thrashing through the brush again. On the move in the wrong direction.

Charlie built speed as she pushed into the pines. There was less to think about here than in the thicket. Just run to the light. Stay between the branches.

The sound of his feet trailed away, just as she'd figured it would. Soon she couldn't hear him at all.

Good. She'd bought herself some time.

Lights glinted through the thinning trees. Even partially obscured, she recognized the glow. Solar landscaping lights and the flood bulb shining down from the top of the garage.

She must be coming up on the end of the woods. That clearing of grass was just ahead.

A fresh plan started to formulate in her head.

The lodge emerged as she broke through the last row of pines. The towering structure forming from the darkness. The light slanting down on the sheets of cladding. Solid. Real. Close.

She rushed for it.

CHAPTER EIGHTY-TWO

Charlie darted back into the house. Her toe caught on the threshold and sent her spilling into the foyer in a stagger.

Choppy steps. Shoulders pitched forward. Not quite falling.

She righted herself. A strange fluttering flailed in her chest. An overwhelming brew of emotions whirring there.

Excitement. Hope. Anxiety. Terror.

White light speared her eyes. Illumination attacking from every angle. So bright after all that dark. But she didn't slow.

She squinted her eyelids to slits and kept moving, kept pressing ahead.

Being back in the well lit space intensified her vulnerability to the point that her skin crawled. She dug the stun gun from her pocket. It might not be much good against Brandon's gun, but she felt better with it in her hand.

She scanned every surface in the big entry room. Vases. Mirrors. Plants. Trophy fish.

No phone.

She veered right. Into the den.

Again her eyes flitted over the surfaces here. Lamps. Magazines. A cigar box.

There. A landline. On the desk.

She zipped toward the beige rectangle. Eyes going so wide they stung along the edges from all the brightness.

She didn't fight it. The pain didn't matter anymore. Only the phone.

She lifted the receiver. Punched those three digits with her index finger—911—and brought the phone to her ear.

Her whole body thrummed with anticipation. She rocked her weight from foot to foot. Fought back the panic.

And she stared down at her reflection on the glossy desktop—this version of her face stained dark like the wood. Noticed the wet beads of perspiration clinging to her top lip. Clear jewels that glittered where the light touched them.

She waited for the sound. Waited for it.

Closed her eyes. Gritted her teeth.

Nothing.

She sucked in a breath. The whole world seemed incredibly quiet. Incredibly still.

And then it hit.

The phone was dead.

The disbelief clobbered her in the center of her chest. Sent the breath whooshing out of her, a hissing sound as the air and hope leaked out as one. Another hole punched into her plans.

She hung up the phone and tried again. Finger stabbing the switch hook several times in rapid succession. Listened for the dial tone.

Nothing.

She panted. Felt the blood beating in her temple, an uneven throb that battered along at a speed-metal tempo.

He'd cut the line. Probably around the time he'd slashed her tires. He'd come here with a plan.

She couldn't dwell here. Needed to keep moving.

She slammed the phone down. Turned just in time to see Brandon standing in the doorway to the room.

Her gaze jumped to the object at the end of his extended arm: his gun leveled at her head.

She froze. Eyes drifting to the barrel of the gun. That gaping black hole that seemed to grow as she looked into it.

A smile spread over the bottom half of his face.

But his eyes were dead.

CHAPTER EIGHTY-THREE

"Looks like playtime's over," Brandon said. "Drop your little toy there."

Charlie could hear the note of amusement in his voice—the faintest lilt of delight—even if he was no longer grinning. She released her grip on the stun gun, watched it bounce once on the rug and go still.

Her chest deflated. A sickened feeling welled in her gut so hard it made her double over as if to retch.

He gestured with the gun, pointing her toward the other entrance to this room.

She obeyed. Walked slowly toward the second doorway between two bookcases as he fell in behind her.

She thought he'd say something. Gloat more. But he stayed quiet.

They passed a formal dining room with a massive table and a set of bulky chairs. Another exterior door loomed against the far wall. They must be heading back outside. Toward the lake.

He hadn't killed her. Yet. There had to be a reason for that.

Perhaps he'd want to make it look like an accident. Just like Dutch. Just like Gloria. Keep all suspicion off of him, even if Marjory was still in the crosshairs of the police investigation.

She felt his shadow creep right up on her as he jabbed the barrel of the gun into the small of her back.

"Go on and pick up the pace, little rabbit," he said. "No use stalling now. No use fighting. Just go on and get what you came for."

He laughed at that last line before he went on, and she could feel his breath on the back of her neck.

"That's right. You came here for this, whether you knew it or not. As sure as fate."

He flicked a switch as they neared the rear entrance. A harsh glow bloomed through the window panels cut into the back door.

Bright floodlights shone down on the massive backyard.

Brandon hustled up in front of her to open the door, still vaguely pointing the weapon in her direction even as he did.

"No funny shit, alright?" he said. "You try it, I promise you'll regr—"

She didn't wait for him to finish. Charlie got low and rushed him. Pushed his gun arm up over her head and gave him a shove, hoping he'd be thrown off-balance enough to give her a decent head start.

And then she was bolting through the open door, bounding down three concrete steps, and careening to the right. Plunging over a patio of fitted flagstone. Racing for the cover of the closest cluster of trees.

But he was on her right away. And with a simple nudge between her shoulder blades, Brandon sent her flying.

She sprawled in the air. She tried to will herself to land in the grass, but it was no good.

She hit elbows and knees first on the slab of stone. Scraping forward on the rough surface. Ripping a layer of skin off.

The pain intensified when she rolled over and the air assailed the wounds. An incredible sting. The hurt shuddered through her. Made her curl up like a crushed spider.

And then she was moving to get to her feet again. Trying to stand. Trying to run.

Arms snaked around her torso. Constricting. Getting her under his control.

He bashed her in the nose with the butt of the gun. Metal crunching against bone. The force of the blow sat her straight down on her butt.

She could feel the pain throughout her entire body. A splitting. A sundering.

Tears flooded her eyes. Made everything blurry.

Two breaths later, the blood came gushing from her nostrils. Red cascaded over her mouth and chin. She could taste the metal of it on her lips.

She tried to blink the tears away. Tried to wipe the blood away. Neither attempt was successful.

She stared down at the thick red smeared over her fingertips. Dark even under the bright lights. Still blinking, even if the tears just kept coming.

"See how that works?" he said. His dark silhouette towered over her, head wagging in a way she read as cocky. "Try running again, and I'll bash it again. Believe me, the second time, with the nose already busted and that piece of cartilage wigglin' around in there, hurts a whole lot worse."

And she knew now that she wouldn't run. Couldn't run. She'd need to find another way.

CHAPTER EIGHTY-FOUR

Charlie staggered across the backyard, and the man with the gun followed closely behind her. Every so often she felt a soft puff of his breath twirl just above the collar of her shirt. It tickled in a way that made her want to cringe.

Defeat crept over her body. Her nose throbbed. Bright flashes of hurt radiating outward from the broken thing. The flesh of it felt hot too. Fevered. She could only imagine what kind of mangled pig snout occupied the center of her face just now.

And blood still wept down from her nostrils. Her back and shoulders ached. The dull pain of fatigue, of exhaustion.

Emptiness occupied her mind. Listlessness. A lethargic daze. That was the worst of it, she thought. The way all the fight had seeped out of her, leaking from a hole she couldn't repair. Draining out along with the blood perhaps.

"Don't even tell me you're giving up now," Allie hissed. "You don't get to quit."

Brandon jabbed the gun into the small of her back to keep her moving. The soles of her shoes scuffed the concrete as she dragged her heavy feet.

Allie continued, "If he wanted to use the gun, he would have done it already. You said it yourself. He'll want it to look like an accident."

They followed a long path, moving away from the house. The trail of pale cement reflected some illumination from the lights bearing down on them, made a splash of brightness over the dim ground. A glowing path that led to what? Death, she supposed.

Charlie knew that it led to the dock she'd seen earlier, even if she couldn't see it just now. The lights didn't reach that far.

Trees jutted up around them now and again. They looked eerie in the gloom. Blackened trunks protruding from the grass. Twisted limbs reaching outward like so many elongated arms.

The dark huddling around the branches looked smoky just now, Charlie thought. All of the shadows turned strangely oversized from the angle of the lights, like when a spider zips across the wall at night and the shadows of the skittering legs stretch out to about ten times the size of the arachnid itself.

Visible or not, Charlie knew the water was out there, the endless blue of Lake Huron some hundred or so yards beyond their current position. She could hear it slapping at the beach, waves surging up to touch the land over and over.

But she couldn't see it yet. The glow of the lights only reached another fifteen feet in front of them.

Inky blackness lay past that point. An ebon wall that revealed nothing. It made her uneasy. Made her swallow hard, her throat sticky and dry.

The sound of the water lapping at the shore grew in volume as they neared it. The wet sounds made her shudder, even if she didn't know why.

They trekked past the borderline where the lights gave way to the night. Moved into the full darkness at last.

At first, Charlie could only see the faint pale hue of the concrete path underfoot in the blackness. That once glowing path dimmed down to almost nothing like a dying ember.

She walked on it. Tried to focus on it. Tried not to gape into the nothingness that occupied all else just now.

But her eyes began to adjust. Form took shape in the void as it always did.

The moon came first. An orb of light above. No longer dulled and blocked by the harsh artificial light.

Then the stars faded in. Glowing pinpricks that occupied the sky from the horizon up.

Those sinister trees re-emerged. Blacker than the rest. Solid things, if twisted.

Soon even the texture of the grass began to show some, if distorted for the moment. Like a layer of peach fuzz lining the ground.

The sound of the lake caught her attention again. The surf crashing against the beach in the dark. Closer than ever.

She could make out movement in the distance. Liquid thrashing that she knew must be the waves, even if she could discern little detail for now.

She remembered the lakefront as she'd seen it in the daylight.

The long dock extended into the water, waves rippling alongside it, the surface of the water a shimmering, chaotic thing that never stopped moving. And then she remembered what lay alongside the dock.

A boat.

A cabin cruiser, as she recalled. Yes. This scene was starting to make more sense to her, even in her deflated state.

He was going to take her out on the boat. If he took her out far enough, he wouldn't need to use the gun at all. A burial at sea made to look like an accident. A drowning. Let the body wash up on the shore, bloated and fish-belly white. Neat and tidy. No forensic evidence to speak of.

And that was if she was even found. Lake Huron was practically a sea, it was so vast. Twenty-three thousand square miles of churning, thrashing water. Her body was just as likely to sink to the bottom where all the marine life would pick her bones clean.

Charlie could see a change in the path ahead. That smooth cement trail receding into something darker, right where the water met the coast.

She marched toward the dark place. Not sure what else to do.

The sidewalk ended and the dock began. The wood sounded hollow underfoot. Thudding and ringing out reedy notes like a giant xylophone.

The smell of the lake came clearer out here in the open. Crisp and fresh.

And a great sprawl of night seemed to spread outward from here. The great wide open. No more trees or bushes around. No more grass. Just planks of wood laid out atop the choppy water. Empty air all the way to the horizon.

Moonlight gleamed down on the top of the boat. The silvery glint changing shapes as the vessel rocked back and forth.

They sidled up to it, and Brandon waved the gun at the deck.

"Hop on board," he said.

Charlie stepped up and on, and the boat shifted beneath her feet. Tilting.

Brandon knelt to undo some ropes, and Charlie gazed over the opposite edge. The water seemed mostly peaceful now that she was closer.

She clenched her fists. Resisted the urge to jump into the shallows. Wade away into the dark.

It'd never work. Running in the water was so slow. He might not want to shoot her, but she knew he would if given no other choice.

He boarded the boat. Feet thumping over the deck as he moved to the captain's seat.

He lifted the cushion and pulled a length of rope from the cavity there. Something heavy thunked down beside his feet. Seconds passed before Charlie realized it was an anchor.

With the press of a button, he fired up one motor. Then he pressed another, and a second growl joined the first.

The grind of the engines leveled out into a purr, and the vibration thrummed upward from below.

Brandon eased up the throttle, and they were off. Moving out into the vast expanse of Lake Huron.

"I figured we'd take a little ride," he said. "Just the two of us."

CHAPTER EIGHTY-FIVE

The boat rocketed out into the nothing. Brandon flicked on a light now and again—a strange wedge of glow slicing into the blackness, shimmering on top of the dark water—but they mostly traveled in the inky gloom.

That made sense, Charlie thought. Fit his plan. He probably wanted to stay as low-key as possible until they got way out in the deep.

Away from the shore. Away from civilization. Away from any lurking Coast Guard types, though she doubted they were even out at night, unless they had a reason. Miles away from everyone, out where light didn't matter anymore.

The wind whipped at her face as the boat accelerated. Cold biting at her cheeks. That heavy lake air turned wintry at night, a humid type of chill that saturated her flesh rapidly.

Charlie flinched when Brandon spoke. His raspy voice rising out of the darkness, sending another kind of chill all through her.

"You know, if we head due north from this spot, we wouldn't hit the shore for, oh, a hundred and fifty miles or something like that. Pretty wild, right? People don't understand just how big a bastard ol' Lake Huron really is. Seven hundred and fifty feet deep, at its deepest. Two and a half football fields of water, straight down."

His silhouette shook its head. And she could see a faint wetness split the shadow face in front, his smiling teeth shiny with saliva.

"You ever swim fifteen miles in rough waters? Thirty miles? Might be a little chilly, though. Or what's the word? Frigid."

Two puffs of laughter vented from his nostrils, and then a few moments of silence passed.

"So quiet," he said, and it was a second before she realized he was talking about her. "And here I thought you'd have questions. You had so many before."

Charlie didn't respond, which seemed to amuse him even further.

"Or do you think you have it all figured out?"

She ground her molars together. She didn't have any real interest in talking to him, but maybe it would buy her some time. Distract him and deliver some kind of opening.

"Marjory's the one who pushed Dutch down the stairs. She'll be broke once Trevor divorces her, so she'd have a few million reasons as far as motive." Charlie pushed a strand of hair from her face. "And you murdered Gloria because she'd found out the two of you are fucking."

The wolfish grin spread over his mouth once again. She'd expected the last bit to rattle him, or maybe for him to show some shred of shame, but if either emotion touched him, she saw it not at all.

"Very good." He made a show of clapping. "I'm impressed."

"And it was you who ran me off the road?" Charlie asked, though this time she was less sure of the answer.

"Right again."

"So all of this was just about money? From the beginning?"

Brandon faced forward and studied the vast blackness before them.

"Isn't it always?"

They rode on for some time with only the sound of the wind in their ears.

"The funny thing is, this probably could have been avoided if you'd just gone out with me," he said.

Charlie scoffed.

"How do you figure that?"

"I have a certain power over women." He shrugged, totally serious now. "Call it an in-born talent."

Charlie wanted to laugh but was too tired. She rolled her eyes.

"What, you think Marjory came up with the idea to give our father a little nudge toward the grave?" Brandon asked. "No. It was my plan all along. Marjory does what I tell her."

"Is that why she tried to kill herself? Did you tell her to do that too?"

One of the tiny muscles under Brandon's eye twitched. He looked annoyed for the first time, and Charlie realized she'd gotten under his skin. Good.

"No. That was… Marjie's always been weak of will." He sighed. "Once she found out we'd gone to all this trouble for a fortune that doesn't even exist… she wasn't happy. She possibly even felt a bit of regret, I suppose. Silly girl."

Charlie felt a new wave of disgust roll over her. He sounded not at all sorry that Marjory had attempted suicide, only irritated that she'd gone off-script. She'd assumed their incestuous relationship meant they loved one another—in all the wrong ways, of course—but now Charlie wondered if the grinning jackal before her was even capable of love.

He throttled the boat down. The vibration underfoot lost its intensity all at once, and that cold wind likewise had its energy drained as the vessel lost velocity.

Then he killed the engines, those throaty growls dying out to silence. She could feel the emptiness where the thrumming in her ears had been.

The boat drifted, slower than before but still advancing. Creeping. The waves began to have their way with the ship, making the thing shimmy and pitch atop the water.

She thought he'd turn on the light now. Out here where no one could see. Shed light on this final task. And she steeled herself for the fight, jaw clenched so tightly it shook.

Instead she lost him in the gloom. One second his silhouette had been standing at the console, small display LEDs glowing up blue to partially light his face beneath the chin. And then he'd vanished.

She squinted. Strained to see his dark figure among the many shades of black.

Instinctively, she backpedaled as she scanned for him. Slow steps. Inching back until her calves butted up against the stern of the ship.

She stopped there. A breath hitching into her. She squinted harder. Tried to flex her eyelids hard enough to see something. Anything.

Forms shifted in the shadows before her. Indistinct drifting. Ripples in the murk.

And then he lurched for her. Something large and angular glinting in his hands.

He exploded forward. Legs pushing. Hips rotating open as he swung his hands in her direction.

Charlie dodged to one side. Head and shoulders jerking back as the anchor grazed the air in front of her nose. She felt the wind of it.

Her top half now leaned over the water. Her balance wobbled. Legs shaky beneath.

She went with it. Rode the momentum. Jumped.

And for just a second she was weightless. The wind held her above the glimmering surface of the lake. Lifting her. Embracing her.

She twisted as she fell. Hit face first. Slapped the water.

And then the lake took her.

Submerged her in blackness. All sound cutting out save for a wet flitting in her ears.

The shock of the cold surrounded her. Gripped her. Squeezed her torso. Sucked the breath out of her. Dragged her into the deep.

CHAPTER EIGHTY-SIX

Charlie's downward drift slowed. Her body hung there, motionless. Like a sample floating in a jar.

She hovered. Arms splayed out at her sides. Gliding up over her head.

Already the cold had faded, her body numb to it. Strange how quickly that happened.

She peered up. Saw the moonlight glittering down through the water. The shape of the glow changed over and over as the waves chopped and lurched and dipped.

And she could just make out the boat's hull—the dark shape amid those dancing motes of light. Solid. Faintly bobbing. Two massive propellers jutted out from the back, looking more like something you'd see on a jet than on a boat.

Something heavy clicked above, and a brighter light joined that of the moon.

A spotlight shone down. A great glowing shaft that angled a few feet into the water, though it died long before reaching her. The darkness squelched it.

The beam shifted around. Kept moving. Scanning. He was looking for her.

And then the engines fired, one after the other. He was ready to pounce once more.

Time to move.

Charlie batted her arms. Kicked her legs.

She swam away the best she could. Going the opposite way that the boat was pointed. Limbs feeling heavy and awkward in the cold, her clothes dragging her down, her breath running out.

She slowly drifted to the surface as she swam. The water lifting her little by little, whether she wanted it to or not.

She'd hit the top before long. And she knew he'd come ripping after her then.

She focused on those kicking legs. Keeping their motions tight. Controlled. Streamlined. Getting as far as she could.

She breached the surface. Sucked in a big breath.

The engine revved somewhere behind her. Purring and then roaring.

She dove again. Got ten or so feet down and gazed up.

She watched the boat circle back, slow as it got above her. Drifting directly over her. Passing her in slow motion.

The spotlight swung all the way around now. Going from behind the boat to in front of it. Brandon must be standing on the bow now. Looking out the wrong way.

This was her chance.

Charlie kicked again. Paddled her arms.

Watching the light angle harder to the starboard side, she surfaced just off port. Stayed low to let the hull mostly hide her.

She clasped a hand around the rail on the side of the boat. Held on. Listened.

Brandon's footsteps thumped, but she couldn't place them very well from this angle. The water kept sloshing against the side of the vessel. Slurping and muffling everything else.

The engine lurched. She could feel its vibration change pitch in that metal bar clutched in her hand.

The thrum grew taut. Strong. Strident.

The boat slowly accelerated. Lifted a few inches higher as the speed built. Hull riding more on top of the water.

He'd drifted past the spot where he'd last seen her, so now he'd probably have to circle back to continue the search. Hopefully she could hold on long enough to see this through.

She gripped the rail with both hands. Pulled herself up, arms shaking.

Then she tucked her legs up to reduce the drag. A small thing huddling against the side of this boat. Hanging there.

The bow split the water. Sliced it off so two wakes rolled off of each side of the ship. Smooth ripples.

And that rolling wet reached for her. Surged up onto her shoes and then her ankles. Higher and higher. Tugging. Trying to wrench her free. If she lost her grip now, she'd be sucked right into the path of the twin propellers.

She'd seen them when she had been under the boat. Massive blades spinning and sucking and chewing up water.

The cold bit into her now that she was half out of the water. Her fingers ached with it, and as hard as she tried to cling tight to the rail, the tiny muscles of her hands began to shake.

Her strength faltered for a second, and she slid a few inches closer to the stern. She clamped down again, fighting now. She glanced back at the churning froth. She couldn't hold on much longer.

And then the vessel slowed. The front half sagging back down. That pulling current dying off.

She lowered herself. Submerged up to the shoulders. Nearly hidden. All the muscles in her hands and arms thankful to be released from the strain.

Another set of heavy footfalls thumped over the deck. And then the spotlight started swinging over the top of the water.

He scanned the light off the stern this time. Swung it back and forth behind the boat. The light sliced a tube in the dark, glared some where it touched the glassy surface.

When the light winked out, she hoisted herself up again, her top half rising out of the wet. He pounded back over to the console and the boat started accelerating again. She knew it was time to make her move. Now or never.

She breathed a few times. Felt the cold lake air sucked deep inside and slowly expelled.

Then she hauled herself up onto the boat, spilling onto the deck like a fish dumped out of a net, water gushing all around her.

CHAPTER EIGHTY-SEVEN

She crouched on the deck on hands and knees. Staying low.

Her eyes took a second to get oriented. Staring. Blinking. The dark shapes slowly drifting into forms that made sense.

His broad shoulders coagulated from the void. Standing at the wheel. One hand on the accelerator.

And then she could see part of one side of his face. The stubbled chin and jaw glowing blue from the little LEDs on the console.

He stared straight ahead. The rising grumble of the engine had covered the sounds of her surfacing. He was oblivious for the moment. Totally focused on steering the ship.

She scanned for a weapon. Needed something hard or sharp or heavy. Anything.

She saw the fire extinguisher first. The large object stark against the white floor in the back corner. The slender nozzle protruding from the fat tank. It was one of the bigger models. Probably weighed fifteen pounds.

That would work.

Her tongue flicked out to touch her lips as she crawled toward it. Tasted lake water as it did. That little hint of algae and scum worming across her palate.

She inched over the floor. Wanted to be quick. Wanted to be decisive. But needed to be soundless above all.

Just a few more seconds now. And then it would be over.

The boat lurched, and she froze. The deck almost seemed to jump and then dip. Slowing. Was he stopping already?

No. He was taking the turn at speed. Everything tilted to the right as the boat leaned. Hard. Rough.

She got low again. Braced her hands wide to keep her balance.

Her right wrist caught on something. Something sharp. And hard. And heavy.

That would work, too. Even better, she thought.

The boat leveled out. That sideways tilt relenting.

Any second now, he'd stop again. She needed to pounce while she still could.

She stood. Wrapped her hands around the anchor. Lifted it.

Charlie crept toward the figure at the wheel of the boat.

CHAPTER EIGHTY-EIGHT

The anchor was twenty-two pounds of hard metal. A curved piece that locked onto a pointed wedge of flattened metal that looked like a stretched-out home plate. It felt heavy in her hands. Awkward.

Charlie slinked forward. Feet light. Chin tucked.

Brandon faced away from her. Arms working the console, the wheel, the accelerator. Flipping switches. Adjusting the throttle ever so delicately.

She kept her gaze leveled on him as she got closer. Locked onto his torso. Unblinking.

The back of his shirt rippled in the darkness. His shoulder blades knifing into the fabric.

She breathed in and out through her mouth. Soundless wind passing over wet lips.

And electricity thrummed in her brain now. The inside of her head prickling and jolting and alive with it.

Aggression. Fury.

She was barely a yard away from him now. Within striking distance.

She adjusted the anchor's heft. Readied to swing it.

And a shiver overtook her limbs. The cold suddenly intensifying. Made her elbows rattle against the bottom of her ribcage.

Brandon turned then. Perhaps sensing her presence at last.

She watched as his stubbled jaw passed through the blue light of the LED as he twisted to face her.

And she swung with all her might. Thrusting the anchor upward from her waist. Arcing it toward his skull.

Every muscle in her body worked as one. Coiling and releasing. Feet and then legs and then hips and then hands, just like she'd learned in softball.

Metal cracked against bone. Hot liquid spattered against her face.

The anchor caught Brandon on the temple just as he came around. Flung him like a ragdoll.

He bashed into the sidewall and toppled over the rail. Tipping and plummeting overboard. Knees banging the side of the boat on the way down.

The splash sounded heavy and hollow at the same time. Impossible.

Disturbed water lurched everywhere. Dark and thrashing.

The surface swallowed him whole. She waited a second for him to bob to the surface, but he didn't.

In an instant he was gone. Vanished into the inky deep.

CHAPTER EIGHTY-NINE

Charlie dropped the anchor, the heavy metal thunking at her feet. Then she moved to the console. Throttled down the boat, the growl of the engines quieting.

Still, the ship drifted forward. Slowly creeping due to the momentum. Leaving Brandon behind.

She turned. Stared at the place where he'd gone into the water.

And an emptiness came over her. A vacancy roiling in her chest cavity.

She felt no triumph. No sense of victory. She felt cold and wet and exhausted.

Her shivering intensified. The chill seemed to reach to the core of her all at once.

She needed to find him. She took little comfort in the roles being reversed.

She pointed the spotlight out at the place where he'd gone under, or the place she thought he had, at least. It was difficult to pinpoint the exact spot, now that they'd drifted.

She moved back to the boat's control panel. Twirled the wheel. Pushed the throttle to give it some speed.

"What are you doing?" Allie said. "It's over. Take us back to shore."

"I can't. Not yet."

"Why?"

Charlie thought a second before she answered. Tried to ignore the icy wind blasting her in the face.

"Because I have to be sure. It's just like he said, right? We have to make sure."

"Make sure he's dead?" Allie seemed a touch confused. "His odds of making it to shore are slim to none. He's dead either way."

They rode on in the quiet. The headlight pierced the darkness before them, made the top of the water glisten.

"What if we get back there and he's *not* dead?" Allie asked.

Charlie shrugged.

"Then we drag him aboard, I guess."

Allie groaned.

"Hold up. You're not actually going to save this scumbag, are you?"

"If I can, but it might already be too late. The anchor hit him square in the temple. I saw the light go out in his eyes."

Charlie slowed as she drew up on the spot where he'd gone under. She leaned out over one side of the boat and then the other.

"You see anything?" she asked.

"Negative," Allie said.

Charlie swung the spotlight around. Watched it shimmer off the swells and dips in the waves. She gave a good long look off all four sides of the boat but saw no signs of movement or life. Just the endless wet.

She swallowed.

Even with the perpetual stirring and chopping of the water, the lapping of it against the sides of the boat, it felt desolate. Empty. Lifeless.

She pushed the accelerator again. Eased the boat forward. Leaning off each side again as it toddled forward. Saw nothing but waves.

And then something thudded on the starboard side of the boat. She pointed the light that way.

Saw him.

Brandon's sopping hand reached up. Clutched that chrome bar on the side of the hull. Then the rest of him emerged from the black water.

Before Charlie could move, his dark figure heaved over the sidewall. Tumbled onto the deck the same way she had, water gushing everywhere around him.

He still had the gun in his hand.

CHAPTER NINETY

Brandon pointed the pistol at her. Slowly getting to his feet.

The gun might not work, she thought. Might not fire after being submerged. But if it did still work? She wasn't willing to stand here, waiting to find out.

The light was aimed at his feet. The glow sheening against the wet of his jeans. Shadows swirled around his face, but she could just read the subtle smile etched on his lips.

"Should have raced for shore while you still had the chance," he said, smiling harder. "Dumb bitch."

His arm shook faintly. The gun quivering at the end of it.

Charlie lurched for the throttle. Jammed it all the way forward. Instinctively squatting as she did to brace for the thrust of the boat's momentum.

The engines roared. Angrier than ever. The boat lifted.

Brandon squeezed the trigger just as the ship jerked to life beneath him. His trembling arm wobbled upward as it shook him off balance.

The muzzle blaze lit up everything for just a second. An orange flare that cast a momentary flash against Brandon's chin and brow.

And then the crack of the gunfire split the wet night air around them. So loud. Percussive. A violent sound rolling out over the open water.

It made Charlie's shoulders hunch. Made her skin flex.

But the shot went high.

And then a choppy wave slammed into the hull. Jolted the ship. Knocked them both to the deck. Flung them like they were nothing.

Charlie blinked. Face down. Confused.

She watched the spotlight swing around everywhere. A beam of light untethered. Touching everything.

The gun. He'd lost the gun.

She'd seen just a glimpse of the fumble as he'd slammed down somewhere in front of her.

She propped herself up on hands and knees. Scrambling forward in a crawl. Fingers feeling everywhere for the cool, hard metal of the weapon.

And then the light swung past. Lit up the deck for a second. And she could see him.

Brandon. A few feet away. He was searching for it too. Hands clawing over the glistening deck. Looking anywhere for the gun.

Only one of them could find it. And it had to be her.

The engine seemed to rev higher, past the point of impossibility. The waves slammed into the hull. Rocking them over and over. Making Charlie wobble in place.

The engine rasped and snarled. Strained for higher and higher notes.

The next time the light swung past, she saw that Brandon wasn't looking for the gun.

He hurled himself at her.

CHAPTER NINETY-ONE

Brandon crashed into her. Torsos colliding. His arms wrapping around her frame and squeezing. The force of the impact lifting her from the deck.

Weightless.

Floating in the dark.

They slammed down. A solid thud ringing out. Bright stars exploding in Charlie's field of vision.

Brandon's shoulder drove into her chest. That pointed piece of bone trying to spear her, pierce her.

They skidded over the wet deck. Water flung everywhere around them. Limbs entangling.

They scrambled in the dark. Grappled. Each trying to free themselves from the knot of body parts, trying to shove and bend and pry themselves away from the other.

Charlie got her feet under her. Moved into a semi-upright squat. Instinct keeping her low in case any more waves jostled the solid footing of the deck out from underneath her.

She sensed that Brandon had done the same. Gotten to his feet. He was close.

She shuffled to her right. Half trying to conceal her position. Half twirling away from his dominant hand. Working the deck of the boat like a boxer in the ring.

She'd lose a fistfight, though. She needed to be smarter than that. More strategic.

The light swung past just in time for Charlie to see Brandon winding up for a big haymaker. She ducked. Felt the wind of the punch swoop overhead.

And then she launched herself into him. Flung her body with total abandon. Legs firing like pistons. Catapulting her.

She drove the crown of her head under his chin. A thick crack ringing out like a snapped femur.

Exploding stars again. Brighter and more plentiful than before. Raining and firing and rocketing toward her.

And she felt him lifted from the deck. Thrown. All of that force guided into his jaw. Detonating there.

The light drifted to a stop just on them then. And she saw him.

Flailing arms. Head thrown all the way back. Limp atop his neck.

His legs bashed into the sidewall of the boat. The force of it folding him in half. Dumping him over the rail yet again.

He seemed to come to life just then. Thrashing his limbs as the water tried to take him once more. Wet splashing everywhere around him.

Most of his figure disappeared into the murk. Swallowed.

But his head and arms still jutted up from the water.

It took Charlie's eyes a second to make sense of what she was seeing.

The rail.

He was clinging to the rail. The same as she had. Knuckles going white as she watched.

And then he slid further down the metal pole. Inching toward the back of the boat. Struggling to regain his grip.

The propellers.

The boat was still hurtling along at top speed, and the propellers were pulling on him. Sucking. Trying to take him.

Charlie didn't hesitate. She reached for him. Arm outstretched to where his hands clung to the metal.

His fingers squeaked a little as he slid further down the siderail. His eyes went to the churning water at the back of the boat and blinked hard.

And then he was gone.

Just gone.

Under.

The boat rattled. A heavy thump nearly knocking Charlie over again as the ship slowed abruptly.

A whir vibrated through the deck. Choppy tremors. Violent. Hateful. The force shook the entire hull.

"Jesus!" Allie said.

The propellers whined and shuddered. Whirring and gritting and crunching.

Charlie winced. Closed her eyes.

It was a terrible sound. Half coffee grinder. Half woodchipper.

It seemed to go on and on. Endless grating. Gritting. Scraping.

And then the noise cut out all at once, and the boat lurched forward again.

Charlie couldn't move. Couldn't breathe.

"Uh-oh," Allie said.

CHAPTER NINETY-TWO

Charlie cringed. She quickly turned the boat around and then slowed the forward momentum. Let it drift back to where the disturbance had taken place.

She killed the engines. Some instinct kicking in. She wanted to be able to hear in this moment.

"Uh-oh," Allie repeated, her voice soft and small.

The silence felt huge. Ominous. Wrong.

Charlie spun the light to shine off the bow. The glow glittered on the water there. And almost right away she found it.

A dark shape bobbed atop the lake. Motionless apart from the water's undulating movement. It came into focus more and more as they glided toward it.

And then she realized that it was more than one chunk bobbing. A mess of them rising and falling with the wet, though she still couldn't get a good enough look to identify any of them.

She shined her spotlight toward the floating shapes. Adjusting for the boat's continual movement, like a cameraman following the action.

A red cloud slowly spread through the lurching water, surrounding the dark objects. Opaque. Bright scarlet.

And then she saw a little piece of a plaid flannel shirt—red and blue.

"Found him," Allie said.

CHAPTER NINETY-THREE

Charlie stood on the shore, feet planted in the sand. A Reflexcell blanket draped over her shoulders, a thin metallic layer of aluminum-foil-type material that was colored bright emergency orange on the outside. Surprisingly warm. One of the EMTs had given it to her. She held it shut in front of her, her right hand serving as a clasp, pinching the two sides of her foil cape together just like she had as she'd watched her car being pulled from the water.

Law enforcement milled around the scene like worker ants. One crew of crime scene techs worked the boat, hands sheathed in nitrile gloves, shining flashlights into the gray murk of the predawn morning.

The rest of the officers waited for the Coast Guard search crew to turn up Brandon's remains, if they did. Charlie wondered if they'd be able to find him, or what was left of him, out there in all that endless lake. The boat's GPS tracker would give them a good starting point anyway.

And for just a second, she pictured those objects bobbing atop the dark water, the wet of them glittering. And that red cloud surrounding them, a pool of thicker, darker stuff.

She shuddered. Pushed the images away.

She stared out over the water, gazing off into the horizon where the choppy waves seemed to end, though she knew firsthand that they only went on and on.

Her left hand tightened around the Styrofoam cup she held, lifting it to take another slurp of coffee. The heat made her tongue and throat tingle.

She was dry at least. She'd found some spare clothes in one of the closets inside the cabin and warmed up in front of the big gas fireplace in the den before coming back out to watch.

Footsteps crunched behind her, and she turned to find Zoe striding over the rocks washed up by high tide.

"Just got off the horn with the sheriff. They're officially charging Marjory with first-degree murder and a boatload of other charges, pardon the expression." Zoe came to a halt at Charlie's side and thrust her hands in the pockets of her uniform jacket. "She's still in the hospital for now, but when she's discharged later today, it'll be straight to a jail cell. I can only imagine the judge will deny bail."

When Charlie only nodded, Zoe went on.

"If I'm being honest, she doesn't seem so tough to me. I'm thinking she'll crack pretty easy. Especially once she sees what's on this."

Zoe dangled an evidence baggie containing the thumb drive Charlie had found in the house.

"I doubt you'll even have to show her what's on it," Charlie said, shaking her head. "Once she sees you've found out all her secrets, she'll spill everything. That's my guess, anyway."

They moved off the strip of sand and over to the dock, the planks ringing out their hollow thuds underfoot.

Charlie could hear the chopper circling way out over the lake. She had watched it ride out, its search light aimed down at the water. It had shrunk in slow motion, disappearing into the distance little by little until it was just a speck above the horizon.

Hearing the propellers chopping the air had made her cringe, and another twinge of that hit her now. She closed her eyes. Lowered her head to her chest. Fought to keep her mind blank.

"You OK?" Zoe asked.

Charlie breathed and lifted the coffee cup again. Steam wafted off the top of it, warming her nose. She took another drink. Felt steady enough to open her eyes again.

"Yeah."

Behind them, she heard the engine of another boat rumble to life. A new crew joining the search.

"Let's go home," Charlie said, heading back up the long walk toward the cabin.

CHAPTER NINETY-FOUR

Charlie had been right about Marjory's confession. As soon as she peered through the plastic film of the evidence baggie the detective presented and spied the small black thumb drive, she agreed to a plea bargain.

Charlie watched it all from behind the two-way glass separating the observation room from the interrogation room. Noticed the way Marjory fidgeted as she spoke, picking her fingernails and twitching her nose.

"Brandon needed the cash," Marjory explained when the district attorney asked her to explain why she'd murdered her father. "He owed some rather large sums to what I understand are some very unsavory people in the gambling world, and their reminders were becoming more and more threatening. And then of course there was my divorce to consider. In the past, I'd always been able to help him out of binds like this, but that wasn't going to be the case this time. Unless we found a way to pay off his debts, I truly believed Brandon's life was in danger. Those are the people you should be after. Those are the real monsters in all this."

This revelation jarred something loose in Charlie's mind, and she let out a thoughtful gasp.

"What?" Zoe asked.

"Back when all this started, someone mentioned that Marjory's house had been burgled a while back. The thief broke in and stole the husband's coin collection. Trashed his study. But that was all he did. Oh. He also peed on the carpet. Marjory referred to it as 'marking his territory.' I think I have an idea of who the burglar was."

Zoe nodded.

"Brandon Carmichael."

"Yep," Charlie said. "I bet he stole the coins to pay off one of his debts. And then caused a little damage just to… I don't know. Make a point, I guess."

When the lawyers on both sides had come to an agreement and wrapped things up, Charlie asked if she might have a minute to talk to Marjory herself. Because there was one thing Charlie hadn't figured out. One nugget she'd neglected to pry from Brandon before their final struggle.

Besides that, she wanted Marjory to see her face before being transported to whatever cell would hold her until the sentencing hearing.

No one objected.

The detective opened the interrogation room door, and Charlie slipped inside. Marjory looked much older without all the makeup. And the prisoner jumpsuit she wore hung awkwardly off her thin frame.

Marjory's eyes slid up when she heard the door opening and narrowed down to slits when she saw Charlie standing there.

"Come to rub it in, have you?" Her tone was acid. Biting. "I hope you don't honestly think you can bring me any lower than this."

Charlie stepped closer to where Marjory sat. There was another chair across the table from her, but Charlie didn't want to sit down. Instead, she rested her hands on the backrest and leaned forward.

"Brandon told me he was the one who ran Gloria down that day," Charlie said. "I know why he did it. I know Gloria had found out about the two of you. But I don't know how she discovered it."

Charlie thought Marjory might refuse to answer, but apparently Marjory's earlier confession had greased the wheels, and the words just flowed out of her mouth.

"She saw us… together. At least we thought she did." Marjory stared down at her hands. "Trevor was gone, so Brandon was at the house. We didn't usually meet there. It was too risky, but… Gloria came by to ask me something about the foundation. She must have seen Brandon's car in the driveway and wondered what we were doing together. She was so suspicious after Dad died, she must have thought we were up to something. Which we were... just not what she thought. She came in so quietly. We were on the back veranda, by the pool. I was in Brandon's lap, and he practically threw me off the way he stood up when Gloria opened the back door. She was always being sneaky like that. Used to listen in on my phone calls when we were kids. Daddy always acted like the sun shone out of her ass. Gave her all this credit for keeping the family together, but I always thought she was just a bossy busybody."

Marjory's lips pursed in annoyance, and then she went on.

"Anyway, I'm pretty sure she saw us. She tried to play it off like everything was normal, but we could tell something was wrong. Brandon hatched the plan for me to go up to the cabin with a friend immediately, so I'd have an alibi. And he took the job of following Gloria."

She said it casually, as if the entire scenario made perfect sense. As if it was all somehow logical to murder Gloria in cold blood just to protect their incestuous secret. Their sister. Their flesh and blood. Charlie didn't realize she was shaking her head in disgust until Marjory's head snapped up.

"Don't you dare judge me. You only think it's wrong because society has brainwashed you into thinking that way. You don't understand how close the two of us were, me and Brandon. We weren't even a whole year apart. We were practically twins."

"Uh, as an *actual* twin, I have to say I don't see how that helps her case," Allie said.

Marjory jabbed a finger into the tabletop.

"We had a bond. He always protected me. And me him. We were one."

Not interested in hearing Marjory rant about the tainted love she shared with her brother, Charlie pushed off from the back of the chair and turned to the door. Just as her fingers brushed the metal of the door handle, Marjory spoke again.

"He never cared about you. I hope you know that."

Charlie paused, trying to make sense of what Marjory was saying. Was Marjory actually jealous at the way Brandon had tried to use flirtation as a way to manipulate her? And did she think Charlie could retain even a hint of warm feelings for Brandon after he'd tried to kill her?

"Jealousy isn't a logical monster, Chuck," Allie said. "And neither is love, as sick as hers is."

Charlie realized Allie was right. Marjory loved Brandon. Whether the inverse was true, Charlie couldn't be sure. The way Brandon had spoken of Marjory in his last hour hadn't seemed especially affectionate. She suspected that Marjory had been just another pawn to him.

Charlie turned the handle and opened the door, but before she passed through, she asked Marjory one final question.

"He really did a number on you, didn't he?"

EPILOGUE

"I don't see why the blindfold is necessary," Frank said. "Why can't I just close my eyes?"

"Because I know you. You'll peek." Charlie flapped the bandana in the air between them. "Put it on."

Frank snatched it from her and wrapped it around his eyes.

"This better be worth it."

Charlie rubbed her palms together then gave Paige a thumbs up, which was her signal to run to the back room and make sure everything was ready.

Taking Frank by the elbow, Charlie led him down the hallway to the back office. He took slow, shuffling steps, like he was afraid he might fall.

"You can walk faster than that," she said. "I've got you."

"I'm supposed to just trust you won't run me into a wall? I've seen you trip over your own two feet, turkey."

When they finally reached the back room, Charlie maneuvered him until he was facing the door.

"Wait here," she said, scurrying into the room and taking her place. "At the count of three, you can take the blindfold off."

"Lotta fuss," he muttered.

Charlie locked eyes with Paige, and they began counting in unison.

"One… two… three…" They held the banner high and waited until Frank had torn off the blindfold before they yelled, "Surprise!"

Paige popped a balloon filled with confetti while Charlie pressed play on her phone. Queen's "We Are the Champions" blared from the speakers she'd set up on the small dining table.

Frank chuckled and read the sign Charlie and Paige had spent the previous day coloring with magic markers.

"'Fuck cancer,'" he said, nodding. "Fuck cancer, indeed."

Charlie turned the music down and pointed out how clean the back room was since she and Paige had finally made their way through most of Frank's packrat stash.

"There's actually, you know, room to walk around and everything," she said. "What do you think?"

"I think I'd like to know what you did with all my stuff. That's what I think."

"Your junk, you mean?"

"Some of that was useful, and not only that, but—"

"I'm going to stop you before you go on about how one day those Happy Meal toys are going to be worth a fortune." Charlie handed him one of Paige's cupcakes. "Here. Try this."

He took a big bite and then licked a smear of frosting from his lips.

"Hey now." Frank waggled his eyebrows. "That's good eatin'."

She glanced over at Paige and found her grinning and blushing at the compliment.

"Is that a fresh raspberry filling?" Frank asked, taking another bite. "I love a good raspberry dessert, but most people screw it up. They make the raspberries too sweet."

"I feel exactly the same way," Paige said. "The original recipe had it all wrong. It called for store-bought raspberry jam, if you can believe it."

Frank helped himself to another cupcake.

"Ludicrous."

They scarfed more cupcakes and listened to the classic rock playlist Charlie had made that was full of Frank's favorites, and Frank told a few of his best P.I. stories, like the time he'd been hired to track down a person who'd been regularly leaving poop in someone's mailbox.

"Turns out it was the guy's own brother, mad about some joint business venture," Frank said. "And he was lucky that his brother didn't want to press charges once he found out who the culprit was. Vandalizing a mailbox is a federal crime, and he would have been in deep shit. Pun intended."

"Oh!" Paige clapped her hands. "Speaking of being in deep doodoo… did you see the news? We're famous!"

Charlie raised an eyebrow.

"We're what?"

"Our case. It was all over the TV last night," Paige said, getting out her phone and bringing up a clip from one of the Detroit news stations.

"Earlier today, the FBI stormed the estate of the late Randolph 'Dutch' Carmichael," the news anchor said.

The studio footage cut to an aerial shot from a drone or helicopter. It showed the Feds swarming around the Carmichael mansion, loading boxes and other items into trucks.

Big bold letters at the bottom of the screen read: MASSIVE PONZI SCHEME.

Charlie shook her head.

"They can seize the lot of it, sell it off, do whatever they can to squeeze every last penny out of it, but it won't be enough. Gloria told me her accounting of the assets at the house totaled a few million dollars. Carmichael Investments bilked their investors out of *billions*. Those people are going to lose everything."

"That's why I invested the bulk of my portfolio in rare Happy Meal toys," Frank said. "More stable than gold is what my financial adviser told me."

"And who would that be, exactly?" Charlie asked. "Ronald McDonald?"

Noting the time, Charlie dusted cupcake crumbs from her hands and grabbed her bag.

"I have to get going if I'm going to make it before the end of visiting hours." Charlie gave Frank a quick hug. "Congrats again on the remission."

"Thank you for this little celebration, turkey. I assume the half-nekkid lady jumping out of the giant cake comes later?" Frank smiled at his joke and held a cupcake out. "Take this to your mother, and give her my best, will you?"

Charlie accepted the cupcake and nodded before heading out the door.

The Cedar Grove Healing Center was located in a setting that reminded Charlie a bit of a summer camp. Down a winding dirt road through densely wooded land. Over a small bridge with a babbling creek running underneath it. Nestled in a clearing with a duck pond and a garden and paths that wove around the grounds.

The buildings were all stately brick affairs with glossy green ivy clinging to the sides.

Charlie checked in at the reception desk, and a nurse led her to her mother's room. It was small, but cozy and neat. It felt more like a dorm than a hospital. Nice enough, but it wasn't home.

Nancy sat in a rocker, watching TV. She greeted Charlie and thanked her for the things she'd brought—her book of crossword puzzles, a framed photo of her and Allie as kids, several changes of clothes—but otherwise she didn't speak much. She did make sure to say Charlie's name several times, as if reassuring the both of them that she was in her right mind.

Charlie convinced her mother to go for a walk around the grounds, thinking that might perk her up. She brightened a bit when showing Charlie the koi pond and miniature waterfall at one end of the grounds. But overall, her mother seemed hazy. Zoned out. Charlie knew Dr. Kesselman and the doctors here were tweaking her meds again, and it would take some time for her to adjust.

They sat in silence for a while, watching the fish circling the murky water. Eventually, Charlie voiced the question on her mind.

"Do you think you'll be ready to come home in a few days?"

Nancy turned her head and looked Charlie in the eye for the first time.

"Actually, I've been thinking I might stay."

"Stay?"

"Stay here. They have a residential program. I'd have my own room, a lot like the one I'm in now, but bigger. And there'd be a communal kitchen I could use too."

"But you have a kitchen, Mom," Charlie said. "At home."

"I know. But… maybe it's time I face facts. I never wanted to be a burden to you."

Charlie shook her head, trying not to cry.

"You're not."

"Yes, I am," Nancy said. "I know I am, and I don't say it for pity. The truth is I stopped taking care of you the day your sister went missing. And I think maybe the part of me that knew how to be a mother died somewhere along the way. It's been you taking care of me since then, and that's not right. That's not how it should be."

A tear slid down Charlie's cheek. There had been times she'd felt bitter about the way her mother had changed since Allie's death. Times she'd resented all of it. But just now she didn't care.

"I don't mind," she said, her voice shaking.

"I do." Nancy took Charlie's hand and closed her eyes. "And it's more than that. I almost hurt you. I could have *killed* you. I can't allow that to happen again. Never."

Charlie sniffed and wiped her cheek.

"OK, just… don't make any decisions yet. Let's see how things go from here before you make up your mind." She squeezed her mother's hand. "We'll take things one day at a time."

Nancy nodded and opened her eyes. As Nancy's gaze wandered back to the rippling surface where the waterfall struck the pond below, Charlie could tell she was receding back into the medicated fog.

Charlie squeezed her mother's hand once more and climbed to her feet.

Kissing the top of her head, Charlie whispered, "I love you, Mom."

But as she walked away, Charlie wasn't sure her mother had heard her over the sound of the water.

A NOTE FROM L.T. AND TIM

Thanks so much for reading *Girl Under Water*. If you enjoyed it, feel free to sign up for the Bookouture Vargus/McBain list at the following link. They'll keep you up to date with new releases in the series.

www.bookouture.com/lt-vargus-and-tim-mcbain/

We can't wait for you to find out what happens to Charlie next time. Salem Island is going to be lit.

In the meantime, we love hearing from readers. Get in touch with us on Twitter or Goodreads, or join our personal email list if you want to hear about all of our other books and reading recommendations. Sign up for that here:

ltvargus.com/mailing-list

Oh, and if you have a second to leave a review, we'd really appreciate it. Even just a couple sentences about your experience reading *Girl Under Water* would mean the world. Reviews are so critical for authors when it comes to finding new readers.

That's all for now. Be on the lookout for more Charlie Winters soon.

L.T. Vargus and Tim McBain

 ltvargusbooks
 @ltvargus
 ltvargus.com

Printed in Great Britain
by Amazon